The troopers from Echo fic from the grunts on the ground as they rushed to assist at over one hundred clicks per hour. *Peg*'s gleaming skids sliced branches from the tops of trees as she dove.

"We've got NVA Regulars here!" the voice yelled through the radio static. "They dug in MG nests around the LZ! My mortar man and RTO are K.I.A. We need arty now, copy?"

"Rodg," the pilot answered. "LZ in dirty sex, ladies!"

Zack swallowed hard and forced himself out of a crouch. "Okay," he shouted, smacking his huge hands together. "Get your asses in gear. *Now!*"

Artillery was already upending palm trees when Gabriel set the chopper down between two tree lines running parallel to each other. Half the cabin emptied seconds after hitting the turf, as the men leaped down into the elephant grass. A few stray sniper rounds zinged off *Peg*'s skids, but there was no firestorm of hot lead like everyone expected. Not yet.

A mortar exploded behind the last two soldiers a few seconds after they jumped from the hatch, knocking them off their feet in a fury of lightning white heat and thick smoke.

The blast flipped the chopper onto its side, the fifty-foot rotors slamming hard into the earth. One of the blades broke in half, slicing down through the cabin, and the rest arced out into the sky, over a distant hilltop. Gabriel and the co-pilot scrambled from the cockpit, uninjured, as a wall of black-pajama-clad sappers stormed over the near hill.

*Includes a complete GLOSSARY*
*of military jargon*

*Other books in the* **CHOPPER** 1 *series:*

**#1  BLOOD TRAILS**
**#2  TUNNEL WARRIORS**

# CHOPPER 1

## #3 JUNGLE SWEEP

## Jack Hawkins

IVY BOOKS • NEW YORK

For Nick and Angie, John and Kwang-Im,
and Richard and Lan, who've managed
to bridge East and West, in their own little way,
using that love and loyalty found and forged
in the heart of tropical cities under siege.

Ivy Books
Published by Ballantine Books

Produced by Butterfield Press, Inc.
133 Fifth Avenue
New York, New York 10003

Library of Congress Catalog Card Number: 86-91842

ISBN 0-8041-0018-7

All the characters in this book are fictitious and any resemblance to actual persons living or dead is purely coincidental.

Manufactured in the United States of America

First Editon: June 1987

# AUTHOR'S NOTE

The following is a fictional account of Operations Masher and White Wing, which took place in the Republic of Vietnam during January and February, 1966. The 7th Cav of the 1st Air Cavalry Division really existed. But there is some disagreement among armchair commandos and military archivists as to whether or not there ever really was an "Echo Company."

The colorful characters of "The Pack," such as Snakeman Fletcher, Em-ho Lee, Nasty Nelson, and Brody The Whoremonger, may remind readers and First Team vets of actual troopers they knew in The Nam, but this novel is a work of fiction. Other than well-known public and historic figures, any resemblance of its characters to persons living or Killed In Action is purely coincidental.

Jack Hawkins
Little Saigon (Garden Grove), California
31 October 1986

"I would use anything we could dream up, including nuclear weapons. . . . We seem to have a phobia about nuclear weapons. . . . I think there are many times when it would be more efficient to use nuclear weapons. However, the public opinion in this country and throughout the world would throw up their hands in horror when you mention nuclear weapons, just because of the propaganda that's been fed them. I don't believe the world would end if we exploded a nuclear weapon. . . . At Bikini . . . the fish are back in the lagoons; the coconut trees are growing coconuts; the guava bushes have fruit on them; the birds are back. As a matter of fact, everything is just about the same except the land crabs . . . the land crabs are a little bit 'hot,' and there's some question whether you should eat a land crab or not. . . ."

Gen. Curtis E. LeMay, Former Commander
Strategic Air Force, and Chief of Staff,
U.S.A.F., at a news conference announcing
his candidacy for vice president, 3 October
1968

# CHAPTER 1

## An Lao Valley

"Take us up! Take us up—we're too low!" No one heard Larson protesting through gritted teeth as he leaned into his Hatch-60, unloading steady streams of tracer down at the sloping hills. "Take us up, you sonofabitch!"

But the pilot kept the gunship low and near the ground as he swooped down into the valley, swerving the Huey from side to side like a madman drunk on adrenaline.

"I knew I should have stayed on the Isle of Stork, I knew I should have stayed on the Isle of Stork, I knew I should have . . ." Larson was repeating over and over under his breath as they grew nearer the ville and explosions on both sides increased.

This new pilot that the C.O., Neil Nazi, had assigned to *Pegasus* was a cockpit jockey, definitely chasing fame, glory, and medals. The Professor—as Shawn Larson was known to the men of Echo Company—certainly needed none of that at this point in his life. Larson was getting "short," which was GI slang for near-DEROS, his Date of Estimated Return from Over-Seas.

"Meltdown!"

The warning coaxed Larson from his own self-pity. He

stopped firing long enough to glance back over a shoulder toward the two newbies manning an M-60 machine gun mounted in the opposite hatch. "Don't burn your—" The Professor started to yell, but it was too late. Chappell was already reaching for the glowing M-60 barrel. *Pegasus* hitting an air pocket created by the nonstop string of explosions was the only thing that saved the teenaged trooper from third-degree burns.

In his peripheral vision, Larson saw Sgt. Zack, his left leg wrapped in battlefield bandages from fun in the Ia Drang, limping from up front toward the two FNG's.

"Get away from that hog!" Black Buddha, the stocky black NCO, yelled above the roar of slapping rotorblades. "You boys are gonna hurt yourself!"

"Shit." Larson shook his head from side to side in resignation as he blasted away, using five- and ten-round bursts. It wasn't the same without Snakeman Fletcher at the hog. Fletcher had run off to Singapore or Hong Kong or Christ-knows-where, on a seven-day R and R, and he'd taken Corky Cordova along.

But worse than that, Treat Brody was absent also—chasing his cunt fantasies to godforsaken Plei Me, of all places. Which left Larson with hog duty when all he wanted to do was hide out his last few days in The Nam, polishing up his suicide note.

Shawn Larson had been writing his suicide note ever since Day One in South Vietnam. It became a nightly ritual until, now, the letter was more like a manuscript, having reached several hundred pages in length. Larson's intellectual growth and spiritual fullfillment was suffering in Southwest Asia, he claimed, and the four-eyed draftee made the men in his squad suffer along with him by forcing them to listen to each new entry.

Larson's shirtsleeves were rolled down because of the clouds of mosquitos that had swarmed through camp during the rescue muster, and he used one to wipe the lenses of his

2

wire-rim glasses. It was raining lightly, and the sticky, humid mist blanketing the valley was causing them to fog up. A squad of sappers carrying satchel charges caught his eye, but before he could get a good sight picture, the craft bucked again, banked sharply to the left, and nearly rolled onto its side.

"Jesus!" Larson let a short burst arc up into the black void above. "What is *with* that bastard up front?" Chopper jockeys! His mind clouded with anger as he fought to keep his balance atop the pile of flak jackets and Saigon phone books.

If only Hal Krutch was still in command of *Pegasus*. But The Stork was dead, and nothing could change that. The chopper levelled out, and Larson sprayed the final approaches to the ville with crisscross patterns of smoking hot lead.

Things were constantly changing in The Nam, but Larson couldn't understand why just this once the status quo couldn't ignore him for ten, maybe fifteen days. All he wanted to do was finish his Tour 365 with as little fanfare as possible. Lay low, and keep a shorter-than-short profile until the day they announced a freedom bird flight manifest with his name on it over the Camp Alpha intercom.

It was a different intercom deciding his fate tonight, however. The metallic voice clicking into his headset was laughing almost demonically. "LZ in zero-five, gentlemen, hey, hey, *hey*! And it's gonna be hotter'n a whore's hole on Saturday night in Sin City! Hold onto your assholes, amigos; pucker factor officially increasing at this time, over."

"Is he buckin' for a Section 8 or what?" Larson called across the cabin to Zack. But the crew chief had taken over Chappell's M-60, and was prepping the landing zone with a shower of glowing red and white tracers.

The Brass Monkey had gone out at 2330 hours—a radio call for help from a medical team trapped in the An Lao Valley, fourteen klicks west of Bong Son.

The team had been inoculating children in villages north of the Iron Triangle when they received word their extraction

3

chopper would not arrive before dusk due to mechanical problems, so they opted to spend the night with their friendly patients. A few hours later, the Cong sent in an assassination team and, after a lookout turned the death squad back with pistol fire, began mortaring the ville.

The pilot brought *Peg* in roughly, pranging across several sandbag-reinforced trenches without flipping over before the gunship slid to a stop sideways. Still cursing, The Professor guided the swivel-mounted heavy machine gun from side to side, firing longer bursts now out at the trees as Special Forces corpsmen wearing grimaces instead of green berets hustled up to the craft, many carrying children in both arms.

"No brats of the indigenous persuasion!" The pilot was screaming above the whine of turbines and *whop-whop-whop* of fifty-foot blades above, but the ashen-faced medics were ignoring him.

Zack was too. He turned the Hatch-60 back over to Nelson and began hoisting both soldiers and children up off the skids. "These kids are comin' with us!" a Green Beret with subdued captain's bars on his collar advised anyone within earshot. "They don't stand a chance with Charlie!"

"As of right now, they're officially orphans!" A stocky NCO with blood streaming down one bulging bicep followed the SF officer aboard. "Their parents are dead. Took some of the first rounds right between the eyes. This whole fucking ville is an orphanage in the making."

"Half the adult population just got *fini*'d by a hellacious mortar barrage," the captain added, trying to pry one of the children from his waist so he could help the doorgunners with the ammo. "I haven't seen anything like tonight since that rampage down in Mytho back in '63!"

Larson glanced at a young girl scampering back into a corner between ammo boxes. Her face was streaked with soot and dirt, and long black hair fanned out across the front of her figure, but he could tell by the whimper and expression she

4

was not even into her teens yet. He wondered how such a child could face the future with such horrors filling her past.

Their eyes met for a brief instant, Larson's and the girl's, and in that ageless moment he understood something new about the war in Vietnam, something he had never encountered before on all the missions he'd flown. There were actually people down there, under the gunships. This girl represented them.

Larson's fingers were still numb from firing the machine gun, and his whole upper body was shaking from the thundering discharges, but he managed to wink at the child as the clanking golden brass of empty shells piled up around his boots. And the girl responded with a bewildered half-smile.

Two more corpsmen piled onboard, and the SF captain gave the thumbs-up. *Peg*'s pilot was not even waiting for a signal from the cabin. He had been monitoring activity on the ground, and as soon as the last Green Beret jumped up onto a landing skid, the craft's tail rose and *Pegasus* pivoted, ascending as she whirled around, nose dipping.

The other six gunships in the rescue muster had been swooping in and out of the area in circular patterns, their crews attempting to keep Charlie pinned down until the extraction of medical personnel could be effected.

"What about the villagers who are still down there?" Private Chappell yelled, wide-eyed, as *Peg* rose up above the treetops, leaving the valley fighting far behind.

"Charlie just wanted us," the Green Beret captain replied, removing a fatigue blouse to reveal several minute puncture wounds from mortar shrapnel across his chest. "Now that we're out of there, they'll pull back into the tree line."

"Well, I don't know." Chappell didn't sound very convinced. He removed thick, black-framed glasses and ran a palm back across short, black, sweat-soaked hair. "Before I came over here, I read about them Victor Charlies in *National Geographic* and I don't think they're the forgive-and-forget type."

"Before you came over here?" The sergeant squatting with two small boys held firmly in his grasp laughed. The children were staring out the hatches at the blur of treetops racing past. They were terrified by the roar of rotors and the manner in which every section of *Pegasus* seemed to be shaking and vibrating out of sync. Yet somehow the huge metallic predator remained airborne. "Just where the hell did you happen to pick up a copy of *National*—"

"Back in . . . uh, well, back stateside," the newby admitted sheepishly. He glanced away, acting as if the pile of phone books that protected doorgunners' private parts from ground fire needed attending to.

"That's what I thought." The NCO and captain both nodded at the same time, exchanging confident smirks. "Well, let me tell you something, son," the sergeant said somberly. "We truly fucking appreciate your pullin' us outta a bind back there and all, but you don't know diddly-squat about Victor-fuck-ing-Charlie—do you catch my meaning?"

Chappell did not immediately respond.

"Sure, Charlie's gonna have a hair up his ass about us gettin' extracted so smooth and all, but he'll get over it. This is a showpiece hamlet, pal. Press corps pricks comin' through here all the time. The dinks don't want any more of a bad name for themselves in this area than they've already got."

The other Green Beret tapped the SF combat patch on his right shoulder. "We've been over here since the CIA was OSS, fella. We use *National Geographic* for toilet paper."

"When we can get it." His commander laughed, then winced as a bolt of pain arced down through his bruised and battered frame.

"It only hurts when you laugh, right?" Zack pulled a packet of painkiller from a pouch on his web belt and handed it to the soldier.

"Something like that."

"I think we oughta drop the kids off back at camp, then

6

return to the ville and *get some*!" The private crouched beside Chappell appeared eager for action.

"Only if you drop us off along with baby-san there." The Green Beret sergeant smiled when he motioned to the terrified girl. She tried to smile back, but her lips wrinkled in distress and the only response became tears. "We've had enough excitement for one night. My MOS is medicine, not misery."

Nelson was definitely disappointed. He'd been in The Nam only a few weeks, but had already heard all the double-vet stories a dozen times each. The youth wanted some VC molars hanging from his dogtags chain. He wanted his Ace-of-Spades deck of DEATH FROM ABOVE playing cards to grow smaller. He wanted a HOG HEAVEN patch sewn across the back of his flak jacket. Enough of this humanitarian crap already; he wanted to kill something!

But the kid knew he was being outvoted. And he was well aware the men making the decisions knew more about The Nam and their options and the right moves than Nasty Nel would know even six months from now. So the private with no time in grade opted to sit tight and quiet.


Army Nurse Lisa Maddox and First Cav medic Doc Delgado were waiting at the rear base camp when *Pegasus* touched down. The Green Beret captain handed the trembling and wild-eyed children down to the lieutenant one at a time before the tired crew members all dropped from the cabin.

"Well, what do we have here?" Maddox held the girl in her arms as the boys huddled around the Special Forces soldiers who had plucked them from the jaws of death. The lieutenant's long blond hair was pulled back in a ponytail, and though her face was free of any makeup, Larson and the others felt she was as beautiful as any doughnut dolly they had ever met in The Nam. She was their own private Miss America. "Do any of you kids speak English?" She swept back the

7

girl's long black hair with slender fingers and kissed her lightly on the cheek. The response was an outburst of tears, and the child wrapped her arms tightly around Maddox's neck.

The captain whispered something in hushed Vietnamese to the little girl—words of encouragement, it seemed to the nurse—but the girl only responded with negative nods and kept her face buried against the lieutenant's neck.

"Come on, honey." The sergeant was beside her now, and Maddox swallowed hard when she noticed for the first time how much blood covered the Americans. "You can tell the lieutenant what you told us. She's your friend now, too. Just like me and Captain Jerry, hon. Really."

More helicopters were flaring in for abrupt landings behind *Pegasus*, and Maddox shielded the girl's face from the wall of dust that billowed out from the flapping rotors. "We'd better get these kids inside," she said, "and get them checked out."

"VC kill mama-san. Kill papa-san!" the girl said finally as Lt. Maddox turned to head for the glowing lights of the aid station. "VC Numba Ten! Someday I join army. *Kill* VC!"

"Sure, sure, honey. No sweat." Maddox kissed the girl on the cheek again as she hustled her away from the whine of turbines and the escalating profanity of the arriving troops. "We're here to help you, child. Everything is going to be all right."

Larson and the rest of his crew stood amidst the hardened and weary Green Berets, watching in silence as Lt. Maddox followed Delgado toward the portable E.R.

"Nice piece of ass," the SF sergeant finally decided. All of the men's eyes were obviously zeroed in on Lisa's shapely haunches as she gracefully sauntered through the swirling gloom. "I wouldn't mind pokin' that a little bit myself."

Zack laughed, not really worried. "Better keep your voice down. Her old man is a general down at Puzzle Palace."

"Saigon?" The captain seemed surprised.

"Disneyland East," the Professor confirmed.

"You'd think with Daddy Brass-Balls in such a high position she'd be treatin' cases of the clap down at 3rd Field Hospital instead o' dodgin' mortar shrapnel up here in the boonies," the sergeant mused.

"Lisa . . . I mean, the lieutenant don't care much for eight-and-skate down in the big city," Larson explained as the group started toward a dimly lit bunker from which the fragrance of fresh coffee was drifting. "She told me once she really digs the action out in the sticks."

"She was with us in the Ia Drang." Zack patted down his four jungle fatigue shirt pockets in search of a cigar butt, frowned, and began checking the thigh pockets of his trousers without slowing his pace. "She's a good ol' broad." He grinned with admiration. "Not like some of your field hospital types who think their shit don't stink."

"That's not fair, Leo." Larson glanced over at the big NCO.

Zack nodded sheepishly, remembering the nurses who had saved his leg after medics bandaged it up at the foot of the great Chu Pong. "Yah, you're right, but fuck it—don' mean nothin', slick."

"The Lieutenant manages to pretty much follow the unit from operation to operation," Larson added for the Green Berets' benefit.

"Well, I'd still like to dip my wick in her—" the SF sergeant began, but Larson interrupted with a dry chuckle and a wave of his hand.

"No chance," he said matter-of-factly. "She's been ballin' that medic you saw helpin' her with the kids since we were killin' commies for Christ back in the Ia Drang."

Zack shot the Professor an icy look of caution, but Larson didn't seem to notice.

"But she's an officer." The Green Beret captain's lower jaw was nearly dragging in the red clay of Bong Son.

"Since when has *that* counted for anything, sir?" Larson sounded proud. He both respected and hated these brave and legendary Green Berets, but it was not in the Professor's personality to pass up a chance to point out a classic case of fraternization between officers and NCOs.

The captain chuckled. "I think I've seen everything now."

Zack sighed with relief. The Special Forces captain's amused grin was proof he was ready to drop the matter.

The SF sergeant was rubbing his meaty palms together as Zack led them all into the mess tent. "I knew the moment I saw her that nurse was my kinda cunt." He was speaking to his C.O. as if the others were not there. "She obviously prefers noncommissioned officers, *sir*." He laughed loudly, grinding it in for the captain's benefit.

"And noncommissioned officers of Hispanic heritage at that." The captain smiled back. He was not about to let his favorite sergeant get the best of him.

"Aren't you two more in the mood for a check-up and scrub-down at the dispensary than the poison they serve in this dump?" Zack couldn't help but notice the trail of blood both Green Berets were leaving in their bootprints. Leo was having second thoughts about the severity of their wounds. The amount of blood looked serious.

"Later." The sergeant dismissed his concerns with a brusk wave of a hand. "The E.R.'s crowded enough with all those Viet kids over there. Right now, my belly's aching more than anything else, and it's got nothing to do with bombs and bullets. Beside, I wanna wait till things quiet down, so I can have that round-eyed princess all to myself."

"Aw, quit your belly-achin'." His C.O. picked an already opened tin from a stack of mess kits and led the line through midnight chow.

"Say!" the mess sergeant supervising the men on KP called to Zack, who was still holding open a tent flap. Two more helicopters were landing in the distance, and rolling clouds of dust from their rotorblades headed directly for the fortified bunker. "You comin' or goin'?"

"Yah, Leo!" Larson spotted the dust rushing toward them. "You gonna grace us with your presence, or you gonna let the

10

red clay of Bong Son spice my serving of ham and mother-fuckers?"

Hands on his hips now, Zack let the tent flap fall behind him as he stepped back outside to monitor the situation developing between both helicopters. Sensing trouble, Larson and the others from Echo Company also set down their trays and ambled over to the crew chief's side, while the Green Berets ignored the proceedings, interested only in their food.

"Is that Lawless?" The Professor could barely make out the two warrant officers arguing in the gloom, fifty yards away.

"Yep," Zack confirmed softly, biting his lip. "I'm afraid so. Lawless and the Gunslinger."

"And they're having a disagreement over something."

"Yep." Leo the Lionhearted shook his head from side to side slowly. "Kinda sounds that way, don' it."

Larson folded his arms across his chest as Chappell and Nelson moved closer, intrigued by the nightly after-action ritual they had grown accustomed to witnessing. "And you think we oughta step in and stop it before it gets serious?" The whine of jet turbines and whirring rip of rotors through the wet, muggy air was decreasing as the two gunship pilots' shouts quickly grew.

"Naw." Zack licked bruised and chapped lips. "Not yet. I don't think it's gonna get serious tonight."

The two pilots were a study in contrasts. Warlokk, or "Lawless" as most grunts called him, was a career soldier of short stature but big goals and dreams. With forearms almost as thick as his biceps, he could dazzle the local maidens with his piercing blue eyes. But when Lance "Lawless" Warlokk smiled, only half his face ever cooperated—the half not slightly disfigured by shrapnel from an RPG that exploded through his cockpit window "the monsoon before." He preferred to keep his blond hair shaved short, and had in the past shown up on missions sporting absurd Mohawk or even Beatles-style wigs. Normally clean-shaven, the man had been known to make his appearance at extraction points wearing a

Santa Claus beard or even a Ho Chi Minh goatee. In contrast to The Gunslinger, whose specialty was unarmed med-evac slicks, Lawless flew the sleek, new Cobra attack gunships—two-man choppers equipped with the latest rockets and armament, and a snout painted with intimidating shark's teeth.

Cliff Gabriel, on the other hand, walked with a limp. His stocky frame was also a bit shorter than the average battlefield grunt, but his reputation and aggressive personality more than made up for any lack of height. His body was covered with scars from numerous crash landings in the past, and the man was a hero to the soldiers in the rain forest, whom he had saved countless times over. Like Warlokk, Gabriel shifted somewhere between his late twenties and early thirties. He had been briefly held as a prisoner of war by the Laotians the year before, and tortured. He commenced wearing a revolver on his hip after the capture and escape, vowing never again to be taken alive by the enemy. Hence the nickname "Gunslinger," which his best friend Lawless Warlokk tagged him with. His best friend, that is, until Nurse Lisa Maddox entered the picture. The lieutenant became the center of attention for both men as well as the object of their dreams and desires, only to quash the pilots' fantasies when she was caught with medic Danny Delgado between her lily-white thighs.

That was several weeks ago, and neither warrant officer had lodged an official report concerning the incident. Maddox was still cordial toward the chopper jocks, and she and Delgado kept their off-duty affair private, but it was obvious to every swingin' dick in Echo Company the head nurse was up for grabs. And that was the only incentive Warlokk and Gabriel needed to stay in the game, however confusing it had become.

"I'm just saying you had no right to cut me off like that," Gabriel was insisting as the two pilots backed out of the stare-down contest and started for the glow in the distance that signaled coffee on the burner.

"Bustin' my balls to get between you and the Cong is my

*job*, Rodney!" Warlokk used his best Dangerfield accent. "I *am* the ace chopper jock of this battalion, ain't I? Last time I looked, *you* was drivin' a goddamned slick, Mister! And slicks are for transportin' the wounded back to the rear, period. I was pilotin' a snake, and—"

"That's another thing I been meanin' to talk to you about." Gabriel held the tent flap back, and both warrant officers brushed past Zack without so much as a nod. "Neil Nazi advised me my request for transfer to Cobras was denied because *you* specifically counselled the Colonel against it. Now what kinda shit is that."

"I told Buchanan you were the best Dustoff pilot I ever saw," Warlokk countered with a sly grin.

"Bullshit!" The Gunslinger ignored the privileges of rank and fell in with the regular grunts at the end of the line.

"No." Warlokk's smile faded somewhat as Gabriel turned back to face him. "He asked me what I thought of your request for transfer to snakes, and I told him that, besides the shortage of Cobras, I didn't think you could be as good a gunship AC as you are a medivac pilot."

"You fuckwad."

Warlokk's hands came up, palms out, in a gesture of surrender. "Hey, cut me some slack, Gabe." He forced a dry laugh for the benefit of the men eavesdropping nearby. "I told him you were the best goddamned Dustoff pilot I ever saw, and that that was where I wanted to see you stay. You're savin' more lives guidin' a Huey slick into hot LZ's then you ever would behind the cyclic of a—"

"You fuckwad," Gabriel repeated. "I'm tired of saving lives. You ever seen that T-shirt The Stork used to wear before. . . . The one with the two vultures sittin' on a tamarind branch, looking down on a Viet farmer and his water buffalo, plowing rice paddy? Saying: 'Patience, My Ass—I'm Gonna Kill a Commie for Mommy.' The farmer's got an AK slung over his shoulder and he's—"

13

"Yeah, so?" Lawless passed up the rations and settled for a mug of steaming coffee.

Gabriel watched him struggle with the decision whether or not to add sugar and milk to the brew. "Well, that's how *I'm* beginning to feel about this chopper war, Lance. Sure, the Air Medals all look nice on your Class-A's back in The World, but this is here, and now is now."

"Huh?" Warlokk cast him a quizzical look.

"We may never make it back stateside," Gabriel explained his theory further. "And I want to smoke some zips before some lucky dink drops his thumper and the accidental discharge blows me out of the void."

"You've got a strange way of putting it, Cliff."

"Screw it." Gabriel stared at the green lining on the powdered eggs as the cook slapped them onto his tray. His nostrils curled slightly in disgust. "I just want you to see where I'm coming from."

"I know where you're coming from," Warlokk began, only to have the other pilot cut him off.

"Then let's trade. Just for a week or two."

"I don't fly slicks."

"You could for a week. A week, or two." There was something desperate in Gabriel's voice, and though Warlokk detected it, he chose to ignore the plea.

"Fucking forget it, Cliff. Dustoffs ain't my style." Warlokk gave up on the other selections the mess sergeant was offering that night, and left the line. He headed over for a cable-spool table in the cramped bunker's low-ceilinged corner.

Gabriel cleared his throat as he followed Lawless. "I'd have thought you'd jump at the chance to fly medivac." He snickered quietly. "More chances of getting to see Lisa at the hospital. More chances to—"

Warlokk did not take the bait. Instead, he laughed in Gabriel's face as both men sat down. "Shit, Gabe, what kinda fantasy world you livin' in, boy? I can stop by and see Lisa anytime my gonads are in need of a little."

Sgt. Zack smiled to himself as he listened to the warrant officers argue. If Victor Charlie didn't cancel their tickets they'd probably do each other in. Eventually. Zack shook his head slowly at the thought: Such a waste. Two good soldiers, their priorities sent asunder by pussy.

The thought brought another chuckle to Leo the Lionhearted, but then his gut contracted and he sucked down the air in his lungs with a start. It was a quiet gasp, actually, and Zack backed deeper into the shadows of the tent.

He had seen something in the bamboo tree line beyond the wire. Something moving toward the perimeter. Something that gleamed yet was as black and elusive as a bayou ghost slithering through swamp reeds.

Instinct told him what he was seeing. Experience demanded he sound the alarm and slam the charging handle of his M-16 into action. But Zack waited a moment longer.

This was a new base camp. They were in a strange land, a weird valley. And the men were all edgy lately. The Ia Drang had made them that way, and respect for the officers and NCOs was on the wane. The troopers were cocky after the seige and survival of Plei Me, and they were making more and more fun of that new Lieutenant Vance's cautious decisions.

That was why Sgt. Leopold Zack waited until the shifting shadows approaching the perimeter became black-pajama-clad sappers, and the sparkle in the night became flashing bayonets, before he slipped the rifle from his shoulder and began firing at pith helmets rushing the concertina.

# CHAPTER 2

## Plei Me, Ia Drang Valley

Raindrops lifting puffs of dust from the red clay subsided to a warm drizzle throughout Ia Drang Valley. Brody The Whoremonger turned away from the swirling mists and concentrated instead on a double rainbow extending out over the jungle.

But a humid breeze racing down through the grave markers seemed to call to the American, and he forced himself to face the mound again. A single iron stake to mark the mass grave, and Treat Brody stared down at it, fighting the tears as helicopter gunships cruised past low overhead, their powerful rotors beating the sheets of rain down on him.

"I'm sorry, Koy." Brody let his rucksack fall from his back. He leaned a blood-caked M-16 against the same tree she has so often draped her clothes from.

The same tree that had so often sheltered her from the prowling Cobra choppers and shielded her from view of the Plei Me tower guards, before she would strip naked and slide beneath the perimeter wires of sparkling concertina to assault the Special Forces camp after dark.

Brody dropped to his knees. He still couldn't believe it. What the Green Berets and Strikers at the outpost told him upon his return from the fighting at LZ X-Ray.

Using torn and bruised knuckles to wipe a tear from his cheek, the doorgunner dropped to his knees and began unstrapping the entrenching tool from the back of his ruck.

I'm sorry I wasn't here when you needed me, Koy." His rasping whisper was all but covered by a gaggle of Hueys floating in off the horizon. Brody did not look up to see where they came from, or where they were going. He unscrewed the keeper, opened the small shovel's blade, then retightened the device. When he plunged it into the mound, the young soldier collapsed in sobs. All strength drained from Brody as the memories flooded back to torture him. The guilt increased tenfold, forcing the weight of a hundred gunships down on his shoulders. *Taunted and teased in Vietnamese* . . . He could hear her voice now, soft and soothing above the roar of thunder rolling through the belly of storm clouds above. *Please come back to me, Treat Brody! Please come back to Koy!*

"I'm so sorry, Koy." He took hold of the shovel again as a new torrent of rain washed across the gently sloping hills rising above the military compound. Brody took hold of the shovel and slowly submerged it into the mud. He was fighting the images. Images that always came back to him when he tried to picture her face in his mind. Images of *Pegasus* hovering above the perimeter . . . images of a cold and uncaring Treat Brody firing down at the naked girl in the wire.

He told himself she could have been anyone, any of a dozen VC women rumored to have helped build the tunnel system that crisscrossed the approaches to Plei Me. The naked guerrilla he had cut in half with his hatch-60 looked like any of a thousand other Vietnamese women from that distance— the long black hair; the smooth, shapely, amber flesh, curves he had aimed at, never paying any attention to the face. Faces were always a blur from that altitude. He preferred the anonymity that wielding death from above the treetops afforded doorgunners. It helped cut down on the nightmares.

Brody told himself the woman he blew to shreds that afternoon they left Plei Me *had* to have been one of the hardcore communists, not Koy. He refused to believe what the Montagnardes told him the day he returned from the operation in Ia Drang in search of her. "She Viet Cong, Bro-dee," they all had insisted. "The woman you search for was VC. We watched you kill her from chopper."

"One final parting shot," a Green Beret sergeant had added with a sly grin. "You really know how to say *Xin-loi* to your whores, boy!" And they had laughed. Every last one of them. "We buried her ripe ol' ass in a mass grave over on the hillside, with the others."

"Typical doggie Cav trooper." Another Special Forces NCO slapped Brody on the back as they led him down toward the compound's main gate. "Goes bonkers with a Hog-60, rippin' up tits and twats, then expects *us* to mop up the mess."

Everyone enjoyed a real laugh over that remark.

Thunder clashed directly overhead, making the hairs along the back of Treat's neck stand up, but he kept digging down into the mud without looking up. He couldn't leave her here. Not with all these slimy, no-good commies.

Dual bolts of lightning threw contrasting shadows across the gnarled fingers that suddenly came into view beneath the shovel. As he sprang back, the shifting shadows made it appear the fingers were moving!

*But that couldn't be!* He fell back down onto his knees and began digging furiously with his hands. *The mass grave had been covered over by a combat engineer's bulldozer more than two weeks ago!*

An arm, and then a soldier's entire left side slowly came into view, but the corpse Brody had unearthed belonged to a man, and he threw the rotting cadaver aside. Strips of spongy, rotting flesh clung to the grotesque claw of a hand.

"Koy!" he called out, a rolling crescendo of thunder pounding at his ears. He resumed digging with his hands, and a second corpse greeted him with flashing teeth as its skull

18

rolled from his grasp, down the hillside, worms and maggots wriggling in the empty, rodent-polished eye sockets.

*How would he know her?* his mind screamed as warm sheets of rain molded Brody's unruly blond hair down over his forehead.

He dug faster, spurred on, it seemed, by a renewed surge of adrenaline. But this was not the adrenaline of action-packed air assaults into Injun country, or the gut-gnawing charge that came with hand-to-hand combat.

Treat was experiencing a terror deep within that only desperate men, who've lost family, can know, a terror that powered his arms beyond normal abilities. Brody was edging beyond control. He was a rancher from the 1800s, whose white woman had been kidnapped by Indians while he was herding cattle, five miles away. A cop on the beat, whose girlfriend was raped and murdered while he sat in a coffeeshop, flirting with the waitress. A father, working nights, whose daughter was molested by a burglar; he was all these men—angry and fearless in his quest for revenge and his thirst for justice, yet helpless. And as he dug deeper into the rotting mass grave, Treat Brody refused to believe *he* might be the reason Koy was dead.

He tried to think it through again as he dug, to recreate those last few minutes as *Pegasus* ascended from the SF camp and the Skycrane trooper spotted the naked girl crawling beneath the wire. He attempted to justify his zeal in grabbing the soldier's submachinegun and showering the perimeter below with countless bursts of hot lead. But the images would not come now. His mind had shifted into defense, and was blocking the memories out.

"You're wasting your time, troop." One of the Green Beret sergeants materialized behind him, and Brody whirled around. The sound of his shouldered M-16 scraping against web belt rungs mingled with the steady din of raindrops striking the helipad tarmac in the distance.

"Bullshit," Brody muttered under his breath, dropping to his knees again.

"You didn't even know the girl," the NCO persisted.

"Leave me alone." Treat's trembling fingers sunk into the mud again.

"Just trying to help, pal." The older soldier turned to leave.

"I *did* know her!" His statement was a protest. Still digging without looking up, he sensed the sergeant had stopped. The soldiers kept their backs to each other, as if any conversation to follow required it.

"Give it up, son."

"I did know her, Sarge."

"I remember." His voice sounded more distant now as he faced the Special Forces outpost. "I remember that night you and Nervous Rex and Stormin' Norman and the others all got shit-faced in Top's bunker after your little escapade in the ville, slick. I remember the war story about eluding the MPs, and being helped by the whores, and—"

"She isn't—she wasn't—a whore." Koy's face flashed in front of him now, crystal clear. He could see her staring up at him in that tiny, dilapidated shack on the outskirts of Plei Me, flickering light from the flares and an elusive crescent moon revealing her shapely, unspoiled figure. And her true innocence. He could hear her voice as he dug down into the grave. He could hear her voice: *Make romance to me, Treat Brody.*

"You did not even know her name."

"Her name was Koy."

"You told us you never knew her name. That she was a great fuck, but no name."

"You're worse than a Vietnamese woman, Sarge." A sly chuckle escaped Brody, but he did not stop digging as another severed limb rose to the surface and he tossed it aside.

"How so?"

"Vietnamese women may forgive, but they never forget."

"I'm not sure I appreciate the comparison. I'll have to mull that one over, slick. In the meantime, why don't we double-time back over to camp and discuss this over an army-issue brew. I'm one old Asian hand who's gettin' too old for this layin'-dog-under-the-monsoon crap."

"Not until I find her."

She had become someone special, that dark evening beneath the flares. Especially after he realized she was a cherry girl—a virgin. A beautiful Vietnamese maiden, who cherished her culture and all the traditional customs, but made the decision to submit to this tall, handsome foreigner, whose hair reminded her of clouds floating over the rice paddies. She had never kissed a man whose eyes were the color of the sky after a storm, Koy had confided in him, and Brody the Whoremonger felt suddenly unworthy. Humbled beyond words, and unworthy. This doorgunner extraordinaire had never been so moved by such a vulnerable and trusting smile.

"I am a soldier, Koy." He could hear his own words now as he saw her tears of contentment become silent cries of disappointment and confusion. "I will always be one. Riding the gunships is what I live for. You deserve better."

And he left her without looking back.

Brody's return to the Ia Drang Valley campaign drastically changed the way he looked at life and death. The 1st Cavalry Division had participated in the first major U.S. engagement of North Vietnamese forces during October and November, and paid a heavy price: Some 240 American soldiers perished defending the Ia Drang. The final enemy body count totaled over 1,800 NVA regulars.

Treat Brody promised himself, Buddha, and any rain forest gods who'd listen that if he survived the valley battles, he would return to Plei Me and find Koy. He had thirty days' leave time on the books, and if it took a month to search every hut in the ville, he'd do it. She had become even more precious to him after the fighting.

Memories of her face, and her voice, and her touch had helped him through all the death, blood, pain, and suffering in

21

the Ia Drang. Koy had become his reason to survive. He would return to her, and do it the right way.

*You didn't even know her.* And he hadn't. But Koy had become his whole world.

The memory of her had replaced his lust for the midnight chopper missions into hell. Brody no longer lived for the smell of gunsmoke and cordite drifting on the jungle breeze. He no longer anticipated the reassuring flap of Huey rotors with each gaggle of birds floating in off the horizon. Instead, he cherished the memory of her fragrance that night. He saw her smile in the dim light. The slowly revolving ceiling fan above her had replaced the all-protecting rotorblades of the only "girl" Brody had ever been loyal to: *Pegasus*.

Treat's breath left him when the crossed arms appeared in the mud. He knew instantly they belonged to Koy.

The Green Beret sergeant helped him rebury the woman's upper torso several hundred meters away from the mass grave in a quiet rain-forest clearing, far away from the main trails running in and out of Plei Me. Koy's body had been nearly severed at the waist when she was killed, and the 'Yard Strikers were not particularly gentle or selective as they flung terribly mutilated and disfigured corpses into the pit.

The sergeant who refilled both of their DEATH FROM ABOVE coffee mugs stared across the empty ammo-crate table at Brody, wondering what visions the young Cavalry trooper chased in the steam rising from the rim.

"Headed back to the Tea Plantation?" The Special Forces sergeant referred to the First Cav's Ia Drang base camp. "I hear tell you boys brought bookoo smoke down on Charlie out there, and—"

"I'm on my thirty-days leave, Sarge," Brody interrupted, taking a long drink of the hot coffee.

22

"You already told us. But you don't wanna spend it here in Plei Me, son."

"I had really planned on finding Koy, and taking her over to Pleiku or Danang. I had a week set aside just to locate her, then another in the big city, then I was going to take her to a place in Thailand where there isn't any war. A place where we could—"

"Come on, son. She didn't even have a passport, did she?" The sergeant brought his mug to chapped lips, but the coffee was still practically boiling. "Hell, I'll bet *you* don't even have a passport."

"Since when have mere technicalities stopped Brody the—" He slammed his empty cup on the table. "Fuck. Gimme a refill, Sarge. And can you spice it with something strong?" A tight grin of resignation warped Brody's exhausted features.

The NCO smiled broadly. "Now that's what I like to see." He laughed. "You're finally starting to lighten up, son. Ain't never been a woman on God's green earth worth shedding a tear for!"

Brody stood and started up the sandbagged steps of the underground bunker before the sergeant could pour any coffee. "The Division's headed down to Binh Dinh Province," he said. "They've probably left already, in fact. I'm only a few days into my thirty. I'm gonna hop a convoy down to Saigon, Sarge. Maybe go AWOL. Move in with one of those hookers down on Le Loi Street or Tu Do—the fifty-piaster all-night girls I've been hearing so much about from Two-Step and The Stork."

"Naw." The sergeant folded his arms across his chest and shook his head slowly from side to side as they emerged topside. Eyes assaulted by shafts of sunlight lancing in off the eastern horizon, both soldiers shielded their faces. "You don' wanna go and—"

"Yah. I'm gonna get me an all-night girl in some fancy bungalow where it's never dark 'cause o' all the neon, Sarge.

And I'm gonna pay her to sit on my face for the rest o' my life."

"They got more MPs down in Saigon than flies on a body bag, boy." The sergeant laughed again. "You wouldn't last two weeks as a deserter. You've got that look."

Brody's smile vanished. He turned to face the NCO. "What look?"

"That guilty look." He knew immediately it was a poor choice of words and slapped Treat on the back lightly. "Aw, hell. Go on down to Sin City. See if I give a shit. But steer clear of them MPs."

They exchanged looks that were both sarcastic and skeptical.

Beyond several P.O.W. conexes, the huge dual rotors of a grounded Chinook helicopter began slowly turning as the craft's monstrous turbines kicked in.

"Maybe I could thumb a ride aboard that jolly green, if it's headed there," Brody suggested.

"I doubt it, dude. But it couldn't hurt to try."

Brody needed little other encouragement. He was quickly off, running through the clouds of dust billowing out from under the Marine helicopter's rotorwash.

"Give my regards to the go-go girls at the Golden Lotus! On Tu Do Street!" The salty Green Beret added as an afterthought, "And send me a postcard, kid!" His words were competing with the rising roar of flapping rotorblades. "I want a tit card of them ladies of questionable virtue! They got a rackful at Tan Son Nhut Airport!"

Against all odds, the Chinook did happen to be headed south. Notorious LBJ (Long Binh Jail) was the final destination, but the crew chief waved Brody onboard, confident he could make connections into Saigon rather easily once they were down out of the Highlands. "We got plenty of room," he

24

was told by a tall and lanky Marine wearing a holstered .45 and a toothy smile.

Glancing about the cabin as he climbed in, Brody noticed there were only a half dozen passengers in the lumbering CH-47, and they all wore ankle manacles. He glanced up at the crew chief, bewildered. "Prisoners?" Brody never thought of The Nam as being a place where anyone concerned themselves with law and order, crime and punishment.

"Deserters, my man," the Marine grumbled matter-of-factly, as the Chinook trembled and vibrated violently, then ascended with a jerking climb.

"Deserters?" He was not sure he heard the crew chief right —the downblast was almost deafening now.

"From that MP raid on the whorehouse in Plei Me couple weeks ago," came the dry reply as the black soldier raised his voice to compete with the rotors.

"Green Berets?" Brody was astonished.

The Marine erupted into laughter. "Fuck, no! Doggies from Danang, my man—no offense." He eyed Treat's 1st Air Cavalry combat patch.

"Danang?" Brody stared at the prisoners, who in turn kept their eyes on their boots. They were beaten, broken GIs, with not a trace of defiance in their features.

"Yep. Danang. Went over the hill and set up shop in Plei Me after they heard about the Honda Honies our Green Beaners were trying to keep a secret. Figured no one would come looking for 'em in Nowhere Land, I guess. Thought they were home free, so to speak . . . assuming they could accept Plei Me as home sweet home from here on out. Every last one of 'em is *dinky-dau*, if ya ask me, friend." The crew chief was using the Vietnamese slang for "crazy." "They shoulda picked Saigon, or stayed in Danang."

But Treat Brody was no longer listening to the Marine sergeant. And he had lost interest in the prisoners.

"Now you take Saigon." The crew chief moved closer and rambled on. "That's a cesspool of three million zips, my man!

25

*Three fuckin' million!* Forty or fifty percent of which are probably hard-core Cong, if ya get my meaning." He winked down at Brody. "With that many VC ridin' scooters sidesaddle, you'd never have a dull moment. Yep, in Saigon, an AWOL could probably get lost in the crowd. For a while, anyway.

"Know some bloods who thought they could outthink The Man, but Saigon's got some badass MPs, too. Shee-it, I heard tell they got military po-lice workin' the street down there who used to have cushy cop jobs back in The World, you know? But they gave it all up to get back to Saigon, can you stomach that? They call it the toughest beat in the world, partner. Those dudes wearin' armbands down there aren't even GIs, bud: they love it too much. Even know some brothers that are workin' patrol down there. Goofiest-talkin' motherfuckers you ever heard. They re-*enlist* to *stay* in Saigon! Can you figure that? Huh? Can you?"

Brody was not thinking about Saigon anymore. The Chinook was taking the same flight path as *Peg* had that fateful day. They would be passing over the spot any second now.

When the sparkling strands of concertina wire came into view, Brody thought he was going to pass out. He spotted the clearing without having to search for it. But there was no evidence of the pool of blood, no darker stain across the red clay. The reeds, the elephant grass, the ancient tamarind— none of it seemed disturbed. The jungle had reclaimed Koy, and now it was reclaiming the clearing.

He wished he had paid more attention to her face before pulling the trigger. So he would know if she had still been alive when the dog trotted forth from the peaceful sea of shimmering elephant grass and began tearing her intestines out with its teeth.

# CHAPTER 3

## An Lao Valley

Black Buddha, as the Arvins often called Zack behind his back, was never so glad he'd been born with a dark shade of skin. The Viet Cong snipers were shooting at the white soldiers, whose faces reflected light from the flares better.

He pulled the four fragmentation grenades off his web belt and lined them up along the edge of the trench he'd jumped into when the surprise sapper attack began. He switched his M-16 to auto, and unloaded on the shadows crisscrossing the perimeter with thirty rounds from the rifle's banana clip. Then he pulled the pin from the first grenade and heaved with all his might, watching, with his mind's eye, as the projectile sailed out over the wire into the heart of Charlie's ranks.

The Air Cavalry sergeant popped his rifle's ejector button, and as the empty magazine dropped into the dust, he rammed a fresh banana clip home, its last ten rounds red tracers.

Zack threw another grenade, and then a third. Screams from the communist sappers filled the night air, and just as the American was about to rise up over the edge of the trench to unload with his M-16 again, a flare popped overhead, revealing hundreds of ghostlike shapes rushing out from the misty tree line beyond the wire.

"Jesus," he muttered under his breath, switching his

weapon to semi-automatic. "No way. No way we gonna make it outta this one, baby. Life's a bitch and then you fry." He chuckled to himself, deciding to save the last grenade for one final surprise he'd keep under his body after Charlie ended his career.

At the same moment Zack resumed firing with his rifle, a burst of green VC tracers stitched through the smoky air barely a few inches above his head, and a body slammed into him from behind.

Visions of Charlie sneaking up on him from the rear rushed through Zack's mind as he whirled around, hoping to get one last bayonet thrust in before he died.

"Sgt. Zack! It's me! *Don't shoot!* For God's sake, don't—"

"I see ya, Lieutenant. I see ya!" Leopold Zack did not appear excited in the least, but merely resumed peppering the distant tree line with hot lead. Shadows in the bamboo dropped left and right. Many flew backwards through the air, out of sight.

"I was just checking our defenses." First Lt. Jacob Vance held out his .45, but hesitated at pulling the trigger. Zack looked him over in a flash: no other weapons, probably five rounds in the pistol and another ten on his web belt. By the book.

Zack frowned. "I thought we'd be all right 'til that flare popped and I saw how many of the zip bastards are out there," he said. They both watched the bright golden flare break away from its silk parachute and plummet to earth, leaving a smoky trail behind in the sky to mark its path.

"Do you think they'll overrun the camp?" Vance didn't sound worried for his own neck but for his men's, which Zack interpreted as a good sign.

"Maybe. It's possible, but I doubt it. The Colonel better get on the horn and order some air support to go, though. I smell death on the wind. I just hope it's dink blood I smell and not ours."

"I catch your meaning on that, Leo. One hundred percent!

Col. Buchanan was crankin' up the field phone as he told me to beat feet for a sitrep. So that's what I'm doin'."

Zack glanced back at the lieutenant. He didn't know much about Vance, but the officer had proven himself under fire at Ia Drang and again at Plei Me, and that was all that really mattered to the big NCO.

Vance stood at around five foot ten, weighing in at 160, tops. He was slender, but physically fit, as were ninety-nine percent of the lieutenants Zack saw come to The Nam fresh from West Point. He had a babyface below a neatly trimmed black crewcut. When Zack first met Vance, the twenty-two-year-old possessed piercing blue eyes despite his obvious innocence and inexperience in military matters. Now, the young officer's cheeks were sunken, and his eyes had dulled, looking like they belonged to a hundred-year-old man. Jacob Vance drifted in and out of that thousand-yard stare as he spoke with Zack, using only the slightest Southern twang. "This sucks the big one, Sgt. Zack." The officer breathed in dust as a mortar barrage swept over the camp and both soldiers became as flat as possible along the bottom of the shallow trench.

"Got that right."

"Wait a minute."

"I hear it."

Jets. The thick, sticky night air was parting for two sleek metal predators. Phantom jet fighters swooped in so low over the camp Vance thought his eardrums would burst when their afterburners kicked in.

"Sorry 'bout that, Charlie!" A grunt who had remained in one of the outpost's corner towers throughout the firefight waved his fist defiantly in the air as four napalm canisters slammed into the tree line, lighting up the darkness with billowing balls of green and gold flame as they floated majestically skyward.

"Yah!" Zack rose from cover and fired off a long burst of shells until the first red tracer appeared. "*Get some*, wingnuts!"

The night filled with the screams of dying crispy critters as the wall of bamboo became a crackling, roaring inferno, eating up anything that moved through it. Smoldering corpses staggered forth, the flesh peeling off their skulls as they escaped the angry rain forest only to topple over, lifeless. "I'm grossed!" Zack and Vance could hear the Professor complaining somewhere in a bunker behind them. "This is mindfuck to the max!" Larson screamed. But he was firing his M-16 from the hip, too.

"Is Shawn freaking out?" Vance solicited Leo's opinion. He sounded serious. Serious and worried.

"That pussy has been a pantywaist ever since the first day I met him." Sgt. Zack didn't seem concerned as he unleashed the last nine rounds on rock-and-roll.

Vance watched, mesmerized, as the crimson glow from the tracers seemed to create a ghostly halo around Zack. But then the NCO's magazine emptied, the illusion faded, and the pitch black of a moonless night closed in again on all sides.

The jets swooped in for another pass, and the men cheered them on, though there was no way the pilots could hear anything but their turbines screaming and ordnance exploding. But they knew. They knew what a relief it was to be saved by air support.

"Oh my God!" The camp went suddenly silent as a brilliant lancelike object rose from the treetops, catching one of the F-4 Phantoms in the belly.

A blinding explosion followed, and though most of the Americans shielded their eyes, Zack watched the jet tumble end over end across the rain forest's triple canopy and disappear beyond a spreading blanket of thick, oily smoke. "Mary, Mother of God," Vance gasped.

"We've gotta get out there!" Zack rose from the trench and began running back toward the CP, Vance right behind him. the sergeant was headed for a radio or field phone.

"Do you think maybe they parachuted to safety?" Vance

asked between heavy breaths. He felt instantly stupid, but Zack made no attempt to belittle him.

"Not at that altitude, Lieutenant!" he replied as they ducked into Buchanan's bunker. "They were flying too low. Add the explosion, and the injuries sustained, and their only hope is *us*!"

Vance glanced back over a shoulder as the second jet swooped in even lower than before, laying down cover fire in hopes any survivors on the ground could make a mad scramble for freedom.

The Phantom vanished in the growing cloud of smoke, then reappeared far off in the murky distance, its afterburners bright orange moons as it climbed back toward the stars.

"I know, I know!" A tall, stocky man in his early fifties with an Adolf Hitler mustache and massive biceps silenced Zack with the wave of a hand. His other fist cradled a field phone under a lopsided helmet. A two-inch horizontal scar ran beneath Col. Neil Buchanan's left eye, but it was barely visible in the dim light of the underground command post. The C.O. was barechested except for a dusty flak jacket he wore unbuttoned over a muscular, sweat-laced chest.

Explosions outside rocked the bunker slightly, and dust filtered down from sandbags in the ceiling. Buchanan's face twisted with irritation, and he tilted his head down farther, trying to hear whoever was on the other end of the landline, but it was no use. The thunderclaps outside were coming nonstop now.

Buchanan glanced up and pointed at a corporal standing guard in the doorway. "Get out there and let me know if the dinks get through the wire!"

"Yo!" The soldier was a lanky Italian youth with a Brooklyn accent. "Yuh c'n bank on it, *suh*!" He yanked back his M-16's charging handle and rushed up through the swirling dust cloaking the bunker's entrance.

Buchanan threw down the field phone and kicked an empty ammo box across the floor. "Charlie cut the goddamned line!"

he complained. "Now what's this my man topside was telling me a Phantom got knocked out of the sky?"

"Right, Colonel!" Vance rushed up to Zack's side. "We saw Charlie shoot it down with a SAM or something."

"I think it was a lucky hit with an RPG, sir!" Zack interrupted. "It has that kind of doublepunch to it. Anyway, we gotta get a team together and—"

"Rescue them Air Force boys?"

"Right, sir!"

Col. Buchanan was sliding M-16 ammo pouches onto his web belt in preparation for leaving the bunker.

"It's the only right thing to do, sir. It's—" Vance began to say, but his explanation was unnecessary.

"I agree, son." Buchanan already had a cigar lit and was balancing it between his lips. "Let me just get some extra firepower hooked up here and then we'll be all set to bring smoke down on—"

"I really don't think you should participate . . . uh, I mean I just don't think you should be leaving the camp, sir."

Buchanan hesitated in midstep, seemingly taken aback. His cigar teetered on the edge of his lower lip.

Vance was expecting Zack to back him up, but the veteran NCO remained oddly silent all of a sudden.

The *thump-thump-thump* of helicopter rotors was reaching a dull crescendo outside. Some of the chopperjocks obviously had made it to their gunships, and had taken it upon themselves to assault the hostile treeline.

"You're right, son." A slight grin creased Buchanan's soot-coated features as he grabbed Lt. Vance's arm, gently turned him around, and guided him up the sandbag steps. "I definitely concur. *I'm* not going to lead the rescue mission out into that. *You* are. Now go with God, kill some commies for Christ, and bring me back some Cong skulls for my retirement mantel back in New Yo'k."

32

# CHAPTER 4

## Bangkok, Thailand

"This is it, Corky...I'm tellin' you, 'Cockbang, here we come!'" Snakeman Fletcher crowded the Boeing 727's fogged-up window as he surveyed the Kingdom of Siam below, rising swiftly to kiss the wheels of their jet. "Yep, they say Thailand's got the most beautiful women in the whole world, my friend. The whole...wide...world." Fletcher held his arms out to make his point, and Cordova protected his plastic cup of orange juice just in time.

"So mellow out, Snakeman." He surveyed the planeload of other GIs jetting to Bangkok for their week away from war. "We've got seven days and seven nights in the land of smiles and tongue jobs. Just hold onto your hard-on, dude."

Fletcher erupted into good-natured laughter. "Smiles and tongue jobs! Love that kinda talk." Snakeman watched row upon row of rusty-roofed squatters' huts spread out along the edges of the airport. The plane floated across several green canals and then—as nearly every soldier on the left side of the cabin stared at a topless teenaged girl sitting on an unmoving water buffalo in the middle of a rice paddy—set down with a scream of burning rubber. Cordova felt the craft tremble slightly, and then their pilot reversed the engines, and the powerful roar reassured him. He was whisked back into another time...another place. The memories worked their way

33

to the surface of his thoughts, protectively caressing him, and he saw another woman . . . felt her touch . . . heard her voice. Then watched her die. Again. Over and over.

"Let's go! Let's go!" A short, stocky Marine was pushing his way through the crowded aisle as the plane lurched to a stop beside the terminal. "I got only a hundred and sixty-eight hours in this town! Get a lot of slanted pussy to eat. Out! Move outta the way!"

Cordova glanced up at a stewardess. She was still smiling, refusing to let the soldiers' language affect her. Must be more than used to horny grunts on this Saigon-to-Bangkok run, Cordova decided. Must develop a real hard crust not to blush after a GI with no class and less brains uses the word "pussy" only a few feet in front of your face. Must develop a real gutter personality, Cordova's thoughts rambled on without direction, out of control as he watched her nipples, taut and erect, press against the fabric of her blouse as she stooped into the next row to retrieve a pillow. Must be a real bitch in bed . . . a real slut in the sack. Corky Cordova could think of nothing more he would love right then and there than to have the green-eyed blonde hike that silver miniskirt up over her hips, drop her drawers—if she was wearing any—and sit on his face. That's all. That's all he wanted for the rest of his R and R. He was in love. Snakeman could have all the bargirls in Bangkok. Just allow him one night with—

"Hands off your cock and up with your socks, soldier!" Fletcher was grabbing his elbow and guiding him toward the aisle. "The massage parlors don't come to you, amigo. You gotta go to them."

After the three-hour air-conditioned flight from South Vietnam, the heat and humidity of the airport terminal was a flashback to their first arrival in a country at war. They were safe now—for a week, anyway—but they were still in Southeast Asia. The faces were still Oriental. There were still temples on the horizon, and military vehicles everywhere. Snakeman seemed to read his mind. "At least you don't have to worry about the whores here inserting bamboo splinters in their *ying-yang!*"

"Don't be so sure." Cordova met the gaze of several prostitutes huddled on the far side of a customs counter as the American GIs entered a cavernous hangar the Thais had converted into a terminal only a few years earlier. The prostitutes were eager for new customers whose pockets were stuffed with combat pay, but no one said they had to enjoy their work. The dark, almond eyes of nearly all the young women were icy and laced with hate. Hate that could be softened somewhat with U.S. greenbacks and a handful of *baht,* but never cured completely.

Fletcher seemed absorbed with the actions of customs officials as he and Corky joined the long line of soldiers preparing to open their AWOL bags for inspection. "Okay . . . okay." He slowly nodded confidently. "No sweat. I got their routine down pat."

"Huh?" Cordova was mesmerized by a top-heavy whore with a Jackie Kennedy hairstyle who seemed absorbed in controlling an ice-cream cone. It was melting faster than she could lick it up.

Fletcher grabbed him gently by the shoulders and moved him two soldiers back. "They're letting every second and fifth GI through without an inspection. I'm number two, and now you're number five."

"I got nothing to hide, Snakeman." Cordova still could not take his eyes off the beauty with the lizardlike tongue. It was obvious she was just showing off her oral abilities, but he didn't care. It had been so long since he'd slept with a woman.

"Just shut up and take your sunglasses off," Fletcher coached him. "You wanna get through and get first dibs on the boom-boom girls, don't you?"

"Well, 'course, but . . ."

Forty five minutes later, after they were both chosen by customs agents for a spot check, the two First Cav troopers exited the security partition and were immediately surrounded by cabbies offering transportation to the hotel strips or notorious Patpong Road.

"Fucking customs dudes." Fletcher was shaking his head. "Never fails. What is it about my face they find suspicious? I can do without this kinda crap. Shit, I'm a fucking *guest* in their country, right? Now what kinda way is that to treat a 'guest?'"

"I doubt it was your face, Snakeman. It was probably the Luke The Gook Sucks Donkey Dick T-shirt."

"Well, shee-it, Corky. It was nothin' personal. Luke The Gook refers to Charlie, not any of these Thai types."

"I don't think those guys back there were in any mood for explanations."

"Fuck 'em if they can't take a joke, okay?" Fletcher waved the taxi drivers off and led his partner over to the woman devouring her third ice-cream cone.

"Well, just don't flash the soles of your boots at anybody, or moon a temple, or spit on the local currency. . ."

"Huh?"

". . . or badmouth the King or Queen . . ."

"Just what the heck are you ramblin' on about now, Corky-san?"

"Remember ol' Griff?"

"Griff? Yah, sure. From Delta Company. I heard he went AWOL couple months back." The prostitute standing in front of them was wearing bright pink hot pants and a blouse with no buttons, and Fletcher's eyes dropped to the swell of flesh pressing forth to get out. The woman's hand came up and she gently took hold of Snakeman's chin, forcing his gaze higher. She winked and blew him a loud kiss. Several customs agents turned at the sound and directed scowls of disapproval in their direction.

"Naw, he wasn't AWOL, Oh Honorable One. Griff took an R and R, just like you and me, amigo. Came to Thailand, too. Got a little boozed up, which is the norm, but kinda went

36

overboard when one of the hookers wouldn't suck on his ding-dong. Brody told me she gave him the 'No can do blow job, Joe' routine. 'Buddha dwell in head, Joe . . . so sorry . . . no can lower head to do that . . . Numba Ten *ching-ching* . . . .'"

"You're shittin' me."

"I wouldn't shit you, Snakeman—"

"I know." Fletcher's hands came up defensively. "I'm your favorite turd. So anyway . . ."

"So anyway, Griff—bein' the Good Ol' Boy that he's always been—grabs the chick by her ankles and holds her over the balcony railing, butt-ass naked, threatening to drop her on her sacred head if she don't comply with the 'oral agreement' he felt was made when the hundred *baht* changed hands.

"The Thai cops came, broke a couple nightsticks over the guy's noggin', then dragged him down to police headquarters after he ripped the money he had paid the girl in half—knowing it would piss off the cops, since you don't deface anything with the king's likeness on it—and yelled something about the king being a fag."

"Which is another thing you don't do in Bangkok, or anywhere else in Thailand. . . ."

"Right."

"Never fear, Snakeman's here." He bowed to the whore, and she responded by licking her fingers clean—slowly and sensuously.

"Why you name . . . 'Snake?'" The woman's lips curled in disgust. "In Thailand, snake kill people. No one like snake. You ever hear of python? You ever hear of cobra?"

Fletcher grinned. At the mention of pythons, he thought of Treat Brody again and the stuffed snake head the gunny had been wearing into combat recently. But he spoke of the other species. "Honey"—he lifted his ring finger for her inspection —"where we come from, cobras are the meanest of mother-fuckers."

37

The silver ring was one of several Fletcher's friend Patterson had presented Brody's people a few weeks back. The stones—faceted royal purple corundum—had been purchased in Saigon and inlaid between the inscriptions HH-100 on top and VC HUNTING CLUB on the bottom. Gunships prowling the rain forest's triple canopy with Viet Cong skulls impaled on their landing skids adorned one side of the ring, while a snarling Vietnamese dragon brought luck on the other.

Fletcher tapped the gunship skids with his finger, producing a Death's-head grin. "You ever hear of VC, Miss *swaymock poo-ying?*"

"Yes." The "very beautiful woman," as Snakeman had just described her in Thai, made her eyes widen somewhat, but Cordova knew she wasn't impressed. "Vietnamese Communists."

"Very good."

"We have Communists here, too." Pride seeped into her wide, sloe eyes, and Fletcher was unsure if it was because she was a sympathizer or simply gauging the danger quotient involved. "In south, near Malaysia border, and in northeast . . ."

"Near the border with Laos." Cordova beamed proudly at being able to participate in the politics and geography session.

"Ooohhh." The woman was totally ignoring Fletcher now as she wrapped her arms around his. "Veddy smart GI. Know *mock-mock* about Thailand."

"Yes, *mock-mock.*" He glanced down at the unavoidable sight of her cleavage. "And I would like to learn more. Especially about the local customs."

"Yah, 'nough war talk," Fletcher added importantly, throwing his chest out. "I wanna see some temples."

"You stay Bangkok before?" The woman was cuddling up close to Corky as he leaned against a concrete pillar, and Fletcher shuffled off to bargain with the cabbies. "You stay *tealok* with Thai girl before?"

"No." Cordova swallowed hard as something that had happened to him back in Vietnam flashed through his head but vanished just as abruptly, like joss smoke on the Bangkok breeze. "But I'm eager to get to know——"

"My name Sugar." The woman lowered her voice, and the tone became no-nonsense and businesslike. "How much you pay come home with me tonight?"

Cordova swallowed again. This woman was still hugging him as if they were in high school and going steady. She ran her fingers through the hair on his wrists. "Sugar?" was all he could think to say. "What kind of name is that for a beautiful Thai girl?"

"You no could say Sugar's Thai name. Too long. Not like Vietnamese name: Kim, Cuc, Xin-loi, Phuc-it. You no could say."

"So try me." Cordova was feeling guilt. He felt obligated to play the berieved widower because of what had happened in Vietnam . . . obligated to keep talking with this woman so he wouldn't have to become intimate . . . obligated to stall for time, so he could figure out where his head really was, and which way was the right way. . . .

"Hey-*hey!*" Fletcher rejoined them with a slender, short-haired hooker on one arm and a shorter, dumpy-looking cab driver under the other. "'Crap' here can give us a good deal on a ride over to Sukhumvit," he announced.

"I think you mean 'Khop,' Snakeman." Cordova frowned. 'Khop' was the equivalent of 'sir,' according to the GI's R and R handbook for Thailand.

"Whatever. Whatta ya say, Crap? Can you take us over to Sukhumvit for less than fifty *baht?*"

The cabbie nodded eagerly, a grubby cigar dangling over his lower lip. He wore no shirt, and his brown khaki pants were torn and oily. "*Ching-ching*, sirrrr. No problem."

Fletcher glanced back at the small man for a moment, wondering what the deal was with the "sirrrr," but dismissed his suspicions just as quickly. He waved Cordova and the women out through the front terminal door. "Only a couple bucks. Not bad, eh, Corky?"

39

Cordova's smiling eyes met the taxi driver's, and the American winked. "Crap" responded with an informal salute and half bow but repressed the grin. In Thai, "sir" translated roughly into "dog."

"Soi Nineteen, Crap," Fletcher was reminding their driver as the cramped taxi left the main, four-lane boulevard and swerved down a narrow alley.

The cabbie responded with the same eager nod. "Oh, yesss, sirrrr. No sweat. Yes sirrrr . . ."

"So why Sukhumvit Road?" Cordova asked as they slowly drove past sidewalk vendors crowding the gutters and often overflowing out into the street itself. "Why not Patpong, or some of those other flashy places I read about on the way over here in that R and R brochure?"

"Exactly that." Snakeman smiled as they stopped at an intersection and a mob of street orphans selling flowers and Thai newspapers crowded around the dented and smoking compact. "Too much publicity. Too many tourists. I always come to Sukhumvit and Soi Nineteen and the Honey Hotel, and—"

"The 'Honey Hotel?'" Cordova laughed. He reached into his pocket, withdrew a quarter, and handed it to a pretty girl with glazed-over eyes in exchange for a glossy magazine he couldn't even read. "*Hey!*" he called out suddenly as the twelve-year-old ripped the watch off his wrist, breaking the band at the clasp. "Hey, you little . . . STOP THE CAR!"

"Nebbah mind." The cabbie braked to a halt, but he was shaking his head in the negative. "She long gone, Joe. I sorry. Never find. Forget."

Cordova opened the rear door and started to get out, but Sugar was holding on to his arm tightly. "No, honey. She gone. He right. You never find. You forget."

Cordova gritted his teeth. They were right—the girl had vanished into the night, darting down a dark corridor in the maze of alleyways, but it was in his nature to pursue. His

40

personality demanded he chase her down and . . . And what? What was he going to do to a starving little kid who probably lost her cherry to child molesters when she was seven or eight and had nothing in her heart but hate? Besides, that corridor was *really* dark. Shadows were shifting at its mouth. Maybe it was a setup. Maybe there were more *cao bois* waiting out there to ambush him. To jump him and steal the rest of his valuables and perhaps his life. No, not *cao bois*. In Thailand, it was *ka-moys*. Cordova shook his own head in resignation.

"Was it Rolex?" the woman sitting in the front seat between Snakeman and the driver asked, compassion in her frightened eyes as she turned to face Corky.

"Rolex!?" He sat down again in the cab, angry now. "What do I look like, a fuckin' Green Beret? Only fuckin' Green Berets wear thousand-buck Rolexes." He folded his arms across his chest and spat out the window.

"Sorry." The girl faced the dashboard again, then glanced up cautiously to gauge Fletcher's reaction.

Cordova cleared his throat, embarrassed at the outburst. "Hell, it was only a twenty-dollar Seiko."

"Still sorry." The woman braved another bad reaction and stared over her shoulder at the American until he smiled sheepishly in reply.

"Me, too." Cordova broke the eye contact first and stared out his window at a long line of sidewalk soup stalls that extended off into the murky distance. Steam from the huge vats and kettles and smoke from the cooking fires rose toward the stars. Storm clouds brewed beyond the concrete-and-stucco skyline but seemed to be keeping their distance for the time being. An orange crescent moon hung on the horizon, waiting for the soldiers' next move.

"'Me, too,'" Fletcher imitated Cordova. "Great. Now that we're all on speaking terms, we can engage in a big cluster-fuckin' orgy when we get to the hotel."

"No talk dirty." Snakeman's "date" nudged him in the side, playing her part.

"But first we gotta *get* to the friggin' hotel," Fletcher continued. "Get my drift, Crap?" he leaned forward in order to get a look at the driver's emotionless face.

The cabbie saluted, and they were off again.

"I love the smell of these soup vendors," Cordova said, rolling the back window down all the way even though the air conditioner was on and sporadic raindrops began pelting the taxi's roof.

"We stop ar.d get soup," the woman wrapped around his arm decided. "This Soi Seventeen. Best place for sour-shrimp soup. You like, you see."

"No, no." Fletcher frowned. "It's straight to the hotel, ladies." He switched to pig latin. "My alls-bay have been raggin'-day for two eeks-way, and it's time to tune-up this ol' door gunner's engine. I need a lube-job at least once a week, minimum, to keep my performance at its peak."

"Boooo." The prostitute seated between him and the driver reclaimed both arms and folded them across *her* chest, imitating Cordova.

"Don't sweat it," Snakeman consoled her coldly. "I know the routine, babe. Sucky-fucky all night, then buy 'em breakfast in the morning. Nothin' more, nothin' less."

"You're Mr. Ice, Snakeman." Cordova tried to chuckle but couldn't.

Fletcher didn't respond with his usual quick wit but seemed to be concentrating on the cabbie's driving instead. "You missed a turn back there, Crap," he said softly. "The Honey Hotel's on Soi Nineteen. You're goin' on up to Soi Twenty. Tryin' to run the meter up on us, eh?"

Unintimidated, the cabbie simply waved off Fletcher's accusation with a grubby hand. He did not look over at the American when he spoke. "Fix street on Soi Nineteen. Must go around. Must—"

"Bullshit, Crap." Fletcher's gun hand instinctively dropped to his hip. A chill ran down his spine when he remembered he was not in Saigon or Danang or Pleiku: There was no holstered .45 on his web belt. He was not even wearing a web belt. "If there was a detour, you would have taken a different route . . . you would have taken Soi Eighteen back there or—"

"Forget 'bout fix street." The driver remained stonefaced. "Just remember."

"You better not be settin' us up, old man." Snakeman's fists became karate chops waiting to happen, and he displayed them for the old Thai man. "Me and my partner back there just came from The Nam. From the jungle side of The Nam. We're confirmed psychos with permission to kill and the blood of a hundred commies on our hands. Danger is nothing new to us. You're not giving a couple tourists the run-around. . . ."

"Jesus, Snake." Cordova leaned forward, resting his elbows on the front seat. "Mellow out. The dude just screwed up, that's all. He doesn't have the meter on. We already agreed on the fare and paid him, remember? It's his loss, not ours."

"I just want him to know 'Murder' is my middle name, and that he better not be plannin' anything hinky. I'm next in line for a Dirty Thirty slot, and—"

Their driver suddenly jammed his foot down on the accelerator, swerved around two slow-moving motorscooters, then took the next corner on two wheels and roared down into a dead-end side street.

"You *fuck*!" Snakeman reached over to grab him, but the driver rammed his foot down onto the brake pedal, locking up all four wheels. The car was thrown into a sideways skid, and Fletcher was slammed back into the passenger door, striking his head against the glass.

Even before the taxi had stopped shaking from side to side, the cabbie had flung his door open, and was running a short distance away from the vehicle.

"It was nice knowin' ya, Snakeman, ol' buddy," Cordova muttered under his breath, sizing up the situation and finding only hell in his horoscope.

"You don't stop breathin' till they plant one in your heart,

43

buddy-boy," Fletcher responded. "And it ain't over till you're six feet under and that first dirt clod strikes your coffin."

Nearly a dozen Thai men were quickly emerging from dark doorways and converging on the stalled taxicab. They did not look like members of the Bangkok welcome wagon. Those that didn't carry small, concealable firearms brandished machetes.

# CHAPTER 5

## Saigon

Rain fell differently in downtown Saigon than it did in the Son Long Valley. Brody made that decision as he stood on the balcony of his fourth-floor hotel room watching slight wisps of the silver droplets swirl down through the narrow back alleys and flower-lined boulevard where Nguyen Hue met Le Loi. In Son Long the steaming sheets of water pounded you into the red clay until you feared you might drown.

"Is the rain always like this?" Brody posed the question to a half-naked bar girl lying on her stomach amidst piles of satin sheets in the bed behind him. "Is it always this damned beautiful?" He watched a rainbow arc out beyond row after row of charred and blackened tenements, and the sight reminded him of Plei Me, and Koy, and his last morning in the Ia Drang.

The bar girl seemed intrigued by Treat Brody's interest in the weather. He was the first American in some time who paid her for conversation and nothing else. Tilting her head slightly to one side, she wondered for a moment what he was really up to—when would he finally hit her with the kinky request, or the embarrassing revelation? Dep had heard it all.

Brody glanced back at her, waiting for an answer, just as she was rising from the huge bed's blue-and-purple satin sheets. Dep's breasts were large and firm—especially for an Asian woman, he decided. His eyes narrowed, focusing on them as they swayed heavily from side to side when Dep slid to the edge of the bed on one knee and jumped to her feet. She glided across the room to a desk in one corner, and donned his gold silk shirt, draped across its chair.

She did not fasten the front buttons, but allowed it to remain open, teasing him with the inner swirls of her nipples, still visible. Brody liked the way the bottom edge of the shirt rode her hips. When she flung her long, black hair out over the collar, it dropped well below her haunches. Her head still tilted slightly to one side as she locked eyes with him, Dep produced that evil grin of hers and sauntered toward him, walking like a whore who was in need of a penis and willing to pay for it.

"Why does rain int'est you, Bro-dee?" She entered the balcony, rested her elbows on the railing, and threw her petite chin into the air, announcing she was bored with what fell from the sky, be it rain or that solitary midnight rocket. She rubbed her hip against his, but the American did not respond.

Back in the bedroom, a lizard, clinging upside-down to a corner of the ceiling, interrupted their conversation with a guttural mating call that sounded uncomfortably close to the English equivalent of "Fuck you!" Over and over again.

"Rain reminds me of the war." Brody sought a more meaningful answer, but those were the only words to leave him.

"You come from the fighting?" Dep still sounded far off and unapproachable.

"I told you that last night." *After picking you up in a real sleazebucket of a bar on Tu Do Street*, he wanted to say.

"I forget. Nebbah mind." She reached down and began massaging his crotch.

"Nebbah mind," he mimicked her. "Don' mean nothin'."

"Don' mean nothin', Bro-dee." She gently took hold of his hand and placed it between her breasts.

Brody did not laugh when she sighed at the touch of his

46

rough fingers, or even when she released an almost convincing moan. The woman was just trying to do her job. "Dep means beautiful. Your parents named you well."

He pulled a yellow carnation from the balcony's flower pot and slid the stem through her silky, radiant hair. Even with the sun up, the strands still seemed as sparkling and midnight-blue as they had beneath flares floating in off the Saigon River the night before.

Dep brushed his hand away, removed the flower, and inserted the stem between her legs. "My girlfriends give me that name." He detected a slight bitterness in her tone. "You would not be able pronounce names my mother and father gave me when born, Bro-dee." She took his hand again and manipulated his fingers so that he was gently pulling off one petal after another while the flower's stem remained inserted between the lips of her vagina. "Bro-dee love Dep," she whispered. "Bro-dee no love Dep. . . . Bro-dee love Dep. . . . Bro-dee no love—"

"You were born in Saigon?" he interrupted her.

"No," she said simply, still using his thumb and forefinger to rip away the petals. Her hips began to sway and rotate as music from the hotel room below drifted up to their balcony. He watched her lips continue to move silently as she counted off the flower petals.

"Bro-dee LOVE Dep!" she cried out suddenly, laughing wildly. Only half-serious, if that, she dragged him off the balcony and back into the bedroom.

She wrapped her arms around him as she backed toward the bed, and the two tumbled onto the fluffy sheets, Dep's legs opening up to him as his weight pressed down against her. She struggled with the velvet belt of his robe, finally stripping the hotel-supplied garment away, but Brody was still not in the mood. Refusing to respond to her excitement and caresses, he just stared down into Dep's eyes, his own expression seemingly lifeless.

Freezing, she allowed him to roll off to the side. Brody

47

almost expected to see tears well up in her eyes, but an angry glare was what he got instead. "Why you no let Dep do what you pay for her to do?" the twenty-year-old prostitute yelled.

"I paid you to spend the night with me. That's all."

"You pay Dep five doll U.S. greenback to talk? To spend whole night just talk—no fuck? What you think Dep is, stupid girl? Soon I have to go. Do your thing now, GI. Your all-night meter running out with this short-time girl!"

Moving to the edge of the bed, Brody placed his elbows on his thighs, leaned over slightly, and stared down at his toes, wondering if the tears would come again now or if he had cried himself dry on the ash-n-trash chopper relay from LBJ to Saigon. "I'm going to be in this town another two or three weeks, my dear," he revealed softly as she left the bed and began sliding the one-piece dress over her head and down onto that sleek, shapely, amber-toned body of hers. It had been "love at first sight" last night, and the dress had helped do the trick. "And I don't want to go through all the formalities of last night again in order to find you. I want a friend to help me forget a few things, that's all. I just want a girl to show me around Saigon."

"Formal'ty?" Dep folded her dainty arms across the dual swells along the top of her see-thru blouse. "You try impress short-time girl with fancy two-dollar word, Bro-dee? You go Pleasure Palace, stare at bookoo girls lined up in glass cage, and pick cleanest-looking *Co* with Numba One boobs—*me!*" She curtsied, then flipped him the finger, and the lizard now clinging to the base of the Casablanca-style fan told him where to go too, right on cue.

"Jesus." Brody erupted into tense laughter and rose to his feet. He pulled one of the satin sheets from the bed, wrapped it around his waist, and started back out onto the balcony. He had come up against Vietnamese women like this before— icy, cynical, and forever the skeptic when it came to the true intentions of a soldier on R and R. There was only one way to break through that barrier.

48

Halfway to the balcony he changed his mind, and rushed over to the pair of jeans draped across the chair.

Brody pulled out his product-of-Vietnam wallet with its map of Indochina molded into the photosection flap. "Here!" He withdrew a moist and crumpled wad of multicolor Vietnamese piaster notes. "There must be two or three thou P in that bundle, *Co* Dep! Is that enough to buy your time for another day or two?" He flung the money in her direction, and it bounced across the bedsheets and dropped to the teakwood floor.

Dep frowned at his gesture, refusing to move except to brace a flaring thigh out provocatively. "You pick up," she demanded. "Dep is a lady! You pick up and hand to Dep like *Gen*-tle-man." She did a trick with her full, red, lotus-petal lips that instantly aroused Brody as they shifted her expression from one of mock fury to silent contemplation.

Fighting back the grin, Brody's shoulders sagged, revealing his intentions. His firm countenance softened, and he dropped to one knee, picked up the money, and handed the roll to Dep with his head bowed.

"Okay." Dep reached over and grabbed two chopsticks from the empty plates piled on a nightstand. She tapped him on the head. "Dep forgive Bro-dee. You rise now."

Without meeting her gaze, he gracefully rose to his feet and returned to the balcony.

"What GI want do today?" she asked him from the edge of the bed, then glanced at a wall clock that hadn't worked in years. "No can do nothing. Bookoo rain soon. No can do nothing but fuck. Can fuck all day, all night, when rain. Make love feel extra good when sound of rain come through window. Romantic, Bro-dee, you *bic*? Bookoo romantic. But GI no want fuck." She lay back against the plush pillows, flexing her chest muscles as she spoke to herself, firm breasts jutting up at the lizard on the ceiling. "GI just want talk. *Dinky-dau.* You *dinky-dau*, Bro-dee. Pay so much P, but no want make romance. You have head problem, Bro-dee."

*Make romance to me, Treat Brody.*

Brody saw Koy's face in the rain. He tried to fight the pain rising in his chest. "Don't say that word again when you're around me."

"What word?" Dep had joined him on the balcony now, and when she held her hands out to try to catch the raindrops, the vision of a weeping Koy disappeared. And Brody knew. He sensed it. This woman standing beside him now held the power in her touch—the power to keep him safe in her arms through the night, to protect him from the ghosts of Ia Drang. To save him from the memory of what he'd done to Koy.


"I want to take you on a picnic somewhere, Dep," Brody said, reaching across the table and clasping her long, slender fingers as if picking up a newborn baby for the first time. "Somewhere outside the city, where it's peaceful and quiet. Somewhere with a river—and a waterfall. We could make love on the riverbank, in a sea of elephant grass." His mind saw them tangled together beneath the waterfall itself, the fine mist hiding their nakedness and vulnerability.

She laughed, but she was not mocking him. "Dep no go outside city, Bro-dee. VC live outside city. VC find Dep with American, they hack off my tits and march me through center of Viet Cong hamlet naked, bayonet in my back. Dep is city girl. No leave Saigon."

"Why do I hear that same story from all you girls?" He shook his head incredulously, glancing up at an old man who was entering the cavernous hotel dining room through a side door.

"About no want to leave city?" Dep had finished her drink and was using her tongue to play with the cherry.

"About bayonets in the back."

Brody slid his chair to the side slightly, concentrating on the old man now. He and Dep were now staying in a section of Cholon, Saigon's Chinese sector, several miles west of their

50

first hotel. The old, bent-over papa-san was carrying something in his hands, something long and sinister-looking, it seemed, but halfway across the empty dance floor, he climbed up onto a stage and ambled over to an abandoned set of drums. The object in his hands was a set of drumsticks, painted black.

Brody watched the man remove plastic covers from the bass and snare. The cymbals began to vibrate, lending an odd tension to the muggy air, but Brody's stance became comfortable again. "Ah, at last," he sighed. "Some entertainment."

"No count on it." Dep spoke without a smile as she continued running the cherry back and forth across the top of her tongue, from one side of her mouth to the other.

"That makes you look very unladylike." Brody watched two young Vietnamese men with long hair stroll from the hotel lobby through the tables in the dining room. They were soon climbing up onto the stage, too.

"If I care what people think, I no be see with American," she responded dryly, smacking her lips for emphasis as she began chewing on the cherry.

"Oh, thanks a lot for your vote of confidence." He glanced away, trying hard not to feel offended.

"*Xin-loi*, GI." She batted her long eyelashes at him. "Just tell truth. Vietnamese people no like see Vietnamese girl with foreigner." *Xin-loi* meant both "sorry about that" or "tough luck" in the local lingo.

"Really?" Brody was watching a strikingly attractive woman in her late forties, wearing the traditional *ao dai* gown, enter the room. Rich, black hair was piled atop her head and held in place with long jade-and-ivory pins. A glittering lightning-bolt design ran diagonally down the dress, and instead of the usual closed collar, a plunging neckline revealed the top halves of her breasts. Perhaps not so traditional after all, Brody decided. The two young musicians reached down and helped her up onto the stage, but Brody was convinced she needed little assistance, if any. The woman

51

wore no pantaloons beneath the gossamer-thin gown, as most Saigonese did, and her shapely calves and flaring thighs were exposed by the side slits running from hip to ankle as she rose off the floor.

"She is the singer?" Brody forgot about the complexities of prejudice in Asia for the moment.

"It would appear so." Dep sounded suddenly fluent, an educated lass from the best family in town, but Brody did not pursue the obvious slip. "She prob'bly main event."

Two spotlights suddenly lanced through the huge room from opposite corners of the catwalk behind Brody's table as the woman loosened a microphone from its stand. Blue and gray clouds of cigarette smoke drifted through the silver shafts, revealing for the first time how crowded the nightclub actually was. Brody glanced around, but didn't see any other American faces in the dim light.

Professionally painted eyes narrowing slightly as she surveyed the crowd beyond the harsh light, the women smiled politely, introduced herself as Thuy, and greeted her quiet audience in both Chinese and English.

Allowing the guitarists to build up for her opening number, she treated her audience to a very soothing, almost hypnotic folk song about patriotism and honor and valor in Vietnam. Her delicate, singsong voice was candy to the ears, and though nearly all eyes in the club were fighting back tears, the audience was also smiling, as Thuy had smiled at the beginning of her performance. She made her listeners feel good.

Thuy's music worked magic on the crowd. Whatever troubles or pain they left back at home, everyone seated in that nightclub experienced a change in their outlook on life as she sang her ballads of love and death, birth and war, lost love and abandonment in Vietnam's cities of sorrow.

For nearly an hour, the music remained melancholy, but then—as if she'd merely been detaining the gang until her true guests arrived—an A-team of Green Berets fresh in from eight weeks in the Delta entered the club, and she launched

52

into a rousing rendition of a popular Doors song currently sweeping the states. The mood rose like a skyrocket after that, becoming considerably upbeat.

Brody noticed four soldiers entering the nightclub through a side door.

MPs. That could mean trouble.

He gently grasped Dep's hand. "Come on. Time to beat feet, my dear."

Dep was not paying attention to happenings outside the sphere of her glass. "I want another drink," she said, swaying slightly from side to side. "You buy Dep one more Saigon tea, okay, Bro-dee?"

"No can do, babycakes. Time to *di-di mau*. Come on, I'll take you to one of them outdoor, backyard Chinese war epic movies."

"Dep no want see movie. Dep want listen music. Stay here. Eat. Drink. Later, go upstairs, make love all night, all day, all night again. You enjoy, Bro-dee. Wait and see. You love Dep more tomorrow than tonight, but less one week from now."

"Huh?" She definitely had had too much to drink, and though he hesitated about attracting attention to himself by making a scene, Brody picked Dep up, intending to carry her out of the night club. The slight shift in altitude was enough, however, to cause the streetwalker to blackout, and she collapsed over his right shoulder.

Holding onto her legs by the thighs, Brody started for the lobby, Dep's chin bouncing off his buttocks.

"Hey, soldier!" Thuy was between songs when the booming voice cut through the din of conversation rising from the audience.

Brody froze, then slowly turned around. Already, the MPs were halfway across the dance floor, headed straight for him.

"Have you checked her VD card?" said a short, stocky military policeman with a baby face and corporal chevrons on

53

the sleeves of his jungle fatigues. He was smiling in anticipation of Treat's reply.

But his partner spoke up first. "Cut the guy some slack, Zriny. Might be his wife."

Zriny's smile vanished, and he glanced back at the buck sergeant wearing blue prescription sunglasses. "Well, I just thought I'd seen her before at the meat market. Tha's all."

"No harm done." Brody nodded.

"Just watch your ass out there," the NCO warned with a sly grin. "Something about tonight, pal. Somethin' in the air. Bookoo VC out there, sneakin' around in the shadows. I can smell 'em and I've never been wrong yet."

"Appreciate the words of warning."

"And use a rubber." The corporal had not been fooled.

"Right."

Wall-to-wall neon, flashing to keep the dark back, assaulted his eyes when he carried Dep out through the lobby into the street. They were staying now at a smaller hotel across the street that didn't have a bar or swimming pool, and Brody didn't relish returning to the sparsely furnished room so early.

The night was still young, and he wanted to see Saigon after dark. His dancing partner was out cold now, however.

"Wake up, *Co* Dep!" He tapped her cheek lightly several times.

"Are we in Horry-rood yet?" She came to with a wisecrack, and Brody smiled.

"No, we're not in Hollywood," he replied, with a kiss on her nose.

Dep's free hand came up from behind, clasping the back of Brody's head. She forced his lips down onto hers for a long, hungry kiss.

Two minutes later, Treat was gasping for air. "Holy claymores!" He gently let her back down onto her feet.

"Pretty good kisser, huh?" she challenged him confidently

54

as she pulled out a pocketbook mirror to check her lipstick. "What you think, Bro-dee?"

"I think you kiss like Tina Turner sings."

"Huh?" Dep frowned, afraid he was setting her up for a joke she would not understand.

"The way your nose flattens out and flares when you kiss, it drives me *dinky-dau*!"

"Who Tina Turner?" A snarl curled Dep's lips, telling Brody his answer would determine whether or not she pounced and scratched his eyes out.

"A singer back in The World."

"Oh." She seemed to contemplate his reply for a moment, then suddenly her hands flew up, slapping him.

"What!?" Brody The Whoremonger recoiled, massaging his chin.

"Why American GI always have refer to stateside as 'The World'? Why Vietnam no count for nothing?"

"It's not that Vietnam no count for noth—I mean, it's just that—"

"Always, Dep hear, 'Ooohhh, baby, someday I take you back to The World with me,' or 'Ooohhh, baby, I'm really missin' The World. . . . I'm really missin' the hamburger and hotdog and hotrod and—"

"Hey, I'm really sorry, okay?" Brody was somewhat taken aback by her display of outright anger, though he knew he should have expected it.

"You shou'd be!" She turned and began walking slightly ahead of him.

They started to cross the street, but a large truck's airhorn warned them back, and they had to wait for a long ARVN military convoy to rumble past.

Several of the South Vietnamese soldiers riding in back of the deuce-and-a-halves showered Dep with catcalls Brody couldn't understand as the vehicles roared by, but she ignored them all, never once looking up.

After the convoy disappeared in a rolling cloud of dust and

55

exhaust smoke, a three-wheeled cyclo puttered down the street toward them, and Dep flagged it down. Brody noticed the seven ornately carved bracelets of Vietnamese gold sliding along one wrist as she moved.

"Very pretty." He clasped her arm as the cyclo driver worked his way through heavy motorscooter traffic to the curb. "Forgive me for asking, but is it real gold? It looks so . . . well, it looks different, sort of, from the gold I've seen before."

"Vietnamese gold, Bro-dee. Twenty-four carat. You not such man of world after all."

He watched her remove one of the bracelets and slide it on the opposite wrist without touching the remaining six. "I am a jungle expert, as the saying goes, nothing else. I was not trained for this concrete canyon." He glanced up at the charred and blackened tenements rising up all around them.

Dep seemed to be ignoring him. "Change one bracelet every day," she explained. "From one wrist to the other, then, end of week, back again."

"Why?"

"For good luck."

"Oh."

"Dep think she like you after all, Bro-dee."

Treat helped her up into the open-air seat mounted across the cyclo's dual front tires. The driver's seat was mounted over a single rear wheel, behind and slightly above his passengers.

"Where are we going?" he said, smiling at her last remark.

"You want to see Saigon. Okay, Dep show you." She turned to face the driver and rattled off several sentences in Vietnamese.

Brody glanced at his watch. Only 2100 hours—still a good three hours until the midnight curfew was clamped across the capital. He glanced over at her, thinking about something she had said only moments earlier. "How do you know a lot of all this GI slang, anyway?"

56

"You forget." Her face met his, and Brody's curiosity cooled before icy, bottomless orbs. "I know many man before I meet you, Bro-dee. Sleep with thousands of soldiers like you—*millions*! Learn something from them all."

"Millions?" He refused to let her spoil his mood.

"You no believe Dep?" Her gaze returned to the road up ahead.

"Well . . ."

"How old Bro-dee think Dep is?" Her eyes narrowed as a taxi approaching from the opposite direction caught her attention. Intoxicated American soldiers were hanging out of three of the sedan's four tiny windows, and Dep seemed to be searching for familiar faces. Brody felt a twinge of jealousy, and he immediately reprimanded himself mentally. "Bro-dee think Dep nineteen, or twenty? Maybe twenty-five?"

"Well . . . okay, that's close enough," he said.

"Dep thirty-five. Thirty-five, but look twenty-five, even on a bad day, you *bic*?" Vietnamese city women keep youth." She tried to explain, sometimes struggling with the English. "Farmer woman look old after first baby-san, but I know city woman in her late fifties, still race with Dep for business."

"Business?" Brody couldn't help trying to paint her into a corner.

"Dep business girl, Bro-dee. You think Dep *new* girl?" She feigned surprise, throwing up her hands as the cyclo pulled to the curb in front of a seedy-looking warehouse.

"What's the difference?"

Dep laughed. "Okay." She caught her breath as the cyclo driver continued to snicker softly. "I explain one time, but we never talk 'bout again, okay?"

"It's a deal." Brody made the sign of the cross, and Dep frowned.

"Okay, 'new' girl means same-same cherry girl, you *bic*?"

"Virgin?"

Dep nodded in the affirmative. "'Business' girl same-same work . . . topfloorhotel." The last three words came out so

57

quickly Brody nearly missed them. He decided it was time to get blunt.

"'Business' woman is polite way of saying whore."

Dep's tentative grin vanished, but she seemed to accept his judgment, and didn't get angry. "Okay, like agree: now you know. No talk about it anymore."

"I want to see some temples," he decided, throwing his arms up to encompass the shadowy skyline. "I want to see the biggest temple in all of Saigon." Brody hadn't even noticed the cyclo was stopped.

"First we go inside here." Dep motioned for him to help her down out of the cyclo, but Brody stepped out the opposite side, ignoring her.

He eyeballed the dark structure, which seemed to be leaning precariously to one side. Banners in Vietnamese, proclaiming everything from freedom to the grand opening of a noodle shop two blocks down the road, hung between the structure and the tenement next door. "Dep wouldn't be settin' Bro-dee up now, would she, honey?"

"Trust," she replied, the bounce in her step announcing a growing anger deep inside. "Trust me, okay? Wait here if you want. I go inside, talk girlfriend only one minute."

"I'm comin'." His jaw was set like that of a man expecting trouble and prepared to combat it.

A burst of noise assaulted Brody's ears when Dep's hand touched a panel in the warehouse wall, and a door appeared where none had been visible before. The noise was hard-rock music. "Ahhh, a private club." He caught up with Dep and patted her on the bottom as blue cigarette smoke swirled out to greet them.

"Yes." She took his hand. "They open one hour ago. Will stay open 'til sunrise. Maybe longer. Depend on if *bookoo* customer or *ti-ti* customer."

"I catch your drift, honey-buns."

He grinned as soon as the cages suspended from the ceiling along an opposite wall came into view—bamboo cages con-

58

taining topless go-go dancers, gyrating to taped imitation American music. The place was packed with people crowded together, dancing with one, two, and sometimes three bumping, grinding partners. Many danced alone, singing along to tunes only they themselves heard in their heads.

Brody saw no other Americans, and he began feeling somewhat uncomfortable as half the faces he passed turned to watch where he went. It seemed as if a hundred hostile, Oriental eyes were boring into the back of his head. But he worked to shake the feeling by memorizing all the sights and sounds inside the single-room building.

There were seven bamboo cages suspended in a straight line from the ceiling. Dep's girlfriend was in the center one. She appeared a couple of years younger than his companion, as well as a bit heavier. But the weight was in all the right places.

"Bro-dee." Dep's hand came out, palm up, and stopped in front of his throat. "Meet Wanda."

He wasn't sure if the body language was a warning for the girlfriend or himself. "The pleasure is all mine." Treat reached up and took her hand, making a point to keep his eyes off her chest as she dropped into a squat—the bottoms of the cages were a good five feet off the ground.

Like Dep, this woman also wore her long hair piled atop her head and held in place by jade and ivory pins. She had high cheekbones, reminding him of the Montagnarde women he'd seen in Pleiku and Kontum, and a razor-thin scar running from the edge of her chin down a couple of inches along her throat—a scar he did not think would be noticeable were her skin not gleaming with a thin coating of body oil.

"Pleased . . . meet you." She shook his hand like an intoxicated man might—too energetically—and Brody watched her face work magic: the lips curled into a half smile while her eyes remained emotionless as glass. She was cold to the touch, despite the hot temperature in the warehouse.

"Hello, Mista." A voice behind and above Brody tingled in

59

his ears. It was a throaty, seductive voice that sent a flash through the Whoremonger's loins. When he turned around, he was not disappointed.

The first thing he noticed was the skimpy G-string riding the woman's crotch. His eyes dropped along firm, flaring thighs for an instant, then shot up to an almost nonexistent midsection and, finally, the jutting underslopes of two bare breasts. He saw an evil smile with cherry-red lipstick above and beyond two bouncing, quivering nipples. The nipples were taut and erect, almost beckoning to him, and Brody felt himself growing hard.

"*This* my friend." Dep grabbed him by the bicep and squeezed, returning Treat's attention to the first go-go dancer. "Not Moanin' Lisa up there!"

"Oh. Yah, sorry!" He bowed again slightly, and Dep launched into a conversation that combined both Chinese and Vietnamese. Her girlfriend remained in a squat, ignoring the frowns from floormen passing by now and then, who were constantly on the prowl, making sure the dancers danced and the bar girls kept the customers happy and their glasses full of Saigon tea.

But as the gossip, or news or request or whatever it was, transpired between Dep and her friend, Brody got bored, and his eyes strayed back again and again to the woman gyrating to the music only a few feet away. *Moanin' Lisa*, a voice laughed in his head.

Every time their eyes locked, she would drop into a twisting squat to the drumbeat, spreading her legs for him, and Brody would blush. No G-string was designed to cover that much crotch, and the dancer knew it.

Dep missed little, and suddenly she was twisting his ear playfully and leading him away. "Hey, knock it off!" Brody lost his temper and slapped her wrist away. "If I wanna overdose on snatchshots, that's *my* business, you *bic*?"

Dep's grin faded with the end of a song drifting down from

60

the ceiling speakers, and she tried to slap him back. Brody caught her hand.

"Whoaaa! Whoa, baby! You're sure a feisty one tonight, aren't you?"

"My girlfriend loan me piaster so I can take you out, Brodee, show you good time. But your tongue drag on heel of Numba Ten butterfly girl back there! Maybe we just *fini* now and forever!"

"Well, maybe we just better," he started to say, when her knee came up. Swift and sure, and he was not fast enough to block it.

Brody The Whoremonger doubled over in pain and slammed face-first against the sticky, beer-coated dance floor. Moments later, explosions on all sides rocked the building.

# CHAPTER 6

## An Lao Valley

The RPG-7 rocket launcher was getting heavy on her shoulder, despite all the excitement and the adrenaline surge that had powered her through many a past firefight. Trinh Thi Kim, a.k.a. Vu Y-Von, a.k.a. Xuyen Thi Vau, had watched the Phantom jet tumble end over end across the treetops before bursting into flames. It was her shoulder-fired projectile that had snatched the F-4 from the night sky, and now comrades in her offshoot cell of PRG revolutionaries were silently congratulating her. "But we must go now," one of the other women in the squad cautioned. Dual sets of rotorblades roared back and forth above the triple canopy, and bursts of red-and-white tracer arced down into the jungle.

"The monkeys will be out in force soon," another guerrilla agreed, this one a boy barely into his teens, yet possessed of a snarl that made him look twenty or more.

"Yes." Kim decided against trying for one of the gunships. Downing the Phantom had been a one-in-a-million shot, and she did not wish to test her luck.

"I hear the monkeys coming." The first woman cupped her right ear with one hand. She had detected the slight change in pitch. "Monkeys" was the latest term the VC were giving Americans, because of their hairy arms and chests.

"Yes." Kim could tell the differences in craft too. The helicopters strafing the trees had been the two prototype Cobras —two-man machines with sleek snakelike designs and sharks' teeth painted along their snouts. But now a Huey was airborne, maybe more than one. And the Hueys carried the grunts.

Kim thought of the First Cav grunts as her cell made its way through the dense rain forest, away from the crash site. She thought of the one named Treat Brody, and of Shawn Larson too. And the one she had to kill out on the island, Hal Krutch—the pilot they called the Stork. She lit a *joss* stick for Krutch now and then—not because she felt remorse, but because she feared meeting his angry, avenging ghost some night on the rain-forest trail.

Born into a life of poverty and abuse in the Imperial City of Hue twenty-two years earlier, Trinh Thi Kim had been recruited into the insurgency at the age of sixteen, after her parents were killed by French "friendly fire" during a dayslong battle with the Viet Minh. Trained at a communist tunnel complex along the Vietnamese-Laos border, then sent to Saigon using the alias Xuyen Thi Vau, she was instructed to seduce and blackmail Americans. Upon arriving in the capital, she promptly botched her mission by falling in love with a young consular official, whom she eventually confided in.

One year later, he left The Nam and betrayed her to MI—U.S. Military Intelligence. Kim was sent to prison for three years, but inadvertently released following the Diem coup and assassination in 1963. She changed her name and disappeared into the jungle for two years, only to re-emerge in the Saigon-Cholon resistance movement in early 1965.

At a petite five foot one and 100 pounds, she was proof small packages can pack a big punch. High cheekbones gave her an almost Central Highlands tribal tint, and some said she had a Eurasian cast to her features, but Kim was full-blooded Vietnamese. She possessed firm curves on an unusually well-endowed figure, but she also sported cigarette and field-phone

63

wire burns on her breasts and other private parts—souvenirs from her stays at Chi Hoa prison and the Con Son Island tiger cages.

Though she had no formal education, an aunt had taught Kim to read and write when she was a child, and she was able to speak pidgin English with a heavy yet sensuous Viet accent —a trait that, in the past, had driven her "long-nosed" boyfriends wild. She was legendary among the American GIs as a beautiful warrior who had outgunned them during numerous prior battlefield skirmishes despite great odds. Her comrades often called her the Dragonlady. The GIs had a dozen derogatory names for her, and a $10,000 bounty on her head.

Comrade Trinh was awarded the Order of Heroes Medal for Merit after successfully attaching several pipe bombs and satchel charges to the undercarriages of U.S. MP jeeps in 1965, and the Valorous Achievement Medal for bringing back the ears she "liberated" from an American Naval officer after seducing him at his hotel, only one block from MACV Headquarters.

"The Cav grunts land!" one of the men in the team announced as the helicopter in the distance pulled pitch, flaring in for an abrupt landing.

"They have found the clearing."

"They have the dogs again."

Kim felt a chill swirl through her belly. The dogs. Some of the Air Cavalry teams had begun using attack dogs to help them on these jungle chases. Before, it had been easy to lay in wait for hours, or days if need be, then strike with blinding ferocity and melt away into the bamboo, leaving not a trace for the rescuers or reinforcements to follow.

But they did leave a trace, it seemed. Whether it was something on the soles of their feet, or the ghosts of their dead comrades following them through the jungle, or possibly even the aroma of *nuoc-mam* on their breath, Kim, didn't know. But the dogs could follow them.

And she had seen what the dogs could do. Big and black,

with white eyes that glowed in the dark. Daw had been too slow and the dogs had caught up with her. The soldiers did not call them off, either, but allowed the animals to rip out her throat and her crotch until Daw was dead and too mutilated to bring back to the caves—no one would carry her body. Bodies violated so grotesquely trailed bad *joss*, and nobody wanted to risk being jinxed.

"Tonight we escape the dogs," their cell leader said confidently as they reached a shallow creek. He pulled two small tins from his belly pack and handed them to separate members of the squad. "You," he pointed to one, "step in and head downstream, sprinkling this powder along bank as you go. And you," he directed the other apprentice insurgent, "start in the opposite direction. Hurry. We will be heading straight across from this point. After you have rushed downstream for twenty seconds, and after *you*," he nodded to one of the wide-eyed youths, "have rushed *up*stream for twenty seconds, leave the water and angle in. We will wait for you one kilometer into the heart of the trees, then double back to the caves after the Americans have left emptyhanded."

The older boy threw his chest out as he took the small can. "You need not wait on our account. I'm prepared to sacrifice myself for the Cause and—"

"Save your patriotism for the victory parade when we move farther south and take Saigon. There is no need for your sacrifice, comrade. This powder will render the dogs' noses useless. Now go!"

They had followed the First Air Cavalry from Ia Drang to Bong Son. Major Minh, of the North Vietnamese Army, would not rest until he had Col. "Neil Nazi" Buchanan's head mounted on a tall bamboo pole in front of his CP, and the high bounty was an inducement for the Viet Cong to follow the Americans south.

The dogs became confused as soon as they reached the water. Though their handlers attempted to coax them beyond the banks, the animals wanted to stray in opposite directions, and began sneezing. Their handlers quickly identified the source of the problem: powdered fish sauce.

When the search was finally called off, Kim and her crew were already several hilltops away.

Kim grinned after they had lain dog for an hour, blending into the bamboo. "I wonder how long it will take them to develop a method to cheat your powder."

"The Americans?" Her leader seemed preoccupied with something in the air, something that seemed out of place.

"Who else would I be—"

"Do not give the long-noses so much credit," the cell leader snapped back. "They are not as—" he began, but his voice trailed off and he held up one hand. "Something is not right." He lowered his voice considerably, sniffing at the air again.

"You smell your own powder." One of the youngest team members giggled, still proud of Kim and jubilant over the fighter jet shoot-down.

"Be silent, you little pip!" The veteran sapper whirled around, his Vietnamese rapid-fire now. "Or I will have your gonads hanging from a pole in the middle of Bon Son's public square."

"Think your threats over, old man." The words, again, were fluent Vietnamese, but they carried a heavy American accent and came from out of nowhere, like the voice of a ghost. Kim and her comrades froze, their trigger fingers tense.

That's when the Green Berets began dropping from trees like flies onto a body bag.

Kim was one of only three Viet Cong guerrillas to escape the deadly crossfire that decimated her squad when the Green Berets began dropping from the trees. Two younger women followed her through the razor-sharp reeds, acting with blind

66

faith and trusting her abilities. And Kim led them straight into a punji pit.

One girl was impaled through the chest by the four-foot-long bamboo sabers. She dangled in the darkness screaming as Kim and the only other survivor rolled to the side, missing the urine- and feces-coated stakes by mere inches.

When they rolled, it was into the old, abandoned spider-hole.

The ancient tunnel complex was alive with snakes, spiders, and rodents for the first dozen yards or so, and had to have been a remnant from the old Viet Minh days, when France was the enemy instead of America.

Kim had played in such underground hide-outs as a child, and knew what to do when she came to what appeared to be a dead end. With her shoulder, she rammed the earthen wall to the left, and the partition behind two or three inches of dirt collapsed inward.

The complex was not large. It was composed of two levels, one running the same direction as the original access tunnel, and the second, lower level crossing below in an unparallel fashion. It appeared to Kim the project had been aborted long before being completed.

Kim smiled at the thought, wondering how many men or women had died down here, along the very spot where she and her companion were now lying. Tears filled the younger woman's eyes, and Kim made no attempt to comfort or reassure her. How was she to know whether or not they would survive this retreat into the bowels of the earth?

The girl in the stakes was still screaming. The Americans would surely find her before she was silenced from loss of blood. Then only the toss of a coin would determine whether or not the Green Berets climbed down into the pit to examine the body for weapons or documents, or continued their sweep of the area. They would notice the spiderhole entrance during daylight. If they searched it tonight, possibly not.

Even now, Kim could hear the boots rushing past overhead. She judged themselves to be five to six feet beneath the surface at most, and glanced over at the support boards. Dust fell now and then from the low ceiling, turning her perspiration-lined features from amber to chocolate brown.

"What are we to do now?" Her companion touched her elbow from behind as weak beams from the senior communist's L-shaped flashlight played back and forth across the tunnel's walls.

Kim glanced back at her and placed a rigid forefinger over her own lips. "First," she whispered, "we remain silent. I do not know where air shafts are, or if they would carry our words to the surface. Second, do you still have your weapon?"

The woman shook her head, and Kim frowned. Keeping a tight grip on her AK-47, she drew a Chinese-made revolver from the holster on her hip. "Do you remember how to use one from training?"

The woman swallowed loudly, stress lines creasing her forehead, but nodded nervously. "Here." Kim handed the weapon to her. "Six shots. If you are brave, you will take a half dozen American bastards with you when you die. But if you are smart, you will save the last bullet for yourself."

Kim did not have to explain. The younger woman knew what she was talking about. For the last two weeks, ever since their unit followed the Americans from Ia Drang, cadre leaders had been filling their heads with allegations of atrocities committed by the U.S. soldiers on VC women.

To rape a Viet Cong woman while she is still alive is a status symbol for the Air Cavalry killers, the cadre claimed at every campfire political session. To mount her from behind and *snap her neck* while raping her makes the soldier a "double vet," the teacher explained, "and to reach 'double vet status' is the ultimate accomplishment of any helicopter soldier."

A burst of shots rang out, and both Kim and the younger woman instinctively dropped the sides of their faces against the tunnel floor, listening intently.

The girl impaled by the punji sticks had stopped screaming.

Boots were running past again overhead. "They are going on," she told her comrade. "They won't search the pit until morning." The muffled bark of dogs could be heard like echoes oozing from the clay walls.

# CHAPTER 7

## Bangkok

Unbeknownst to Snakeman Fletcher or Corky Cordova, the woman they knew only as Sugar carried a .38 Special in the bottom of her hotpants.

"Get down!" she ordered them in a commanding, no-nonsense voice. "On floorboards!"

Fletcher glanced at Cordova, whose expression displayed more shock and surprise than even his own. It was against their nature, but both unarmed soldiers sheepishly complied.

"What the hell's goin' down?" Cordova whispered to Fletcher as they lowered their bodies against the bottom of the cramped taxi. The prostitute Snakeman had teamed up with was also pulling a pistol from concealment—this one, a small automatic, from between her breasts.

"Hell if I know, Corky, but our best bet is to get those guns from the broads and start bustin' caps on—"

His plan was interrupted by the squeal of tires and sirens as four unmarked sedans roared around a corner down the street and skidded up to the scene.

Sugar and her friend were already out of the taxi and standing between it and the hoodlums, screaming directives in Thai at the men carrying machetes and grease guns.

Cordova and Fletcher both slowly raised their heads at the same time and peeked over the dashboard at the weird scene unfolding beyond the windshield. Sugar and the other "whore" stood with their high-heeled feet braced apart in defensive stances as they confronted the street gang. Their long, lean legs stood unshaking, and their arms were locked out straight, bracing firearms in combat holds.

Behind the taxi, a dozen or more uniformed Thai police carrying submachine guns were piling out of black sedans, racing to back up the two women.

"What the flying fuck is going on!?" Fletcher demanded of Cordova as both GIs watched the girls wave the uniformed patrolmen past.

"Hell if I know, Snakeman!" Corky was wild eyed as they watched several of the hoodlums dropping their weapons and lying spread-eagle across the wet blacktop. Some of the policemen zigzagged through the prone figures, chasing those who opted to flee down the alley. "This is the strangest clusterfuck I've ever seen!" But it wasn't a clusterfuck at all. The police—and the women Cordova and Fletcher had been lusting over for the last half hour—had taken down the punks smoothly and quite professionally. And without a single shot being fired.

"You can get up now." Sugar was slipping her snub-nosed revolver back down into the seat of her hotpants. Fletcher and Cordova both watched in silence as she holstered her hardware.

"Don't say it." Corky couldn't surpress the grin.

"I won't," Snakeman complied.

"I assume you two are all right?" Sugar opened the back door to look in on Cordova. He and Fletch quickly exited from the door on the other side of the car.

"Fine, fine!" Snakeman stretched and glanced about nervously, obviously somewhat concerned about their immediate future—from a legal standpoint.

Cordova didn't seem so upset. "Just suffering from a little loss of face, I guess. We were about to help out . . . I mean, we

71

were intending to jump out and break some knuckles for you ... ladies, when you came up with the firepower."

Sugar's partner watched the uniformed officers handcuff the last prisoner, then slowly sauntered back to the taxicab, smiling slyly. Snakeman frowned, reading her mind. He was sure she enjoyed this part the most: humiliating the prospective johns.

Cordova half expected her to return to his arm, then realized the fantasy was over.

She ceremoniously flipped on a safety, then slipped her automatic back down between her breasts and pulled an ID-card holder from the back of her shorts. "Bangkok Metropolitan Po—"

"We surmised as much." Fletcher held out his hand politely, but there was a disappointed glaze in his eyes. The policewoman shook it confidently, with a no-offense smile spreading across her features. Snakeman knew the look: She was still riding the adrenaline high, was still charged from the action ... the close brush with death. He was intrigued. He had never considered the possibility that a woman could experience the adventure and danger that kept men the world over in elite teams within law enforcement and the military. And he had never balled a cop before.

"Meet my partner, Officer Chatsungnoen." Sugar introduced the woman with the tight and well-filled halter top. Her partner curtsied, and several of the uniformed patrolmen rounding up suspects chuckled at her antics. Blue and red roof lights flashing madly and throwing surrealistic beams across the walls of buildings rising up on both sides, a police Land Rover roared by and disappeared down the alley in the direction where several of the officers had gone in foot pursuit of the gunmen. "And I am Sergeant Prasertkwan."

*"Sugar* Prasertkwan?" Fletcher challenged her good-naturedly.

The policewoman laughed lightly. "Yes, believe it or not,"

72

she said. "You can call me that. Most of my friends in the department do."

"Because she is so *sweet*." Sugar's partner teased. Sgt. Prasertkwan responded with an obscene gesture that only a Thai cop could understand.

"Actually, my true first name *is* very difficult to pronounce." She lowered her gaze somewhat but kept her eyes locked on the American's as she recalled their conversation back at the airport terminal. "The Thai word for "sugar" is also, believe it or not, "sugar." Fletcher did *not* believe that, but it was all water under the bridge. He wondered why they were even bothering to explain anything to two GIs on R and R. He would have expected a stern lecture and deportation, and that was if they were lucky. But these women were still acting sociable.

Fletcher watched two young patrolmen emerge from the darkness of a side street, escorting the cabbie back to the scene. His nose had been flattened, and blood covered his chest. Snakeman smirked as their eyes briefly met. "That's *nothin'* compared to what you would have received if *I'd* gotten to you first, asshole!" he taunted the prisoner, who responded with a glob of spittle that fell several feet short.

"I suppose we're going to jail now." Cordova put Fletcher's earlier fears into words.

"What forever why?" Sugar slipped back into Pidgin English, adding a British, Hong Kong whore accent.

A smile crept across Corky's face. He glanced over at Fletcher for guidance but read no eyeball command for silence. "Well, for . . . soliciting, I guess."

"Prostitution is not illegal in Thailand, Mister Cordova." Officer Chatsungnoen's smile faded somewhat. "Unfortunately, it is the only way some women here survive . . . support themselves and their families." Cordova's lower jaw dropped, and he wondered how she knew his last name. The policewoman pulled Corky's wallet from the front of her hotpants and handed it over. Even in the dark, despite the sea of flashing red lights that now lit up the alleyway, he could tell she was blushing.

True to form, Cordova ran the wallet beneath his nose and licked it. "I will cherish this old flap of cowhide the rest of my life." He slipped it into a back pocket, took her hand, and gently kissed the dainty knuckles. "It will remain a constant reminder of the brave manner in which you and Sergeant . . ." He glanced over at Sugar.

"Prasertkwan," she helped him out, the hint of a grin returning to her ruby-red lips.

Cordova struggled mentally with the pronunciation for a moment before continuing. ". . . in which you and the sarge here risked life and limb to protect two mere foot soldiers of the American military and—"

"We're gunnies, douchebag!" Fletcher interrupted. "Not foot soldiers. *Door* gunners! And don't you forget it."

Sugar laughed, and Chatsungnoen hastily withdrew her hand as Corky started to work his way up along her wrist. "Actually," she explained, "we are members of an anti-robbery squad, working in cooperation with your government and CID in hopes of stemming the tide of recent muggings and assaults involving American GIs here on R and R."

"The whole thing at the airport was a setup?" Cordova asked innocently.

"Whatta you think, numbnuts?" Snakeman ribbed him with an elbow.

"Well . . ."

"What if we hadn't gotten hijacked like that?" Fletcher folded his arms across his chest smugly. "Would you have remained . . . uh, undercover until we had you . . . under the sheets, so to speak? I mean, just . . . how . . . far . . . will a Thai PO-licewoman go in the line of duty?" He tilted his head to one side mischievously and cocked an eyebrow at her.

"We happened to have been conducting surveillance on the cab driver for the last forty-eight hours," Sugar explained.

74

"He is a known robbery suspect, and we expected him to perpetrate a takedown tonight."

Cordova glanced over at Fletcher: He didn't trust a Thai woman who could speak English better than he and Snakeman combined.

"From there," Sugar continued, "it was just a matter of guiding you two to the right taxi."

"And you had backup following us the whole time?" Fletcher was becoming more and more impressed.

"Of course." Her partner pulled a thin shawl from her purse and draped it around her shoulders. "We watch the mandatory eight hours of *Adam-12* per week, you know. . . ."

Sugar laughed again and rattled off a light reprimand in Thai. Chatsungnoen responded with a mock frown.

"In other words, you were counting on a robbery going down, so you wouldn't have to walk us up to a hotel room, eh?" Fletcher grinned like a devil on parole.

"We *knew* a robbery would go down." Sugar's eyes became sad, and Fletcher wondered if he was being taken for a different kind of ride now.

"We haven't had to drop our hotpants for a GI yet." Her partner arched her eyebrows, daring Prasertkwan to reprimand her again, but Sugar only burst out laughing. It was a schoolgirl kind of laugh. For the next minute or so, both policewomen launched into a nonstop conversation in rapid Thai, and Fletcher wondered if they were reliving close calls in the past, or just deciding how to best deal with these two sex-starved Americans.

"So what happens now?" Cordova asked.

Sugar glanced over his shoulder, down the street, as if scanning the traffic passing in the distance. "Well, there was supposed to be a CID agent involved in the backup. They usually take the GIs away. . ."

Cordova swallowed hard, and his eyes shot over to Fletcher.

Sugar waved his concerns away. "Oh, don't worry," she

75

said. "It's just to get your written statement. One of the guys told me they give you an added five-minute lecture about the evils of attempting to pick up prostitutes, show you a VD film, then cut you loose to resume your R and R. No sweat, Gi," she said mimicking a bargirl, and winked at Snakeman.

"You two came from Vietnam, right?" her partner asked. Cordova nodded, and she said, "Okay. No problem. They make special concessions for jungle GIs."

"After all," Sugar added, "if you fuck up again, where can they send you for 'punishment' that you haven't already been?"

"Germany," Cordova muttered.

Fletcher's eyes had lit up when Sgt. Prasertkwan finally used a four-letter word. "I love it when you talk like that." He moved closer to her, but Sugar held her hand out, and the open palm pressed against Snakeman's chest.

"We are on duty," she warned, feigning a stern countenance. "And I'm sorry about the slip. Working with cops twelve hours a day can ruin a lady's vocabulary sometimes."

"When are you *off* duty?" Fletcher challenged. He glanced at the rings on all five fingers. They looked like cheap costume jewelry. None appeared to be genuine wedding bands.

"I think you're out of line, Snakeman," Cordova cautioned him.

"Whatta ya mean, I'm outta line? The Snakeman ain't never outta line, doofus."

"They're beautiful ladies." He did not lower his voice to continue the conversation. "What makes you think they don't have husbands waitin' for 'em at home, or a dozen boyfriends knocking at their door each time they get off work?"

Both soldiers glanced over at Sugar for her response, but she spooke to Chatsungnoen instead. "Check with Sirikhan. See what the delay is regarding CID." She kept to English as a courtesy to the Americans.

Her partner nodded and walked over to a uniformed sergeant. A portable radio was constantly squawking on his black

76

leather belt. "I don't know what could have happened to them," she continued. "You may have to ride down to the station house with us."

"Only if you sit on my face the entire trip," Fletcher couldn't resist adding.

"Jesus, Snakeman." Cordova shook his head in resignation.

Sgt. Prasertkwan tilted her head to one side, slightly confused. "Sit on face?" she asked, nostrils wrinkling in disgust as her mind conjured up a picture.

Cordova was relieved that Fletcher didn't have time to elaborate: Sugar's partner returned with a long-winded explanation regarding the fate of CID.

After listening patiently for several minutes, Prasertkwan turned to face Cordova. She would not look at Fletcher. "Your CID people have wreck couple miles back."

"They're not *my* CID people," Snakeman protested, but Sugar seemed to be ignoring him now.

"Nobody hurt," she said. "We will take you down to police headquarters for a statement, then arrange transportation back to your hotel."

Chatsungnoen motioned them over to an unmarked police sedan, and Sugar pointed a forefinger back at Fletcher sternly. "You behave!" she warned. "No hanky-panky. No 'Sit on face'!"


"I told you they wouldn't wait for us," Snakeman Fletcher said, frowning after the CID agent was through interviewing them about the robbery attempt.

"You didn't really expect them to, did you?" Corky Cordova stood in the doorway of the Combined Patrol Force briefing room on the third floor of Bangkok Metropolitan Police Headquarters. He hesitated venturing out into the brightly lit corridor. There was too much foot traffic scurrying past, even at this late hour.

"Well, Sugar—or whatever her name really is—promised to be here when we were through. Was it my imagination, or did she say she and Chat-whatever-her-name-was would drop us off back at our hotel? Huh? Was I dreamin', or what the fuck, over..."

"What's the *problem*, over?" Their friendly CID agent had left his desk.

"Uh, nothin' really, Mister Reilly." Cordova drilled a don't-blow-it look into Snakeman.

"'Nothin' really, Mister Reilly,'" the tall, stocky warrant officer mimicked him. "I kinda like the sound of that." He laughed. "And I wish more of you men would leave Thailand with fewer problems. That's what Bangkok's all about, right? I and I."

"Don't you mean R and R?" Fletcher took the bait.

"Nope, I and I: Intoxication and Intercourse."

"Oh ..." Cordova forced a laugh.

"You know, I hope you weren't waiting for those two lovely policewomen who escorted you up here." Reilly had a thick, reddish-brown mustache, trimmed vertically on the sides, and he tugged at the edges when he spoke, almost as if he missed a curl the military had made him shave off. He wore gold wire-rim glasses, and with his other hand he removed them and concentrated on scratches in the lens as he spoke. "I mean, I see those two ladies a lot ... I work with them all the time and ... well, I'd hate to see them get—"

"They're sure a couple of lookers, aren't they, sir?" Fletcher cut in. "They promised to come back up here when you were done with us and take us back."

"Well, they didn't actually promise to escort us back to the hotel," Cordova reminded the Snakeman.

"God, I'd give a month's pay just to have Sgt. Sugar sit on my face for one night. Just one everlovin' fornicatin' night!"

Reilly frowned. "I kept you gentlemen busy with witness statements for nearly three hours." He glanced at his watch

78

again before sliding the glasses back onto a slightly crooked nose. "You can't really expect them to stand around waiting for you."

"Just ignore the Snakeman, Mister Reilly." Cordova shook the CID agent's hand and ventured out into the corridor finally. "He's just got a perpetual hard-on that needs servicing, and Miss Sugar and her partner came onto us kinda hot and heavy before we realized they were decoy cops or whatever you call 'em. You understand."

"Sure, I understand." Reilly draped a muscular arm around Fletcher's shoulder. "Just a word of advice," he said. "Forget them." Two short but exquisitely proportioned matrons walked between the door gunners, and one of the policewomen glanced back over her shoulder provocatively at Elliot.

Cordova was afraid Fletcher was going to float up off the floor and glide after her, chin out and lips puckered. "Why do you say that, sir?" He latched on to one of the Snakeman's biceps.

"Well . . ." Reilly did not want to overstep his bounds. After all, they were all lonely GIs, this *was* Southeast Asia, and anything with a skirt on was fair game—excluding Moslem holy men, of course. "It's just that they've got enough problems in their lives right now, bein' female cops in this cesspool and all."

"In other words"—Cordova was finally getting the message—"the last thing they need is a migraine in the form of two no-account gunnies with one thing on their mind."

"No offense."

"None taken." Cordova produced a sad expression that told the agent he'd almost been accepted as one of the boys. Then, still guiding Snakeman away from the bottom-swishing matrons, he turned to leave.

"Look"—Reilly scratched at a jagged scar on his chin—"they're both nice ladies. And parents, if you get my drift."

Cordova stared at the scar and not Reilly's eyes. He had another scar on his throat, too—a long, wide burn scar that disappeared beneath his collar. The agent wore civilian clothes—a khaki safari suit—but there had been a plaque on his office wall with Viet script across the top and a framed Purple Heart beside it. That told Corky the man had been around and deserved the last word. After all, this was his town—so to speak.

"Parents?"

"Sgt. Prasertkwan's husband was killed three years ago in a shoot-out between TPs and some black marketeers."

"TPs?"

"Thai Police. The black marketeers just happened to be of the round-eye persuasion, but they got away. To this day, no one is sure whether or not they were even American.

"She was home caring for their newborn daughter when she got the knock at the door. I'm told she doesn't hold it against the U.S. GIs. She's always been cordial toward me, anyway."

"And her partner?"

"That's a sad case, too. Sawang—that's Miss . . . uh, Officer Chatsungnoen's first name. Well, she was out on a ferry-boat with her common-law husband—they were never really married . . . just lived together, I guess. Anyway, it was that time of year when the klongs are swollen from monsoon rains, and the ferry was hit by a barge. It overturned. She managed to cling onto her youngest son—he's five now. But she lost her two daughters. And the old man, of course. It was a real tragedy. That was in sixty-two, I believe. Before she was hired by the TPs."

Cordova was touched, but he tried not to show it. "That's a real heartbreaker, Mister Reilly, but what do you expect from us?"

"Just a bit of compassion." He folded his huge arms across his chest. It was body language that spoke tomes to Cordova.

80

Brody would have called it "mindfuck to the max." Reilly flexed his wrist muscles, and that started a chain reaction that rippled all the way up along his biceps. "The last thing they need right now are promises of paradise when all you want is a one-night stand."

"We'll keep you posted on our progress." Fletcher decided he'd heard enough and started toward the stairwell.

"I don't know what"—Reilly's voice rose slightly—"but they obviously saw *something* in you two. It's the first time I ever had them escort any *phalang* crime victims all the way up here before. Just don't take advantage of 'em. Okay, troops?"

Both door gunners nodded, and after they were a few steps down the stairwell, Snakeman said, "He's just pissed they ignored *his* advances."

"Probably."

"I didn't wanna date no widowed mothers anyway."

"Yah . . . Patpong Road, here we come!"

But once they reached the main lobby, both soldiers found themselves in front of the desk officer.

"We were hoping to speak with Sgt. Prasert—"

A short, bald Oriental with a pencil-thin mustache and thick glasses smiled politely but waved them silent. He pointed over to a younger man whose full head of black hair was slicked down from front to back with grooming oil. The Thai sat at a small desk beside a teletype machine. A sign hanging from the front of the desk said TRANSLATOR. The two door gunners shuffled over to it, and Snakeman cleared his throat.

"Excuse me, sir." Cordova took it upon himself to be their spokesman. "But we were hoping to speak with—"

"Military ID card, please," the translator interrupted sternly.

"Huh?" Fletcher stared at the pistol grip protruding from a shoulder holster.

"He wants to see your green card," Cordova interpreted.

Both soldiers fished the laminated IDs from their wallets.

"Orders." The translator remained cool and detached as he studied some paperwork on a clipboard, ignoring the cards.

"Orders?" Fletcher folded his arms across his chest and wondered if he looked as intimidating to the policeman as Reilly had to them.

The young plainclothes officer glanced up for the first time. "Military Orders. Are you on leave? TDY? R and R? AWOL?"

Fletcher let out a loud laugh that turned several heads in the lobby. "Oh, hell, buddy . . . we're definitely not AWOL," he said, glancing over at Corky, who was searching his pockets for the R and R pass, and commenced checking for his own. "Not yet, anyway."

The translator set down his clipboard and presented them both with an irritated frown. "What exactly is it can I do for you?" he asked, the lines across his forehead evidence he was not happy in his job.

"We, uh . . . we participated in a . . . a decoy bust this evening," Cordova said deciding to try a different approach, "involving Sgt. Prasertkwan and Officer . . ." He turned to Fletcher. "What was her partner's name?"

Snakeman's eyes bulged. "You're askin' *me*? Hell"—he searched his memory—"Chatsworthdam or something . . . I don't know."

"That's it." Cordova beamed, remembering now. "Chatsungnoen. Officer Chatsungnoen."

"And?" The translator was beginning to look intrigued. Intrigued, or amused.

"Well, they promised to . . . I mean, they were going to give us a lift back to our hotel."

"The decoy squads are back out on the street. It only takes them an hour or so to book their prisoners and fill out all the paperwork. Even on a big catch like they had tonight."

"I see . . ." Disappointment clouded Cordova's eyes.

82

"It is doubtful they will be back in here tonight." He glanced at his watch. "They work nineteen-hundred hours until zero-three-hundred hours. That's seven P.M. until three in the—"

"We're on military time, too," Snakeman reminded him sarcastically.

The translator didn't seem to take offense. "And since it's almost three o'clock now, and they haven't dragged in another paddy wagon full of criminals, I'm sure they'll be calling it a night very shortly."

"Don't they return to the station before officially going off duty?" Cordova remembered something from a *Dragnet* episode.

"Must police in all country copy American way of doing everything?" His eyes narrowed slightly, and the thick lenses made them appear somewhat sinister.

"Fuck it." Fletcher was the one to do the grabbing this time. "Let's get the hell outta here. I knew all along, there was something snooty about them two cunts."

Cordova watched the translator's eyebrows arch slightly. "Snooty?"

"Uppity. You know—they were playin' us for suckers, Corky. Shit. We oughta have our ding-dongs slapped."

"What the heck are you talkin' about, Snakeman?"

"'We come get you after CID done with questions,'" He imitated Sgt. Prasertkwan's voice as well as he could. "'We take you home to hotel room . . . *hee-hee!* . . . show you Bangkok on the way. . . .' My ass."

"Aw, lighten up. They probably *are* bustin' their buns out on the beat, tryin' to make the streets of Bangkok safer for tourists like you and me." Cordova forced a laugh, trying to ignore the fact that almost half of their first night of R and R was already shot.

"Shit. They're probably on their backs somewhere ballin'

their boyfriends. Ain't no PO-lice*women* that work this time of night, Corky-san. Give . . . me . . . a . . . break. Fuck 'em."

"Yah." Corky decided there was no reason why he should stand up for Prasertkwan and Chatsungnoen. Time to beat feet over to Patpong Road, Cockbang's famous red neon night club district and get to the whores before the best ones were taken.

# CHAPTER 8

## An Lao Valley

"Lieutenant, I've got an SF Lurp team on the freq! They've made contact with Charlie and are pushing him back our way!"

Vance listened to a dull crescendo of automatic weapons fire rising in the distance. Now and then, fierce M-33 explosions could be heard. Screams of the wounded and dying also carried on the breeze, and that told him he was getting his battle back *rikky-tik*!

"*Our* Charlie?" he yelled above the swish of rotorblades all around—four gunships had just set down, and the troopers were eager to pursue the enemy.

"Roger! The same Victor Charlie that shot down the Phantom, best we can guestimate!"

He glanced up at the stars, searching out the sliver of crescent moon. It would stay dark. "Okay! Spread your men out along that berm there. I want half your people to gimme a Lima ambush, and the rest to double-time down that ravine and around to the northwest."

"The northwest, sir?" A tall, stocky buck sergeant towered over the lieutenant.

"That's right, Sergeant. If the Berets are kickin' ass like it sounds they are, Charlie'll panic and beat feet the easy way out, and that's through here. If he remembers we were chasin' him first and may have left a sniper team behind, then he'll dick around till he finds the only avenue of escape left, and that's through that gorge. Where I want you to take some men and set up an X ambush."

"I don't have enough men for an X-Ray, Lieutenant. Besides, I don't think these dinks are from around here. They're actin' weird. I think they're just passin' through. Maybe strayed from the Ho Chi or something."

"Improvise."

The discharges were rapidly getting closer.

"But—"

A glowing green tracer sliced through the gloomy mist, striking the sergeant in the forehead. A stench in the air followed the round past Vance's nose, like death itself blowing gunsmoke in his face.

Jacob Vance dropped into the prone position, then crawled over to the sergeant, checked his lifeless form, then rolled back against a log as the roar of discharges increased and a wall of flying lead ripped out from the bamboo.

A shoulder slammed into his back, and the lieutenant whirled around, ready to slash with his survival knife. "Sorry, sir! Didn't know anyone claimed this tree already!"

"Larson! What the hell's going on?" Vance slipped the blade back into its ankle sheath. "I thought we were preparing to counterambush a small squad of sappers the Berets were pushing back."

A rocket-propelled grenade exploded against the other side of the tree trunk, sending a shower of splinters into the air. Both Vance and the Professor curled up into the fetal position, covering their heads with their arms as more RPGs screamed in. "Near as I can make out, sir, our counterambush got counter-counterambushed!" Using one hand and holding the weapon like a pistol, Larson lifted his M-16 over the edge of the log and held the trigger in without aiming until half the magazine emptied with a bouncing clatter.

86

"What!" Vance demanded.

"Right! Charlie lured us into a trap! We're catchin' hell on two sides, near as I can make out! I think we stumbled into a main force of battalion size or larger!"

"Well, shit," Vance muttered under his breath as he listened to the flap of distant rotorblades fading. The gunships had lifted off at the first sign of trouble.

"Right-o, sir. We're fucked. Truly fucked."

"Shut up, Larson, while I think this through." He rolled over on his back and ejected the twenty-round magazine from his M-16. From his ruck he pulled out two banana clips of thirty-rounds each, taped together, the business ends opposite each other. Vance rammed one of the mags into the rifle's well and sent the charging handle home.

But Larson wasn't one to comply with orders when his hide was at stake. "You better call those choppers back in, sir! Then *we* better dig in and wait for the Cavalry!"

"The birds were low on fuel. No way could they fly some loops for you, Private. We're on our own until—"

"Then you better call some arty down on top of us again, sir! 'Cause this time you got a legit excuse!"

The entire tree line was ablaze with muzzle flashes, and the log they were using for cover was becoming smaller and smaller. Each time another burst of lead impacted against it, the force on their shoulders was greater, until it actually started hurting.

"Fuck!" Vance already felt black and blue all over.

"Corpsman up! *Medic!* We need a medic over here— *Now!*"

Larson recognized Chappell's voice instantly. He waited for a lull in the constant shooting, then chanced a glimpse around the edge of the bullet-riddled tree trunk. He could just barely see Chappell's helmet in a clump of bushes twenty yards away, halfway down the gentle slope of a hill.

Larson glanced around as much as he could without

presenting more of a target, but there was no one rushing to their aid. "Doc!" he called out. "Doc Delgado! Corpsman up!"

There was still no answer, and he felt a sudden sick and sinking feeling in the pit of his gut.

Vance grabbed his wrist and Larson began sliding out of his ruck.

"Somebody's gotta help 'em!" The Professor pulled two smoke grenades from his web belt.

"You won't be any help to them—nobody can!" Vance argued. "Not right now! You'll just get yourself zapped half-way there!"

"They're just newbies, Lieutenant!" Larson was not slow-ing as he readied the gear he would need and tucked the rest away.

Larson had thrown the smoke grenades and was leaping to his feet when the ground gave way partially beneath them.

"Jesus!" Vance all but screamed as the huge boa shot up out of the earth. They had collapsed a snake hole, and the reptile, already irritated by all the gunfire and concussions, wasn't in the mood for uninvited company!

His ankle twisted, Larson left Vance with the hissing con-strictor and limped through the smoke down to the hillside. Unable to see very well because of the milky gray screen, he tripped into the trench the newbies had hastily dug, spraining his other ankle, too.

A soldier Larson couldn't recognize lay on his back next to Chappell, groaning and trembling violently. His nose and one ear were gone, and his face was a bloody pulp. His right arm was twisted behind him unnaturally, and his left leg was man-gled into shreds below the knee. Chappell was trying unsuc-cessfully to apply a tourniquet to the man's shaking thigh. "Where's Nelson?" The Professor broke out his own first-aid pouch as thunder erupted overhead. A fine mist suddenly cov-ered the steaming battlefield.

"I don't know!" Chappell screamed, tears in his eyes. "Over there somewhere, with the others! What are we gonna

88

do with this guy, Shawn?" The mist was quickly turning to huge drops, and within minutes blinding sheets of rain pounded down on them.

"Well, so much for a Dustoff!" Larson referred to the medical evacuation choppers.

Chappell reached across and grabbed Larson by the arms. "Do you have any morphine or whatever they give you when you get zapped? This guy's really in pain!"

"I can see that, Aaron!" Larson's head dropped back, and he yelled at the top of his lungs, "Corpsman up! We need a medic over here!"

"Corpsman up!" Chappell joined him.

"Doc Delgado! Where the hell are you?"

Neither man wanted to confront the obvious: Delgado was probably out there somewhere lying face down in the mud and muck, dead.

"Give him something for the pain!" Chappell repeated.

"I ain't *got* anything for the pain!"

"What!"

"Only Delgado carries that stuff around. Delgado and some of the dopers!"

The wounded soldier was suddenly sitting bolt upright and trying to grab Larson with both hands, though one wouldn't respond properly. "Waste me, Professor!" he pleaded. "THE PAIN!"

Larson recoiled, but he couldn't get away. The man's fingers were like metal vise grips. "Please, Professor! I can't stand it! Shoot me, you son of a bitch! PLEEEEEASE!"

"Don't listen to him!" Chappell tried to pull Larson away, but he couldn't free him from the wounded soldier's hold.

"Easy, man!" Larson pushed Chappell back as he argued with the bleeding GI. "You're gonna be all right! We're gonna get some help in here! You just wait."

Blood bubbled forth from the lower half of the soldier's face—where his lips used to be.

Larson and Chappell both knew that, even if a Dustoff

managed to make it in despite the zero visibility, the man would never make it back to an aid station in time. Larson prayed for painkiller to drop from the skies.

A long, drawn-out scream left the soldier as mortars crashed down near their position and the blasts pushed Larson onto his severed leg. He screamed forever, it seemed, and then he was gasping for air and, as soon as he caught his breath, screaming again. "Kill me! Kill me! Kill me!" he chanted. Desperate pleas from a man in so much pain that Larson feared his own heart would stop at any moment from the agony of just watching the man and not being able to do anything for him.

"No!" Chappell yelled as he and Larson locked eyes for an instant and, chin set firmly, The Professor slowly drew the .45 pistol from his hip.

One of the mortar rounds had sent a fist-sized chunk of shrapnel into the wounded soldier's neck, ripping his throat open, yet still his body clung to life against his will.

Chappell's hand shot out and grabbed Larson's wrist as he brought the pistol up. "No! Let him die!" He had to struggle to get the words out, so intense was the rain now. "Don't shoot him!"

"He ain't gonna die on his own!" Larson could not believe what he was saying. The words were coming out, but he had no control over them. "His body's got the curse! It's got the rain-forest curse! It ain't gonna *let* him die!"

"But—" Chappell grabbed his arms again, but Larson jerked his gunhand free.

"And I ain't gonna let him suffer another second!"

The single discharge was like thunder echoing between their ears compared to the snapping fingers of distant shots zinging in to kick up dirt all around the Americans, two living and one dead.

Larson had placed the .45's barrel against the wounded man's temple and gently squeezed the trigger.

90

"Fuck." Chappell couldn't believe what he had just witnessed.

"Shut up." Larson quietly holstered the pistol, ignoring the ricochets bouncing in on all sides.

"I knew Nam was gonna be bad, but I never thought I'd see this."

Larson reached over and grabbed him by the front of the shirt, exposing them both to enemy fire. But it was doubtful anyone could see the two GIs for the rain and drifting pall of gunsmoke. "You didn't see *nothing*, newbie! You got that?"

Chappell swallowed hard, eyes bulging behind the thick lens of his black-framed glasses. "Uh . . . right, Shawn. Nothing."

The Professor pushed the younger soldier away as if repulsed by the sight of him, and the two troopers waited out the rest of the battle back to back, convinced they would be dead meat, too, in a matter of hours.


Following glorious victories in the Ia Drang Valley campaign the month before, 1st Cavalry Division Commander Major Gen. Henry W.O. Kinnard found himself confronted by the problem: where next to seek and destroy the enemy.

After his troopers returned to their western Binh Dinh Province along Highway 19 in An Khe, MI agents in early 1966 suggested he try the western highlands once again, in hopes of catching Charlie with his pants down while he regrouped and licked his wounds following the loss of face at Ia Drang.

The Air Cav's own Intelligence staff had confirmed that the Sao Vang, or "Yellow Star" Division, was operating in northeastern Binh Dinh Province, and Kinnard wanted to leave a lasting impression on their commanders also. Yellow Star was actually the North Vietnamese Army's 3rd Division, which was a combination of the 18th and 22nd North Vietnamese Regiments, along with VC Main Force 2nd Regiment, and the

General could smell another rat's nest that needed to be cleaned out.

Binh Dinh Province was an area of treacherous mountains and highly populated plains stretching to the coast. The South Vietnamese 22nd Division was experiencing problems keeping the region secure, as they did not have enough men to both keep vital Highway 1 open and complete pacification duties as well.

Gen. Kinnard knew that Binh Dinh Province was where he would bring the Airmobile concept of gunship warfare next.

Shawn Larson stood at the position of attention, along with several hundred other soldiers, as the awards presentation neared an end. Private Aaron Chappell stood beside him, but neither soldier had really looked at each other in the three days since they had been rescued by the Green Berets from Bong Son.

They had hidden in that grassy ravine for over twenty-four hours, listening to bullets whistle past overhead, before the rain stopped and reinforcements moved in.

Over one hundred enemy corpses were left behind by the North Vietnamese Regulars and VC guerillas they had clashed with. Also left behind was a booby-trapped flag—which killed the three newbies trying to retrieve it—and a note that read, in part: "WELCOME TO LAND OF YELLOW STAR. NOW GO HOME."

The Professor watched a general staff officer, who had flown in aboard an all-black Loach and would leave shortly in the same helicopter—its rotors were still twirling lazily on the helipad in the middle of Bong Son's Special Forces outpost—pin the Distinguished Service Cross on recently promoted Col. Hal Moore. But this was not an awards ceremony for bravery displayed during the recent battle outside Bong Son. Colonel Moore was receiving his DSC for leading the troops to victory in Ia Drang, though they had had to go back twice since declaring the Valley secure, and were planning a return for one final search-and-destroy sweep after this business in Binh Dinh Province was attended to.

There had been no investigation into the death of the soldier Larson had put out of his misery. It was assumed he died from wounds inflicted by the enemy—and justly so: communist shrapnel had added several pounds to the trooper's weight. Larson's bullet had left only a small purple hole.

Doc Delgado was found alive and uninjured after the gunsmoke cleared, pinned down with a dozen other soldiers a hundred yards from where Larson had unholstered his automatic.

"Gentlemen." Light applause and a few whistles filtered through the swaying formations as Col. Neil Buchanan stepped up to the makeshift podium. He would be the fourth officer to address the troops this afternoon beneath the blistering Asian sun. "You have just survived the opening stages of Operation Masher, and on that I congratulate you!" Another round of semi-sincere applause rolled up and down the countless rows of GIs clad in jungle fatigues and bush hats.

"It is our job to exterminate the VC terrorizing the twelve provinces of II Corps, and by God we're gonna do it!" The raucous cheers he might have been expecting did not materialize, but Buchanan went on unabated. "With the help of some Airborne and 22nd Division Arvins, as well as a few good ROKs, we've been able to launch the Bong Son campaign with a roaring start!"

*No shit.* Larson blew disenchanted beer-tainted breath through his teeth. The Professor had been scheduled to depart Vietnam a couple of weeks earlier, as the Ia Drang campaign wound down, but he had been involuntarily red-flagged without his consent: Due to high casualties and low number of replacements, many of the soldiers who had completed their year overseas were being kept on. "Extension was at the request and for the convenience of the government," the crumpled set of orders in Shawn Larson's thigh pocket read. That was now two Christmases he'd missed because of duty, honor, and country.

But the Professor wasn't so angry anymore. These last few days, he was beginning to have second thoughts about returning stateside. He didn't want to go back to The World now. Not after what he had done. Not now that, every waking minute, Shawn Larson saw that young mutilated teenager's pleading eyes moments before he placed the pistol barrel against the youth's temple and pulled the trigger. The Professor hadn't slept well in days. And when he did doze off, nightmares woke him—nightmares that brought the whole tragedy back with crystal clarity.

Larson missed his young sister desperately. She was confined to a hospital bed back in Seattle, suffering from a childhood disease that left its victims handicapped and virtually helpless. A disease the scientists had found a vaccine for— but too late, in his sister's case. The family—or what was left of a family—had deteriorated and eventually split up over the emotional trauma and medical expenses. Shawn never forgave his parents for abandoning the girl to the state. And now the insurance had run out, Ma and Pa were nowhere to be found, and the bills were coming to Private S. Larson, United States Army, Vietnam.

He shipped marijuana home by the duffel bag, using a cousin in Washington State as the middleman. The sales kept his sister out of a welfare nursing home. He just didn't care about what was legal anymore. All that mattered now was his sister. She was all he had left. She and the friends he had made here at Echo Company, though Larson had shied away from relationships ever since Hal Krutch was killed.

"As this last week in January approaches, I want to remind you our mission in the Republic of Vietnam is far from over, and that we must never forget those who made the supreme sacrifice that helped bring us to the point where we're at now." Buchanan removed his helmet, and every man standing below him knew what the colonel was referring to: Forty-two members of the 2nd Battalion 7th Cav's Alpha Company were killed during the first day of air assaults on Deo Mang Pass, when their C-123 crashed during a thunderstorm. Morale had been sinking fast among certain elements of the First Cavalry ever since.

"Now it's time to get back down to business, gentlemen." He replaced his helmet. "It's time to"—Buchanan reached down and picked up an M-16 rifle that had been leaning against the podium and began waving it in the air over his head—"*rock and roll*!"

Half the formation waved their fists in the air this time, but the Colonel was not through charging up the troops. "The politicians back home are not very happy about the title we've chosen to give this latest little Airmobile experiment: Operation Massshhher." He drew the word out until most of the enlisted men were laughing. "They've even called upon good old LBJ to change it. Seems the press—you remember the Press Corps, don't you gentlemen?" Visions of false or misleading stories about some of the Division's activities sprang into the minds of nearly every man there. "Well, the Press Corps is having a field day with Operation Massshhher! Don't ya jest love it?"

"Monster the media! Monster the media!" the chant rose, and Buchanan's smile grew. The soldiers were referring to an elaborate jury-rigged antipersonnel mine that involved exploding over a dozen claymores simultaneously. It was called a "monster."

"Well, despite the *news* media, we're gonna wipe Charlie's ass for him, gentlemen. And we're gonna use a *bayonet*!"

Buchanan certainly knew how to get his troops excited. Now, despite earlier boredom or indifference with the muster, nearly all of them were jumping up and down, ready to go back into battle. War cries and animal grunts filtered up to him from every section of the vast formation. But some of the senior staff members who outranked Neil Nazi did not seem enthusiastic about his presentation. Pep rallies were better left back in The World, they felt. Larson watched a few of them confer with each other in whispers behind shields of closed fingers.

"Well," the Bull, as he liked to be called, continued, "Charlie's gonna have hell to pay now that we've got everyone together for our little field trip in the boonies. Let me see here." He consulted a clipboard. "We've got the 1st of the Seventh, the 2nd Battalion, too. And we've got the 12th Cav's 1st and 2nd battalions as well. Hell, we've even got those gunship recon commandos from the 9th Cav's 1st Squadron. Now, you can't rightly beat that, can you?

"Taking into account the boys in aviation and arty, I'd say that adds up to nearly 6,000 men in our combined little brigade—give or take a couple hundred. Now I find it hard to believe Charlie would dare challenge that many First Team warriors, do you?"

Someone released a purple smoke grenade, and the section along the rear of the formation began falling out.

"Okay! Awright, I get the message!" Buchanan prepared to dismiss this rowdy group of grunts and gunnies who had permission to kill. "It's a hundred and twenty in the shade, and there ain't no goddamned shade! But before I dismiss you clowns, I want to remind you about something.

"The three-day Tet truce with the Viet Cong didn't go over too well, as we all know. Somehow the Lunar New Year made it to The Nam. And 1966 is"—he tapped the First Division combat patch on his right shoulder—"the Year of the Horse!"

Several more cheers went up as the men began to disperse, heading back toward their chopper pits. The Air Cavalry emblem was the largest in the Army, and featured the head of a black horse.

"Keep that in mind. Do the First Team justice!"

# CHAPTER 9

## Saigon

Dep's thighs were tangled around his head when Brody the Whoremonger finally fought his way up from the bottomless pit of all-consuming pain. Screams from several women became yelp and high-low sirens from a dozen police land-rovers. His head throbbed beyond description. The sirens died, leaving only echoes bouncing back and forth off the tenement walls, and the echoes again became women's screams.

A severed arm was lying on the sticky dance floor, inches from his nose, and he instantly thought of Dep. But there was hair on the arm. It was a man's arm, and even from here he could read the inscription on the green and gold ring: U.S. ARMY MILITARY POLICE SCHOOL—FORT GORDON, GEORGIA, 1964.

"Bro-deeeee...." A weak voice, the voice of a child in search of her mother, reached Brody's ears, and stiffly, a groan escaping him, he untangled Dep's shapely but blood-splattered legs from around his head and lifted her by the shoulders, into his arms. He brushed her hair back.

"Thank God," he whispered. Her eyes were swollen, black and blue, but there were no deep cuts on her face. Dep's blouse had been ripped off by the explosions, but her long hair fanned out below a bruised throat, covering her breasts.

"Are we dead?" She brought her head back slightly, confused by her inability to open her eyes.

"I don't think so." Brody glanced around. The nightclub was filled with a rolling blanket of black smoke that remained at table level, swirling about with each movement of the survivors but refusing to disperse.

Bodies lay everywhere, some alone, lifeless, others bleeding or stunned, friends crouching over them. The dance floor was becoming slick with blood.

"Everyone stay calm!" One of the military policemen was moving through the building slowly, his .45 automatic out, the barrel pointed at the ceiling. There were no sappers anywhere to be seen, but a secondary assault was on his mind. "Somebody threw a satchel charge through the windows. Help is on the way! Remain calm—help is on the way!"

"I think you've got a Mike Papa wounded bad over here somewhere!" Brody called to the MP, using the military phonetic for army cop. He stared at the glowing Academy ring on the severed limb.

"Right. Thanks." The soldier moved in the opposite direction. "I already checked. That's all that's left of him."

"Jesus."

Dep had forced her swollen eyelids apart as Brody started to lift her up off the ground. "Gotta get you to a hospital, honey. Gotta—"

Dep let out a scream that sent a bolt of terror through Brody, and he whirled around, expecting to see a suicide squad of Cong charging them from the back corridors of the building. But Dep was pointing at his own arm, and that was when he felt the pain for the first time. Blood spurted like a weak fountain in front of his eyes.

It was a stabbing, ripping pain, as if an invisible demon had taken a liking to his elbow and clamped down tight with razor-sharp teeth. Brody felt himself blacking out again and

98

losing his balance. He leaned against the bar, still holding Dep in his arms.

"Set me down!" she cried. "I'm okay. Really! Set me down, Bro-dee!"

He not only set her down on the closest bar stool, but collapsed immediately thereafter, watching the floor rush up to meet him. He never felt the impact.

When he awoke, it was to the sight of a mosquito net drooping inches above his face from four bedposts rising in a dark room, in some low-ceilinged, ramshackle hut. The sound of a canal rushing past outside the window filled his ears.

"Dep," he whispered, not sure he should move. Was he being held prisoner somewhere? Had the VC actually overrun the nightclub and kidnapped all the roundeyes?

"No talk." Her voice drifted over to him from a back room. He could distinguish the two sources of running water now as he painfully lifted his head: the canal outside, and faucets filling a bucket.

The pain returned along his entire left side, and he wondered for a moment if he'd suffered a heart attack. Brody had read about healthy men younger than himself who'd dropped dead from cardiac arrest without any warning. And the sapper attack on the Cholon nightspot had surely been shocking enough to elicit at least a skipped beat or two.

"You lose bookoo blood, Bro-dee." She reappeared in the bedroom, moving slowly because of her black eyes.

"Where are we?" he asked, feeling safer now that he was no longer alone with the darkness.

"My hooch," she said simply, dropping into a squat beside the narrow bed. Her fingertips were touching his chest lightly. "Lie back," she whispered, "you have *ti-ti* fever." Brody complied, and she placed a cool washcloth over his forehead.

"Your hooch?" He tried to mask the surprise. He'd thought

a woman like Dep only lived from day to day, night to night, hotel room to hotel room.

"Yes." She attempted to smile, but her trembling lips would not cooperate. "You think I stay streets?"

"I thought . . ." he began.

"Nebbah mind, Bro-dee." She placed a fingertip over his lips. "I know."

"Why is it so dark in here?"

"Power out again. Happen bookoo in Cholon." She glanced at the lone window in the room as a jeep passed by outside, its headlights throwing eerie shadows across the street.

"Oh." He watched her reach up and wind the shutters closed.

"No sweat. I light candle. Make you warm again."

"Don't leave me!" he said, clasping her wrists gently as she rose to leave.

"Just go bathroom," she told him. "Get new bandage for your arm."

And then he remembered. Before passing out back in the nightclub, he had noticed the long gash along his left elbow. Whether inflicted by shrapnel or breaking glass, he was not sure.

"Maybe you should take me to the hospital," he suggested when she returned to change the dressing. "The American hospital: 3rd Field, or 17th, or whatever it's called down here."

"Not that bad," she advised him.

"Then why the hell did I pass out back in the club?" He stared up at the mosquito netting, the slowly twirling fan in the ceiling, and the temple tapestry hanging over a rice cooker on a small table against one wall. For the first time in months, he really felt like he was seeing the true Asia.

"We sleep long time after bomb blow," she explained.

"Sleep?"

"*Vang*! Yes. Long time. Then you try get up, no see noth-

100

ing wrong . . . try carry Dep. You lose bookoo blood, Bro-dee. No strength. Fall down. Ker-*plop!*" She slapped her palms together loudly, and Brody winced.

"Thanks for your diagnosis, Doc. But what about the arm? Won't it need stitches? You know: sew it up?" He tried to raise both arms to imitate someone sewing by hand, and intense pain lanced down through his side again.

"No move!" she rushed back over, reprimanding him. "No worry. Dep already sew Bro-dee back up. Good as new," she said matter-of-factly.

"Jesus." He rubbed at the elbow before she returned with the bottle of antiseptic. "No wonder I feel like a skunk that's been run over by a convoy of—"

"Quiet." She squatted beside the bed again, draped back the mosquito netting, and began removing the old bandages.

Brody wanted to look at the wound, but she would not let him. "Don't worry," she whispered. "Dep do good job. Blood stop. But you owe me fifty P for *soi chi*."

"*Soi* what?"

"*Chi*. I no know American word." She made the motions he had just attempted.

"Oh, thread."

Dep nodded. "Yes. T'red."

Brody tried to slid backwards across the sheets, but the pain only immobilized him more. Dep did not appear to be affected by his groans.

A few minutes later, after she had the new bandage on, Brody rolled onto his back. He watched her limp across the small room to a table in the corner. It was the kind of table his sisters kept on the patio to play house with. A hotplate sat between two tall piles of packaged noodles.

Dep carried a bowl into the bathroom, filled it with water from one of the faucets, and returned to the hotplate. "No have rice this week." She poured the water into a pan and placed it on the hotplate. "You want share noodles with Dep?"

"Noodles?" He felt himself falling back into the daze.

101

Brody had no appetite whatsoever. "No . . . no thanks. But you go ahead. Just ignore me. I'm gonna crash, baby-cakes."

"No hungry?" She glanced back at him and frowned at the nod. "No sweat. Cook extra. Maybe you want later. Tell Dep. Make hot for you again."

Brody thought he was about to pass out, but as soon as he laid his head back against the pillow, the dizziness left him. He was in too much pain to get any sleep, so he tried concentrating on his surroundings.

The room was half the size of a small hotel room back in the States, yet it appeared to be Dep's entire world, when she was at home and not out hustling johns. Aside from the Chinese-style bathroom—no toilet and no tub, just a washbasin with cold water faucets, and a screened pipe that eventually led down to the sewer—there were no other rooms.

Along the wall to his left was a small, secondhand bureau supporting a cracked mirror. Yellowing and faded photographs of Dep posing arm in arm with American and Vietnamese men were taped to its corners. Above the mirror was a red-and-yellow banner proclaiming something in both Chinese and Vietnamese. The only thing Brody could recognize was the date 1963.

Against the far wall was an unpainted child's desk, piled high with American and French glamour magazines, though Brody could not make out the covers from where he lay. On one corner of the desktop was a stack of letters held together with a strip of green silk. Brody wondered if they were from her lovers, from the men in her past. GIs she had spent a year with, who just never came back one night—usually twelve months to the week after she first met them. Maybe Dep liked it that way. No long-term relationships. No sad farewells. Just, suddenly—gone.

Some had surely given in to second thoughts after a week back in their winter wonderland. They had written her, promising to return, or promising to get her out. Cold, uncaring America could do that to the vets—bring back the memories

102

of Saigon and their little "pearl of the Orient," the steaming sugarcubes at midnight, standing on the balcony together, watching firefights on the edge of the city and flares floating down through the castlelike cumulus; making love through the night with a slender, amber-limbed enchantress who knew nothing but to please. The dull routine of day-to-day life in a country at peace became emotionally debilitating, even cancerous. Many vets would return, eventually—those who were not tied down to women they'd married long before their Vietnam experience changed them forever.

Brody, feeling some strength returning, rose onto his elbows and watched Dep closely as she knelt in front of the table supporting the stacks of noodles. She was unwrapping a small package and withdrawing two long, narrow sticks, lighting a match.

The strong aroma of *joss* incense quickly reached his nostrils, and he watched as she held the two sticks between her fingers and brought clasped hands to her forehead before bowing to a small statue of Buddha sitting on a wall shelf. Dep bowed all the way to the floor, remained silent and unmoving for several minutes, then inserted one of the *joss* sticks in a small planter filled with silver ash directly in front of the Buddha. She then rose and went over to a doorway at the end of the window by Brody's head, slid a bamboo partition back, stepped out onto a balcony, and placed the second *joss* stick in an identical planter sitting on a small altar adorned with fresh fruit. Tangerines, bananas, and grapes also formed a wreath around the foot of the altar on the wall shelf.

"Feel better, eh, Bro-dee?"

She stepped in off the balcony, moving slower this time, and walked over to the bureau without comforting him. "Go sleep, soldier-boy. 'Morrow Dep take you to Aussie R and R hotel. Think Saigon too tough for Bro-dee. Maybe he should go Sydney, or Queen'land."

"I want to stay with you, Dep."

She had been pulling open a drawer and did not freeze as

he thought she would, but kept going through the motions. He watched her slowly remove the shirt she had draped across her shoulders back at the nightclub. His shirt. It was bloodied and torn, and she dropped it into a basket beside the dresser. Treat stared at the upturned slopes of her breasts, made larger and more exotic by the flickering candlelight.

"No talk *dinky-dau*, Bro-dee."

"I'm very serious." He tried to sit up, but the pain returned and he had to settle back against his elbows.

"No make Dep sad with crazy talk, okay?" Her expression showed no emotion, but her eyes were desperate, shifting back and forth between the face in the mirror and the man in her bed.

He watched her turn her back to him and slide out of her panties. Totally nude now, Dep walked into the bathroom, picked up another washcloth, and soaked it in a bucket, never once taking her eyes off his. Then she returned to the foot of the bed and began rubbing the soot and blood and sweat from her face and chest. Brody watched her wipe the dried tears from her cheeks and run the cloth along her arms, then down between her breasts and along a flat belly and over the mound of jet-black hair where her legs came together. He watched in silence as she worked the cloth over the curves of her thighs and calves, and decided he had never before been so excited by a woman simply cleansing herself.

"Let me stay with you, Dep."

She did not respond for a long time, but kept wiping away any evidence of the hell they had gone through back at the nightclub. Brody was not sure if she was taunting him or not—she spent more time toying with her nipples and crotch than was necessary—but he didn't care.

Finally, the washcloth nearly dry and new tears appearing along the edges of her dark, almond eyes, Dep moved closer to the bed and knelt beside him. "How long Bro-dee have left in Saigon?" she asked softly.

"Over three weeks." He ran his fingers under her chin,

then along those proud cheeks, wiping away the first tear to fall. "You know that."

"Plenty time." She took hold of his hand and kissed the bruised and scraped knuckle. "For fall in love. For fall out love. Kiss goodbye. *Fini.*"

"No."

"Yes, Bro-dee. For next week, Dep take care of you. Make you new man. Then, two more weeks, make love all day all night. You never forget Dep. Then you go back Army, be good soldier, fight for U.S.A. Fight for South Vietnam. Make Dep proud. Send her letter from hell'copter GIs. Stay friend forever."

"I think I love you, Dep," he started to say, but she slapped him. She slapped him hard, and it stung.

"No talk *love*," she nearly hissed, and Brody felt he could read her mind, could see the flashback she was experiencing even then: dozens of different American faces, one after another, telling Dep they loved her. "Never again!" She grabbed his shoulders and shook him, ignoring the severity of his wounds.

"I'm sorry," he said after she finally released him. "I'm not playing jokes on you." He was explaining as much to himself now as to her. "And I'm not some cherry boy falling in love with his first fuck."

"No . . . can . . . work, Bro-dee," she said slowly, regret in her tone.

"I want to tell you about myself, Dep." He leaned forward despite the pain, and his lips brushed her cheek. "I want to tell you my secret. The story that is . . . that is killing me inside. And then, if you still want me to go, I will go."

"I do not want hear 'bout wife back in U.S.A.," she said. "I do not want hear 'bout too many baby-san stateside, or—"

"I killed my last girlfriend," he told her.

Dep did not react the way he thought she might. There was no gasp, no shock in uplifted eyes.

"I killed her, but it was an accident."

Her hand came up, and she placed another washcloth against Brody's forehead. "Lie back," she said. "Go ahead an' tell Dep story. Talk all night if you want. But lie back. I do not want sick GI die my bed. Bad *joss*, you *bic*?"

He nodded, and continued. "I shot her from far away. I was high above her." He felt his upper lip start to tremble. "I did not recognize her, Dep."

"You were high in sky?" she asked. "In hell'copter?"

"Yes." Brody felt a sob working its way up through his chest, and he tried to turn away from her. But Dep took hold of his chin and forced him to face her.

"We have war my country, Bro-dee. Many people die. It is sad, but it is Vietnam."

"She was Viet Cong."

Dep recoiled slightly. "VC?" She was not sure she heard him correctly.

"I did not know . . . until after. Long after. They threw her in a mass grave. Without her legs."

"Treat." She leaned across the bed, trying to take him in her arms without hurting him.

"Without her legs, and now I see her face whenever it becomes dark."

"Unless you are with me."

Brody locked eyes with her, and Dep kissed him on the lips, then rubbed the tip of her nose against his in the Vietnamese fashion of showing affection. "Yes." The word left him as a whisper.

"I have heard this talk before," she revealed.

"Oh." In his mind, Brody saw Dep in this very bed, on her back, legs spread, a line of soldiers waiting at the door for their turn.

"Many GIs are brave on battlefield, but later, when ghosts follow them home, not so brave."

"It's not my imagination, Dep." He sought the right words to explain. "It's not all in mind. She's *there*. I see her face at

106

the foot of my bed, or my rack, or my cot or bunk or whatever it might happen to be. She's *there*."

"You need talk to her. You need tell her, 'Go away!'"

"I'm serious," he said, even though Dep did not sound in the least like she was joking.

"Dep same-same serious. Why you think she . . . *thuong-toi*." The woman lying against Brody switched to Vietnamese, searching for the right word. "Haunt. Yes, why you think she *haunt* you, Bro-dee?"

"Because I left her behind. Because I abandoned her in Plei Me."

"You were her lover? You loved a Highlands girl, Bro-dee?" Dep remained straight-faced, but he saw silent laughter in her eyes—a peculiar trait he had noticed only in Asian women before.

"Yes. Well, no. I mean—"

"Yes, no, make up mind, soldier-boy." Dep tilted her head to one side, challenging him to make up a story that would impress her.

"I . . . fell in love with her. But we never *made* love."

"So what Bro-dee do impress Highlands girl so much she want haunt you forever?"

This time it was Brody who swallowed. His head dropped. He could no longer look into Dep's eyes. "I shot her. With a machine gun."

"Machine?" She ran her fingers along the hair on his chest.

"Shoot bookoo bullets quickie." He snapped his fingers.

"Ah. M-16."

"Kind of," he said. "The bullets tore her in half." Dep stared at him as if she did not fully comprehend the words. "Tear in two," he added, lifting an old newspaper from the nightstand and ripping it down the middle.

"Ahhh." Dep nodded. "Highlands girl lose her head. No wonder she haunt Bro-dee."

"Not her head," he said. "Her legs. The bullets cut her in half at the waist." He ran the edges of his hand along his belly.

107

Dep nodded again, this time with more certainty in the movement. "Highlands girl mad because part her body gone?"

"I tried." He was seeing himself kneeling at the mass grave, in the middle of a monsoon downpour, digging through the mud, searching for Koy's legs. "I tried, but I couldn't find them."

"Mass grave same-same everyone stay one hole?" she asked him. Brody nodded, and Dep stood and walked over to the table holding packages of noodles and a bag of *joss* sticks. From a drawer he hadn't noticed before, she took several candles and began placing them about the room.

"You see Highlands girl my home yet?" she asked him. Brody didn't want to admit to that, but she said, "It's okay. Tell truth. You see her this room?"

He nodded, and pointed toward the foot of the bed. "When you were out on the balcony. I think."

"S'okay, Bro-dee. Maybe you see, maybe you no see. I believe ghost bother you. Dep see ghost before, did you think poss'ble?" She smiled for him as she began lighting all the candles. "Sure. You forget: This Vietnam. Everybody see ghost. Everybody *talk* ghost sometime. Tonight we talk ghost."

"No," he said firmly.

"Tell go away. Leave Bro-dee alone."

"No."

"You want have two womans in your bed all time—one warm and horny, one cold and ghost?" She was not smiling, but there was that odd twist to her lips that made Brody wonder if she was putting him on.

"No." He used the back of his hand to wipe sweat from his brow.

"Okay," she said, pulling a black nightgown from a middle drawer in the dresser. She slipped it over her head, and it fell to her ankles. "What Highlands girl's name?"

Brody hesitated, and Dep, bare feet braced apart, placed

108

her hands on her hips, assuming a restless stance. "Okay," he finally answered. "Koy."

She hurried over to the small family altar and took the largest picture frame from the wall. Brody watched her clutch it to her breast and wondered if it was meant to be a charm to protect her. "Koy!" she addressed the ghost in Brody's head, raising her voice without yelling. "Listen Dep."

"What do you want me to do?" he asked, but she ignored him now.

Moving from one side of the room to the other, in a circle, she stared up at the ceiling. "Koy! Listen Dep," she repeated. "Leave Bro-dee 'lone! Bro-dee stay with Dep now. Go back spirit world. Return *tinh tanh*!" She switched to Vietnamese and rattled off what Treat felt was a rough translation, and then her singsong voice changed slightly, and he knew she was speaking Chinese.

"Bro-dee bookoo sorry you die." She soon returned to English. "But you die accident! Bro-dee no know. Bro-dee make wrong. But Koy make wrong, too: No tell she VC!"

Dep held the framed photo up over her head and turned in another complete circle. "Now Koy leave," she ordered. "Dep family dead, too. *Fini*. More power than Koy. Stay my home. Protect Dep. Protect Bro-dee."

She turned back to face him, and winked, obviously confident the ceremony was going well so far. "Now leave, Koy. Leave Bro-dee heart. *Fini*!"

She skipped over to the ancestral altar and returned the photo of her parents to its rightful place above the other family pictures. "Tha's all," she announced, brushing the palms of her hands off, then walked over to each candle and doused them with her fingertips.

"That's all?" He sat up, expecting to feel something. A tingle in his body, the hair rising up along the back of his neck—anything.

But the room remained the same.

"You better now?" She was standing over the only candle that remained lit, providing light for the room.

"I don't know. I think so."

"Find out now," she whispered, snuffing out the flame. Brody watched her walk away through the darkness, out onto the balcony. Moonbeams lanced in, revealing the outline of her curves through the sheer nightgown for a moment, and then she was gone.

Dep remained on the balcony for several minutes. She did not return until he called for her softly. He had not felt the fear while she was away, leaving him in the dark. He felt free, finally.

"Better now?" she asked, lying down on the bed beside him.

"Yes," he whispered, trying not to break the spell.

A gaggle of choppers passed in the night outside, several miles away, and their flapping rotors failed to shatter the eerie calm in the room. The dull whump of giant blades even seemed to add to the numbing experience Dep's exorcism had left him with.

"Much better?" she teased, dropping her head slowly until she kissed his chest.

"Much."

Her hand took his, and he let her guide his fingers into the nightgown until he was cupping the edge of a breast. Brody ran his thumb back and forth over the nipple, feeling it grow warm and taut. Dep sighed as his hand moved to the other side of her chest, working it too.

After a few moments, he slid his hand up over her shoulder and began caressing the back of her neck, massaging the tightness out. "Feel good," she cooed, dropping her lips onto his belly as she curled up beside him. "Feel veddy good, Treat Bro-dee. No stop, okay? Harder."

With his one good hand, Brody rubbed Dep's neck and

shoulders, bringing moans of pleasure from her throat each time his touch found a new sore spot.

When his fingers started down her spine, kneeding the shallows and bone, her face moved lower, to make his work easier. Before he realized what was happening, she had taken him into her mouth and was working her lips up and down, slowly at first, sucking him erect, then roughly, like a cracking whip.

Brody's hand soon fell away from her backbone, and his pelvis rose, accommodating Dep this time. His head fell back, the flesh along his throat tight, and when he began to groan, losing control, her mouth slid off and her face turned toward his.

"Tell Dep you love her, Bro-dee," the Vietnamese woman said, breathing quickly.

"I love you," he said, running his lips across the top of her head, basking in the joy of her perfumed hair tickling his nose, breathing in her fragrance, her scent. *"Em yeu anh mai mai,"* he whispered, thinking he'd said, "I'll love you forever."

Dep giggled over his attempt at Vietnamese and added to his excitement. He rolled her onto her back, and using his knee to spread her legs, he entered her quickly, roughly, bringing a gasp from Dep's throat. She closed her eyes tightly, trying to match his rhythm. Brody stared down at the exotic lids, and watched her lips part as she began breathing harder.

A smile slowly returned, and she opened her eyes to find him still staring down at her, his own eyes bulging slightly now with each thrust.

"No hurt Dep." She pursed her lips, submitting totally to his control and dominance. "Make love Dep." She pretended to beg, bringing her shapely legs up and locking the ankles over his hips. Her long, slender fingers took hold of his haunches and pulled. They pulled harder with each stroke, forcing her thighs farther apart, drawing him deeper into her, closer to her soul.

Dep's hands slid up over the curve of his buttocks and along his back until her wrists were wrapped around the back of his neck and she was able to pull her face up. She devoured him with her lips, forcing her tongue deep into his mouth. Dep hugged him fiercely, and when her head dropped back finally into the pillow, she said, "Make love Dep all night, all day, all night again. Okay? Make you feel good. Make you forget past."

She unlocked her ankles and dropped her legs as he began thrusting harder and faster, losing control again, and she slid the soles of her feet flat against the moist sheets, arches touching the swell of her hips. Keeping her knees bent, she took hold of her ankles, feeling every vibration now, letting him penetrate her to the root.

Dep felt her loins swirling for the first time in years. She felt her womb preparing to explode against the man inside her, and tears broke loose along the edges of her eyes. "*Anh . . . yeu . . . em . . . nhieu . . . lam*, Treat Bro-dee. I . . . love . . . you . . . very . . . very . . . much. . . . "

"Open your eyes," he whispered, the words merging into a gasp yet filled with strength and power.

"What?" she asked softly, forcing the lids apart, flushing at the thought he was still staring down at her, and now she, up at him.

"I want to look into your eyes when I come," he said, blowing a kiss down at her as he sucked in the room's humid air with those final thrusts. "And I want you to stare into mine."

Dep smiled. She would do anything in the world for this man right now. "You are *dinky-dau* GI, Treat Bro-dee."

"I want us to become one with each other."

Dep swallowed hard, losing the defiance in her eyes. Her proud features began to melt, as if she was no longer in con-

112

trol, as if she was experiencing something new. "I . . . think . . . Dep . . . come . . . now." She swallowed again, drinking him in with her eyes.

When the schoolgirl whimper left Dep's throat and the sensations of bliss and euphoria consumed her body, Brody's release came too. He thought he would find something of himself in Dep's eyes, an answer to his questions. But all he saw was Koy's face, reflected in their depths.

# CHAPTER 10

## Special Forces Camp, Bong Son

The First Cav strategy against insurgents of the Yellow Star Division involved hammer-and-anvil-type operations. Assisting units would hide in ambush until Airmobile troopers, launching from the Bong Son Green Beret airstrip, could chase the enemy into their traps, not unlike tribesmen flushing game on the dark continent of Africa. That was how Shawn Larson viewed Operation Masher, anyway: like wild tribesmen flushing dangerous game.

The AO—area of operations—involved four sectors surrounding the Special Forces outpost: the An Lao Valley to the northwest; the Eagle's Claw in the southwest (actually the Kim Son Valley; its nickname was derived from the area's ariel appearance: seven smaller valleys within the Kim Son looked like a claw); the Cay Giep mountain range to the southeast; and the Cavalry's first target: the flat stretch of plains running along the northeast from which the SF encampment took its name.

When the Japanese left Indochina twenty-one years earlier, Viet Minh forces took over Binh Dinh Province, and it had remained a communist stronghold ever since. The Viet Minh became the VC, and when France left in defeat following the 1954 Geneva accords, the communists attempted to have

Vietnam divided into north and south *below* Binh Dinh—they could not accept losing territory to the Saigon government which they had controlled during the first Indochina wars. Binh Dinh, which meant "pacified," remained a part of South Vietnam, but it also remained, for the most part, under control of the insurgents.

Nearly a million Vietnamese lived in this province, which the U.S. Central Intelligence Agency pronounced "lost to the communists" in 1965. Since nearly 50,000 of the "refugees" who went north in 1954 were from Binh Dinh, a favorite phrase for the area was, "If a farmer in Binh Dinh was not Cong, he was at least related to one." Such beliefs were fueled by military intelligence that revealed many of the northerners were returning south. The province was becoming a maze of underground tunnels. Village sweeps saw few draft-age men —they were already in the ranks of the Viet Cong.

On January 25, 1966, the First Air Cavalry Division mounted a blatant challenge to Major Minh, his North Vietnamese cell leaders, and their VC suicide squads. The American gunships were going to clean up Binh Dinh Province. And they were going to start with the Bong Son Plains.

"No way." Private Shawn Larson shook his head in Lt. Vance's direction as he surveyed the drizzle moving into the area. "No way are the birds gonna be able to lift off, sir." Fog was rolling in across the Special Forces airstrip on all sides, also.

"Second of the 7th oughta be boardin' their ships back in An Khe right about now." Vance glanced at his wristwatch. "They're gonna meet us at the staging area. You don't wanna miss all the glory, do ya, Professor?"

Larson was slightly taken aback by the Lieutenant's use of his nickname, but that didn't keep him silent for long. "I still say no way, sir. The *crachin* is gettin' worse. Looks just like acid rain, Lieutenant—Detroit drizzle. This shit eats chopper

115

blades for breakfast." *Crachin* was a French word for "spit," and the Parisian soldiers of the fifties used it to describe the season of drizzle and fog that followed the June-to-January monsoon in Vietnam. The *crachin* wasn't quite as bad as Larson made it out to be, pollution-wise, but it could keep a gaggle of gunships away from a free fire zone.

"Second of the 7th is comin' in on twelve C-123's, Professor. They'll make it, all right. C-123's don't give a shit whether it's drizzlin' or dry."

"C-123's?"

"Roger that, slick."

"Oh."

Vance stared after Larson as the Professor saluted, turned, and walked back toward the group of grunts waiting to move out. Just when he thought he had the Private E-Deuce figured out, Larson started acting like a soldier. Vance shook his head in resignation, wondering what the draftee was up to. He used to be so anti-authority. Now he just moved with the flow, keeping a low profile, observing military courtesy and obeying all the rules—even the "chickenshit ones," as he used to refer to the busywork details and ridiculous regulations that seemed to govern the often boring routine of day-to-day GI life between missions.

"What's the latest, Lieutenant?"

Vance whirled around to find Col. Buchanan standing behind him. He started to salute, but the C.O. waved it off. "Looking good, Colonel. Second of the 7th's 600 are proceeding down through the An Khe Pass without incident, so far. They should have that forward supply base at Phu Cat set up by this afternoon." The camp he spoke of would be about forty-five kilometers south of Bong Son.

A radio man rushed up to the officers as Vance started to tell Buchanan about the latest weather forecast. "It's the general, sirs!" he said, worry and anxiety creasing his expression. "They've got contact with Charlie down at Phu Cat! The—"

"Who's made contact, soldier?" Buchanan toyed with his gig line.

"The ROKs, sir—the Koreans!"

South Korean troops were scheduled to link up with members of 2nd Battalion, 12th Cavalry and secure the Phu Cat base, while ARVN soldiers patrolled the Highway 1 area south of Bong Son.

Buchanan's battalion—specifically, Echo Company—was tasked with ferrying shock troops from suspected VC village to village, intimidating the communist sympathizers while the hammer and anvil of Operation Masher was set into action. Echo's secondary job involved rescue missions and gunship support, and now it appeared they were needed for the latter.

"Shit." Vance loved the Airmobile action, but he had really been looking forward to testing his deployment skills against the enemy strategists. Now it looked like another shoot-'em-up swooper would end the day instead.

"The General wants you to send a team, sir." The radio man held his microphone out to Buchanan.

Before conferring with the Operations CP, Buchanan told Vance, "Scramble seven. I'll fill you in as soon as I get more. For now, just get airborne!"

Vance was already running toward *Pegasus* and the other gunships.


The wind was knocked from Trinh Thi Kim's chest as she fell from branch to branch, finally regaining her hold on the prickly limbs only after dropping several dozen meters. She was still a hundred feet off the ground, though, and the foliage was thick all around her. She doubted the rifleman who had blown the platform out from under her feet could see her now. She doubted he saw her when he fired the random burst into the trees, either—it had just been a lucky shot. But she still had her AK-47, and a ruck full of ammo clips.

Phu Cat was only a few klicks up the road. And for several

117

miles, the roadway passed through this dense stretch of rain forest. Those Americans who rode the truck convoys instead of Hueys into Phu Cat would come under fire from a hundred snipers in the treetops.

But before the team of guerrillas was completely set up, the Lurp team, reconning the area in advance of the First Cav, had spotted the black-pajama-clad VC climbing from branch to branch with their shooting platforms of bamboo strapped to their backs.

This Delta team consisted of only seven SF troopers, however. They were clearly outgunned, and the Vietnamese had the better angle of fire, quickly pinning many of them down. The distant *whop-whop-whop* of rotors sent a chill through Kim's heart: The helicopters were on their way. It would be only a matter of minutes before they were shooting down into the treetops with their mini-guns and rockets. With the convoys, Kim's people could remain in the trees, climbing from branch to branch with considerable impunity, but with Cobras hovering overhead and those First Cav madmen rappelling from Huey hatches right down on top of them, her team didn't stand a chance.

"Kim!" A young woman made her way through the collage of branches and man-sized leaves along the lower level of the double canopy. "What are we to do?" The Green Berets were ignoring the threat from above—motivated, perhaps, by the increasing crescendo of flopping blades on the horizon—and firing long bursts of tracer up into the trees now.

"Are you ready to sacrifice your life for The Cause now, Dinh?"

The young woman stared back at her with wild eyes, trembling as she clutched a bloodied assault rifle. "No!" she cried. Her wrist was bleeding from a flesh wound.

"Then you must climb down to the ground and—"

"*No!*" she glanced down at the Special Forces soldiers zigzagging between the tree trunks a hundred feet below.

118

"—And run. Run away from this war as fast as your feet can take you. Hope the Americans don't catch up to you!"

"If we stay, the Cobras will kill us."

"They will kill some of us," Kim yelled above the scream of a teenaged guerrilla who stopped a stray round with his forehead and plummeted to earth, arms and legs flailing until the last ten or twenty feet.

Dinh watched him crash into a stump that had been destroyed by lightning weeks earlier. His chest was impaled by a shaft of splintered, charcoal-black wood.

"Buddha save us." Dinh closed her eyes tightly, then concentrated on aiming at the men on the ground.

"Buddha does not visit the battlefield, Dinh." Kim watched the first gunship arrive, swooping past low overhead without warning, and she sent a ten-round burst up at its sparkling skids. "Count on Kim, and you might survive this."

Another Huey rushed past above them, only a few feet over the treetops, and Dinh could see the boots of several soldiers dangling casually over the side as they crowded the hatch, eagerly awaiting permission to locate, engage, and terminate the enemy. She took aim at a blur of a camou-painted face, but they were gone in an eyeblink, and she nearly lost her balance and fell from the branch.

"Come closer." Kim waved her to a position on a broad branch only inches away. "This is a good place—the best place. I cannot be seen from the ground, and we cannot be seen from the air."

"We are going to lose again." Dinh aimed at one of the Green Berets, but her rifle's firing pin failed to detonate the primer, and she began fighting with a jam. "We should have stayed in that tunnel. We would be better off. We should stay there until the war is over."

"This war will never be over." Kim fired a three-round burst down at a tall Green Beret with red hair, but he was quick and the bullets only burrowed down into the rotting carpet along the jungle floor behind him. With each slug of

119

lead striking the dead leaves and branches covering the ground, two or three snakes would slither off in opposite directions. From this height, the businesslike manner in which the serpents darted about made them appear even more deadly and fearsome than up close.

"The last Vietnamese to die in this war has not yet been born," Kim continued after ramming a fresh magazine into her AK-47.

"You give nice speeches." The girl jerked back her weapon's bolt and they both watched a mangled cartridge pop out and twirl down through the leaves, sparkling like fool's gold as it dropped into the midst of the Green Berets. "But what are we to do now?"

"We wait." Kim pulled an M-33 American-made grenade from her chest straps, withdrew the pin with her teeth, and dropped it after the brass cartridge.

A muffled explosion ripped through the rain forest, shaking the trees around them, but not the sturdy mahogany monster they were clinging to. Screams followed the rolling blast and swirling smoke, but only for an instant. Kim watched two soldiers drag a third to cover of several fallen logs.

"I want to go back to the caves, Vau." Dinh called Kim by her formal name, and the older guerrilla responded with a harsh slap.

"Shut up and concentrate on the enemy below us!" she snapped. "Or I will shoot you myself!"

"But I only—"

"I am tired of listening to your whining, Dinh! Do as I say and we will get out of here."

A third helicopter gunship swooped past overhead, and Kim caught sight of the crossed sabers painted along the bottom of its snout. A shiver corkscrewed through her, and for an instant, she saw another place, another time. She herself was aboard one of the Hueys, floating out over the South China Sea, racing toward an island, with two GIs and seven Vietnamese whores laughing and joking as they escaped the war at last. Or so they thought. . . .

Too late, she fired after the craft, and in response, a burst of red tracers tore up through the leaves. Somehow, she had betrayed their perch—a puff of gunsmoke or flash of steel. None of the rounds reached either of them, but Dinh screamed as a dead gibbon crashed down onto her shoulders, its face a pulpy, misshapen mess, and she nearly dropped her rifle.

"We must change to another tree." She frantically pulled the bloodied animal off while calling over to Kim.

Kim disagreed. "They do not know. We are too high up—the forest is too dense. Even if they knew, they could do nothing. Stop shooting for now. Just stop shooting and wait. Watch the ground below, and wait."

They monitored all movement across the jungle floor a hundred feet down as Cong in other trees, far away, continued the battle. The Green Berets could no longer be seen. They had moved off, out of the kill zone.

That meant it would only be a matter of seconds before the gunships returned in force to pulverize the tree line with their rockets and mini-guns.

They would have the area surrounded by foot soldiers, also. Waiting. Waiting for the pyrotechnics to flush out her brothers and sisters. And many of them *would* flee. Others would attack the Americans in suicidal charges.

There were no tunnels in this stretch of woods. None that Kim knew about. She and Dinh would remain in the tree. They would weather the air assault out. Time would tell if they would live to snipe at the imperialists another day.

Already the leaves all around were trembling as violent vibrations in the muggy air announced the gunships were returning. Kim felt an icy, two-pronged fear in the pit of her gut. They were no match for the metal predators. And guerrilla warfare no longer held the excitement and flavor of past missions. The adrenaline was still coursing through her veins, but it was an animal instinct preparing her to "fight or flee," not the thrill of battle. Kim was tired of spending her nights waiting in trees or tunnels, holding a cold weapon to her bosom. She was feeling suddenly old inside, as the rotor downblast from seven choppers turned her lush green world into a whirlwind storm of flying twigs and thorns. Dual rockets roared down through the trees only a few meters away, exploding with a fury that hurt her eyes and ears.

Dinh crossed back over to her tree, keeping close to Kim, and they watched a green and gold fireball rise up through the branches. Flames began crackling in the network of interlocking rosewood and rhododendron below their sandals.

An endless stream of mini-gun fire ripped down through the jungle's roof to their right, and a tree that reached into the low louds crashed down against their own refuge, striking Kim and Dinh with small branches and twigs that gouged their flesh and nearly knocked them from their perch.

It seemed a hundred more helicopters were converging on the patch of jungle, but Kim knew it was just the same seven, circling around and around, taking turns at terrorizing the treetop snipers, playing around, toying with them before moving in for the final kill.

"I've had enough," Kim muttered to herself as she watched Dinh pull a twelve-inch splinter of crimson-coated wood from her fatigue blouse. It had impaled Dinh, passing all the way through her right breast, and blood spurted from her chest.

For the first time since she could remember, Kim felt sick at the sight of blood. She was getting too old for this.


## Bong Son, South Vietnam


"This ain't gonna be no picnic!" Pvt. Aaron Chappell listened to one of the experienced gunnies as the whole chopperload of Cav troopers watched the twin-rotored Chinook descending

122

swiftly only five hundred meters ahead of *Pegasus*. The CH-47, which appeared to have something suspended beneath it, was smoking heavily.

"Is that bird gonna crash, or what?" Shawn Larson was gripping his hatch-60 as he followed the larger helicopter's path down through the treetops.

The craft disappeared from view, but a few seconds later a terrific shock wave shook their Huey, and the men watched as a column of billowing smoke rose toward the storm clouds. "Yep," someone added dryly. "I think it's gonna crash."

"Scrub the old game plan," Sgt. Leopold Zack yelled over a shoulder from up near the cockpit. "Prepare to deploy. We're going to secure the crash site."

"I knew this was gonna be a romeo-foxtrot." Larson shook his head. "A rat-fuck all the way around." "Rat-fucks" were missions which the grunts felt were doomed from the start.

"So do we know if it's a hot Charlie-Sierra, or a cold Charlie-Sierra?" Gunslinger Gabriel was *Peg*'s pilot this trip around.

"I don't think it was mechanical failure," his peter pilot clicked in. "Spotted some tracers from that clump of palms on the november-whiskey."

"Rodg." Gabriel hit the intercom. "Square-dancin' in dirty sex!" he announced, which was a private little joke in Echo Company. Hal Krutch had always warned the team when they were 'thirty secs" out from an LZ, but the ride was often so rough and noisy the words came across as "dirty sex."

"I'm gonna miss ya, Peggy-baby!" Nasty Nel Nelson stood up and began dry-humping a support beam in the cabin wall, and some of the men cheered him on. Half of the remaining troopers began grunting like animals and psyching each other up for the jump down into the LZ. The rest remained stone cold silent. Aaron Chappell was one of these men, as he watched The Professor from behind.

Larson would not be leaving the ship. He was one of two doorgunners who would remain aboard *Peg*, showering the hostile tree line with M-60 rounds. It was a dangerous job: Gunnies stood a better chance of going home in a body bag than the grunts who were actually jumping down off the skids into a blazing, smoke-enshrouded hell.

"Take care, brother!" Shawn muttered to Chappell as the chopper pranged across some logs hidden in the reeds and the newbie waited his turn to un-ass.

Aaron glanced back at The Professor, but didn't reply. Their eyes locked for a silent instant, and then Nelson was pushing him out the hatch, and the whole team was gone, zigzagging down through the reeds toward the crippled Chinook.

Fog, mist, and drizzle had been plaguing Operation Masher from the start, and Col. Buchanan feared he would not have the necessary air support at his disposal should Echo Company run into concentrated resistance by the enemy.

The plan originally called for 3rd Brigade to hit LZ Dog, north of Bong Son, and sweep the area along the south end of the B.S.—or Bullshit—Plain, as the troops were beginning to refer to it, eventually positioning blocking teams in a northerly manner before dusk.

Buchanan's escort ships, and other squads from Bravo Company of the 7th Cav's 1st Battalion, concentrated on Luong Tho village when the Chinook went down. Gabriel's chopper was the first to set down, and he delivered Larson's people onto a hell known simply as Landing Zone Papa.

"We're receiving mortar and small-arms fire!" Lt. Vance and his RTO sprinted across a desolate hilltop as geysers of dust erupted on both sides. They dove against an embankment where Zack, Chappell, and Nelson were already laying down fire.

"Along that tree line there, Lieutenant!" Zack's red tracers showed Vance where the snipers were. "I still haven't been able to tell where the mortar pit's at!"

124

They were huddled approximately seventy-five yards away from the downed Chinook, south of where its crew had fanned out and commenced returning enemy fire from behind logs and anthills. The helicopter had not crashed with any great ferocity, but the belly landing ripped large strips of fiberglass and magnesium away. The object it had been transporting was a 105mm howitzer, and the cannon's barrel had not been kind to the Jolly Green Giant—as the troops referred to Chinooks—when it dropped on top of it.

Vance began calling in artillery, and after several hundred cannon shells decimated the surrounding terrain, the sniper fire ceased. "Fan out along that ravine there!" He ordered a corporal to take Chappell, Nelson, and three other men toward the tree line.

Thirty seconds after the shelling stopped, several additional slicks brought the rest of 1st Battalion into LZ Papa, and a hut-to-hut search of Luong Tho began.

The corporal was "Saint Pat" Patterson, a medium-sized soldier with a boxer's mug and slightly sloping forehead. Patterson possessed a perpetual sneer that entertained the grunts and kept the officers wary. NCOs like Zack felt that if they could take one platoon of Pattersons into Hanoi after dark, the war would be over by dusk.

Patterson pointed directly at Chappell. "This is your debut, cherry!"

"Me?" Aaron swallowed hard and nodded, gripping and regripping his M-16 nervously. He was the perfect picture of inexperience as he stared bug-eyed at Patterson from behind those thick, black-framed glasses. His helmet was low across his forehead, riding his dark eyebrows, and the steel pot's chinstrap gouged the flesh along his chin.

Only a low hilltop separated them from the tree line now. Patterson watched *Pegasus* swoop past low overhead. Larson stood in the open hatch, unloading on the trees with his Hog-60.

Saint Pat waved Gabriel off. "Okay!" he told Chappell.

"The Professor already fuckin' did your job for ya! Low crawl over this hill and recon that first clump of trees. We'll be right behind you."

Nelson stared at Patterson, trying to decide if he was serious, but Chappell was up and running before anything more could be said. He dropped into the dirt just below the hilltop's rim and started low-crawling as Patterson had instructed him to.

"Okay, let's go!"

When the others caught up to Chappell, he was standing over the bodies of seven VC riflemen, strewn across the clay between the silent palms. The newby's rifle barrel was not smoking.

*Pegasus* dropped from the clouds for another pass, and Larson could be seen leaning out the hatch now, held aboard by the monkey straps hooked to his web belt.

Patterson and the others laughed as the gunship circled even lower, and Nelson flipped his favorite doorgunner a thumbs-up. The Professor's zipper was open, and he was urinating down onto a mortar pit thirty feet away from the snipers, where another four Viet Cong lay bloody and mutilated from a single burst of his swivel-mounted machine gun.

# CHAPTER 11

# Bangkok

Wide, golden shafts of sunlight filtering through the bamboo shades struck Cordova's face, waking him. First one, then the other eye popped open. A slurping, sucking noise reached his ears. He waited for his eyes to focus on the wallpaper: dragon and phoenix designs in purple on white. Corky tried to remember where he was. This definitely was not the inside of a tent in the Ia Drang Valley. The aroma drifting through the air was not gunship diesel or the usual oily smoke from an exploding ammo dump fire. Corky Cordova smelled pussy. He lived for that fragrance, and felt himself growing hard again at the realization, but still couldn't remember where he was.

When he rolled over, his head began pounding. "Shit," he muttered, closing his eyes tightly. When he reopened them, the watch on his wrist read: 6 A.M. "Jesus, two lousy hours of sleep." That much he remembered.

A woman's coppery back was against his nose now. He slowly lifted the flowered sheets slightly off her hip and gazed at a very shapely set of tight haunches. She shifted her bottom about on the mattress as the warm breeze caused her to stir. Cordova listened as she moaned in her sleep softly. The woman started grinding her teeth.

His memory returning, Cordova slowly raised his head above the shallow outline of her waist and gazed out at the two bodies tangled together on the opposite bed. An involuntary chuckle escaped him.

"*Sawatdee*, Crap!" Snakeman Fletcher was sitting up in his bed, back against the headboard. A nude woman's face was buried in his crotch. Corky watched the mass of long, black hair bob up and down obediantly: the source of the odd sounds. The woman's crotch rested across Fletcher's chest as she balanced herself on her knees, propping her buttocks up, inches from his face.

Cordova laughed again. "You take the cake, Snakeman!" he proclaimed. Balanced atop the beautiful woman's haunches was a laquerwood platter, and on the platter was a bowl of Thai soup from which Fletcher was noisily slurping.

"And I eat it, too!" Snakeman grinned evilly, patting the swell of flesh a few inches beneath his chin. "Ain't this the life?" Using chopsticks, he played with the noodles in the soup.

Cordova slid his left arm under the woman lying in front of him and cupped the breast over her heart. It was not large, but very firm. She was a young one. Nineteen. Maybe younger. He could remember almost nothing whatsoever about their expedition to Patpong Road.

Still half-asleep, the woman shook her shoulders mildly in protest and tried to push his fingers away, but Corky brought his other arm across, effectively capturing her.

"Take no prisoners!" Fletcher raised a fist in the air as he monitored his buddy's progress with considerable interest.

Corky slid his body closer, until she could feel his lower body against the crack of her buttocks. "Uhhhmmm." The woman was awake now, and she shifted her bottom about again, getting comfortable.

He rolled her onto her stomach, pressing her breasts out flat against the palms of his hands as he mounted her from behind. "Gentle . . ." the woman whispered, working her arm under her body as she lifted her haunches against him. She took hold of him and guided it against the lips of her vagina,

128

working herself into a feigned frenzy before letting him enter. "Gentle . . ." Her voice was throaty, now. Sensuous. But she ruined it with, "Pussy still asleep. . . ."

Fletcher burst out laughing. "*What* did she say?" he asked.

Frowning, Cordova drew the sheets up to the middle of his back. "She said her hole's still dry." He glanced over at Snakeman, who seemed to be ignoring the girl working feverishly below the platter of shrimp and rice noodle soup.

"Just don't start a fire." Fletcher finished the last steamed prawn and started licking and smacking his lips.

His own hips thrusting rhythmically now, Cordova still stared at Fletcher's woman. "Isn't she ever going to get your rocks off, Snake?"

Fletcher lifted the platter out of the way, feigning surprise. "Hell!" he exclaimed dramatically. "Is that what she's been doing all morning? I've been numb below the belt since that quickie in the back seat of the cab!"

"Shit . . ." Cordova shook his head and returned his concentration to the slender doll pressed flat beneath him. With his knees against the insides of her thighs, he spread her legs apart farther and dropped his lips against an ear.

As the woman sucking Fletcher began giggling—perhaps understanding enough English to comprehend what he'd just said—she rolled off his crotch, gasping for air. "*Fini!*" she whined, legs spread slightly as she lay on her back.

Staring at the beads of perspiration forming along the slopes of her breasts, Fletcher set the tray on the nightstand, and rose to his knees. "Hell, baby-san," he warned. "We've only just begun!"

And then the Snakeman pounced.


Later, as the two door gunners lounged alongside the hotel pool, watching their whores frolic topless in the shallow end, a young boy entered the high-walled compound, newspapers under both arms. "*Sawatdee*, Joes!" he greeted them both in Thai. "You buy paper?"

Fletcher, who sat beneath a colorful umbrella, hiding behind dark Air Force aviator shades, was dead to the world. He had hired two more lobby-lurking prostitutes to stand behind his deck chair and fan him with palm fronds.

"Whatta ya think, Snakeman?" Corky checked the tiny pocket on his swimming trunks for change. "Should I contribute some *baht* to this juvenile's delinquency?"

"All I want from you is silence"—Fletcher rubbed his temples—"or the favor I asked thirty minutes ago."

"No way." Cordova grinned, shaking his head. "My nuts ache so bad I can't walk as it is. The elevator's out, and I ain't humpin' three flights of stairs just to get your camera."

Fletcher had purchased one of the fancy new Instamatics from a cute cherry girl in the Century Hotel's giftshop on Rajaprarob Road who showered him with compliments about his crewcut. "I just gotta get a snapshot of these ladies of questionable virtue fanning me like this," he said. "Brody and the boys ain't gonna believe this unless they see evidence."

"Maybe later." Cordova located a soggy, one baht note. "Here, kid." He held it out with both hands. "Sorry 'bout its condition—"

"No sweat, Joe." The boy routinely laid it out over one of the deck chairs to dry beneath a simmering Bangkok sun. He handed Corky an English-language paper, the *Bangkok Post*. "You want boom-boom girl, Joe?" The kid was either blind or ignoring the girls fanning Snakeman and the bulbous tarts splashing about in the water.

"Whatta ya think, Snake?" Cordova glanced over at his R and R mate. "Should I pay this miniature pimp to deliver some new doughnut holes?"

Fletcher did not hesitate. "Well, I'm not itchin', and I ain't got the drips, so maybe we oughta stick with a good thing, you know?"

130

"I concur." He looked back at the newspaper boy. "Sorry, friend. Maybe tomorrow."

"How long you stay Thailand, Joe?" the kid persisted.

"Five more nights, I think."

"No sweat. Ding return tomorrow. Checkee-checkee again. Cheap rate for cherry girl, too. Two-hun' *baht*. You like little girls?" He winked at Corky.

Two hundred *baht* was about ten dollars. Cordova asked, "How young are you talkin', Ding-dong? We're not lookin' for any jailbait."

"Thirteen . . . fourteen." He rubbed his chin in thought like a junior businessman.

"I don't stoop below seventeen, kid. Even in never-never land. Bring me an eighteen- or nineteen-year-old cherry girl the night after tomorrow and I'll give you *three* hundred *baht*.

The boy's eyes lit up for a moment, and Fletcher erupted into laughter. "Eighteen?" He gagged on a mouthful of green grapes. "In *Asia*? They're gonna have to sew it back up."

"Can do . . . can do!" The boy waved Snakeman silent. "No sweat."

"Fine." Cordova was skeptical. "Not tonight . . . tomorrow night. I'm not tired of Miss Beaverlips yet." He laughed at memories of a rare talent his girl possessed.

"Which one?" Ding the newspaper boy surveyed the women in the swimming pool critically.

"The one with the pink bikini bottom."

Ding's smile vanished, and he directed sad eyes at Corky. "Oh, sorry 'bout that, Joe," he said. "Numba ten *poo-ying*. Call her Vicki VD."

*"What?"* Cordova sat up in the lounge chair, spilling his glass of pineapple juice, and Fletcher reacted with another discharge of laughter.

Ding rushed over and patted Corky's wrist. "Just kidding." He smiled. "Just kidding!" And he turned to walk away.

"You little fuckwad." Cordova wiped the juice off his newspaper.

"See you in two nights." The youth waved before disappearing through a barbed-wire gate topped with glass shards.

"Goddamned *nitnoi* gangster..." A picture on the front page caught Cordova's eye, and he quickly read the caption beneath it. "Whew-weee!" He blew a long-winded sigh through clenched teeth.

"What the fuck, over..." Snakeman removed his sunglasses. Have the NVA crossed through Laos into Thailand?"

"No, but the First Cav is really kickin' ass around Bong Song. Check *this* out." He started to hand the half-page photo over to Snakeman. It was shot by an army correspondent from the ground and depicted several grunts jumping down from skids into man-high elephant grass even before the choppers had set down. "Wait a minute." He noticed something else in the headlines.

Fletcher watched him speed-read through a story for several minutes. "So I repeat: What the fuck, over? The suspense is killing me."

Shock and disbelief in his eyes, Corky got up, walked over, and handed the paper to Fletcher. "You lowlife..." he muttered.

Fletcher snatched up the newspaper. "Whatta ya mean 'lowlife'?" He couldn't tell whether Cordova was serious or not.

"And *you* called 'em cunts last night. . . . I hope you feel like shit now."

Frowning at his *ex*-friend's behavior, Snakeman snapped the newspaper like a whip, holding his arms out in front of him. "Manila put OFF LIMITS to sailors and airmen in The Philippines due to shortage of penicillin. . . ." he started to read.

"Not *that* story!" Cordova had taken to pacing back and forth along the poolside, but now he rushed over and stabbed at the correct article with a rigid forefinger. "This one!"

Snakeman Fletcher focused on the unsmiling file photos of Sugar Prasertkwan, Sawang Chatsungnoen, and a third Thai

132

policewoman he didn't recognize. His grin slowly faded as he began reading the story.

## THREE METRO COPS KILLED IN
## TEMPLE OF DAWN SHOOT-OUT

A predawn confrontation between Bangkok Metropolitan Police undercover officers and a heavily armed gang of robbery suspects ended with the death of three veteran policewomen and five ex-convicts on the banks of the Chao Phraya River overnight. The shooting ended a four-hour stake-out involving the controversial decoy units, which use policewomen disguised as prostitutes in an attempt to arrest known felons and other underworld elements who prey on foreign servicemen visiting the capital.

The victims were identified as Sgt. Butzarakorn Prasertkwan, 27, and Officers Sawang Chatsungnoen, 25, and Chit Suriwong, 32. All three women were pronounced dead at the scene. The gangsters involved were not identified pending notification of next of kin. Inspector Korat of the Officer Involved Shooting teams refused all comment except to say the investigation was continuing and more arrests were expected within 24 hours.

Officers Prasertkwan and Chatsungnoen, both widows according to sources within BMP, are survived by young children. Officer Suriwong's family was killed by communist insurgents in March of 1961. Her fiancé was reported in seclusion early this morning.

Please see COP KILLERS on page 32 for background report on the gang involved and profiles of the policewomen murdered.

Even without the black armbands, and the black sashes across the badges of uniformed officers, Cordova and Fletcher could sense the change at Bangkok Metro's Decoy Division. There was none of the lighthearted chatter that was present even during hectic shifts in police buildings the world over. Someone wrestled with a cursing, wildly thrashing *katoy* in a back corridor of holding cells, but otherwise there was only silence. Corky and the Snakeman felt as if they had tread into a tomb.

"We're really sorry about the three policewomen," Fletcher said, standing in front of the same interpreter's desk of the night before.

"The three policewomen?" The young man seemed even more fatigued as he removed his glasses and rubbed sore eyes, but he had lost some of his earlier arrogance.

"You know." Fletcher motioned at the Thai's armband. "Sgt. Prasertkwan..."

"And Officer Chatsungnoen."

"And the other lady." Snakeman pulled the carefully folded newspaper article from his shirt pocket. "Officer..." He scanned the print for her last name.

"Oh, yes, yes..." The translator's eyes narrowed slightly, as if he'd just been caught in the middle of a lie. "It was very tragic. Very tragic, indeed."

"Well, we..." Cordova was carrying a large basket of flowers.

"Go ahead," Fletcher urged him on.

"Yesss?" the translator sat back in his chair and crossed his wrists over his crotch disapprovingly.

"Well, we've asked all around, but nobody seems to be able to help us."

The translator was staring at the flowers now. "You want to go to the funeral," he deduced.

Cordova read the suspicious gleam reflected in the lenses as the man replaced his eyeglasses. "Well, if it wouldn't be intruding..."

134

"We could leave this at their graves," Fletcher decided. it at the cemetery, but no one will even tell us where they are being buried, or—"

"The memorial service and burial have already taken place," the translator revealed, slamming his logbook shut.

"But." Fletcher glanced at his watch.

"I'm sorry you missed it," he was told. "It was a very touching affair. I will extend your condolences to the families of the slain officers." And he stood up, walked over to a corridor alongside the desk sergeant's station, and slowly disappeared up a winding stairwell. Each time he rose another loop up the stairwell, his eyes met those of the two Americans, until he was out of sight.

"Well, this sucks the big one," Cordova complained.

"Fuck it." Fletcher set the flowers down on the translator's desk. "We came, we saw, we conquered—and we struck out."

"But . . ."

"Look, we tried, Corky. Forget it. Let's beat feet back over to Patpong. The Snakeman's pecker's splittin' the seams of his pants, and his balls are a draggin'."

"Christ! Show some respect, okay?"

Fletcher shrugged and rolled his eyeballs. "Whatever. I just can't see cryin' over someone who never even got to pull on my pud."

"Jesus." Cordova shook his head and started walking back over to the desk sergeant. "They saved our ass when those fucks up on Sukhumvit tried to rip us off, remember?"

"Well, okay . . ." He raised one finger in the air and scored a point for the policewomen on an invisible tally board.

"We'd like to know which cemetery Sgt. Prasertkwan and her partners were buried at today, sir," Cordova asked an aging police NCO with hashmarks from his elbow to his wrist. Like the translator, he wore glasses, but they were thicker and didn't seem to help: He leaned out over the raised platform and squinted down at Corky. His crewcut was completely gray yet thick as a new brush.

135

He glanced to each side, gauging the reactions of his subordinates, then resumed correcting some paperwork. *"Bai!"* He shooed them away.

"Come on." Fletcher grabbed his arm. "Let's get outta here."

"What the *fuck* is going on?" He locked eyes with Snakeman.

"These people view life and death differently than we do, sport. Come on. Forget it. They probably burned their buns and spread the ashes over *Wat Phra Keo.*"

*"Burned* them?" Cordova was aghast.

"You know, cremation. The Buddhists are big on that."

But he wasn't convinced. "Well, there's no excuse for the way everyone's behaving."

"Indirectly, they probably hold *us* responsible, amigo." Fletcher lowered his face at Corky compassionately. "You know what I mean. If it wasn't for us bein' out there on the bricks in the first place, hustlin' for some cheap meat, Sarge and her Honda Honeys wouldn't have had to come to the rescue of lowlifes like us, *savy?*"

"Oh great, Snakeman." Cordova looked like he wanted to crawl down into a hole and die. "I really needed to hear something like that, pal."

Fletcher patted him on the back as they walked through the police building's cavernous lobby. "Fuck it," he said as they both watched several lovely matrons glide past. "I figure if we get back over the Patpong by four o'clock, we'll have our choice of the half-decent crowd who only lost their cherries in the last dozen years or so."

Cordova nearly responded with an insulting retort, when something in the lobby caught his eye. "Wait a second." He started over toward a large display near the front doors. "Are these . . . *yah!"* Small wallet-sized photos of what must have been every police officer, both male and female, assigned to the district, were displayed in a locked glass case. "See if you can find Sugar and Sawang."

136

"Are you kidding?" Fletcher glanced at his watch and then at the line of taxis parked along the curb outside. "There must be a thousand photos here!"

"Just check the ones with long hair, dipstick!"

"Okay, okay." Fletcher began following the departmental tree where it branched out from administration into patrol and investigations. "You don't have to get personal, prick."

"Here they are!" Cordova found the file photos of Prasertkwan and Chatsungnoen in less than a minute.

"They're running this place ass-backwards." Fletcher seemed startled by the display in front of them. "Why the hell would they have these photos all displayed like this? Especially the undercover cops?"

"I doubt *all* the 'undercover cops' are on this board," Cordova said, glancing around at the passersby. He and Snakeman were the only people showing any interest in the display. "And these don't really look like Sugar and Sawang and the way they look now . . . I mean, the way they used to look." His head dropped, and he began shaking it. "Fuck." Corky sounded on the verge of tears. "What a waste."

Fletcher felt a chill run down his spine. Was Cordova going to break down on him in public over a broad? He moved closer to his friend and took a good look at the pictures. Cordova was right: there was no way anyone could connect the women in the file photos—probably taken while the girls were young recruits years earlier—with the heavily made-up and scantily clad decoy hookers straddling a curb on Patpong or Sukhumvit. For one thing, the customer would most probably be looking at their attributes below the neck. "So what do you intend on doing now that you've located the pictures?" he asked.

"You've gotta create some kinda disturbance so I can slip the lock on this case and snatch these snapshots," Corky replied, scanning the passersby.

"Create a 'disturbance'?" Fletcher was showing little enthusiasm for the plan thus far.

137

"Right. There's too many people milling around in the lobby."

"That's what lobbies are for." Fletcher cocked an eyebrow at him.

"Spare me the comedy, okay, Snake? Just trot on down to that aperture separating the lobby and the complaints counter and keel over or something. . . ."

"Keel over?"

"Faint. Pass out. Drop like a rock right in the middle of the doorway. Get everyone's attention." Cordova was examining the lock again. "It's simple. I'll have it open before you hit the floor."

"I don't plan on 'hitting' any floor." Fletcher's best frown came to the surface as he sauntered back toward the desk sergeant's station.


After they had the photos, Cordova paid a taxi driver to take them down to one of the black-market bazaars. The vendor stalls extended for several blocks in the shadow of the largest *wat* in Bangkok. Colorful umbrellas and long tarps protected the merchants and customers from a merciless sun. Piled high on rickety tables was everything from blue-and-white PX fans to jeep windshields and tank treads. Some of the GI items had American markings, but most were Thai, Khmer, and South Vietnamese. Here and there could be found actual legitimate items such as watermelons and Thai silk, but most of the browsers were interested in all the military hardware.

"Just what exactly are we looking for?" Fletcher asked after they had spent over an hour bartering for different types of police equipment: a web belt and TCP whistle here, a billy club and empty holster there.

"Now I just gotta find me an MP armband and helmet, and we're all set." Corky was rubbing his hands in anticipation as

138

they neared a corner stall piled high with helmet liners and unit patch collections.

"A *what*?"

"Actually, we gotta get two, amigo. One for you, also."

"Wash your mouth out with soap, skuzzball. I'm an eleven-Bravo, and don't you forget it. Besides, Uncle Sammy don't pay me enough to put up with the shit them Mike Papas come up against every day."

"Ahhh, wonderful." Cordova was ignoring him as he ran his fingers over the creased elephant tusks of a Sattahip Command patch. "Yah, yah . . . a couple of these will do," he told the vendor, a short, elderly woman with silver hair sticking out at odd angles. "And do you have any Eighteenth Brigade patches?"

"Eighteen?" The mama-san scratched her brow. "MP?"

"Yah, yah, mama-san. MPs."

"MP Vietnam?"

"Right, right. Have you got? I give you twenty *baht* each."

"No got," she said matter-of-factly.

"What?" Cordova looked crushed. "Well, what about armbands. Do you have any MP armbands?"

"No got," she repeated her earlier answer with even less energy.

"No got?" He turned to face Fletcher.

"If she says she no got, I guess she no got." Snakeman laughed. It was a semi-insane little laugh. Corky Cordova was driving him *dinky-dau*. It would definitely not be long now: a section-8 or ten months at the Fitz 609 psycho ward was surely just around the corner. "What the flyin' fuck do we need MP armbands for?" he murmured.

"It's part of the plan, Snakeman." Cordova remained calm.

"*What* plan, you bastard son of a Bangkok water buffalo! I don't like bein' kept in motherfuckin' suspense."

"Okay . . . okay, mellow out, clit-breath." He gently took hold of Fletcher's wrists. "Here's the plan. I got the idea from an MP back in Saigontown who—"

"When'd *you* ever get down to Saigon?" Fletcher threw his chin out.

"Listen-up, slick. Do you wanna hear it, or not?"

"Okay, okay. But this better be good. I'm tired o' always gettin' my tit in a wringer 'cause you cherry boys fall head-over-heels in love with—"

"So anyway. . ." Cordova smiled for the first time since they'd learned about the deaths of Sugar and Sawang. He'd been talking rapidly the whole time, moving quickly from stall to stall, as if slowing down to relax would mean his death, too.

"So anyway. . ." Fletcher was fast becoming impatient.

"This Mike Papa back in Saigontown—this is how he found out where this *canh-sat* chick he was tryin' to date lived. Dude's name was Sgt. Cain. A sly, conniving devil if you got on his wrong side, yet your typical all-around, good guy if you stayed straight. I think he's with the Two-hundred-eighty-first MPs down at Camp Samae-San now."

"A good ol' boy." Fletcher wished he smoked. He wished he could light up, take a deep drag, and blow the smoke in Corky's face.

"Yah."

"So's anyway."

"To make along story short . . ."

"Me and my testicles appreciate it."

"We ain't MPs, but it's gonna work just as well for us."

"I think you want the location of that cemetery just a little bit too much, Corky-san," Fletcher decided as they examined the plastic helmet liners. "I'm beginning to worry about you. It just ain't healthy."

Cordova was ignoring him again. "So you don't have any MP armbands, huh?" he asked the mama-san.

"No can sell." Her eyes scrunched up with irritation, and Fletcher feared for a moment she might try to punch him in the nose.

"Feisty little bitch," he muttered, stepping back.

140

"Why you no can sell?" Cordova waved him silent.

"MPs come check. If find, go jail." She was tapping her own chest with a rigid forefinger.

"Okay, so you don't keep an inventory." Cordova was well aware she didn't know what he was talking about, but it didn't matter. "Can you make me some, though? Right now."

"Make?" Her eyes lit up. "Sew?" Her fingers came together as if she were working a needle and thread.

"Yes sew."

"One hun' *baht*," her tone returned to an all-business one.

"What?" Cordova asked incredulously.

The old woman held up a finger. "One hun'."

"That's highway robbery," but he seemed to be considering the offer. One hundred *baht* was approximately five dollars. "Can you paint me up some of these liners, too, to make them look like MP helmets?"

"No sweat, Joe!" She snapped her fingers for him, fished through a boxful of junk, and came up with two cans of spray paint: one white and one black. "*Two* hun' baht."

"I think we're in business." He licked his lips and saluted an unsmiling Snakeman.

# CHAPTER 12

## Saigon

Treat Brody stared at the photograph of First Air Cavalrymen jumping from hovering gunships into the elephant grass of Bong Son, and felt pangs of guilt gnawing at his gut. Here he was in the heart of the capital, with a beautiful woman at his table and the aroma from a seven-course meal tickling his nostrils, and his buddies were up north dodging bullets and trying on body bags for size.

Dep read the look in his eyes. "Throw away newspaper. Throw it away, okay, Bro-dee? We have good food tonight. Enjoy. You go back soon enough. No think about now."

They were dining at an open-air cafe on Nguyen Van Thoi Street a few blocks down from one of the busiest warrooms in the country, and the sidewalks were crowded with MPs and QCs on foot patrol, but few gave Brody a second look. They were all staring at Dep.

She wore the traditional Vietnamese *ao dai*, a gossamer thin gown, closed at the throat and slit along the sides from waistline to ankles. The outfit was worn over silk pantaloons. Dep's were white tonight, and her *ao dai* was a floral pattern of gold, green, and blue. Small dragons decorated the stiff collar.

The military policemen were mesmerized by Dep's beauty,

while Brody was intrigued by the women lining up across the street. "What are they doing over there?" he asked as their roast duck and pork ribs arrived. "In the park."

Some twenty or thirty Vietnamese women stood in a snakelike line beneath the park's leaning tamarinds, waiting to see a small man who was seated at a portable desk and bent over a typewriter.

"They have papa-san send letter America," she explained.

"America?"

"They speak Vietnamese. He type English," she said simply. "They pay him each page. He put envelope. Girls send go U.S.A."

"Oh, a translator." Brody glanced down at a tray that had arrived: fishheads and shrimp spread between sliced cucumbers on a plate of steamed rice. The shrimp still had their heads and legs.

"Yes. Translator." Dep took her chopsticks, picked up one of the fishheads, examined it closely for a second or two, then opened her mouth.

A crunching sound reached Brody's ears, and he couldn't resist. When he looked up, Dep had crushed the fishhead between her teeth and was sucking out the contents.

Treat Brody closed his eyes tightly.

She reached across the table and tapped him with one of her chopsticks. "You should try, Bro-dee." She urged him on, lifting one of the fishheads off the tray. Still using the ivory chopsticks, she held it out to him. "Taste no worse than pussy."

Brody laughed. "How would you know what . . . Never mind." He held up his hands. "I don't wanna know."

"Oh, Dep know." She nodded seriously, eyes dropping to the dish of vegetables and twice-fried pork. "Dep Numba Ten girl, Bro-dee. Have to do bookoo bad thing during life. Someday I scared maybe Buddha not forgive. Then what happen Dep?" She shook her head from side to side now. "But, nebbah mind: all bridge in water." She examined a slice of octopus, put it back in the shark fin soup, and went after another fishhead.

Brody glanced at his watch.

"Don' worry 'bout time, Bro-dee." She wiped juice from her lower lip absentmindedly with the edge of her pinky finger. "In Saigon, time mean nothing. Relax."

"But, we're running late. If we don't hustle and wolf this stuff down, we're gonna miss the flick I promised to take you to." He took a look at the check and was pleasantly surprised: less than five dollars, and they had been eating for nearly an hour already. Good Old Saigontown.

"No sweat, loverboy." She winked at him. "First ten mintes always newswheel an' anthem."

"News*reel*," he corrected her.

"Same-same. Now eat, or Dep's legs stay locked tonight when we go home."

Brody had moved her out of Cholon to a semi-respectable neighborhood near Gia Dinh, where there was less chance of being raped, mugged, or murdered. He had traded in one of the gold coins he kept in an ankle pouch for six months' rent. There were ten more of the coins where the first came from— his entire life's savings. He promised Dep she wouldn't have to trick again, regardless of what he eventually decided to do with his own future, and she hadn't been the same since, treating him like royalty, waiting on his every need. It was heaven on earth. Treat just wondered how long it could really last.

"More *dau xanh banh lot*, sir?" A pretty cocktail waitress in miniskirt and long-sleeved blouse appeared at his elbow. She motioned toward Dep's chilled glass of coconut bean drink. It was empty, while his own was still full.

Brody noticed the girl was wearing a gold locket where her plunging neckline became deep cleavage. He reached up, and she did not protest when he gently touched the locket and popped it open. As he suspected, photos of the girl and a young Vietnamese soldier were inside. "Very handsome," he

144

said. "Your boyfriend?" A dull blast sounded in the distance, several blocks away. Ears perked all around, but the conversation continued as if nothing had happened.

"Yes." She smiled politely, glancing over at Dep first to make sure Brody's woman did not object to the conversation. "He fight Mytho. In Mekong Delta."

"Yes, I know. Very handsome man. I wish him best good luck." Brody shifted into pidgin English, and the girl bowed slightly, flushing. "Someday he will return and marry you. Have bookoo children . . . baby-sans."

She laughed and glanced over at Dep again, covering her mouth with fingers that opened like an Oriental fan. Dep rattled off something in nonstop Vietnamese, and the waitress nodded, picking up her empty glass. Brody stared at the slight bulge inside Dep's cheek and, not wanting to know what she was storing there, he decided it was time for something stronger than coconut bean drink. "A bottle of 33, please, my dear."

Dep was the one glancing at her wristwatch this time, and it was a flashy timepiece at that. Treat had hocked one of the battlefield war trophies in his AWOL bag—a Soviet automatic he had taken off a dead NVA officer on the outskirts of Pleiku six months earlier—to purchase it. "I no think we have time," she decided, sliding her chair out and motioning the waitress back to their table.

Brody did not object, but merely replied with a knowing grin. Dep had been prepared to stay at the cafe another hour, until Treat began talking with the girl. A week ago, Dep wouldn't have raised even an eyebrow at his antics, but now she was staking her claim. "You can take your beer with us." The cool smirk curled only half her features.

"No problem." He blew her a kiss, and she kicked him under the table again.

Five minutes later, Brody was flagging down one of Saigon's notorious blue-and-yellow Renault taxis. The cabbie glanced back over a shoulder at Dep after they got into the back seat, ignoring Brody completely. Dep said, "Rex Cinema," without giving a street address. The cabbie held up three fingers and a crooked thumb, Dep nodded, and the taxi pulled away from the curb, tires squealing.

They were bogged down in traffic almost immediately.

"Oh my goodness." Dep's fingertips rose to her lips as they passed the scene of a restaurant bombing.

"The explosion we heard." Brody was thinking back. It had sounded like a satchel charge.

A white delivery truck sat on its top in the middle of the street, and two policemen in white shirts, mint-blue trousers, and storm-trooper caps, dwarfed by their American-made revolvers, were directing traffic around the vehicle on either side.

This restaurant had also been an open-air affair. Tables lay on their sides all around, and Dep counted seven bodies lying amidst all the debris. The taxi crawled past the security barricades that had been hastily erected, and she poked her head out the window as they approached a police matron directing traffic. Dep exchanged a few hushed words with her, then hugged Brody tightly, shivering. "VC," she confirmed his suspicions. It was always VC. One out of a hundred was extortion related. The rest of the terrorist bombings in Saigon were engineered by the communists. "*Canh-sat* she tell me VC drive by Honda-50. Throw bomb. *Di-di.*"

"Satchel charge." Brody sniffed at the air.

"Yes, Satchel." She shivered again, rubbing her breasts against his arm.

Countless motorscooters waited for a signal light to change at the next intersection ahead of them. Theirs was the only sedan around, and Brody suddenly felt vulnerable. All the windows were down, and the bikes passing by on either side of the car were loaded down with two, three, even four passengers apiece, half of which were bending low to gaze into the cab. Taxis were a luxury. Only the wealthy or prostitutes with GIs took them.

146

When the light finally turned green, their driver laid on his horn, maneuvering in and out of the scooters and bicycles. For a half block, they actually attained some speed, but then another traffic jam appeared. People were shouting up ahead.

"What's going on?" Brody stuck his head out to get a look.

Dep rattled off a question to the cabbie, who responded with a shrug of the shoulders. He leaned against the driver's door, getting comfortable as they crawled along at a snail's pace. Soon they could hear a loudspeaker, and Dep craned her neck in an attempt to find out what was strangling the heart of Saigon now.

"It is protest," she relayed to Brody after only a few seconds.

"Anti-war protest?"

"Buddhist student movement."

"Same thing."

"They talk 'bout secret police harr—harr—"

"Harassment?"

"Bother monks."

The *canh-sats* had set up a security buffer around the noisy demonstration, which was being held in front of a minor government building. Police in riot gear were assembling in the shadows, and Brody could taste it on the warm, evening breeze: Violent confrontation was brewing. "Tell the driver to get us through this as quickly as possible," he requested of her. "I feel some bookoo bad vibes about this group, and I don't wanna get caught in the middle of—"

But it was too late. Several bonzes in gold and orange robes were walking down the steps of the courthouselike building, directly into the paths of passing cars. Tires screeched as many of the vehicles skidded to a stop or swerved to miss the oblivious monks.

"What the hell's that crazy idiot doing?" Brody began shaking his head as a tall, skinny bonze in his fifties or sixties sat down in the middle of the street and began pouring liquid from a plastic container over his head. Several women in the

147

crowd were rushing up to him, falling to their knees and dropping their faces against the blacktop in prayer as if Buddha himself had just appeared.

Suddenly they found themselves staring at a brightly burning bonze, who had just immolated himself in the name of democracy. Dep screamed at the sight of charred skin peeling from the man's expressionless face, and she jumped out of the car. Brody was right behind her as they darted in and out of traffic, the monk's popping eyes permanently melted into memory. When Dep glanced back over a shoulder, he was toppling over onto his side, a blackened shell, and women in the crowd of onlookers were running up to cover him with blankets, trying to snuff out the flames.

Dep was in tears when they reached a park and Brody stopped to catch his breath beside a kiosk. She was gasping too, and holding her side. "Sorry, Bro-dee. Dep afraid. Bad *joss*."

"Come on." Brody took her hand as two dim yellow headlights appeared in the mist up ahead. He led her down through the trees until they came to a hillside. Below, the Saigon River sparkled in the moonlight.

"No." Dep was firm. She did not like the sound of water rushing in the dark.

"Just for a while." He tried reasoning with her. "Until we get out of this neighborhood."

As soon as they reached the bottom of the hillside, a South Vietnamese helicopter appeared upstream. Its powerful spotlight sliced down through the creeping fog, back and forth, side to side, as it patrolled the riverfront, searching for Cong sampans.

Brody led Dep down into a clump of high bushes that, by day, concealed a grassy picnic area. The gunship passed overhead without spotting them. "Fuck," Dep muttered, and Treat did a double take. "They even send hell'copter come find Dep!"

He didn't feel like contradicting her, but it was hard to

148

suppress the smile. It was a warm smile, from the heart. Brody was falling in love with this woman.

He was suddenly feeling comfortable, too. The ground beneath them was soft, the grass long and thick. The spot commanded a beautiful view of the river twenty feet away, and he no longer felt in danger. "Kinda romantic, isn't it?" He wrapped an arm around her shoulder, pulling her close as they caught their breath while watching flares float across the edge of the Saigon on the far side of the swollen waters.

Silver moonbeams fanned across Dep's face when she looked up at him. "Yes," she had to admit. "Nice for now. But we no can stay here all night. Curfew soon. I hear snakes in the grass."

"We're the only snakes in the grass around here," he replied, pressing his lips against her ear. Brody ran his hand along her thigh, up under the *ao dai*'s side slit, and began massaging her crotch through the filmy fabric.

She started to push him away gently, but he resisted. "I no can be romantic here, Bro-dee. Dep too scared."

"No need to be scared, beautiful." He pulled her down onto her back slowly, kissed her long and hard, then said, "Treat will take care of you." He kissed her again, and began fumbling with the *ao dai*'s intricate snaps and latches.

"You're doing what?" She couldn't believe he was trying to remove her clothes.

"Nebbah mind." His voice was a harsh rasp as he whispered against her cheek, fingers working frantically to peel the front of the gown away. "I always wanted to do it in public."

"It?" Dep's hooded lids grew round. *"Public?"*

"But this isn't really public, so to speak. No one's around, and it's dark, and—hey *hey*!—we're in the bushes, woman!"

Dep's breasts sprang forth suddenly and his mouth dropped between them, consuming her with hot breath, taking control of Dep.

Her head dropped back and she sighed as the fingers of his right hand slipped into her pantaloons. "I no believe we do

149

this." Her voice cracked slightly with apprehension as the warm night breeze sent a sensuous, billowing flap through the garment, but he could tell by her own frantic movements that the heat and excitement was coursing through her loins now, too.

Dep raised her haunches up slightly out of the grass and slid the waistband of her pantaloons down over her hips. Brody caught it between his toes, helping guide the silky trousers off her thighs and ankles. Startled, she glanced over at him. Treat was already naked below the waist, and his shirt was completely unbuttoned. She laughed lightly, kicked the pantaloons free, and pulled him onto her.

Dep was feeling evil now. Evil and wicked, and he slid easily into her.

She enjoyed the feel of her buttocks being pressed into the cool, moist grass with each thrust and, instead of raising her legs as she usually did, Dep slid them back and forth against the earth with scissorlike motions, feeling the impact of his body against hers even more—much more roughly than when they made love in bed, she reflected. There was even pain now—a little, anyway—from the unyielding ground against her buttocks and backbone. But the sensations swirling about in her loins were more intense than they had ever been, also. She felt seventeen again. Seventeen, and vibrant. Alive for the first time in years.

Dep and Brody held a contest in those bushes that night. They devised new positions and techniques, trying to outdo each other. Hour drifted into hour, and they forgot about the curfew.

It was while they were tangled together like a human pretzel and she was just about to concede defeat when the powerful flashlight beams struck them both in the face, then quickly roamed the outline of their bodies to inspect other parts. For concealed weapons, of course.

"Well, whatta we have here, Sgt. Cain?" A hearty voice erupted into laugher and satisfied anticipation.

150

"Funny you should ask, Sgt. McClellan."

It was two military policemen. "Should we shoot 'em both, right here and now?"

"It would be a waste of energy to 'cuff 'em and go through all the motions."

"We'd have to transport 'em all the way back to PMO, and book 'em. And I'm due off at the end of Cover shift."

"And I hate paperwork, partner-san."

"Nobody'd notice another couple bloated corpses floatin' down the *Song Saigon*."

"I concur, Ol' Honorable One. It would sure save a lot of time."

Treat Brody stared up at the two flashlight beams blinding his eyes. "If you two are gonna do it, then do it," he muttered coldly. "And quit jawin' about it." He shielded Dep's supple torso from their view. "Save us the suspense."

One of the military policemen's flashlight beams passed over her bare shoulders to examine something floating along the riverbank only a few yards down from their feet. "Well, looky who drifted in with the tide tonight."

"Told you nobody'd notice another floater in the *Song Saigon*, Sgt. Cain."

"As usual, you were right, Sgt. McClellan."

Dep screamed when she saw the bloated corpse staring up at them from out of the shadows as it bobbed about in the riverbank suds. Thorns from bushes hanging out over the water had snagged onto a torn and shredded ear, refusing to let go. The dead man's mouth was stuffed with riverbottom trash, and his scalp had been ripped back partially, revealing skullbone. What had once been baby-blues were now white flaps of eyeball where rodents had ripped the flesh apart.

One of the MP sergeants turned his flashlight off and dropped into a squat only a couple feet away from the lovers. "That's what I love about Saigon. Never a dull moment."

The other military policeman kept the bright silver beam in

Brody's face. "I don't believe we've been properly introduced."

"How 'bout a raincheck on the formalities," the off-duty doorgunner muttered.

The MP still holding the flashlight chuckled. "Oh, we've got a comedian in our midst tonight, eh?" he asked patiently.

But his partner's tone turned suddenly angry. "Lemme see your army ID, scrotebag! And a set o' your orders."

"You're not one of the local REMFs, that's for sure."

"No, he's definitely not your average, run-of-the-mill Saigon commando." The sergeant played flashlight beams across a recent tattoo Brody had acquired. Decorating his right bicep, it depicted a hawk in flight, tearing a dove apart with its talons. Below the two birds was the motto: FIRST TEAM and PLEI ME—RVN 1965.

"Plei Me, eh?" The sergeant with the nametag CAIN turned off his flashlight so that the small patch of grass was illuminated by starlight and passing flares only.

"Yep." Brody did not volunteer any further information.

"You have a unique taste in fine art." The other MP tapped the tattoo lightly.

Brody immediately thought of Hal Krutch, who was officially Missing In Action but Presumed Dead. "I got it in memory of a close friend."

"K.I.A.?"

"Right."

"Sorry to hear it." The sergeant tapped the tattoo again. "'First Team,' eh?"

"That's a rodg, sarge." He shifted his haunches in the grass as wet blades began tickling the crack of his buttocks. "First Air Cavalry Division. Echo Company of the—"

"Happen to know an eight-and-skate by the name of Saint Pat?"

"Patterson?" Brody's eyes lit up slightly, showing some interest. Maybe there was still some hope left here after all.

"Yah. Goofy-lookin' fuckwad. Made corporal, last I heard.

152

Kinda looks like a cross between Neanderthal Man and Cro-Magnon."

Brody's grin came out. "That's our Saint Pat!"

"He used to be a 95-Bravo, too," said the other MP, gazing off at a green-and-gold starburst exploding over a small housing project on the other side of the river.

"Patterson?" Treat had never heard that one before.

"Yah. Damn good cop, too, till he got the killin' fever in his blood."

"Yah, the killin' fever," Cain agreed.

"Transferred to the grunts and went Airborne. All that crap —the whole nine yards."

"Takes a special kind of mentality to get a hard-on jumpin' out of perfectly good airplanes."

"Yah."

"I'll never forget the time the P.M. caught him ballin' one of the CID secretaries in the back of his unit." The sergeant chuckled as the memory drifted back to him.

"On duty?"

"Yep."

"Good ole Saint Pat."

"A hillbilly after my own heart."

"I really hate to change the subject." Brody risked interrupting the stroll down memory lane. "But were you guys gonna blow us away or cart us off to the monkeyhouse?" Dep kicked him in the shin with the heel of her bare foot.

Cain laughed. "We're gonna cut you some slack, my friend."

"Seein' as how you're one of the jungle crazies out there keepin' Saigon somewhat safe from the undesirable elements." His partner glanced over Brody's shoulder at Dep, who quickly lowered her eyes.

"You're releasing us?" Brody felt beads of sweat trickling through his eyebrows, and they weren't from the heat of earlier spent passions.

Cain glanced at his Rolex. "I've still got a bit o' compassion at the bottom o' my heart when it comes to you grunts spendin' your R and R's in the city of sorrows," he said. "Just watch your ass gettin' back to wherever your hotel is. It's well past curfew, and the *canh-sats* don't have the same sense of humor that we got."

"Let's beat feet." His partner was already leaving. "Some FNG's callin' for assistance at the Hotel Majestic!"

Brody watched them sprint off down the street. He had no idea where they'd parked their patrol jeep. They darted down into a maze of murky alleys and vanished in the swirling gloom of midnight mist. A few seconds later, he heard tires spinning, and a siren calling to the cold, uncaring stars.

Despite the dead man bobbing about in the riverbank foam, Brody and his woman decided to spend the rest of the night exactly where they were. Cain and his partner were right: It would be too dangerous to attempt hiring an outlaw Honda to take them all the way back up to Gia Dinh.

Martial law curfew lifted with the first golden rays of dawn, and the two lovers emerged from their lush, green hideaway with renewed freshness in their expression and energy in their gait, despite the hours on the ground. It had not been all that bad, Brody would reflect later, thanks to the thick carpet of grass.

A groggy cyclo driver took them through the waking metropolis, past sidewalk vendors setting up their curb displays of colorful fruit, fresh fish, and stolen tape recorders, and weary militiamen marching back to the barracks from a graveyard shift, into Gia Dinh.

The ancient mama-san, spending her last years on earth camped out in the apartment house courtyard, rose to speak to Dep as she and Brody started toward the stairwell that would take them up to their room. "What is it, old woman?" Treat wasn't in the mood to listen to an hour's worth of gossip.

The mama-san ignored him, jabbered at Dep for several

154

seconds in a Chinese dialect he could not come close to grasping, then handed her a small pink envelope.

"Ah-*ha*!" Brody pointed a finger at her in mock reprimand. "Love notes from one of your old boyfriends, eh, Deppie honey?"

She was not amused by the jest and turned away from him in a huff, throwing her chin in the air as she sauntered toward the stairwell, her *ao dai* none the worse for wear despite their overnight romp near the riverbank. "From girlfriend Cholon," she snarled.

"And my ding-dong's nine inches long, too," he countered sarcastically.

Dep held the envelope back over a shoulder as they started up the metal steps. "See," she said. "Write Vietnamese. Write like girl."

"Oh." Brody did not take the letter from her.

"Girlfriend from my old room Cholon. She send message. Say letter wait for me from Quan Loi. Letter from family."

"I thought . . ." He hesitated for only a moment. Dep was hard-skinned. "I thought your family was all . . ."

"Parents *fini*." He could not see that Dep had lowered her eyes as they continued up the stairwell. "Brothers *fini*. Have *mot* sister left. Quan Loi. Tha's all."

"Quan Loi up north, near the Cambodian border?" He moved past her on the last flight and slipped the key in the lock of their corner apartment.

"Same-same."

"Well, forgive me for asking what will probably turn out to be just the latest in a long series of stupid questions, but why didn't she just send the letter along with the note here?"

Dep pulled a string by the door and a blue fluorescent lamp over the bed's headboard came on. "What?" She teased him with her trademark: an innocent straight face.

Brody decided he'd obviously used too many words in this latest question. "Why didn't—"

"Because girlfriend Cholon not sure Dep live here fo' sure,

155

Bro-dee. Girlfriend Cholon want check first. She no want lose letter from sister Quan Loi, you *bic*? Woul' Bro-dee want someone lose precious letter that way?" She pronounced the word "pre-shess," and the twinkle in her eyes, laughing at him, brought passion back into the young soldier's words.

"I suppose Dep doesn't want Bro-dee to make her feel good again, eh?" he said slowly, rubbing his body up against hers as he draped his arms over her shoulders. "I suppose Dep want Bro-dee take her all the way back over to Cholon to pick up the letter."

Dep filled her eyes with mock sadness. She lowered her head and made her voice crack slightly as she spoke. "No see sister, five, six years."

He began unfastening her *ao dai* again. "Then I think you can wait another two or three hours." Brody jerked on the light's string a second time, plunging the room into darkness again. He picked Dep up, carried her over to the bed, and dropped onto her. They sank into the cool satin sheets.

"Dep shoul' be so lucky," she taunted him, fluttering her eyelids as she began turning the lever that closed the window shutters, sealing out Saigon.

# CHAPTER 13

## LZ Papa, South Vietnam

Larson was leaning over the buttplate of his swivel-mounted doorgun, enjoying a Vietnamese Blue Ruby cigarette as he watched Zack, Patterson, and the others double-time back to the chopper. *Pegasus* was sitting on a hilltop overlooking the Chinook crash site, the downblast from her rotorblades pressing the elephant grass nearly flat as Vance's team sprinted away from the Cong body count along the tree line. A huge skycrane hovered overhead while soldiers on the ground hooked chains and cables up to the downed Jolly Green.

"Welcome back! Welcome the fuck back!" Larson slapped the men on the shoulders as they climbed aboard, grimy, exhausted, and still breathing hard from the adrenaline charge. They'd been on the ground only thirty to forty minutes, yet it had seemed like thirty hours.

"No W.I.A.'s!" Nelson gleamed proudly as he and The Professor brushed knuckles. The team had suffered zero Wounded In Action.

"Great, Nelly baby! Fucking fantastic! What was the body count? Bet you hotdogs can't even count that high, right?"

"Hey *hey*!" Patterson rushed aboard and began slapping

157

Larson's face playfully. "Thirty-two zipperheads, Professor-san!"

"That's all?" Larson feigned disappointment.

"Hey, shove it in and break it off!" Saint Pat's elbow and wrist came up in a Sicilian obscene gesture, but the broad smile remained intact.

Lt. Vance was the next one aboard. His face was grim, even ashen, but his eyes seemed to spark a bit when he looked up and saw Larson. "Good shootin', Shawn!" He clapped The Professor on the back and was gone, headed up toward the cockpit to confer with Gabriel.

"I'm writin' you up, boy!" An ebony-black, chiseled-from-granite face, lined with beads of sweat, was nose to nose with him next. It was Zack, who hadn't missed Larson's display of M-60 expertise either. "Writin' you up for a promotion to Echo-4!"

The Professor forced a tight grin as something in the back of his mind sent up warning flags, gnawing at his conscience. "Don't do me any favors, Leo." He was not sure if that was meant as a joke or not, but everyone on board was laughing.

"Bet *that* would help, eh?" Zack dropped against the ammo boxes beside the M-60. Piles of empty brass crackled beneath his weight. The NCO was referring to the raise in pay, and Shawn's kid sister back in Seattle. At first it had been a secret, with Larson confiding in Treat Brody only, but The Whore-monger quickly spilled the beans during one of their drunken binges back in the Ia Drang hellhole, and now all the men in the platoon seemed to know.

"Glad to have you back in one piece!" Larson reached down and grabbed Aaron Chappell's wrist. He was the last man up onto the skids, but Chappell jerked his hand away, climbing aboard on his own. Someone in the back of the cabin whistled at the gesture.

"Fuck off!" Chappell snapped at The Professor, brushing past him toward the rear of the craft.

"Hey, I was just tryin' to—"

158

"Well, *don't*! Just stay outta my face!"

Zack stared hard into the young newby's face as Chappell stomped past him. He had noticed some friction between the two soldiers earlier, but had attributed it to anxiety over the move from Ia Drang to the even more notorious Binh Dinh region. Whatever was wrong, he didn't have time to baby-sit the two now. They would have to work it out between themselves.

"You fuckwads up back there?" Gabriel glanced back over a shoulder. Without waiting for a reply, he maneuvered the controls that lifted *Pegasus* off the ground.

"We're up," Nelson finally said as they cleared the treetops.

"Back to Bong Son?" the peter pilot clicked in, and Gabriel nodded.

"Need some fuel and the gunnies want ammo resupply."

"Right."

The call for help went out just as they were landing back at the Special Forces airstrip. Elements of 2nd of the 7th were receiving heavy automatics weapon fire in the vicinity of Phung Du Village.

"Let's book!" Zack monitored the call and rushed up toward the cockpit as they pranged across several loose tarmac plates. "What's the hold-up?"

"We need ammo and fuel," the peter pilot responded as Gabriel kept his eye on two jeeps racing out to the helicopter from a heavily sandbagged CP.

"Not for Phung Du!" Zack protested. "It's just a couple o' hops over those hills there!" He pointed toward the mist-enshrouded northern horizon. "Larson and numb-nuts can wing it. We've got enough ammo left over and—"

The two jeeps were skidding up sideways in front of *Pegasus* now, and for the first time Gabe and his crew chief could read the dust-covered words along the bottom of the windshield: MILITARY POLICE.

"What the fuck are *they* doin' out here?" The peter pilot's

159

lower jaw dropped as four MPs brandishing M-16s hopped out of the vehicles behind a uniformed CID agent.

"It's The Man!" Abdul Mohammed, the unit's registered radical, announced. "*Some*body's ass is in the rice cooker, and it ain't ol' Elijah's!"

Larson craned his neck to get a better look. At first he didn't think much about the MPs' appearance, but then fear shot through him, the flashback of placing his pistol against the wounded GI's temple rushed in front of his mind's eye, and he glanced back at Chappell.

Aaron was acting no different from any of the other grunts aboard the helicopter: exhausted, but mildly interested. MPs in the boonies like this—in the middle of a large-scale mission where there were no tank TCPs, anyway—was not all that common, and many of the men treated them like a curiosity.

The warrant officer in charge of the law enforcement detail was holding out his hand, motioning Gabriel to remain on the ground.

"We got a motherfuckin' Brass Monkey to respond to, goddamnit!" Zack was leaning out the hatch. "This better be good!"

"Hold onto your jockstrap, sergeant!" The CID agent and one NCO climbed aboard, a fearless, dangerous look in their suspicious eyes. Larson glanced past them, through the craft's windshield. For the first time, he noticed the military police vehicles were gunjeeps, and stocky corporals leaned against M-60s mounted in the rear seat, eager for confrontation, judging from the leers on their faces. They had an evil gleam in their eyes, too—we fucking *dare* anyone to resist.

"You got an E-Deuce by the last name Larson, first name Shawn, in this battlebucket anywhere?" The agent gave everyone the critical once-over. "Serial number 7145468."

Larson's eyes darted over to Chappell, his knuckles growing white on the hatch-60's handles, and the newby responded with an open mouth. "It wasn't me, Professor—I swear it!"

160

The CID agent drew his .45 pistol so fast few aboard saw it come out, but the automatic was soon pressing Larson's nose flat.

"Take your hands slowly off the bitch." The warrant officer feigned a sort of temporary insanity. His eyes bulged out slightly. "I don't like leavin' Pleiku," he added. "I get nervous when crime and punishment and all that crap takes me out to the sticks, and this *pistola* just might go off if you don't comply. Now!"

Larson's hands rose slowly, and he placed them on top of his head, fingers locked together, like a prisoner of war.

"Cut the dramatics," the gorilla of an NCO crouching beside the agent said. "Out that hatch right there, and spread-eagle on the ground." He pulled a set of handcuffs from a pouch on his web belt. "Keep your hands where I can see them at all times."

"What's the meaning of this?" Gabriel turned the controls over to his peter pilot so the rotors could remain at take-off pitch.

"He's under apprehension," the agent said blandly, a disgusted look on his face yet a combination of let-down and relief in his eyes.

"For what?" Gabriel glanced over at Chappell as if he should be able to shed some light on all this.

"You have the right to remain silent!" the NCO was yelling above the roar of the downblast. "Anything you say might be used against you in any military court martial."

"You have the right to die for your country," Nelson whispered sarcastically under his breath as he and the soldiers around the hatch watched the body frisk taking place on the steaming tarmac. "I didn't think you could get arrested in The Nam—at least not way in the fuck out here."

"What did he do, Aaron?" another newby asked Chappell, who glanced around to find Zack, Lt. Vance, and the CID agent waiting to see how he would respond.

Chappell almost spoke, when the agent admitted, "We've been watching him for quite some time."

"Watching him do *what*?" Vance sounded ready to explode.

"Drugs, gentlemen. High-grade hash. The doper's been sendin' duffel bags full o' the shit back to The World for several months. We're takin' him down to LBJ, where he can learn a new skill and get reha-fucking-bilitated. At Long Binh Jail, they'll teach him a thing or two. Your Professor's gonna be turnin' big rocks into little rocks until it snows in Saigon."

Col. Neil Nazi Buchanan's C&C Loach slid sideways through the dusty tarmac for several meters, like an emergency vehicle arriving at the scene of a violent crime a bit too dramatically. When the Medal of Honor winner jumped from the small black craft and sprinted over to *Pegasus*, the imminent confrontation had all the makings of a Hollywood gunfight about to go down. "What's the goddamned hold-up!" Buchanan glared at a handcuffed Larson as two of the MPs, grabbing him by the elbows, lifted him roughly from the prone position to his feet. "We've got men callin' for help at—"

"I know, sir!" Vance saluted, and the C.O. ignored it. "Like I told you on the horn—"

Buchanan waved him silent. He directed his next question at the warrant officer in charge of the arrest detail. "I wanna see some goddamned orders on this, Mister! We in The Cav cooperate with the MPs, but this isn't the time or the place for—"

"We're takin' this lowlife in, Colonel." The CID agent was already leading Larson away from the gunship, toward the military police jeeps.

"Fine! *Wonderful*, in fact!" Buchanan threw up his arms but pulled them back in just as abruptly when several of the men glanced up at the powerful rotorblades slicing through the thick, sticky air. "He's been nothing but a pain in the rectal

162

cavity since being transferred from some doggy platoon down in the Delta to Airmobile!" The Colonel temporarily forgot about the strides Larson seemed to be making in the attitude department. "But this ain't, I repeat: *ain't* the time or place to be screwin' up my crews! What's he bein' arrested for, anyway—did he snap some VC whore's neck back in Plei Me or something?"

The agent stopped, turned, and gave Buchanan a strange look, as if he was contemplating whether or not to make note of the C.O.'s remark. "Dope."

"What?" Buchanan rested massive hands on his hips.

"He's been sending drugs back to The World," the investigator elaborated. "We've been watching him since—"

"Shit!" Buchanan shook his chin from side to side violently. "Is that all? *It can wait*, Mister!"

"Sir, I suggest you don't attempt to interfere."

"I'm not attempting." Buchanan gave Gabriel a hand signal, and the chopper jock, with a cocky nod, lifted *Peg* a couple of inches off the ground. "I'm *doing*!" During a brief hover, she turned 45 degrees until her nose cannons and strut pods were pointed directly at the two MP gunjeeps.

The CID agent and his enlisted men stared in disbelief at the turn of events. "He's the only man I've got capable of handlin' the hatch-60!" Buchanan exaggerated as the big buck sergeant, without having to be coached further, brought out a tiny key and began removing The Professor's handcuffs. "You can have him back when—and if—we make it back from this rescue mission!"

"You're making a big mistake, sir." The agent was keeping his eyes on the two pilots in the cockpit. "I'm gonna have half the 18th MP Brigade waitin' here when you get back, and I guarantee you your schmuck doper there"—he motioned toward Larson—"won't be the only one headed for the slammer."

"I appreciate your candid opinion!" Buchanan shouted above the protesting roar from *Pegasus*. "But once again,

163

you're wrong. You and your troops aren't going to be waiting here when we get back."

"Don't say?" The agent folded his arms across his chest defiantly, rippling the muscles of his wrists and biceps. This goofy C.O. was overstepping his bounds tenfold. Enough was enough.

"Nope. You're going with us."

The agent lowered his brow somewhat and stared out at the Colonel from below the edge of skeptical lids. "In a rat's ass," he muttered slowly but firmly.

"We're undermanned. Second of the 7th is catching hell over the hill there"—they could all hear distant, non-stop explosions—"and I'm using *my* authority to dissolve your MOS status, Mister! You can leave two men here to guard the jeeps. The rest had better get onboard that gunship right now!"

None of the MPs immediately complied with the Colonel. "Are these fucks serious, Mister Hail?"

The CID agent chewed his lower lip for a moment, then waved the army policemen over toward the idling helicopter. "This is going to be fucking interesting, Colonel." He walked up and tapped the black eagles on Buchanan's collar.

"Oh?" The officer threw his chest out slightly.

"This is going to make the military history annals!" The agent sounded confident.

"You think so?" Buchanan did not flinch. He harbored no self-doubt either.

"I know so! And when it's all over, and you're breaking big rocks into little rocks alongside Larson the Lowlife there, *I'm* gonna be wearin' your full-birds!" He tapped Buchanan's collar emblems again, and the Colonel knocked his hand away.

A large cemetery separated the two landing zones where 2nd of the 7th Commander Lt. Col. Robert McDade had earlier directed his gunship troopers to land. The LZs were also

164

split by a three-kilometer stretch of rice paddies, and McDade's men were to sweep through the villages interlacing the swampy fields.

A fine, misty drizzle harassed the roaring Hueys as they swooped in. An understrength Alpha Company—low on men because their unit had been the one involved in the C-123 crash a few days earlier—landed without incident at the southern landing zone, designated LZ-2, and began working their way north along the paddydike berms.

The routine artillery bombardment by the Americans prior to operations of this sort had been avoided for this mission, due largely to the close proximity of the planned landing zones to the villages. Arty was often called in to soften up an LZ prior to a gunship troop insertion, but that was only when risk to innocent civilians was minimized and it was felt the only persons who would be in the target area were hard-core guerrillas.

LZ-4, where Charlie Company intended to deploy north of the huge Viet cemetery, was a flat, sandy area rising slightly above paddy hamlets on three sides, and the village of Phung Du to the east. It was hard to see many of these hamlets because most of the homes were hidden by thick tree lines, walls of high bamboo, and other improvised fences of camouflaging flora.

Sniper fire from the ground began striking Charlie Company's gunships even before they landed, however, and the decision was made to deploy the troops south of the target LZ. Enemy fire along the northern edges of the cemetery was so intense, in fact, that the choppers landed in four separate clusters, the northernmost group nearly a mile from the men seeking cover toward the south.

Charlie Company's platoon leaders were ordered to make their way back to the original landing zone designated LZ-4, but a mortar barrage began falling on all sides of the Americans. Survivors of the shrapnel were quickly pinned down by

165

several machine-gun nests positioned throughout the strips of foliage encircling the plain of sand.


"We're in a hornet's nest!"

The Cavalry troopers from Echo Company monitored radio traffic from grunts on the ground as they rushed to their assistance at well over a hundred miles per hour. Larson, hugging his hatch-gun, watched *Peg*'s gleaming skids slice branches from the tops of trees.

"We've got NVA Regulars involved here!" The voice yelling through radio net static was loud but still in control. "They're entrenched in MG nests all around the LZ! My mortar man and RTO are K.I.A. We want arty at this time, how copy?"

"Is that Fesmire's voice?" Zack listened to Gabriel and the peter pilot exchanging words over the intercom.

"Rodg. Good ol' Cap'n John."

"Good man."

"Rodg."

Gabriel glanced back over a shoulder. "LZ in dirty sex, ladies!"

Zack swallowed hard, and forced himself out of the crouch. "Okay!" He smacked huge, meaty palms together. "Let's go! Get yo' funky asses in gear!"

Artillery was already upending palm trees when Gabriel set the chopper down between two tall tree lines running parallel to each other just under a hundred feet apart. "Out! Out! Out!" Zack was yelling. "Let's go! Let's go! Let's go!" But half the cabin was already empty as men leaped down into the reeds and elephant grass. Many sank in hot sand to their calves, and were breathing hard and sweating even before they'd made it to cover. A few stray sniper rounds zinged in off *Peg*'s skids, and a bullet shattered the plexiglass in front of the peter pilot, but there was no firestorm of hot lead everyone had been expecting. Not yet.

166

Zack stared at the MPs as they pushed and shoved their way to the hatch. He had been afraid he might have to force them into battle at gunpoint, but these guys were charged up and eager to *get some*! for a change, as the ole Nam slang goes. They were growling and cutting loose with war cries, psyching each other up as each man got nearer his appointment with destiny.

"Finally!" One of them flashed his eyes in Zack's direction. "I finally get to waste some commie-fucks! No more barfights! No more VD card checks! No more paperwork! No more—" And he was leaping out the hatch, screaming like a madman for NVA blood.

"I love it!" CID Agent Hail was beside Zack now, and the black NCO noticed, for the first time, a C.I.B. over the investigator's heart. "I almost forgot what it was like."

Leo The Lionhearted handed him an M-16. He pulled a flak jacket from the pile Larson was sitting on and threw it, along with a spare steel pot, to the agent. "And you're the first soldier I ever saw go into ville combat wearin' khakis!" Zack's laugh was a hearty one as they prepared to follow the last of the grunts out into the violent unknown.

"Maybe it'll mindfuck 'em enough to see me through this thing!" Hail was wearing an ear-to-ear death's-head grin.

A mortar exploded behind the two soldiers a few seconds after they jumped down from the helicopter's hatch. The blast knocked both men off their feet and, in a fury of lightning-white heat and billowing smoke, flipped *Pegasus* over onto her side.

"Christ!" Zack risked but an instant keeping his head up to look back at the craft. Its fifty-foot rotors slammed down into the earth with a ghostly scream of twisting and collapsing metal. One of the blades broke in half, slicing down through the cabin near the center side hatches. The rest of the rotor arced out into the sky and floated off over a distant hilltop. "I hope that fucker don't blow!" He watched Gabriel and his co-pilot scramble from the cockpit, uninjured. The Gunslinger had drawn his revolver and was firing back at a wall of black-pajama-clad sappers storming down the nearest hillside as he sprinted toward Zack and the others.

Lt. Vance ordered a concentrated effort of cover fire be laid down by every man at his disposal, but during the ten-minute firefight that followed, and before the Americans were driven back away from the disabled gunship, Private Shawn Larson failed to climb out of the smoking wreckage.

# CHAPTER 14

## Bangkok

Snakeman Fletcher was sweating over this. Walking down one of Bangkok Thailand's busiest thoroughfares ten minutes before midnight on a Saturday night was not the Snakeman's idea of a good time—especially since they were decked out in the uniforms of American MPs. And that could get a grunt five-to-ten years hard labor at LBJ.

"What happens if we actually have to enforce some military law or something?" Fletcher nudged his "partner" as they approached a Thai police kiosk near the intersection of Samesen and Pitsanuloke Roads.

"Highly unlikely." Cordova sounded confident. "I picked a neighborhood where there's little GI activity but bookoo Thai policewomen. The National Library rose from the mist down the block. "And cherry schoolgirls, too," he added as an after-thought.

"Not at midnight." Fletcher glanced at his watch.

Cordova's plan entailed confronting one of the younger policewomen and trying to convince her Corky was Sugar's old boyfriend. They'd flash the file photos, which both door gunners had trimmed down to an even smaller wallet size, and try to smooth-talk the deceased officers' "current addresses" out of the rookies. They might be able to convince the women

169

they were legit. And they might end up behind bars for impersonating MPs.

When they reached the kiosk at the busy intersection, all they found manning it was a grizzled old, bent-over security guard who didn't speak any English. "Wonderful, Mister Genius," Fletcher muttered as they turned to walk away. "What other brilliant tricks do you have up your short sleeves?"

Two Thai policewomen on a foot beat chose that very moment to glide past in their dull brown skirts and black blouses. Corky made eye contact with the shorter officer—he considered them both to be extremely beautiful, despite the unflattering tunic tops—and she glanced back over a shoulder at him as they continued down the sidewalk without slowing. Her partner, reading the mutual attraction in their eyes, grabbed the girl by the arm, giggled, and pulled down on her wrist, seemingly trying to jerk her from her trance, as they increased their pace shyly.

"Those two." Cordova slowly nodded his head, sure of his choice now.

"The chase is on!" Fletcher raised a fist, and they lowered their upper torsoes as they took after the women in pursuit, chuckling at their good fortune.

An intoxicated American, exiting the dark alleyway, bumped into them the instant they stepped down off the crumbling sidewalk. "Get the fuck outta the way, you pogue." Snakeman grabbed the young GI by the front of his khakis more to steady him than anything. He completely forgot they were dressed like military policemen.

Cordova helped him maneuver the stocky Caucasian to the side of the narrow corridor, but the youth—his head wobbling uncertainly atop his shoulders—locked onto the crossed-pistol brass gleaming in the moonlight and reached out to take hold of Fletcher's shirt as well. *"Just* who I wanted to see!" his words were slurred. The odor of alcohol was heavy on his breath. *"MPs!"*

170

"Don't light a match," Cordova warned. He was not smiling.

The drunk airman patted Fletcher's MP armband. "We're busy right now, bud," Snakeman told him. "If you got ripped off by some *katoy* or something, the MP Station is down on—"

"I wanna surrender," the teenager blurted out, his cheeks puffing suddenly as if he was about to vomit. Fletcher glanced past the kid, searching out the shadows for feminine outlines.

"And just what exactly did you do, pray tell, to warrant surrendering?" Cordova asked, drawing his nightstick. He patted it against an open palm convincingly as two older American couples—obviously tourists, he decided, gauging the men's hair length—passing by stopped to watch the confrontation.

"I'm AWOL," the airman told them.

"What?" Fletcher shook his head from side to side and closed his eyes tightly. This can't be happening, he thought to himself.

"Actually, I'm probably a deserter by now. Been gone since New Year's Eve. Now I'm outta *baht* and my *tealok* kicked me out."

"Gone from where?" Cordova glanced over at the tourists, who seemed in awe that they were actually witnessing something as dramatic as the surrender, in mysterious and raunchy downtown Bangkok, of a dangerous-looking deserter to such handsome MPs. One of the women was appraising Cordova's trim, muscular frame, and he winked back, basking in the limelight. It had been some time since he'd interacted with civilians. For so many months, his days and nights had been composed of jungle missions and rain-forest respites. But little socializing outside the ranks of gun-happy grunts who were too exhausted or burnt-out to engage in small talk, or sleazy Honda Honeys who popped gum bubbles and stared at the clouds passing overhead as they kept their thighs spread for

171

winding lines of restless eighteen-year-old vets. "AWOL from where?" he repeated, returning to the present.

"Utapao, amigo." The deserter beamed, bowing suddenly when he spotted the tourists watching. "You know where Utapao is?"

Fletcher was shaking his head in the negative, but Cordova said, "Yah, down by Sattahip. That's considered part of the war zone, isn't it?" He worked on putting a scare into the airman.

"Well, I . . . don't . . . know 'bout tha—"

"I oughta put a round between your eyes right here and now," Corky threatened, resting his gun hand on a black, laminated rainflap. There were no pistols in the holsters.

One of the women's hands shot up to cover her mouth. They had obviously overheard Cordova's threat. The man who appeared to be her husband started over.

"I'm retired Ninety-five-Bravo," he introduced himself with the MOS occupational specialty code for military police. "Can we be of any assistance?"

Cordova gave him the once-over: nearly six-foot-three and about 250, a slight paunch, but biceps and thigh muscles that still bulged. He obviously enjoyed his brew, but still did his best to work it off the following morning. "We're on the job," Corky said, grasping for lines from an old police movie he once saw.

"Obviously." The retired cop motioned toward the armbands. His grin faded somewhat, and Cordova spotted that twinkle of suspicion he'd seen in every provost marshal he ever came across.

"We were following some suspected black marketeers and don't have time for this clown right now," Fletcher added, regretting the remark the instant he made it.

"In uniform?" The other male tourist joined his traveling companion. He had caught the slip.

"Well . . ."

"And the black marketeers were wearing brown skirts and

172

boob-stretchin' black, eh?" The retired MP folded his arms across his chest.

Beyond the confused, cross-eyed deserter's fuzzy outline, Cordova spotted the MP jeep. Headlights out, it was cruising in their direction, and fast.

"Let's split!" He grabbed Fletcher's arm and dragged him down into the alley. Both impersonators sprinted deeper into the dark, leaving two dumbfounded couples in charge of a suddenly sobbing deserter who picked that particular moment to throw up on the ex-army wife.


The MPs from the MAC-THAI Bangkok Detachment did not take it upon themselves to drive after Fletcher and Cordova. Thailand was a fantasy land where anything, it seemed, was possible. The two khaki-clad soldiers could very well have been on a case far more important than a simple AWOL transport, though it was indeed strange that they could not wait the additional minute or so for the district patrol to take the prisoner off their hands. And Cordova and Fletcher were lucky in another respect: The real MPs were two troopers who were scheduled to depart the Kingdom of Siam in two weeks. They had no desire to work up a sweat, get involved in anything more complex than misdemeanors, or even consider the possibility that impersonators were working their beat.

When Snakeman and the Cork caught up to the policewomen, it was almost as if they'd walked into an ambush. The girls rushed out from opposite dark doorways, confronting the two Americans. Their hands raised slightly, Cordova and Fletcher were backed into a wall, only to notoice neither policewoman had her .38 out. "You follow us?" The shorter one, who had winked sensuously at Cordova earlier was still grinning, but her eyes had gone cold. Her partner looked hungry for a man, but not sure if these two would do. The manner in which her eyes never seemed to blink sent a chill down

173

Corky's spine, and he briefly flashed back to an execution he had witnessed a long time ago.

It had been before the air assaults into Ia Drang Valley the year before, at Quan Loi, some fifty klicks north of Saigon on Highway 13.

He had been with a tunnel-searching team whose mission was to intercept a squad of sappers seen preparing rocket tubes pointed at the airport runway east of the villes. The Americans had approached the mission with little enthusiasm, initially— Cordova himself could not recall when last they'd actually caught a missile team red-handed. *Before* their projectiles were launched. There were those rare occasions when rockets blew up unexpectedly on their bamboo launch pads, killing every Cong within a fifty-meter radius, but this was the first instance they were actually fortunate enough to round up a "trio of twats with their tits still intact," as the NCO-in-charge had put it.

The South Vietnamese interrogator had captured them, actually. While the Arvins and Americans were out beating the bush, searching for ventilation shafts, and falling victim to booby traps and poisonous snakes, their jovial, overweight question-and-answer man, while venturing behind some bushes to relieve himself, stumbled across the trio as they exited a spiderhole.

The women—nearly sixty percent of the insurgents below the DMZ were alledged to be female—had been preparing to detonate an "animal" when Sgt. Lee drew his automatic and began shouting for assistance.

Actually, he had tried to shoot all three scrawny, filthy VC, but a cartridge jammed crosswise in the chamber when he jerked the slide back instead of pulling it smoothly. Dust and bright sunlight in their faces, none of the women realized the .45 was inoperative and, formidable AK-47 assault rifles still suing over their backs, they interlocked fingers over their heads and surrendered.

A guaranteed promotion was not enough for the interroga-

174

tor. Charged with that overpowering adrenaline rush by the first real excitement he had experienced in the field in two years, the Arvin took it upon himself to sentence the women to summary execution, on the spot, when they refused to answer his questions.

That was what Cordova remembered: the defiant, unblinking stares of the women as their leader spat into the soldier's face seconds before he pressed her nose flat with the .45, and calmly pulled the trigger.

The two other women remained brave as their turns came, and when the last one turned away from the interrogator, realizing perhaps, at this last precious instant, the futility of it all . . . the waste . . . she locked eyes with Cordova. In his peripheral vision, he watched the interrogator place the gray barrel against her temple, but there was no way he could tear his eyes from hers. He tried desperately, and for a moment he even attempted to bring himself to protest, but then the deafening discharge flung her head back, fragmenting that frozen moment in time forever. He thought her accusing, contemptuous glare would remain locked on him until her face struck the earth, but it was not that way at all. The instant the bullet slammed through her skull, the woman's eyes flew up into their sockets, and Cordova meant nothing to her anymore. Nothing mattered to the girl anymore. It was over, ended with a slug of lead the size of his thumb.

The entire scene reenacted itself in the blink of an eye as Cordova returned the policewoman's stare, now. He swallowed hard, unable to move, visions of himself and Snakeman being executed here, on the spot, at that very moment—unable to defend themselves because their holsters were empty.

"We were hoping you might be able to help us find someone." Fletcher spoke up first.

The policewomen appeared to be in good moods, out to have some fun with their brothers-in-arms, the MPs. "Help find someone?" The taller officer cocked a dark eyebrow at Snakeman suspiciously.

Both women were slender, with what was obviously long, black hair, pulled back into unflattering buns behind their heads and held in place by splinters of ornamental ivory or black bamboo.

"Our girlfriend . . . uh, girl*friends* . . ." Fletcher stumbled verbally.

"Are they in jail?" The shorter policewoman held her hand over a growing smile.

Cordova pulled out his wallet and proudly displayed Sugar Prasertkwan's photo. "I've been gone." He made a point of looking them both in the eyes. "Away. Up north."

"Routing the Communists?" The senior policewoman remained skeptical.

Before Cordova could respond, the other officer noticed who the picture was of. She touched her partner's wrist to get her attention, and the two launched into a rapid torrent of high-speed Thai. She pulled the wallet from Cordova's hand to study it closer in the dim light radiating from tenements rising up on both sides.

Fletcher sensed a problem . . . a gut feeling that their scheme was falling apart . . . slowly going awry, and he nudged Cordova with his elbow.

"You know how it goes: Thai woman, American GI . . ." he said, rolling his shoulders.

"No good." The shorter officer frowned for his benefit, but her eyes were still smiling.

"Right . . ." Snakeman agreed.

"But we had a good thing going," Cordova persisted. "Problem is, I return from TDY in Nakhon Phanom and Sugar's gone. Moved out."

The policewomen launched into another foreign-language debate—foreign to the two MP imposters—and the shorter one ran her eyes from Cordova's face to his bloused boots and back up. "Sgt. Prasertkwan never tell us about you," she said, finally.

"We kept it all secret." Corky placed his left hand over her

176

heart. "She didn't want to anger or embarrass her family. You know . . . her being a widow and all. Her kids really took a liking to me, though. . . ."

"And how many hot-to-trot MPs you ever met who were willing to marry a Thai woman who's already got a bunch baby-sans running around the bungalow? Huh?"

Their smiles gone now, the two policewomen whispered this time, but for only a few seconds, then the shorter one drew close to Cordova. She gently took hold of his chin, pulling his face down.

Fletcher felt himself growing hard as he watched her rise slightly on her tiptoes. For a moment, he thought she was going to kiss him.

"Now listen to what I am going to say to you." She spoke fluent English. "I am sorry." Her voice was laced with compassion but without any other emotion. "Sgt. Prasertkwan . . . Sugar . . . she is dead. . . ."

Cordova and Fletcher both feigned the required amount of shock. "What?" Snakeman threw up his hands.

"They were killed two day ago," the other officer revealed. "We sorry have tell you in street like this."

"But the chil—Sugar's kids! Who is—"

"Mama-san take care." They anticipated his question. "Don' worry. They okay, *ching-ching*."

"I want to see them," Cordova said.

"Impossible." The shorter girl moved back slightly, remaining courteous but firm.

"Why not?" Cordova kept the distance between them short.

"Police protect them. No one can see."

"They know me." Cordova lied, suddenly wondering why he was getting so deeply involved with all this. "Sugar's kids would want to see me. . . ."

"He could take them back to America," Fletcher cut in loudly. Cordova directed a cautious glance his direction, but Snakeman rambled on. "Yah! Corky could adopt 'em all and take 'em back to good ole U.S.A. for some hamburgers and fries at a beachball party. He could cart 'em all off to a drive-in movie, too, spoil 'em with dilly-bars!"

Cordova's look of concern became an irritated glare, but the policewomen seemed to be falling for it. They resumed a running dialogue in untranslatable Thai, waded through a brief argument, then came to a decision. "Okay." The shorter one spoke despite being outranked by her partner. She had seniority in these affairs of the heart, it seemed. "We give you address. You go see kids. But keep secret where you get or we end up NKP too."

"Oh, no problem." Cordova crossed himself as he watched slender fingers guide a pen across her ticket book.

"Here is the address. She stay at bungalow on Soi No-kyung. Not far."

"Behind Wat Po," her partner added. "You want us show you?"

"No . . . no problem." Cordova graciously accepted the slip of paper. "We can find it. We know Bangkok like the back of our hands." He hugged the shorter woman and kissed her on on the lips. It was a short peck, however, and she lingered on her tiptoes afterward, looking as though she wished the brief contact had not ended so quickly.

"Thanks again." Snakeman backed off into the gloom with a casual half-salute.

"Just follow Maha Rat Road along the Chao Phraya River," the seduced law officer said, sighing despite reprimanding taunts from her partner. "If you've reached the Klong Lot at Richini Road, then you've gone too far. . . ."

"I think we've already gone too far," Fletcher muttered to himself. He raced to catch up with Cordova, whose shadow had vanished in the swirling fog.

# CHAPTER 15

## Phung Du Village

Snatched from the jaws of death mainly because the gunship he had landed in rolled over onto its side—not from the force of mortar explosions, but because the underground tunnel running beneath the craft's right landing skid collapsed—The Professor, stunned and disoriented from the concussion of the initial blast, opened his eyes to find himself lying at the bottom of his own grave. *Pegasus* lay on her side above him, and helicopter fuel was pouring down into the deep trench. What saved Larson was that he kept a cool head in spite of the rapidly deteriorating circumstances. He remained calm and, as the dust began to clear, realized he was not in a pit at all, but in an old Cong tunnel that offered two routes of escape. Escape from death by fire, should *Peg* eventually blow, was a third alternative he did not want to consider. But he had no idea what awaited him down in the tunnels.

Gut instinct screamed at him to make a choice, and no sooner had the doorgunner scampered down into the dry chamber than pith helmets appeared from the end of the fork he had not chosen. The North Vietnamese tunnel rats never noticed him crawling away, however. They were too upset over the stream of gunship fuel swirling about their ankles.

Larson low-crawled faster than in any of his worst nightmares, where scorpions the size of tomcats filled his tent and sleeping bag. Larson moved, snakelike, on his belly for over five minutes, until he dropped down into a vast chamber filled with rifles and ammunition—which was a godsend, he decided, since he'd been unable to remove his M-16 from the gunship.

A tiny lantern burned in a distant corner of the chamber, so it was obviously being used in connection with the ambushes topside. But no one seemed to be around at this time.

The chamber was approximately twenty by thirty meters in size and five feet from floor to ceiling, so he had to prowl about stooped over. Crates of arms lined the earthen walls, and a silk parachute suspended from the packed-clay ceiling kept dust in the weapons cache to a minimum. An exit tunnel was beside the softly glowing lantern.

Larson was torn between two emotions: suicide and surrender. If he waited the battle out—and assuming his side won, or at least survived it—he could return to the surface and turn himself in to the MPs. He'd read accounts in the *Stars & Stripes* about GIs who'd been busted shipping dope home from a combat zone. Most received life sentences at hard labor.

On the other hand, he could imitate some of his favorite writers, and go out with a bang. Jury-rig the ammo crates in the weapons cache so that he could detonate them as soon as enough VC or NVA Regulars retreated underground. Blow everyone, including himself, beyond Bien Hoa. There surely had to be something better waiting for him in the hereafter.

Larson cautiously moved over to a crate containing AK-47 assault rifles. He sat beside it, braced his jungle boots against some planks, and pulled on boards in the middle until the rusty nails squeaked loose. Within five minutes he had one of the AKs out and fully loaded.

Then he commenced searching for the best explosives and some det cord to set it all off.

Shawn Larson held the wires an inch apart, but the desire to end his life suddenly drained away, and he found himself staring at odd Chinese characters on an ammo crate instead.

The parachute nailed to the ceiling of the underground bunker moved up and down slightly as countless boots charged across the surface, three meters above his head. The battle must surely be raging toward a climax by now. He wondered if anyone remembered about him, if Zack or Vance or any of the others realized he hadn't made it out of the chopper like the rest, hadn't retreated from the rolling blast with them, anyway. Had *Pegasus* been destroyed? He recalled her swishing rotors and powerful turbines affectionately, as if she'd been a powerful horse on which they all rode merrily into battle. But all that meant nothing anymore, and the reality of his situation sank home once again.

He was a man without a home. He hated army life, and had been unable to find his niche like so many other washed-up world wanderers. Oh, he had been getting into the thrill of the kill recently, but that high could only last for so long. There was nothing waiting for Shawn back in The World. He loved his kid sister, but watching her wither away was like staring at jungle rot without a beer. He did not want to go back to that. The drug money had been his wall. He did not want to be Big Brother anymore.

He focused on the hot wires again—the crude detonator he'd rigged up, using the insides of a field phone and a prick-25 battery. It was time. Time to end it all. He would go out with a bang, taking as many commies rushing past overhead with him as possible.

A sound reached his ears. The slightest scrape of metal against canvas, and then golden shards of light were revolving around the room.

He peered up over an ammo crate from where he was squatting. Someone had entered the chamber quietly, picking

181

up the lantern as he exited the access tunnel. Maybe more would follow. He would wait until the storage room was full of VC or North Vietnamese, and then he would ram the wires together.

There was no more noise or movement through the access tunnel, and Larson thought perhaps he was imagining it all. But then he saw the boy.

A child, really, perhaps six or seven at the most. He was wearing baggy GI shorts, small tire-tread sandals with strips of inner tube for toe loops. The boy was barechested except for the cloth ammo bandoliers drooping from both shoulders, Pancho Villa style. The bandoliers were not filled with magazines, but something even more solid. Probably plastic explosives. The kid was a walking satchel charge. The Professor knew what the Cong had planned for him: they would send the boy out after one of the gunships. And it would probably work. Both the child and two million dollars in advanced technology and expensive equipment would go up in a ball of flame and volcanic blast of smoking helicopter parts.

Larson watched the boy walk over to a corner of the bunker, drop into a squat, and begin playing with an M-33 hand grenade.

"Psssst! Hey, kid!" he whispered harshly. *"Lai day!"* Come here!

The boy's head whirled around, but he did not move from the crouch. In startled yet curious Vietnamese, he asked, "Who are you?"

Total innocence. Total innocence despite the ten pounds of C-4 wrapped across his heart and soul. The American accent did not seem to frighten him. He did not run away, sounding alarms. *"Lai day!"* Larson repeated, his eyes shifting back and forth from the boy's backside to the chamber doorway.

Slowly, the youth rose and began wobbling over in Larson's direction. He seemed slightly off balance because of the heavy bandolier.

When he reached the ammo crate and saw Larson's Cauca-

182

sian features, his eyes went wide, and he pointed at The Professor accusingly. *"My!"* American!

"Yes, *my*," Larson nodded slowly, motioning him closer. *"Lai day*, boy. Come to Shawn." He was risking discovery for two reasons: he wanted to learn what type of firing device was hooked up to the boy—if the plastique was detonated by radio waves from another location, or if the child himself had to yank on a wire as soon as he reached his target. And he did not want the boy to be down in the bunker when he committed suicide, which was what it all came down to, rationalizations aside.

"You go!" The youth was still pointing his finger at Shawn, and when he grew near enough, The Professor grabbed his arms and pinned them behind the boy's back.

Screams were not the result. He merely grumbled as Larson rolled him roughly onto his stomach and began checking the bandoliers for a firing mechanism.

"Hmmmm," he muttered after locating the Chinese-made firecracker. "Crude."

The equivalent of a cherry bomb was taped against the boy's sternum. Its fuse was pointing straight out. Larson found two stick matches tucked into the bandolier's end pocket. That was all.

And that was all it would take.

A tear edged down the boy's grimy cheek, and he began to tremble as Larson began unfastening the bandolier. "Don't worry, kid," he said gently, forcing a smile. "Shawn's not going to hurt you. I'd just feel a lot better if this bomb of yours was on the other side of the bunker, you know?"

"Toy." The youth tried to retrieve the plastique as Larson unwrapped the last of it.

"Not toy." He brushed his hand away. "Bad! Bombs are bad, kid. Didn't anyone ever tell you that?"

Pouting, the youth responded with a tiny, obscene gesture. Larson merely frowned and glanced down at the bandolier. "Where the hell'd you learn English, anyway?"

183

"From his papa-san, stupid."

An icy voice sliced through silence. An American's voice.

Larson felt the tip of a bayonet against the base of his skull when he started to turn around. It was an NVA bayonet, the kind shaped like a screwdriver. "Slowly," the voice commanded.

When he summoned the courage to glance back over a shoulder, Larson found himself looking down the barrel of an M-14. It was being held by a bare-chested black man, whose hair hung to his shoulders in beads and braids. M-60 ammo belts crisscrossed his sweat-soaked chest.

"Does youz know what one o' these mamas can do to a scrawny white boy like you at this range?"

Shawn Larson stared up at the black deserter aiming the M-60 heavy machine gun at his face, and slowly nodded.

"Then I suggest you very carefully place yo' hands on top of you' head. And no funny business. I don' know 'bout these zip mo-fucks behind me, but *this* nigger got nothin' to lose." He glanced around at the crates of weapons and ammunition, well aware what damage a single burst from the MG could inflict.

Larson had heard about this deserter before. Originally captured by the Viet Cong years earlier, while on a long-range recon, the guy had gone over to the other side. Stories were rampant about the "black dude with the Hog-60" being sighted at battlefields, elusively drifting through the bamboo, or climbing ridges overlooking fire support bases, never without his M-79 grenade launcher.

But he was supposed to run with a white deserter, who had also gone over to the enemy under similar circumstances. Larson scanned the pith helmets bobbing about beyond the black machine gunner, and found the man: ashen-faced and hollow-cheeked, with dazed eyes of walking death, he stared back at The Professor, looking right through him with no expression whatsoever. Despite the weary-looking face, his body was tanned a mahogany brown, and hard muscles rippled beneath

184

droplets of sweat along his entire frame, underweight as it was.

"Keep yo' eyes on the floor, mo'fuck!" The machine gunner jabbed the M-60's barrel into Larson's stomach. The metal was still warm, and he could smell gunpowder and cordite lingering about the weapon.

"Are you going to kill me?" Larson felt the earth all around them shudder as ordnance exploded above the surface, the battle topside still raging.

"Don't speak unless you're spoken to, brother." The white deserter had moved up through the Vietnamese, and now stood beside the machine gunner. He spoke gently, but as if his thoughts were preoccupied.

"From now on," the machine gunner added, "yo' my slave, white meat. Understand? You do whatever I say."

Larson felt no anger, strangely enough. He did feel as if he were caught up in a weird dream, where he'd lost control of all his faculties. Dumbly, he glanced up at the white deserter, who nodded back slowly in the affirmative, though he was staring at something behind The Professor.

*"Well?"* The barrel of the M-60 was jabbed into his belly again, and Larson doubled over.

"Right!" He gasped for air. "Okay! What do you want me to do?" The explosions overhead were getting louder, more powerful, becoming one long, continuous string of sharp reports as their ferocity increased.

"We're going down through a tunnel that will take us away from this ravine." The white deserter's thumb went up, motioning toward the surface. "We're not going to tie you up."

"Yo' on th' hono' sustem, so t' speak." The machine gunner laughed, but it was a bitter, twisted chuckle.

"We gotta lotta climbin' to do, but one false move, and we blow you away—got that? You are a prisoner of war, from this point on. You must understand that."

"Can I say something?" Larson shielded his face as he lifted his eyes and the machine gunner brought the M-60 back as if to strike him with the buttplate. But he balked, and the other deserter motioned for The Professor to continue. "I just wanted to say that . . . well, I will not fire any arms against American soldiers."

The black deserter leaned forward, leering in his face. "Did we motherfuckin' ask you to?"

"Like I said." His partner held him back again. "You are a prisoner. Just act like one, and you might make it through this mess. You might actually make it back to The World someday."

"But don't count on it." The machine gunner pushed the other deserter aside and rammed the M-60 barrel into Larson's stomach, slamming him back against the earthen wall. The Professor doubled over again. It had felt as if the barrel jabbed all the way in to his backbone!

The white deserter issued a directive in Vietnamese, and three privates rushed up to Larson. They proceeded to strip him of his weapons and uniform, striking him on the top of the head with closed fists whenever he looked up.

The Professor was a slow learner. "If I'm a prisoner of war," he asked slowly, after they left him clothed in nothing but a set of baggy, o.d. green GI shorts, "may I ask who I am a prisoner of?"

He half expected to be struck again, but the black deserter merely laughed. It was a hearty laugh this time, and he lowered his machine gun, dismissed Larson's question with a wave of his hand, and turned to leave. "You see the little red stars on their helmets?" The other deserter motioned to the NVA Regulars mingling with the Viet Cong guerillas.

"He asks too many questions." An older man with a heavy Asian accent spoke from the rear of the underground chamber. "Let's get moving before the long-noses notice their gunship opened up one of our tunnels and bring in their flame throwers."

Larson saw that the surge of confidence and self-esteem in the white deserter's face quickly drained when he heard the

186

Oriental's deep, commanding voice. It was becoming evident to The Professor that these two turncoats were not in charge of this mixed platoon at all, but were just putting on a show until the real commander tired of their games. "Okay!" The white deserter acknowledged the directive with a raised hand. "Move out." He pushed Larson toward the access tunnel where the lone lantern had been placed earlier.

Larson managed to catch a glimpse of the mystery man as they descended deeper into the bowels of the earth. He appeared to be a North Vietnamese major, in his late forties or early fifties. He turned slightly to hide his face as Larson passed by.

Less than five minutes later, the tunnel began to ascend again, and the group soon emerged on a distant hillside overlooking the battle for Phung Du. His captors allowed little time for sightseeing, however, and as Larson was hustled through the dense woods and over the hilltop, he watched the first wave of Phantoms swoop down into the valley. They seemed to pull up abruptly, however, never releasing their ordnance or napalm, and if at first he wondered why, in his gut he knew the true reason: The Air Force couldn't strafe the area yet because American soldiers were too close to the enemy positions, in many cases engaging Charlie and the NVA in hand-to-hand combat.

Two hours later, after they had hiked up and down through several valleys, thick with nearly impenetrable bamboo stalks and rife with pit vipers and two-step kraits, Larson's detail began their climb up a small mountain, and the flat plains of Phung Du village and the deceptively tranquil South China Sea in the distance once again came into view.

There seemed to be a lull in the battle, for helicopter activity had increased dramatically, and a Sikorsky Skycrane was hovering over *Pegasus*. Heavily armed soldiers scrambled around the downed gunship, stretching cables and chains over her crippled fuselage. Larson could see all the hectic activity taking place even from this distance.

187

"Oh my God," The Professor whispered to himself as he spotted the small Vietnamese boy emerge from a golden field of bamboo. Wrapped in the bandoliers of plastic explosives again, he raced out toward the soldiers working to raise *Pegasus* up out of the collapsed tunnel so they could ferry her back to base camp for repairs.

"Come on, keep movin', keep movin'!" The machine gunner rammed his M-60 barrel into the small of Larson's back, and he never saw what happened to the half-breed child wired up like a human satchel charge.

Like his childhood days when he'd lie out in the middle of a meadow during a storm, trying to judge the distance of lightning bolts, Shawn Larson began slowly counting; *One thousand one . . . one thousand two . . .*

Halfway down the hill, a thunderous blast, no doubt muffled somewhat and delayed by the many miles of terrain, rollled across the land, reaching Larson's ears.

# CHAPTER 16

## Saigon

"She want me come to her." Dep folded the single sheet of purple paper and slipped it back into the envelope without letting him see it.

"I've got no problem with that." Brody stood at the entrance to the balcony of her Cholon girlfriend. "But I'm going with you, and I don't want an argument about it."

"They no like Americans in Quan Loi." Her words told him she did not want to go alone.

"It won't be the first time I've met with a cold reception in The Nam."

"Maybe they want kill you, too," she tested him, locking eyes with the woman leaning in the doorway. "Bookoo VC Quan Loi."

Brody happened to know there was a large contingent of South Vietnamese soldiers in the small town fifty kilometers north of Saigon. But he said, "No sweat, baby-cakes."

"No sweat?" She sought to reaffirm his commitment to her in front of the woman.

"Right. Treat Brody would die for Dep, remember?" He blew her a kiss from across the room, then stepped out onto the balcony.

The woman in the doorway was a couple of years younger than Dep. A swollen belly was proof she would soon bring an eighth child into the world. Smiling slightly, she nodded to Dep: Her new man was truly a rare find. He didn't beat her, gave her back massages late into the night, and stated in front of a witness that he would die for her. The woman in the doorway was impressed. She and Dep exchanged light small talk for the next few minutes, and then a swarm of children arrived home from school and chirped like little birds around her skirt until she led them into the kitchen where the rice cakes were waiting.

"What keeps Dep's man on balcony?" She joined him now that her girlfriend was busy with sons and daughters. "Pretty girl in street below?"

"Well, there was this slender little lass in a see-thru *ao-dai* sitting at that bus stop there, winking up at me like she was hoping that I would—"

Dep grabbed one of his nipples without warning and twisted hard. "Geez!" He tried to break free, sliding to the side, and with her other hand she reached between his legs from behind and latched onto Treat's one good testicle. "Okay, OKAY, *OKAY!*"

"For man with only *mot* balls"—she used the Vietnamese word for one—"you keep Dep bookoo happy, Bro-dee. Maybe I twist off, you make love even better!"

"Hey, mellow out, okay?" He froze, breaking out into a sweat, but she would not release him. "If you rip it out, there won't be baby-sans, you know?"

"If I break off Bro-dee's balls," she continued, using the plural, "then you can no 'shoot wad,' eh? Dep have hard-on to play with all night!"

Brody brought a rigid forefinger to his lips in an attempt to silence her. "Not so loud," he said. "On the other balconies, or in the kitchen, somebody might hear."

"No pwoblem, lover." Enjoying the control she maintained over him with two small fingers, she drew him close and

190

pressed her lips firmly against his, forcing her tongue deep into his mouth. After a few seconds, she released him, sighing as she melted in his arms.

Brody had lost one of his testicles during a firearms accident as a teenager, long before he entered the military. A relative allowed a pistol to accidentally discharge during a round of horseplay. Though quite a painful wound, he had suffered no disabilities, serious injuries, or long-term side effects. He had breezed through many a romantic conquest in the bedroom, too, without the woman noticing half the plumbing was M.I.A.

Later, on the bus ride north along Highway 13, Dep held tightly onto Brody's arm. She loved him more and more as each night passed into day and they were still together. In her heart, she knew she was fast reaching the emotional point where he would become the most important man ever in her life, and that thought frightened Dep. She had always been so in control of her affairs after those first few years as a naive lover, falling in love with her tricks only to be dropped between dusk and dawn. "Thank you for what you say back there, Bro-dee." She kissed his ear affectionately, feeling almost like a young, carefree girl again. "In Cholon."

"Whatever are you talking about, my dear?" He gazed down at her and ran his lips against the edge of her broad nose.

"You know." She tickled him lightly. "In front of my girlfriend."

"Oh."

"You say Bro-dee would die for Dep." She winked at him seductively.

"Yes, I guess I did say that, didn't I?" He gazed out the window at large raindrops that were beginning to pelt the glass as they started up a steep hill with row upon row of rubber trees on both sides extending out as far as the eye could see.

"Thank you for sweet-talk that way. It very important to Dep. Make Dep look almost same-same wife, you *bic*?"

"I think I *bic*." He smiled at his reflection in the window as it began to steam up.

"I jus' wish you had meant it." She feigned a deep sadness in her heart, glancing down at her knees as she continued to hug his arm.

"Oh, I probably did." He reached over and brushed the strands of hair back from her cheeks. "But it's no big thing, *manoi oi*."

"No big thing?"

"Treat Brody has nine lives, honey-san—didn't you know that?"

"Nine lives?" Her eyes flew up to search his.

"Sure. Like a cat, you know? Nine lives." Dep frowned. "I can see I'm gonna have to teach you all our American customs and culture." He laughed softly. "Poor Dep. So much to learn about Brody's people."

"*You* the one must learn bookoo," she countered. "You want stay Vietnam rest life, huh? Then forget 'bout 'Merica. You must start speak, think, sleep like Vietn'mese people."

"Says who?"

"Dep tell you this because she love you bookoo, Bro-dee."

"If you loved me, you wouldn't call me Bro-dee all the time."

"I just called you honey-san. Special word, just Dep and her man. Secret word."

"You'd call me Treat."

They both glanced at the couple sitting on the bench across the aisle from them. The man, wearing an old ARVN uniform with the pants leg folded up where his right leg was missing, was one of the toughest-looking Vietnamese Brody had ever seen, despite the handicap. Scars crisscrossed the bridge of his nose, yet he was very handsome, with broad cheeks and a thick, drooping mustache. He was seven or eight inches shorter than Treat, but his biceps were thicker. His hair was trimmed short, but not in a GI cut, and Brody judged his age

192

to be somewhere between thirty and thirty-five. Two crutches were leaning against his seat.

The woman sleeping against his left side was in her late twenties, tops. Wearing filmy white pajamas with red rose designs all over them, she was a sensuous picture for men like The Whoremonger, who seemed to have sex on their minds eighteen to twenty hours a day. Brody had still not been able to get over the Saigon practice of wearing pajamas in public. True, it was hot and humid in the capital, and the garments were light and comfortable, but the Viets wore them the way Americans wore blue jeans and T-shirts.

"So are you going to tell me what was in the letter from your sister?" he asked her, after they had listened to the intense rainfall beating against the bus's roof for five or ten minutes.

"She need talk me." Dep had to speak up because of the racket caused by the sheets of rain sweeping down through the hills north of Saigon. She held her lips against his ear, seeking some privacy. "Dep think Lin have baby soon."

"Her name is Lin?"

"Yes. Lin born nine months after Dep. Not true sister, but make-believe sister, you *bic*? Call her star child."

"Star child?"

"This is story." She held her fingers out, as if to help her keep track of the chapters. "When Dep new baby, aunt and uncle come over home to visit. After see baby-san Dep, one day old, aunt and uncle want make baby, too. Go home and make love all night and—"

"How do you know they went home and made love all night?" he challenged her with a grin.

Dep elbowed him hard. "This family story, Bro-dee. Listen, or I break nose."

Brody cleared his throat in reply and stared out the window at plantation workers carrying buckets from the rubber trees through the rain.

"So anyways," she had taken to using one of his phrases,

193

"aunt finish make love late nighttime, just before sun come up. She step out on back balcony where water is, to bathe. And see star fall, Bro-dee."

"Star fall? I mean, falling star?"

"Yes. Very romantic. And she know. Nine months later, baby come. Lin born. Star child, you *bic*?"

"Yes, I *bic*, I *bic*. But I thought you said she was your sister."

Dep paused, searching her vocabulary. "Aunt and uncle killed 1950s. Fighting between French and Viet Minh, you know? Many people die. Aunt and uncle not army, but they die. Lin become stair sister. Stay our family."

"*Step* sister," he corrected her calmly.

"Yes. Okay, stepsister. One year later, Dep's family die too. Only have Lin left. Lin and Dep."

"Then why Dep stay Saigon and Lin stay Quan Loi?" he teased.

She trembled, and Brody brought an arm up, around her shoulder. "Lin no like what Dep do. Dep no like what Lin do." She sounded very bitter, but did not elaborate.

He pulled her close, well aware what Dep, at least, had been doing when he met her. "Well, you have me now, too, honey-san."

"Lin need Dep now. She have bookoo trouble, say if I no come Quan Loi she *fini* everything. Kill self. That not like Lin. Nothing so serious for her before. I have to talk her. Find out problem. Fix."

"Is she half as pretty as you?" He smiled, hoping to lift her spirits with a taunt.

Before Dep could use her elbow to reply, the bus went into a skid, sliding sideways across the rainslick roadway. It came to rest completely blocking both lanes, and when Brody looked out the side windows, he saw the bus was not the only thing blocking Highway 13.

Someone had piled railroad ties up in the middle of the road and rolled a burning ARVN troop transport behind it.

That someone was now emerging from the tree lines along both sides of the road, and they were all carrying Chinese-made assault rifles.

Brody held Dep close as he watched the armed men rushing toward the bus. Because of the heavy rainfall, he wasn't sure if they were communists or just bandits. Either way, the passengers could all wind up very dead, but there was a better chance he could talk his way out of a grave if mere highwaymen were involved.

A young male in his early twenties with a long, drooping mustache and hideous scar covering half his face rushed up and began banging on the door. The bus driver glanced back over a shoulder, saw no passengers in uniform or producing firearms, and quickly complied, jerking back on the latch that swung the folding door open.

"Welcome to Binh Duong Province!" he announced in both Vietnamese and English, after a fast headcount of the passengers showed about a half dozen occidental faces besides Brody's. "You are close to Ben Cat! But not close enough! You have entered the domain of Nguyen Van Truc, who assists the Provisional Revolutionary Government as often as is possible, and yet you have failed to pay the appropriate taxes!" He began walking back through the bus, pausing near each Westerner to intimidate him with a rifle muzzle pressed gently against the nose or temple. Other gunmen, toting American-made M-14s, were boarding the bus now. "So break out the billfolds, gents." The ringleader was wide-eyed and enthusiastic, as if he was running a carnival and soliciting tips to get the fat man to squeeze into a cannon. "And you ladies: start removing the jewelry, if you were stupid enough to wear any on this trip."

Dep glanced over at Brody for guidance, but his attention was focused on the Vietnamese with the drooping Fu Manchu mustache and machete scar. "Since when do revolutionaries steal money?" he challenged the gangleader, all too conscious

195

of the large number of gold coins hidden in an ankle pouch as he rubbed the insides of his sandals together.

The man was temporarily taken aback, but then the smile broke to the surface again. "Ahhh, a troublemaker." He returned to Brody's section. "We need money to finance a revolution, Mister Know-All." He jabbed the M-14 barrel against Brody's ribs.

"Why don't you ask Hanoi for financial assistance?" Treat replied sarcastically, and Dep nudged him sharply.

"Don' bring attention to us." Her whisper was a harsh one.

The gangleader lost patience quickly with Treat Brody, and, pausing to search his thoughts for a quick-witted answer, he drew a blank and suddenly brought back the rifle butt.

Without rising from his seat, the one-legged Arvin veteran sitting across the aisle reached out and grabbed the scrawny thief by the throat, jerking him backwards off his feet. The M-14 came up, and a burst of rounds stitched across the ceiling of the bus, causing many of the women and children on board to burst into screams. An old mama-san began sobbing loudly.

Two of the gangleader's men rushed back and filled the South Vietnamese vet with several dozen bullets. The smoking rounds passed through his chest and into the passengers seated behind him before Brody could even react. The dead man's wife began wailing as she clutched her bloodied husband, and Dep latched onto Brody like an anchor, preventing him from moving.

"Your fault!" The gangleader regained his footing, rubbed at his throat, and lashed out, slapping Brody across the face. Blood dripped from Treat's nose, but Dep still kept him from resisting.

"Don'!" She pressed her lips against his ear, keeping her full weight into his shoulder. "You have no gun! Don' die for nothing, Bro-dee! *Please!*"

"Listen to your woman, coward!" the hood taunted him.

Treat glanced over at the sobbing wife leaning into her

196

dead husband, fingers soaked in crimson as she tried to shake him back to life.

"You bastard." He locked eyes with the gunman. "*You* are the coward. Put down the rifle and I'll rip your face off!"

He could feel Dep's fingers gouging into his arms, pleading by touch for him to act passive, but he didn't care. More than anything right now, he wanted to rise up and kill this Cong creep with his bare hands, adding another notch to his Dirty Thirty tally.

"I am coward because I yellow-bellied, no?" The gangster pulled his muscle shirt up, revealing a rock-hard stomach as he laughed like he'd heard the insult a hundred times before. "Well, we stop bus not only for your money and jewelry, but for your *woooo-mens!*" As if he were the hammer of a half-cocked pistol, the gunman suddenly went off, swinging the riflebutt against Brody's jaw with blinding speed before he could block it.

It was as if someone threw a thick, black blanket over The Whoremonger's head. He felt like he was dropping backward, into a bottomless pit. The pain was all-consuming, swallowing him up, muffling out Dep's screams as he felt her torn from him.

His head told him it was days later when his right eye finally popped open, but his gut instinct told him his mind was deceiving him, that he had only just crashed against the floorboards of the bus. The side of his face was lying in a pool of blood, and the picture of bodies and carnage extending out beneath the seats all the way to the front of the bus was no less a scene straight out of hell.

Brody forced his head up far enough to register on the bulging, betrayed eyes of the dead South Vietnamese vet, and he remembered. He remembered about the insurgents, masquerading as folk-hero bandits, and he saw Dep's face, screaming to him from beneath the raindrop ripples of a deep,

197

murky lagoon. *Bro-dee would die for Dep....Bro-dee would die for Dep....*

He forced himself to his feet, realizing for the first time that most of the other passengers had been unaffected by the robbery—were still sitting in their seats, frozen with terror yet watching his every move. Dep was gone. The Arvin veteran's widow was missing too.

Their screams reached him—had been ringing in his ears all along, really, yet he had only now understood them for what they were . . . realized Dep was no longer his woman . . . that she belonged to someone else.

Brody stumbled to the side window and saw that the gang-leader and his men were dragging a half dozen young women toward the edge of the rain forest.

Dep was with them. Her blouse was already torn away, her breasts flapping wildly from side to side as she fought them all, kicking and screaming and punching, resisting to the end.

Brody searched frantically for a weapon, anything—a misplaced rifle, an abandoned pistol. But there was nothing. He stumbled to the door, choking on his own blood. But when he reached the bottom of the steps, the bandits and the women they had kidnapped from the bus had vanished into the jungle.

# CHAPTER 17

## Bangkok

The fact that they were still wearing the MP uniforms enabled Cordova and Fletcher to pass through the security checkpoints at the entrance to Soi Nkyung. A few minutes later, they were standing in front of the address the Thai policewoman had scribbled onto the sheet of note-pad paper for them.

"Can you imagine growing up in a fairy-tale setting like this?" Fletcher gestured out beyond the swollen river, to where the famous Temple of Dawn rose up through crimson mists of dusk.

"It's certainly not Omaha, Nebraska," Cordova remarked, staring up at the high-walled compound their trek had taken them to. He had not been expecting this, either: sagging loops of sparkling concertina wire above the twelve-feet-high iron-grilled gates. "Check out the tops of these walls," he muttered in awe. Jagged splinters of glass rose up two and three inches above the delicate sweeps of green, blue, and gold Oriental architecture.

"Yah, the Thais are like the Viets when it comes to fortifying their housing projects." Fletcher seemed to be knowledgable in such matters. "They plant bottles in the tops of the walls when pouring the concrete or mortar, then, after it all dries solid, break the bottle tops off at the halfway mark.

Leaves quite a nasty impression on any *cao bois* trying to climb over in the middle of the night."

"I can imagine. But this isn't exactly what I was expecting, you know?" Corky compared the address on his slip of paper with the numbers over the gate again.

"How so?" Fletcher shrugged.

"This place is fucking *huge*, Snakeman. Do you think they were into graft and corruption."

"I don't think this pad is owned by any one person." Fletcher motioned to a submachine-gun-toting commando who appeared on the other side of the gate.

At first routinely grim-faced, the Thai policeman smiled when he saw the armbands. "Ahhh"—he began unlocking the gate—"American MP! Welcome! Please enter."

One glimpse of the barracks-style outlay inside the walled-in compound, and Fletcher made another deduction. "I bet these are all police families that live in here," he said, rubbing his chin in thought.

"Really?" The Thai officer handed Corky a clipboard and he signed in, using a phony name, as if he'd been through the procedure a hundred times before.

"Yah. It's a popular method of protecting the cops' wives and children in countries with insurgency problems like Thailand's. I've read where they've got similar arrangements in Manila and Saigon, not to mention *bookoo* Moslem countries down south."

"Who is it you seek-to-speak?" The sentry did not appear interested in their small talk. He kept glancing at their holsters, intrigued by his inability to spot the usual protruding gun handles. Was this some new type of *phalang* weapon? He was dying to ask but managed to maintain his composure.

"Well, actually, we want to see the children of two of your officers . . . policewomen . . ."

"Oh?" The guard's smile remained intact, as he waited for them to elaborate.

"Sgt. Prasertkwan and Officer Chatsungnoen," Fletcher as-

200

sisted his friend. "We understand their children are staying here while—"

The sentry's smile slowly faded, as if they were playing a nasty little joke on him and He was just now feeling the humiliation. "Sgt. Prasertkwan?" He swallowed hard, glancing back at some women in colorful sarongs and peasant blouses passing between the three- and four-story buildings.

"Yes." Fletcher nodded. "And Officer Chatsungnoen."

"But"—the Thai's cheeks seemed to sink in slightly as he tried to conceive of the true purpose of their visit—"they *dty hlaa-oh, khop*," and he ran his forefinger slowly across his throat, knifelike, as if to emphasize his point.

"Yes, yes," Cordova nodded impatiently, "we know that, *khop*. We want to see their children, that's all. Their children."

"Veddy irregular," he began shaking his lowered head from side to side as he started back to guard the kiosk. "Veddy irregular, *khop*. I check. You wait."

"Whatta you think?" Corky asked Fletcher as they watched the short, heavily muscled policeman pick up a field phone and twirl a bolt of electricity through it. The whirring sound sent a chill through Cordova, and he saw another scene far away, in a place called Cho Gao. His team's interrogator had a female VC suspect strapped naked to an empty cable spool table. She was flat on her back, arms and legs spread, with field-phone wires attached to her nipples and inserted into her vagina. He could still hear her screams, even now, these many months later. And he had thought he was past that point . . . beyond those memories. They had caught her in the act of peeling the skin off a captured Arvin's penis, along with four other Viet Cong, but the rationalization that they were only dishing out what she had coming to her didn't ease the guilt. He could never convinced himself "an eye for an eye" meant a tit for a tit, or that any of it applied to torture.

Before Snakeman could offer an opinion, an older official with "scrambled eggs" on the brim of his high-peaked cap and seven rows of combat ribbons on his brown uniform emerged from an administration building and started walking casually in their direction.

"Colonel will help you." The sentry's tone was apologetic. "Sorry, but—"

"We understand." Fletcher waved the excuse off. "No sweat. Channels, clearance, *chonh woo-uh!*"

"Yes, yes!" The man was all smiles again. *"Chonh woo-uh!"* He bowed slightly, then backed off, making room for the police colonel's appearance.

"What the hell does '*chonh-whatever*' mean?" Cordova asked.

"It's the closest thing in the Thai language to 'bullshit,'" Snakeman explained as they both saluted the colonel.

The colonel returned their salutes crisply, producing a curious smile. "And what can we do for you gentlemen this evening?" he asked politely. "My man here tells me you want to see the children of Officers Prasertkwan and Chatsungnoen. May I ask why?" He was focusing on their shirt pockets, noting the absence of name tags and campaign ribbons.

"We were friends of theirs." Cordova presented his most trusting image, well aware the colonel was highly suspicious of their true intentions, but able to hide it well. "We read about their unfortunate accidents...the shoot-out, and all. Well, sir, we just wanted to pay our respects to their children."

"I see...." The colonel's wrists crossed together against a rock-hard belly, and he took a few seconds to size them up. "You worked with Sgt. Prasertkwan and her partner in the combined police patrols, did you?" he asked.

Fletcher, sensing a trick question, shook his head in the negative. "Well, not exactly, Colonel. You see, we met them in Bangkok Police Headquarters cafeteria one day, while we were delivering some paperwork for..."

"PMO," Cordova summoned the abbreviation for Provost Marshal's Office from the depths of his memory.

202

"Right, PMO . . . and . . . well, you must admit they were two of the most beautiful women on the metro force. . . ."

"And you . . . 'put the hustle' on them." The colonel rested his chin in the crook of one hand, unsure about these two military policemen now.

"Well, no, sir—we bought them coffee, and introduced ourselves, and all that."

"And talked about the differences and similarities in our jobs," Fletcher added.

"We made plans to take them . . ."

"And their children, of course."

". . . up north for a picnic."

"To Chiang Mai," Fletcher decided at that very moment.

"Where they have the elephant festival," the colonel reminded them.

"Yes!"

"Sugar really wanted to see the elephants!" Cordova said. "She was really looking forward to it."

"I'm sure she was." The colonel grinned shallowly. "Considering she was born and raised in Chiang Mai."

"Ahhh, yes . . ." The smiles on Corky's and Snakeman's faces both dissolved, but the colonel seemed to be dismissing their antics as harmless.

"I don't see any problem with the two of you talking with the children," he said. "After all, you are both police officers, aren't you?" He winked at them, his face straight now, and Cordova hoped the blood rushing to his face was not visible in the dim glow of twilight.

The colonel gave the gate sentry instructions in Thai, and they were led toward one of the apartment buildings. "Oh, and gentlemen!" he added, before returning to the administration building. "Go easy on the kids, okay?"

"Sir?"

"Thai children are different from American children. I know. I happened to have studied criminal justice and police

203

science in Washington, D.C. Please don't baby them. And don't mention the shooting, I beg of you."

"We won't, Colonel."

"And whatever you do"—he made one last request before passing beneath a tri-colored flag flying at half-mast—"please don't ask them if they'd like to go to America. It's just not fair to them at this stage of the game."


"And what is your name?" Cordova handed the universal ice-breaker, a stick of bubblegum, to the small boy squatting between two young girls.

"His name Jim," the child's older sister answered for him.

"Ahhh, American name." Corky smiled warmly.

"Jim is Thai name, too." The girl sounded slightly offended. "Is what-you-say? . . . 'nickname' for longer name."

"Yes." Cordova tried to ignore the defiant, anti-foreigner streak in the girl's dark, unpenetrable eyes. Not even in her teens yet, but ready to take on the Western World. Good, he decided. She'll need that kind of courage.

The sentry had ushered them into a large, ground-floor lobby where children from several families had gathered around a Chinese *Go* gameboard on the floor. Except for an empty bookcase, there was no furniture in the room. Iron bars protected the windows. Bug screens covered the exterior, but there was no glass in the frames. Small turquoise lizards clung to the outside surface of the screen and looked in, their tails curling and uncurling with the warm breeze.

"And do any of you belong to Sawang Chatsungnoen?" Fletcher asked softly, scanning the youthful faces. No one responded, and the sentry translated without either American asking him to, but still no hands went up.

"Are any of you children of *Mrs.* Chatsungnoen?" Cordova's fingers searched his pockets for more chewing gum,

204

but even that ploy was not incentive enough to interest anyone in the sullen-faced group.

"They stick together, as you can see." A woman spoke from shadows in the back of the room. Cordova and Fletcher glanced up to find a slender policewoman approaching. "It is all a game to you," she further explained. "They think, because you are American, or white . . . because you are different, that they should not speak with you."

"Otherwise it will only bring further ill-fortune down upon them." A second female officer had entered the room from an unnoticed hallway. She was heavier, but the weight fell into all the right places.

"I see." Cordova nodded, watching the women closely as they drew nearer. Neither wore makeup, but both doorgunners found their sharp Thai features extremely attractive. Fletcher was beginning to wonder if there was anywhere in Asia where he could go and not be bewitched by these women.

One of the officers rattled off a list of instructions, and the children began lining up in alphabetical order. "We are taking them to a movie," she explained. "Would you like to come along? You are more than welcome."

The other policewoman took them aside when both Cordova and Fletcher declined. "You are here to talk to the Chatsungnoen children and the Prasertkwan children," she observed. "But why? Why do their interests concern you?" She remained polite, sounding more curious than defensive.

"You know, to tell you the truth, I'm not really sure about that myself anymore." Cordova smiled down at her. "We were friends of Sugar and Sawang, and we just wanted to make sure their kids were doing all right."

"Frankly," added Snakeman, "this is not at all what we were expecting."

"And just what exactly did you expect to find?" She chuckled lightly. "That we would have them working their skins to the bone, dawn to dusk?"

205

"Actually, we were not aware they were living in a housing project like this." Cordova motioned toward the grilled windows and barbed-wire beyond. ". . . Didn't realize they would be so well protected . . . so well taken are of. . . ."

"We Thai police are not unlike your officers stateside." She winked at the two Americans. "We, too, take care of our own."

"It's just that, well, I was kind of expecting to locate these starving little kids, floating in a dark dinghy on some polluted *klong* somewhere, abandoned . . ."

"We were really hoping to do the Good Samaritan skit and . . ."

"And what?" she looked genuinely perplexed. "Take them back to U.S.A. with you? *Adopt* them? Do you really think that would be best thing for them now?"

"Well, no, but . . ."

"Believe me, gent'r'men, but they are best left alone with their own people. Thailand their homeland. They have 'nough problem adjusting now, with their parents gone. They don't need Chicago wind and Co'ro'rado cold and teasing American children who don't like the way their eyes look. . . ." Her tone had turned suddenly sour.

"You sound like you've been to the States." Fletcher hid his smile by rubbing his lips with a clenched fist.

"University of Denver," she admitted. "One year. Seem like one hun'red. When I quit, give up, come back Bangkok, I feel . . . reborn. No more . . . prej'dice. No more Communist professor talk 'bout stupid things have nothing do with my education, you unders'and?"

Fletcher and Cordova exchanged knowing smirks. "Honey, we certainly do." The Snakeman patted her upper arm gently.

"I surrender all hope of be college girl," she revealed. "Come back Thailand. Join police. I hate Communists. Someday they will take over Thailand, but I will be waiting." She sucked in her lips at some distasteful memory, glaring down at the floor's teakwood planks. "Anyway"—she shook her head back and forth, dismissing the thoughts and startling Cordova —"all that is 'past history.' I am home, love job . . . love our children. None of them really mine, though. But maybe someday. Would you like go to movie with us? It is children's show an' in Thai language, but mos' prob'ry have English subtitles. I think you like."

Both soldiers politely declined—they were obviously out of place and unwanted there. As she escorted them back to the main gate, Fletcher asked the policewoman, "Why didn't you go to college here in Bangkok?"

"I have consider that"—she nodded—"and maybe someday I do. But now, I can help my country more by work for police."

"I understand," Cordova said, taking her hand warmly in his. She shook with a sincere smile, and his eyes searched hers, but there was nothing hidden behind the long lashes . . . no invitation to come back . . . no permission to ask her first name. She was both warm and cold, friendly yet distant.


The two doorgunners waited along the curb, down the block from the police family compound, for ten or fifteen minutes before a taxi came into view, but it was filled with old mama-sans on their way home from the floating market and didn't slow for them.

Cordova watched the children start filing from the heavily fortified compound and march down the sidewalk toward a brightly lit cinema three blocks away. The two policewomen they had spoken with earlier, as well as two commandos armed with automatic weapons, escorted the children.

"I smell trouble." Snakeman sounded very apprehensive as they both spotted the three unmarked pickup trucks cruising, silently but swiftly, into the street from a back alley. Cordova

207

and Fletcher began running toward the children, but they were not quick enough.

Men armed with rifles and shotguns jumped up from behind wooden partitions mounted in the beds of all three trucks and began firing at the two commandos. Both were cut down before they could get off a single shot.

"Jesus Christ!" Fletcher dove under a parked truck as ricochets began bouncing in their direction with sickening whistles. Unable to do anything else, Cordova followed him under the chassis.

One of the policewomen drew her two-inch .38 but was felled by a shotgun blast that nearly severed her gun arm. She was knocked backward through the plate-glass window of a brightly lit Thai pharmacy. Several of the pellets struck the children closest to her, and they all began screaming as they huddled together under the lone streetlight on the block, rays from the open storefront behind them sending golden shafts over the crimson-streaked sidewalk.

"What the hell's going on?" Cordova was fumbling with his holster. His heart sank when he remembered they were not in The Nam, these were not VC, and they hadn't found the need to buy firearms on the black market.

"Damned if I know!" Fletcher felt particles of rock from the asphalt scrape his cheek as he slid closer to the truck's engine block.

Several of the gunmen, dressed in civilian clothes and wearing bandanas over their faces, had jumped from a truck and were surrounding the surviving policewoman. "We have to do something!" They watched her slowly lay down her revolver and raise her hands over her head as gunmen swarmed in to subdue her.

"No shit! You got any bright strategy to fit *this* situation, Mr. Idea Man?" But before they could react further, the masked men had dragged the surviving policewoman and five

208

of the children over to the middle truck and herded them roughly into the back cab.

In a clamor of roaring engines and smoking tires, they screeched around in the middle of the road and disappeared down a side street as officers emerged from the compound and began running to the aid of the traumatized children cowering in the shadows of doorways and filth of the gutters.

# CHAPTER 18

## Sisters of Mercy Orphanage, Phu Cat, South Vietnam

Nurse Maddox held a purple lollipop out to the little girl, but she refused to let go of Corporal Patterson. "Come on, honey," the lieutenant pleaded softly as soldiers lying in blood-soaked gurneys with chest and belly wounds were wheeled past her on both sides. "Come to Lisa, so I can take and get you cleaned up. Get you some food, okay? Now how does that sound?"

"I don't think she understands much English, ma'am." Patterson grimaced as he watched a dazed soldier carry a dead infant into the shelter. The child was missing both arms and a leg, and appeared to have been dead for some time, but the GI didn't seem to notice.

"Where do I put the baby, sir?" He stopped behind Maddox, and she rose to take the corpse from him.

"Corpsman!" The lieutenant called one of the medics over. "Take it." She rolled the dismembered, faceless body into a buck sergeant's outstretched arms and turned to lead the shell-shocked trooper back out of the shelter.

The Sisters of Mercy orphanage at Phu Cat, south of the

fighting, had been converted into a medical aid station to help with the flood of unexpected casualties. To Maddox, worse than seeing the long lines of homeless refugees and walking wounded was watching the new orphans filter in. She had witnessed it before in Duc Co, outside Pleiku: The pain in their hearts would silence many of them for a long time to come. Many would grow into adulthood severely damaged psychologically, never to recover—those who were "lucky" enough to make it through the relocation from family ville to refugee camp or orphanage.

After she saw to several additional casualties, Maddox passed through the triage area again and found Patterson still trying to convince the little seven-year-old girl she would be safe here. But the child refused to let go. Just when he was successful in prying one of her hands loose from his wrist, the other would wrap around him, or her legs would lock onto his calves, and he would have to sit down again or drag her along the ground.

"She's like a little monkey," Maddox observed with a sad smile, bringing coffee over for her and Saint Pat.

"You're tellin' me!" Patterson didn't know whether to laugh or cry.

"She's really growing attached to you," the lieutenant persisted in taunting him. "You ought to adopt her, Corporal."

"What?" Patterson did not display the shock she expected to see, but spoke rather calmly. "Yah," he laughed, "don't get me goin' on that subject, ma'am. Believe me, I've considered it."

"I imagine so." Maddox's heart went out to Patterson and all the other soldiers who were arriving via Dustoff from the fighting at Phung Du. Their jobs were made doubly difficult by the innocent villagers who were being caught in the crossfire. True, Binh Dinh Province had long been a communist sanctuary, but women and children without weapons were turning up dead or wounded as more and more huts were burned to the ground by ricocheting tracer fire, and the Ameri-

211

can side was doing its best to evacuate civilians to the rear areas. They could determine loyalties after the gunsmoke had settled and Charlie retreated.

"I truly believe"—Patterson was forming thoughts in his head now that took on greater importance the more he pondered the situation—"that little Tamminh and I just went through something we will remember every waking moment for the rest of our lives, Lieutenant. Maybe if we stick together, we can survive it."

"You're alive," Maddox reminded him. "That's a start."

Patterson smiled in reply. "And I'm short, ma'am. Only nine days and wake-up, if I don't extend. I could take her back with me. Wouldn't that blow my parents' minds? They pull up to the airport, and their Numba One Son is standin' there in the terminal holdin' a genuine war orphan from The Veeyet-Nam! Hometown U.S.A. would have a heart attack, let me tell you, but it'd be worth it just to see the looks on their faces."

"Don't do it for the wrong reasons," Maddox cautioned him lightheartedly. "She's not just another souvenir you picked up overseas. And adoptions of Viet children aren't that easily arranged, despite the turmoil we've gone through here. Down in Saigon, it's another world altogether. Most of the time, anyway. It could take months. And money, Corporal. Lots o' bucks."

"That just gives me another reason to extend." Patterson did not sound worried. "Evenin', ma'am, I 'ppreciate your guidance." He whipped an informal salute and turned to leave. "Come on, Tamminh. Let's see if we can find that barrel of Kool-Aid Doc Delgado was tellin' us about."

Her upper lip trembling slightly as she watched Patterson disappear down a corridor, she fought back the tears. These guys were all like her own kid brothers, always wanting to help everyone and save the world from the great red menace. The trouble was, she wondered if tiny little innocent Tamminh wasn't part of the great communist horde too.

212

Rotors on the sticky, humid air reached her ears, announcing the arrival of more wounded and homeless. Maddox wiped the edges of her eyes, took a deep breath, and started for the helipad outside.

Corporal Patterson sat between two crouching, heavily armed grunts in the middle of a gunship cabin, listening to the rotors roar overhead, feeling the craft's thin fiberglass and magnesium skin vibrating beneath the punji-proof soles of his jungle boots. They were racing back to Phung Du at over 100 miles an hour, keeping close to the treetops, each man making peace with himself as the din of gunfire and clamor of exploding ordnance grew quickly nearer.

He did not want to return to the fighting. As a single-digit midget, due to be rotated back to The World in less than two weeks, he could probably have avoided boarding the gunship altogether. But Saint Pat felt a duty to his buddies still pinned down out there on the god-forsaken plains surrounding Phung Du. Patterson already knew about "survivor's guilt." He was suffering it from many past encounters with the enemy where he had barely escaped with his skin after a ruthless engagement. And he didn't want to add the sands of Phung Du to the bad memories.

He missed little Tamminh desperately. She already felt like a first daughter, but they had said their pidgin-English goodbyes, and now she was many klicks behind him, with Maddox.

He didn't like the rumbling vibrations of this Huey, either. She was a strange, new ship. This was Patterson's first ride in her, and he longed for *Pegasus*, her smooth, powerful gait, out-of-sync rotorblades adding to her mystery and attraction. She was a mean-spirited, arrogant cunt, but bullets couldn't bring her down, and the grunts of Echo Company all loved her. The Huey he was holding onto now, on the other hand,

213

was cruising tight, like a naive, inexperienced cherry girl, and that could only mean a bad omen.

He rubbed the VC skulls on the gunship skidpoints engraved across the side of his Hog Heaven ring, and hoped for a good, productive night in The Nam.

The pilot's voice clicked into the intercom, and a smile creased Patterson's rugged features: Gabriel The Gunslinger. A good sign.

"Hold onto your gonads, gentlemen!" Gabe warned the young troopers in the back of the chopper. "Lima Zulu in dirty sex, and it's definitely gonna be another sizzler!"


Lt. Jake Vance watched troopers from Company A zigzagging through the cemetery tombstones northeast of Phung Du-3, reinforcing the half dozen men left from his platoon. "Damn, am I glad to see you cats!" he yelled, laying down cover fire with his M-16 on full-automatic.

A wiry captain with a patch over one eye proned out in the sand beside Vance. "What's the poop?"

"There's a goddamned machine-gun nest in those palms over there! He's had us pinned down all day. I've had my men direct wave after wave on rock-and-roll, but without effect. They've been picking us off, one by one."

"We'll handle it for you, sir!" A stocky, energetic-looking sergeant waved his squad up to their position. Vance read the blood-streaked nametag: BERCAW. "We'll rush 'em, with bayonets fixed! The shock oughta turn the tables on 'em! Then your people can pick them off one at a time after we charge and they scatter!"

"We've been practicing this since Christ was a corporal!" A PFC behind Bercaw grinned enthusiastically.

"I've been waiting for this all week!" The grunt beside the Private First Class slammed a fresh banana clip into his M-16 and popped the slide release lever with the edge of his hand, karate-chop fashion.

214

Before Vance or the other officer could really say anything, Bercaw and his squad were on their feet and charging. They fired long bursts from the hip and yelled war cries as NVA bullets kicked up handfuls of sand all around their boots.

"Christ!" Vance and the others, laying down cover fire, watched Bercaw's squad sprint over fifty meters before being driven to cover by intense machine-gun fire.

They had rushed to within a few yards of the MG nest, but the communists hadn't bugged out as they'd hoped.

"Sir." The captain's RTO handed him the field-radio mike. "Trouble."

"Dang," the officer muttered, after listening to directives from the CP on the cemetery's southern quadrant. He started to explain to Vance, but decided there wasn't time. "Sgt. Bercaw!" He rose slightly from behind the sand bar as the shooting died down. "Pull your men back! I repeat: *Pull your men back!* Charlie Papa advises arty on its way in! Repeat: They're going to try and knock the nest out with arty!"

Vance could see the disappointment and irritation on Bercaw's face, even from this distance: so close and yet so far! But how was he going to pull his men back safely out of the artillery's kill zone without risking casualties?

"What's he doing now?" The captain watched Bercaw rise to his knees in full view of the machine-gun nest. But the communists were unable to fire because of the smoking hot rounds flowing nonstop from the gutsy sergeant's rifle into their position.

In all, over 200 bullets left his M-16 muzzle, peppering the machine-gun nest, as his men left the protection of cover and ran back to Vance's spot. They watched Bercaw change clip after clip—eight magazines in all—before the enemy could muster the courage to rise up out of their foxhole and fire back.

Snipers in the nearby treetops attempted to take out Bercaw. Vance watched enemy rounds rip his helmet strap D-ring off, blow a hole in his canteen, and strike his boot with a lucky shot, but then it became clear the machine gunners never would return fire: the fearless sergeant had routed the entire MG squat by himself. Add five more to the body count.

"I just had a duel with an enemy machine gun!" he yelled, breathing hard, water spouting from the bullet-riddled canteen, as he sprinted back across the sandy clearing and slammed against the ground between Vance and the captain. "And I won!"

"You sure did, sergeant!" Vance slapped him on the back as another wave of NVA bullets swept across their position from the opposite tree line. The lieutenant glanced down at Bercaw's boot. A puff of blue smoke floated over a hole in the tread, but there was no blood adding color to that mental picture Vance would carry of the elated sergeant for years to come. He wouldn't have to present the NCO a Purple Heart.

A Bronze Star Medal would do.


That afternoon, the First Team Cavalrymen popped yellow smoke, blanketing the cemetery with an eerie, tracer-swept haze, and six gunships from LZ Papa, loaded down with Bravo Company reinforcements, swooped in to LZ-4 under heavy hostile fire. Two choppers were driven off before they could land.

Friendly artillery fire saturated the constantly shifting perimeters, but every Huey that tried to help Alpha Company was riddled with Viet Cong and NVA bulletholes. The single platoon of infantrymen who did manage to dive from smoking hatches into the sand was immediately pinned down in a crossfire between North Vietnamese and American machine-gun nests. Col. Buchanan's counterpart, Battalion commander McDade, landed to assess the situation firsthand, and was nearly killed less than a minute later as Cong lead showered the ridgeline near his head. He soon discovered that their standing looked bad, if not hopeless. His 2nd Battalion was surrounded and cut off from the rest of the Airmobile opera-

216

tion, and no one could raise Charlie Company, on the other side of the Viet graveyard, by radio.

"We're going to have 2nd Battalion of 12th Cav here by tomorrow morning," Vance was told, "but we're on our own for tonight." The lieutenant shook his head apprehensively as he scanned the menacing-looking storm clouds floating dark and ominous along the northern horizon.

"We've got to get up to the north side of the cemetery," he advised Sgt. Zack, "and help Charlie Company rejoin the rest of us. Then we'll be ready to kick butt by morning."

Leo The Lionhearted stared at the castlelike thunderheads rising in the distance. "It's gonna be a bitch," he said simply. "But I guess that's what Uncle Sammy's payin' us for, ain't it, Lieutenant?"

"Yah, I guess it is, Leo."

There was no twilight that evening. The rains swept in, as predicted, and the shooting continued. Fog and swirling gray mists cloaked the hamlets of Phung Du, and visibility grounded the gunships at less than 750 feet.

From midnight until pre-dawn, with U.S. artillery softening up the enemy positions, Vance and officers in Alpha Company led their men through the tombstones, braving bursts of fire from fellow Americans expecting suicidal sappers instead of a rescue party. But nearly every last Charlie Company survivor was eventually located and led back to the Cav buffer zone.

At dawn, golden balls of exploding napalm burst forth at the same moment a sizzling Asian sun broke free of the eastern horizon. The rains had stopped, but shrapnel still fell from the sky as B-57 bombers and A-1 Skyraiders hit the NVA and VC positions with everything they had.

The eastern perimeter was saturated with artillery strikes between the bombing runs, and at a few minutes before eleven hundred hours, 200 men from the 12th Cavalry choppered in south of the main battlefield. They were led by Col. Hal Moore and Sgt. Major Basil Plumley, who were bent on

217

showing McDade how to teach Charlie a lesson. The Brass at Disneyland East might have been forced to change the operation's name from Masher to White Wing because of public pressure in Washington, but Moore would still pound the Cong into the ground using his hammer and anvil.

The reinforcements met relatively little resistance as they headed northeast through several rice paddies, muddy water up to their knees. But as the first gravemarkers rising from the mist came into sight, heavily camouflaged enemy machine-gun nests opened up on the troopers.

Numerous pitched battles ensued, but Moore was able to maneuver his people so that nearly all the NVA positions were surrounded and annihilated by crack teams of shock troops. They soon reached the survivors of Alpha and Charlie Companies, many of whom were taking cover in a deep trench filled with the bodies of both American soldiers and Vietnamese civilians. Most of the men wore bandages on their heads and extremeties. Many had entire torsoes wrapped. Village women and children huddled beneath the protruding roots of a bullet-riddled palm, sobbing.

"We've got bookoo W.I.A.'s need to be med-evaced out!" Vance told one of the first officers to reach his position. "We had a good company or two of NVA entrenched twelve hours ago." He pointed out hidden machine-gun nests. "But I think most of the dinks beat feet during the night, and we're down to 'bout a platoon or two o' doped-up crazies! I'm tellin' ya, I don't know what it's gonna take, brother!"

Col. Moore had an inkling. He had to get these men, even the walking wounded, out of the trench. He had to get them all on their feet and fighting again, sweeping through the burial mounds in search of Cong! He scanned the helmets extending up through the trenchline for several dozen meters. The men from Charlie had black circles painted on their camou-covers, and the Alpha troops triangles. They were about evenly numbered, and he was sure if he could just get

218

them motivated again, they would follow him against the enemy.

"We got problems, Colonel!" The Sgt. Major rushed up with their RTO. It was a Brass Monkey from the Delta team CP back at Bong Son's Special Forces outpost. Green Berets in the An Lao Valley were being decimated by a surprisingly large number of NVA sweeping through the area. The Delta team leader, a major, had even been shot. They needed help bad, and they needed it now!

The First Cavalry Division had the only gunships in the region that could mount a rescue.

# CHAPTER 19

## Bangkok

Two of the children were dead.

The policewoman who had been catapulted backwards through the plate-glass window by a shotgun blast would lose her arm, but she would live. The fate of the other female officer and the five children who were kidnapped was still unknown.

Fletcher and Cordova sat before the plain, unassuming translator's station at Bangkok Police Headquarters. "I'm beginning to get a little sick of this place, Corky," the Snakeman admitted after the interpreter left to check on a teletype from CID in Tokyo. Uniformed officers walking past stared down at the two "detainees." "Everyone's giving us the eyeball as if it was *us* did all the damage!"

"I know, I know," Cordova agreed. "All we were trying to do was help. It's not your fault you drive like an idiot."

"Aw, shove it to the limit, then break it off, okay?"

They had chased after the three pickup trucks on foot until a taxi, swerving to miss them as they raced through a busy intersection, skidded up against a gutter curb and was commandeered by the two Americans.

Snakeman took over the wheel, and for nearly an hour they chased one of the trucks through Bangkok's narrow back alleys, knocking over vendors' stalls and sideswiping countless vehicles until the overheated brakes on the cab finally went out, and they crashed into a souvenir gift shop. It was a gift shop crowded with valuable jade and ivory statues, and ships constructed from blown glass, encased in special laquer-wood cases. Final tab: 600,000 *baht*. That amounted to slightly over 30,000 U.S. dollars.

All three trucks got away. The owner of the gift shop nearly shot them with a World War II carbine, and probably would have had several officers on foot patrol in the area not responded so quickly to the sound of precious antiques and artifacts breaking.

"Well, at least you're not AWOL." The translator returned waving a long teletype hardcopy over his head. "According to the Pacific Command people in Japan, anyway."

"I've already told you a hundred times," Fletcher said, "we're from The Nam. We come under the USARV or MACV brass, and they don't answer to nobody except Westy himself, who don't answer to nobody but el-Presidente, so you might as well—"

"If you're so convinced we should check with Saigon," the officer interrupted him, "then maybe we should. South Vietnam is closer, but the teletype will take even longer. Perhaps as much as forty-eight hours. Meanwhile, we would have to keep you detained in one of the holding cells, of course."

"Of course," Fletcher said sarcastically. Their Leave papers and R and R authorizations had mysteriously disappeared from their hotel room during their visit to the police family housing project. Fletcher's camera was also stolen, to make it look good.

"I think we're happy enough with the Tokyo teletype," Cordova cut in quickly as he stood. They had managed to ditch their counterfeit MP uniforms after crashing into the gift shop and prior to the arrival of Thai police, and Corky didn't want to have to talk with any military police from the Bangkok detachment.

"Then I think you'll agree it would probably be best if you

both returned to your R and R hotel"—the translator's smile seemed to shift back and forth beneath exhausted, bloodshot eyes—"and leave the detective work to us from this point on. Do I have your promise on that, gentlemen? Enjoy your last four nights in Thailand. Go sightseeing, take in a movie . . . even a floor show or two. Go down on Patpong and get laid, but please disassociate yourselves from this shooting incident. Murder in Bangkok can be a very bloody business."

"So can death in Phung Du," Fletcher rolled up a newspaper and slipped it under his arm without expounding on the comment.

"Can't you tell us what you've found out?" Cordova was suddenly not so eager to sever their ties with the case. "I mean . . . what the hell is it all about?"

"It is totally unrelated to the Prasertkwan and Chatsungnoen shootings, if that's what you were getting at," the translator claimed.

"Totally unrelated?" Cordova didn't believe it. "How can you stand there and say—"

"Just another example of the communist insurgency problem in our country, I'm afraid." The interpreter's shoulders seemed to sag in resignation. His hands came up in a gesture of surrender, palms out. "But what can we do but hope Thailand will someday be as free and safe a democratic society as the United States?" He spoke sincerely, though Cordova and Fletcher both read the cynicism on his face. Corky seemed to see the reflections of a million New York City muggings in the translator's eyes.

"Have you received any ransom demands regarding the children?" Cordova persisted. "Any information about the policewoman they took?"

"It has only been a matter of hours." The translator gestured toward the door. "Now why don't you go out there, climb into a taxi or *baht* bus, and go see a Thai kick-boxing match."

"What about the license-plate number we supplied you with?" Cordova decided he was not ready to leave after all.

222

"We busted our buns tryin' to get that sucker for you, and the least you can do is tell us who that fucking truck was registered to!"

"You're lucky we haven't charged you with damaging the gift shop," the translator countered. "Do you have that much spare cash in your pocket, my friend? Luckily, the district commander was impressed with your desire to get involved with the initial crime scene drama. And, since the safety of police officers was involved, he has 'seen to it' that the shopowner has been compensated. I truly think you should count your blessings and get on with your vacation, *Mister* Cordova."

"The number," Corky replied softly.

"We have overlooked the fact that you keep ending up involved with women on our department who turn up dead or missing, and—"

"Now *that's* a crock, and you know it!" Fletcher defended his buddy.

"The license-plate number." Cordova walked over to the translator's desk as he sat down behind it. The American braced his hands on the desk top's edges and leaned down close to the Thai's face. "Just tell me who the fucking number comes back to, or I'm going to the *Bangkok Post*. They've got a lot of nosy *phalangs* who work there, and I'll bet they'd just love to jump in your shit, *Khop*! I smell funny business here, and so will they."

"Actually . . ." The officer didn't seem the least bit intimidated. Either that, or years working the low criminal subcultures and underworld had left him a good actor. ". . . We don't think you copied that number down accurately, I'm afraid."

"What?" Cordova lifted a fist slightly, wanting to pound it against the desk top, but he restrained himself.

"The plate cames back to a subject by the name of Anukul Thaweekarn of Chiang Mai, so you must be mistaken."

"Why do you think I'm mistaken?" Cordova raised his voice. "I know for a *fact* I got the right number. I *memorized*

223

it and I *carved* it into my hand!" he raised his palm to show the razor-thin scabs again where he had applied the P-38 C-rations opener hanging from his dog-tags chain.

"You saw three pickup trucks pull up in front of the pharmacy, and their occupants begin shooting."

"Right."

"The license-plate number you supplied us with comes back on a four-door sedan."

Cordova was not discouraged. "Big fucking deal!" he said, throwing his hands in the air. "Do you think cop killers are gonna give a damn about improper registration violations? I'm no police officer, but I know the first thing I'd do if I was going to shoot up the town and kidnap some kids would be to switch the plates on my vehicle with a stolen set!"

"Thus far we don't have a . . . 'cop killing' on our hands, Mr. Cordova. Let's keep our fingers crossed that Patrolwoman Samphaognaun will eventually turn up alive and unharmed, all right?"

Several uniformed officers had stopped what they were doing in the headquarters building and paused to gather behind the two Americans in an intimidating semicircle. "Come on"—Fletcher grabbed Corky's arm—"let's get outta here. The man's right. We've done enough."

"The fucking brakes overheated and went out," Cordova reminded him.

"I know. Let's just leave the police work to people who get paid to do it."

"You've done more than would ever have been expected from an uninvolved onlooker . . . a private citizen." The translator patted Cordova on the shoulder, but he knocked the man's hand away. The Thai did not seem offended, but merely kept on talking as if nothing had happened. "Especially a foreign national. Bangkok Metro and the Thai National Police extend our sincerest thanks, Mr. Cordova."

"Fine, fine!" Snakeman grabbed Corky's wrist and began pulling him toward the door. "*Sawatdee*, and all that."

224

"*Sawatdee*, Mr. Fletcher. "*Khop-koon mock, Khop!*"

"*My-bpen-fuckin'-ry, Khop! My-bpen-ry!*"

"Those fuckwads ran an enema in one ear and out the other," Cordova said after they'd left the headquarters building. "There's something smellin' damned fishy in the Kingdom of Siam, Snakeman, and it ain't Thai pussy!"

"Don't get so bent outta shape about everything, Cork. Like the Man said: Let's trot on down to Patpong and get our flutes cleaned again. Say! Wasn't that Ding character supposed to get you an eighteen-year-old cherry girl for tonight?"

"I've kinda lost track of what's supposed to be happenin', Snake, you know?"

"Aw, don't get feelin' sorry for yourself and pullin' a sober on me, pal." Fletcher kicked an empty *Singha* beer bottle as they approached an intersection, and they watched it ricochet along the gutter and bounce off the side of a fast-moving police car.

"Oh, motherfucking wonderful." Cordova wanted to sink into a manhole, but the unit kept going, even accelerating after it passed through the intersection. Sparks flew from the Peugeot's undercarriage as it took the dips at a good forty kilometers an hour, and the officers only glanced over at them for a second, hardly noticing the thump against one of the back doors.

"They must be on a hot run," Fletcher sighed, "goin' to a call or somethin'."

"'Or something.'" Cordova frowned for Snakeman's benefit. "Fucking lucky for us, *huh*?"

"Hey, so cut me some everlovin' slack, okay slick? Jesus! I'm only subhuman. . . ." The Snakeman flagged down a taxi, but Cordova kept walking.

"Sayonara," he told Fletcher. "Have an 'everlovin' good one."

"That's Tokyo, honorable dipshit-san. Here they say *sawatdee!* Aren't you coming back to the hotel?"

"Naw. . ." Cordova kicked another empty beer bottle. It

225

shattered against the side of a parked troop carrier, and he winced. "I need to take a long walk. Gotta think this thing through, Snakeman. Go on without me."

"Okay." Fletcher got into the front seat of the taxi. "If you say so."

A few seconds later, Cordova noticed that the cab was coasting alongside him. Fletcher's smiling face was sticking out the passenger-side window.

Cordova glanced up ahead to see if there was any oncoming traffic, then remembered that driving in Thailand is done on the left side of the road—the opposite of South Vietnam and, of course, Hometown U.S.A.

"If Ding-dong or whatever his name is pulled through for us and delivered the dame, can I have her?" Fletcher asked with an ear-to-ear grin.

"Sure." Cordova frowned on seeing the glowing roach hanging from the cab driver's lips.

"Thanks, pal." Fletcher smacked his own lips loudly.

The taxi started to pull away, Cordova said, "Hey, Fletch!" and the brake lights glowed red.

"Yah?" Snakeman stuck his head out the window again.

"If she shows, save a sample so we can take it back to Nelson."

"A 'sample?'" Fletcher's smile faded.

"Yah. You know: A pussy hair sample. For his collection."

Fletcher laughed. "You gotta be kidding."

"No, seriously." Cordova wore a straight face.

"Hell, Corky—you know as well as I do these Thai cunts are smooth as peaches. Where'm I gonna come up with some genuine pubic hair?"

"They got hair, Snakeman." Corky seemed adamant. "You just gotta look in the right places."

Cordova smiled for the first time. "Bribe the housegirls, if you have to. I just don't wanna leave Bangkok without a contribution to Nasty Nel's egg carton."

"Uh, right . . ." Fletcher waved and ducked back inside.

226

"Don't rub it raw."

"Nebbah happen, GI!" The taxi pulled away from the curb and turned down a side street, heading for the Honey Hotel.

"Crazy fuck." Cordova smiled to himself as he watched the taxi's taillights fade into the growing gloom. He and the Snakeman had been through a lot together, but he would see this thing through on his own if he had to.

Cordova walked for two hours, making his way to Sukhumvit as the eight o'clock movies were letting out and young Thai couples and tourists crowded the sidewalks, heading for the one ice-cream parlor in miles.

He basked in the multi-hued neon signs, trying to lose his thoughts beyond the strange Thai script, but the faces of the Thai policewomen kept returning to him—the heavily made-up faces he had first seen at the airport terminal—and he couldn't enjoy the carefree sounds and tantalizing sights and smells for long.

He purchased a stick of Malay *satay* and munched on the spicy slices of beef, covered with rich Malaccan sauce, as he walked through a late-night, open-air bazaar, complete with snake charmers and brass gong salesmen. But it was at a corner newsstand that the bold headlines caught his eye and the events of the last couple of days returned to haunt him.

### SON OF SLAIN POLICEWOMAN
### BELIEVED KIDNAPPED BY SHAN ARMY
### GANGSTERS

Sources within the Thai National Police requesting anonymity have told this reporter that their primary suspects in the shooting of a Bangkok-Metro policewoman and the disappearance of a second officer late last night are linked to members of the Shan United Revolutionary Army, based in northern Thailand and believed responsible for much of the opium traffic plaguing the Golden Triangle area of Burma, Thailand, and Laos. Five children were also kidnapped by the hoodlums, using three American-made pickup trucks.

The children were taken from the vicinity of a Thai Police family housing project after a shoot-out and bazaar chase which witnesses claim involved U.S. military police. American officials at MAC-THAI's Bangkok Command refused to confirm or deny this. Sources close to the investigation have revealed that a license number connected to the crime registers to a Anukul Thaweekarn, well-known reputed drug kingpin with headquarters in Chiang Mai and connections to the Shan United Army, an offshoot of the SURA.

One police official who did not want to be identified, stated that one of the five children kidnapped at the shoot-out in front of Aeng's Pharmacy at the corner of Thai Wang and Sanam Chai roads was the son of slain policewoman B. Prasertkwan, whose shooting death 48 hours earlier near Wat Arun remains unsolved. Police have not been able to tie the two cases together, and as of yet have refused to comment on reports a ransom for the kidnapped child and policewoman received this morning had been discounted as a hoax.

When Cordova finished reading the short article, he knew immediately what had to be done. On the flight over from Saigon, he had noticed on the Bangkok travelguide map that a railway ran north to Chiang Mai. It was a popular tourist resort, with many splendid temples and exciting elephant roundups. The area was only a few miles south of Burma,

228

and well known for its drug wars between feuding opium warlords.

Cordova would return to his hotel room, pick up the booklet, and take a cab down to the train depot. He could read up on the mountainous northern regions of the country during the overnight, eighteen-hour trip. And he could formulate a plan of action.

It was time to pay a visit to Chiang Mai. He had a gut feeling Sugar Prasertkwan's killer, and his own destiny, awaited him there.

# CHAPTER 20

## Phung Du Village

Larson yelled until his lungs ached, but the guards would not stop. Again, the wooden cane struck the soles of his bare feet, Larson screamed, and his captors laughed and giggled.

His arms were tied back by the elbows with strong twine, and he was lifted off the ground until one of his shoulders was dislocated, but his pleas for medical help went unheeded. "Each time you scream, we hit your feet ten more," the guard warned.

Larson bit into his swollen lower lip until it bled, thinking back on how relieved he'd been when Buchanan ordered the MPs to allow him to accompany the rest of the team into battle. Now, he wished he was sitting in the safe security of a Long Binh stockade cell. Even solitary confinement would be better than this.

They had led him through the rain forests for two nights and three days to reach these mountainside caves, yet even a disoriented Larson could tell they were going around in circles.

He hadn't seen the white deserter or Zulu-blooper since they split up two or three hours before reaching the caves. His torturers consisted only of Vietnamese. Strange as it seemed, he hoped desperately the wild-looking black and his dazed companion would return. Surely they would stop all this mistreatment.

Larson knew why they were beating him. It wasn't as if he was a big Intelligence catch. He didn't possess any top secrets vital to U.S. national security. It was revenge, pure and simple.

When they had captured him, Larson was wearing a flak jacket with the Hog Heaven patch sewn across the back: proof positive he had machine-gunned over a hundred of the enemy into oblivion from the hatch of a prowling Huey. They were going to have a little fun with him before they sent him up the Ho Chi Minh Trail to the Hanoi Hilton.

"Enough."

He thought he heard a soft, feminine voice through the sonic waves of pain bouncing back and forth between his temples. A very, very feminine voice—seductive, in fact. Seductive in the manner of a woman saving her man from death at the hands of another spurned lover. Strange thoughts, but Larson even thought he could place the voice, could see her smooth, amber body naked in the warm, monsoon rain, somewhere in his not-so-distant past.

Tricks, he told himself. Tricks of the mind. But then she spoke again, and he knew it was not a hallucination. He had tasted the breasts that went with that cool, detached voice. And they had been delicious.

"Leave us."

When she cut the ropes holding him suspended from the ceiling, Larson struck the earthen floor heavily. His entire body had been numb for days, and in his mind, he fell in slow motion—even saw himself bouncing back off the ground like a ball of feathers, unaffected by gravity and pain and hands bound behind the back. But then he felt the earth shake as it snapped up, striking him, and his separated shoulder felt like it would split his back right down the middle. Excruciating pain lanced down through his body, but then it faded almost as quickly. He went numb again, and he knew that was a signal from his brain that he was in big trouble.

"Long time no see, sucker."

She stood over him, legs braced apart, feet on either side of his face. She was wearing black calico pants, not a dress or skirt, but she still painted as sensuous a picture for his pleasure as ever.

Slowly, Larson was able to focus on the jutting points of her breasts within the harsh camouflage blouse, and then the face looking down between the firm slopes.

"It . . . has . . . been . . . long . . . time," Shawn said painfully, his thoughts drifting back to the island and its waterfall.

"Yes, quite a long time. So small a world. Did you ever think we would meet again?"

"I . . . I certainly didn't think . . . you . . . were running with hard-core VC." He saw himself aboard *Pegasus*, riding beside The Stork fleeing the war with eight whores in the cabin behind them, bound for paradise off the coast of South Vietnam, their own uninhabited island. Yet it turned out to be someone else's hiding place too: A communist soldier had also deserted from the war, and picked Hon Trau as his sanctuary, and people started turning up dead in the night. First the prostitutes, one at a time, then eventually *Peg*'s first and best pilot, Warrant Officer Krutch. The Professor was a skilled enough pilot —thanks to hundreds of hours in the cockpit with The Stork on ash-'n'-trash details—and he managed to get the chopper and two of the women back to the Vietnamese mainland. During the crash landing, one girl was killed, and the other—the long-haired beauty standing over him now—had darted off through the rain forest without waiting for him.

"Your . . . name." Larson was still trying to catch his breath as he lay on his side. "It was . . ."

"Vau, Xinh, Y-Von, Kim—take pick, GI." She laughed an evil little laugh. "VC girls have many names."

"Ahhh, yes."

232

"I think you are going to die here, GI." She nudged him backwards slightly with the toes protruding from her tire-tread sandals. "You look weak. I do not think you will last very much longer." For no reason Larson could think of, she placed the bottom of the sandal against his face and rubbed it back and forth, as if wiping off the water buffalo dung from between the black treads.

"You . . . could . . . help me." Larson's voice was a harsh rasp.

"I don't think so—'Professor,' was it? Yes, Professor. I don't think I hold the memories dear enough to help you today, foolish man. You should have stayed An Khe, where safer."

"I . . . saved you, Vau. Remember the island? I took you away from there. I . . . saved . . . *you*."

Trinh Thi Kim threw her head back, filling the cramped chamber with a wicked laugh. "You!" She pointed down at him. "You brought me back from Hon Trau before I could finish my mission."

"Your . . . mission?" Larson realized the truth now, as if for the first time. "You were the one doing the . . . You killed Hal?"

"And now I am going to help them kill you. Eventually. More slowly."

"But the wildman. The wildman . . . on the island."

"An inconvenience, who just happened to get in the way. He served his purpose."

"And the girls? You killed . . . all . . . the . . . girls?" Larson was running out of breath again.

"They were a disgrace to all Vietnamese!" She spat in the dust beside Shawn's face. "Selling their bodies to foreigners! I enjoyed hacking their hearts out." Her tone became twisted, as if she was trying to convince herself more than the American. "I enjoyed burying them up to their necks in the sand." She forced another laugh. "I can still remember how the little sand

233

crabs were dancing about in their eye sockets the next morning!"

"But you, Vau. What about you?" Larson waited for her eyes to drop from the ceiling of the limestone cave and focus on his again. "You slept with the foreigners, too. And you did not charge a single *dong* coin."

For several seconds, she stared down at Shawn Larson in silence, contemplating what he had said. And then, desperately searching for a way to save face, she grinned that evil flash of teeth again. "And I am not going to charge 'a single *dong* coin' tonight, either." Her fingers loosened the rope holding up her pantaloons. The trousers dropped in fluffy piles around her scarred, jungle-girl ankles. "I'm going to suffocate you, Mr. Professor." Her English grew choppy as she became excited. "I am going to suffocate you to death, slowly, but surely. Maybe you die now . . . tonight. Maybe I save you for long time. Kill little bit tonight, little bit tomorrow night. But event'lly you no can breathe anymore, and you go to meet the Buddha."

She stepped from the pile of black cotton at her feet, never breaking eye contact as she slowly dropped into a squat, forcing her crotch down onto the helpless prisoner's face.


"Is he strong enough, yet?"

"I don't know. The guards have been rough, but he is as defiant as that first day at Phung Du."

"That is a good sign."

"I suppose."

"What about his toes?"

"They are healing."

"Good. You should have never gone that far."

"I could not resist."

"You knew he was going to have to make a long trek to

234

Laos. You are lucky they did not become infected. You could lose favor over that."

"But they didn't, and I have not. Now what else would you like to discuss? Or did you climb all the way up here just to squeeze my breasts?"

Larson listened to Kim and the NVA sergeant giggling as they talked about him at the mouth of the cave. He glanced down at his toes and shuddered again. He shuddered each time he saw the swollen, scab-covered appendages at the end of his feet. Kim had not really been the one to pull his toenails out, but she had been there, observing from the shadows, and now she was taking credit for it.

His legs still possessed the strength to carry his weight, but several ribs felt cracked, if not entirely broken, and both his shoulders had been dislocated by the guards—dislocated, and left that way. As punishment for biting Kim during their first session three days earlier. Biting the soft folds of flesh where her thighs came together. The soft folds of flesh she had tried to "suffocate" him with.

"We are moving out tonight. After sunset." He heard the NVA sergeant breathing hard with the words as a wet, sliding sound—flesh slapping against flesh—reached his ears. She was on her back for him again. Larson slowly shook his head, smiling only in his thoughts as his face, heavy as rock, dropped to the ground from fatigue. It was becoming their daily ritual. Insults just inside the mouth of the cave, a short discussion about his own condition, then a quickie boom-boom session.

"I wish you were coming with us." The sergeant's voice became stronger again, more confident, as their movements grew slower, less desperate. They were pausing, making it last, taunting and teasing each other so that it would not end so quickly this time.

"My place is with the team, here in the south."

"This trip will keep me in Hanoi several months."

"As you warned."

"You will not miss me?" He must have done something special with his hips, Larson decided, because she groaned with surprise and delight. It was a long, satisfied moan, from deep within her.

"Yes . . . I . . . will miss . . . you."

Larson was leaning against an ammo crate, his back to them. The cave was large, as big as the armory in An Khe, he reflected, and small water-covered tunnels seemed to run off in the dark. But they were small tunnels—too small for a man his size. Only bats lived down there. He had heard them squealing after the sun went down. Bats and other cave dwellers that creeped and crawled while he slept, trying to nibble through the scabs on his toes.

The entrance to the limestone oddity was about fifty feet away, he judged. They kept him blindfolded most of the time, but he used his ears a lot. His ears told him the cave's mouth was high up off the ground. Probably in the side of a cliff. The wind, and singing birds told him that. There was no ocean breeze, however. No hum of waves crashing against the beach. The South China Sea was far away now. They were considerably inland. Probably Laos. Maybe even North Vietnam.

He had heard them talking. Other prisoners were being taken to offshoot tributaries of the Ho Chi Minh Trail for the long journey north. A P.O.W. camp was the ultimate destination, he overheard the NVA sergeant telling Kim. Either in Hanoi or near the Chinese border. The NVA sergeant had made the trek several times, but many of the prisoners—and even some of the weaker, malnourished soldiers—died from malaria and disease along the way. Bombing runs by the American planes—Rolling Thunder—took its toll on the foot convoys too, even though they walked beneath the thick triple-canopy of the rain forest most of the time.

Larson did not look forward to the journey. He had heard

236

stories about the vicious Minh Trail from some of the Kit Carson scouts, and he wanted nothing to do with it. But who was he to protest. Shawn Larson was now a prisoner of war, and no amount of self-pity or regret was going to change that.

It was too late to change one's mind and get off the merry-go-round of war just because you were dizzy. From now on, every waking moment was going to be pure hell, every breath was going to bring him that much closer to another session with the guards. He was going to be the highlight of the trip, their punching bag of boredom. He hoped it was not going to be a long journey. The Professor had read somewhere that half the male population of the North Vietnamese military was homosexual, and he did not want to be anybody's pretty-boy.

"Son of a diseased dog!" The edge of a boot connected with his temple, and Larson felt himself sinking from the plains of reality again, far away from the pain, almost escaping, only to have them break his fall with more kicks.

"He is daydreaming again!"

"Daydreaming? Who gave the son of a diseased dog permission to skate?"

"He was thinking about *her*!"

"The one they call Xinh?"

"Yes!"

"Ahhh, yes. I have spent my hours alone thinking about her, too."

"It is not allowed."

"I agree. It shouldn't be." And they both kicked him again, laughed, and walked away.

Larson rolled over, feeling his own blood coat the side of his face. He wasn't sure how much he had imagined. Voices of the two men who kicked him were real enough—but had it happened yesterday? The day before? Did he really listen to Trinh Tri Kim discussing his future with the NVA sergeant, before they made love within the lip of the cave's mouth, or had that been another trick of his mind?

237

Larson felt himself curling up into the fetal position. He felt the tears in his eyes, and the pain lancing through every fiber of his being, almost shorting out his thoughts. But he clung to the last vestiges of control, refusing to die yet wishing it was over. Finished. So he could get on with his next life.

# CHAPTER 21

## Highway 13, North of Saigon

Treat Brody had no idea what he would do if he ever caught up with the bandits. He had no firearms, and his head was still throbbing from the rifle butt against the temple. His vision shifted from blurred to super-sharp and back again, and with each footfall he nearly stumbled. He feared he would soon black out again.

When he reached the tree line at the edge of the roadway, he heard screams from one of the women, and the thought of Dep being abused spurred him on. He pulled a shaft of bamboo from the ground and slammed it against a tree trunk until it shattered along the end, leaving a sharp splinter. Now he had a weapon, but it was still no match for their automatic rifles. If he caught up with them, he would have to fight dirty. He resolved himself to the probability that he would most probably be dead within the hour, if not much sooner.

His ears perked for a moment, and he thought he heard distant rotors—a helicopter. But this was Vietnam, and there were millions of gunships, and none of them knew about him or his troubles.

Row upon row of the neatly aligned rubber trees extended up over a hilltop, and he kept to these after forcing his way through the wall of bamboo and gnarled tamarind. He began running, ignoring the taste of blood in his mouth, and when he reached the top of the hill, he tripped and fell against the earth, gasping for air.

A wide valley spread out before his eyes as he gazed down the other side of the hill. The rubber plantation gave way to lush rain forest and wild jungle across rolling hills for as far as the eye could see, but there was a small clearing at the bottom of the mound he lay atop, and the insurgents had stopped by some motorcycles hidden there.

Brody could see Dep clearly. She was standing tall and proud in the middle of a circle of laughing men, her breasts jutting straight out. The gangleader had a long bowie knife out, and was running the edge back and forth between the slopes of her breasts as his followers cheered him on. The outline of Dep's ribs could be seen faintly as she took each breath, heart pounding, fingernails extended. She would claw their eyes out before she would let anyone touch her!

She was taunted and teased in Vietnamese, many of the hoodlums exposing themselves to her as their gangleader ran the gleaming blade along her flesh, and although Brody could not understand all the words, he knew what they were saying.

"Pretty girl likes foreign dicks! Thinks she's too good for local boys."

"Thinks she's a banana, huh?" they jeered. "Yellow on outside, white on inside!"

"She needs to be put in her place! She needs a yellow dick in that smart mouth of hers—teach her some respect!"

"She needs a yellow dick between her legs, too, and wherever else there's room, to remind her. To remind her what a yellow dick feels like!"

"She needs to be stuffed by a *lot* of yellow dicks!"

"Yah!" they were all chanting now as belts flew apart and trousers began dropping.

"Then quit dicking around and *do it!*" one of the punks shouted.

240

Dep wore little jewelry, but she did keep a modest gold chain Treat had given her draped around her neck. The gang-leader reached out and grabbed hold of it, ripped it away. The necklace cut into her flesh, and she kicked him in the groin. He dropped to one knee, but managed to rise up again. And now he was no longer just amused. He was angry. Very angry.

The South Vietnamese gunship exploded over the treetops at the same time Brody began charging down the hillside, yelling at the top of his lungs. He truly thought this would be the last great escapade, that the hooligans would cut him down in his tracks before he even made it down through the trees. But now a huge metal bird with helmeted parasites clinging to the Chopper 1 sidepockets beneath its wings was hovering over the clearing, showering bullets down on the laager of parked motorcycles.

The Arvins in the burning troop transport *had* managed to radio for help during the ambush, before they were fried by the Molotov cocktails. They *had* contacted one of the Huey pilots, and three more choppers were on the way.

The insurgents completely forgot about Dep as soon as the doorgunner overhead began firing down on their Hondas. They scattered through the rubber trees as one scooter's gas tank exploded with a terrific metal-warping roar, but soon the air was one single chopping vibration, and more helicopters were setting down on all sides. Infantrymen armed with auto-matic rifles, grenade launchers and machine guns fanned out, and a fourth craft, a smaller, black Loach, pranged across the clearing, and a stocky Vietnamese holding onto a vicious at-tack dog's leash hopped out. The barking animal quickly caught the scent, and went after those bandits who hadn't already been rounded up.

Brody stood in the middle of the clearing hugging Dep close as they both watched the swirl of activity taking place all around them. He had never seen such a precision operation involving only ARVN troops before, and was genuinely im-pressed. He owed their lives to these soldiers, in fact, but

241

none of the commandos were checking on him or Dep. The young couple obviously seemed safe and sound, so the rescue team was attending to the women cowering alone and terrified in the bushes, eyes wild, minds out to lunch.

"I love you, Bro-dee!" Dep clung to him, her arms wrapped around his neck as if she would never let go.

"I love you, too, honey-san." His hand smoothed her unruly hair back down, over and over. "I love you, too."

"You saved Dep!" The tears were flowing freely now. "You say Cholon you woul' die for Dep and now I see with my own eyes! I see you run down hill, want to fight these men! You want do this for me. No man ever care before."

"It's over, now, Dep. Don't worry. We're okay. Now we can continue on to Quan Loi."

"Where?"

She really meant it. Where? She had no idea where they were, or what they were doing there in the middle of the Michelin rubber plantation. He did not think Dep even realized that she was naked from the waist up.

Brody took his shirt off and draped it around her shoulders. "We'll go see your sister now, Dep. In Quan Loi."

She was still trembling, but the wild streak left her eyes, and when she looked at him, Brody knew she would be okay after a few nights in his arms, together, alone, safe beneath a roof away from war, yet still in the eye of the storm.

Several soldiers were returning to the clearing with the gangleader in custody. Brody wanted to rush over, disarm one of the soldiers if he could, and kill the man. His mind rehearsed the deed a thousand times over in the mere blink of an eye, but in the end, he did nothing. They already had him handcuffed, and were leading him over to one of the helicopters.

His nose was smashed flat, and one of his arms looked crooked and broken too, but the worst was still ahead for this prisoner. He had killed a disabled vet, back in the bus, and was ringleader of the gang that torched a truckload of Arvins. It was a long chopper ride back to Saigon.

Dep and Brody watched the gunship ascend in a brisk, businesslike manner toward the dark storm clouds floating overhead. Dep's pained, somber eyes followed the craft for a long time, but Brody looked away.

He did not want to see the man step out the hatch, and have to remember his flailing arms and legs.

"Do you think you would ever want marry Dep?"

Brody kissed the tip of her nose, but did not answer immediately. He would make her earn every word. "The thought has crossed my mind," he finally admitted.

"And would it be Buddhist marriage, or Christian?"

"Well, I am Catholic, you know, but . . ."

"You? You are a Catholic, Bro-dee?" She stared at him incredulously.

He stared over at the blood stains on the bus bench across the aisle. "Yah, sure. What's wrong with that?"

"Well, I just didn' think . . . you just don' act like . . . I would think you were man with no faith, no religion."

"I believe in the power of the jungle and the power of pussy," he said with a serious face.

Dep ignored the taunt. "How many children we should have do you think?" Her pidgin sentence structure brought the grin back.

"Oh, a hundred, at least. To plow the rice paddies I'm going to buy down in Mytho. We're gonna be reapin' and sowin' twenty-four hours a day, rakin' in the P. They can work shifts, of course. Twelve on and twelve off."

"Of course." Dep smiled up at him with a wink. "But what if I bore you only daughters. Would you be angry?"

"Not if they're cute. I mean, if they have their mother's good looks."

"You would open whorehouse instead of rice paddy?" Mock hurt crept into her features.

"Of course not. But I would invite all the strongest, most handsome men from the surrounding villages around as soon as they became of age. Then we could marry them off, and become secure in our old age."

"Marry them off to wealthy men only. City men would be best," she decided.

"Okay, fine. City slickers. I just hope we could find some who would want to marry Amerasian girls with long noses." Brody elbowed Dep lightly, and she laughed. "Would you still love *me* if they had blond hair instead of jet-black hair, like yours?" His fingers slid through the long, thick strands fanning across her shoulders. It felt so cool to the touch, and was one of his favorite pastimes. Brody loved to spend time late in the evening brushing her hair, too, sometimes for nearly an hour or more, as they talked about their dreams and future together.

"They will not have blond hair," she advised him, "though I would not be upset if happen."

"Oh? And how are you so sure?"

"Already check with soothsayer," she revealed, gauging his expression from the corners of her eyes.

"Soothsayer?" Brody scratched the stubble on his chin and rubbed at the tender bruise on his cheek. "You mean, like a fortuneteller?"

"Yes. In Cholon. Old woman, everyone our block go to her many years now. She have special sticks."

"Sticks?" For some reason, Brody thought of the nightsticks MPs carried.

"Sticks with future written on them. Old mama-san keep them in magic can, shake them around after she feel bumps on your head and check hand lines. Shake them around and let them fall on table."

"Ah, yes." He nodded. "I've seen them in action before. Up north, in Pleiku, I think it was. At the USO. The old Viet

244

dude who hacked off our hair also read our fortunes from the sticks—for a price, of course."

Dep frowned as a picture of the old man in Pleiku formed in her mind. "How much?" she asked.

"Five hundred P, maybe a little more."

"Rip-off."

"I'm sure. But it was fun. He told me that, since I was in Indochina now, and it is Vietnamese custom that a man can have more than one wife if he so chooses—"

Dep elbowed him hard, and Brody responded with a painful groan that was not feigned. "Hey!" he complained, tasting the blood in his mouth again. "I just been through the wringer a couple hours back. Be gentle, okay?"

"Hmmph!" Dep folded her arms beneath her breasts and pretended to watch row after row of rubber trees passing by out the windows on the opposite side of the bus.

"Well, don't you want to hear what he said?"

"Not if have to do with Numba Two wife, Bro-dee."

"Hmmph!" he mimicked her, groaning again when it hurt to fold his arms.

Dep locked eyes with Treat. "You *American* man, lover. Not Vietnamese! No need follow Vietnamese custom, okay?"

"Guess I'll just have to quit walking on your back every night after we do it, then, huh?"

Dep's smile returned, and she grasped his arm again as the thoughts flooded her. She always felt so good after they made love and Treat spent another half hour or more massaging her back. Then, on nights when he'd had some *ba-muoi-ba* or rice wine, walking along her spine, China style, kneading the soreness from her back with his toes. She preferred not to wonder what woman in his past taught him the rare and somewhat odd talent. "That is not Vietnamese custom," she told him. "You have Dep's permission to continue."

"Oh, that's mighty tight of you."

"What?"

"Nebbah mind." The straight face saved him from a knuckle punch.

She snuggled up to him and stuck the tip of her tongue into his ear. "Dep never have man before give her massage almost every night, Bro-dee."

"Knock it off." He tried to push her away, but she clung to his arm.

"Really." She licked his cheek once, then kissed his nose. "Bro-dee spoil Dep."

"You more than make up for it." A grin crept across his face finally. "Magic mouth."

Dep did not seem to be listening anymore. She was staring at the bloodstains on the bench seat across the aisle from theirs.

"Anyway," she said after a long moment of silent reflection, "soothsayer say I have two children someday. Maybe more, if want, but two fo' shoo're. She say have black hair and black eyes, same Dep. Same face. Same eyes."

"Sounds like your everyday, pure-blooded, all-Viet kinda kid." He smiled down at her. "Very nice."

"Very nice?" She looked up at him with her eyes growing large and sad. "Bro-dee not get mad if baby-sans have face, eyes, nose same-same Dep?" She took hold of the outer edges of her eyes and pulled on them slightly, pouting.

"Stop that." He was not amused. "Right now the most important thing in our future is seeing to it your long-lost sister is okay, and somehow paying next month's rent without cashing in one of my gold coins, okay? We'll worry about baby-sans when and if they ever decide to tap-dance into our hearts."

Dep sat straighter as she spotted a police checkpoint up ahead. They were nearing Quan Loi.

They did not get a chance to see much of Quan Loi. It was already dark when their bus wound its way through the conglomeration of ramshackle huts and two-story tenements rising along the town's southern edge.

Dep pulled on the stop wire after they passed the first wide

246

avenue intersecting Thunder Road. She seemed to know right where to go.

Dep grabbed hold of his hand as the bus pulled over to the side of the highway and led him down the aisle to the front doors. She exchanged a long goodbye with the bus driver. He still seemed dazed and shaken from the robbery, and sounded very apologetic to Dep, but Brody could not understand all the conversation. As they climbed down the steps to the ground, the driver smiled at Brody and produced a thumbs-up. Brody reached back in and shook the man's hand.

"I take it you know where we're going?" Brody caught up with Dep just as she was about to start down into a maze of dark alleys. She was glancing back and forth between unpainted or fading street signs and a crude map her sister had apparently drawn on the back of the letter.

"Follow map, Bro-dee." She spoke in a low tone. Nearly every dwelling they passed seemed dark. Now and then Treat spotted a candle or lantern burning in a back room. "Play game, just like army."

"Well, at least you can read." He laughed. "That should say something for the IQs of our future—"

She placed a finger against his lips. "Not talk so loud, okay, Bro-dee? Dep no want anymore trouble with anymore people today."

"No sweat." His lack of energy forced him to comply with her wishes. Besides, Brody's quick wit had abandoned him, it seemed. "But I'm pretty sure we're safe. Ain't this an Arvin town?"

"Daytime only."

Brody allowed a giggle to escape. "Oh. I think I've heard that one before. The night belongs to Charlie, right?"

"Sometime true. Saigon, Cholon, Mytho, *bic*? But Quan Loi true *all* the time."

"I see. Even with the Arvin garrison here, eh?"

"They patrol daytime. Stay barracks nighttime."

"You know quite a bit, for a Cholon chick." He draped an

247

arm over her shoulder. Rather than brush it off or push him away, as she usually did in public, Dep took hold of his fingers with her right hand and squeezed them affectionately.

"Thank you for save Dep today, honey-san," she whispered as helicopter rotors beat against the sticky heat pressing down on Quan Loi, and flares floated down through the night sky several miles in front of them, directly in line with their path.

"My pleasure." He kissed the edge of her ear—something he'd often do without warning, which he knew she hated— then suddenly plunged as much of his tongue in as he could.

A muffled squeal left her, and she slapped him lightly, slipping loose. "Don't!" she demanded.

"Let's find another clump of bushes overlooking a river, what do you say, honey-san?" he teased her.

She was comparing her map with another intersection, but vandals had torn the street signs off the pole long ago. "I think this is it."

They started down another narrow side street. At the bottom of the hill below, dozens of yellow lights extended off into the darkness, forming a sort of box-shaped perimeter that Brody estimated was about a mile square. "That would be the garrison," he surmised.

"And I think this is where Lin live." Dep smiled, pleased with the three-story apartment building rising through the night mist in front of them. A high, concrete wall, topped with coiled strands of concertina wire, encircled the housing compound.

"Looks like a bunch o' giant cracker boxes," Brody observed. He judged there to be about twenty or so units in each building.

"Crackers?" Dep pulled open an iron-grill gate without any trouble.

Warning bells sounded inside Brody's head: all the barbed wire and glass shards, yet they leave the gates unlocked. But he didn't have the energy to worry about it. There were plenty

248

of apartment complexes back in the states that were just as lax. It would have been nice to at least find a sleeping guard, but the concrete kiosk inside the gate was empty and filled with trash bags. "Well, let's get this over with and find out what your kid sister Lin's gotten her *ying-yang* into this time."

# CHAPTER 22

## Chiang Mai, Thailand

He thought it would take longer to convince Snakeman to accompany him north into the hills along the Burmese frontier, but the off-duty doorgunner was tiring of the unlimited supply of Thai women and itching for some action. Burma was communist, the last Fletcher had heard, and he'd just love to mix it up with some of Ho Chi Minh's cousins. "I never expected all the goddamned 'skeeters, though, Corky-san!" He slapped as another one landed on the back of his neck. "This is worse than those nights in An Khe when we had LP duty in the middle of that swamp, remember?"

"Yah, I remember." Cordova rubbed more bug repellent across the exposed parts of his skin before rolling over inside the curtained-off berth. "But I'd just as soon reminisce later, if you don't mind. I haven't slept in about forty-eight hours."

"Suit yourself." Fletcher opened the curtain of his bottom berth just enough to let air from the squeaking ceiling fan in. "But I don't know how anyone can sleep with these kamikaze divebombers on red alert." He slapped at another huge mosquito.

The overnight express had left Bangkok's train depot at eight o'clock. One of the porters told them the 500-mile trip along winding mountain track would take eighteen hours, but the locomotive broke down twice, and they had already spent two nights sleeping in the train. Cordova hoped to spend these last few hours of darkness in a blank, dreamless void. Fletcher had orders to wake him at dawn.

Snakeman didn't have to carry them out. The early morning Chiang-Mai chill thrust Cordova from his berth with a start. "Where—" he started to ask, rubbing his arms.

Fletcher was already sitting up in his berth, the mattress rolled away and curtains drawn back. He was wearing his poncho liner for added warmth and sipping on a steaming cup of coffee one of the porters had brought him. "Where are we?" Snake grinned at Cordova's discomfort. "Oh, I'd say about four or five thousand feet up."

That explained the mountainlike chill in the air. "Chiang Mai?"

"Just pulling in."

Cordova jerked down on the thick window shade and watched it snap upward, out of sight. A colorful masterpiece of grandeur, unequaled anywhere in the world, met the Americans' eyes.

Shafts of crimson sunlight were fighting to pierce a thick mist that covered the land. The train was laboring up a steep valley between two huge mountain ranges, and every few seconds, gold and copper temple spires hundreds of feet high rose majestically through the mist. The bright greens, reds, and browns of the valley flora were fused together into a mosaic of color by the explosion of dawn, and entire herds of deer grazed peacefully and unmolested at the side of the railroad tracks. Some glanced up at the passing train as they chewed on the purple flowers, but most ignored the noisy intrusion.

"Mount Doi Pui." An old, wiry East Indian, sitting cross-legged in the berth next to Snakeman's, pointed to the overpowering mountain peak that occupied the center of Cordova's live painting. Fletcher nodded at the turbaned fellow.

They found the "City of Roses"—as Chiang Mai is known because the flowers, along with hydrangeas and rhododendrons, grow so abundantly in the brisk, temperate climate—

quite invigorating, its cool, refreshing climate a welcome respite from the sticky heat of Bangkok.

When the train finally pulled into a depot crowded with children selling fruits and tribal delicacies from platters balanced atop their heads, they took a three-wheeled *samlor* to the Suriwongse Hotel on Changklan Road, showered and shaved, then stopped by the veranda restaurant for breakfast.

"So what's our next move, Mr. Idea Man?" Fletcher took his plate of *kau-paht* and dumped it over onto a bowl of pineapple cubes.

Cordova watched him dig in with slippery, plastic chopsticks. "First, we stock up on energy." He pointed to his *gang-pet* dish of curried, sweet-tasting fish and shrimp. "Then we see if they have phone books in a place like this and start looking up every Thaweekarn listed."

"What if they don't have phone books up here in the sticks?" Fletcher's eyes were on a woman sitting at the bar whose figure-hugging sarong left little to the imagination.

"Then we visit the local town square or wherever folks in Chiang Mai get together to shoot the shit, and we start asking around about—"

"What if they've got one of them funky codes of silence up here?"

"Then we check in at the local police station and see if they can help." Cordova poured them both steaming cups of green chrysanthemum tea.

"I don't know if that's such a good idea."

Corky slammed the teapot down loudly. "I don't think coming to Thailand for R and R was such a fucking good idea."

"Amen to that, brother!"

"We coulda gone to Hong Kong, or Taipei ... even Honolulu, but Snakeman had to stick his forked tongue in some Thai *poo-ying!* Had to sample some of the 'most beautiful women in the world'—just for the record. So he could keep up with Brody."

252

"Say helleluja to that too, brother!" Fletcher had finally locked eyes with the woman at the bar.

"But we're here, so we might as well make the best of a bad situation. Hell, who knows . . . if we solve this mystery, we could be front-page news, amigo—the big time. We could have some decent jobs waitin' for us in The World when we get out."

"Don't hold your breath." Fletcher was motioning the woman over to their table, Thai style: fingers waving like limp leaves in the breeze, palm down.

"You're payin' for her tab." Brody sighed when he saw her start over.

"No sweat, Cork. The Snakeman's got it covered."

"You know how they are. They eat enough for two, then go out the bathroom window before you can get the rubber on."

"Good reason not to use a rubber?" Fletcher laughed. "Shit, that's like doin' it with a rain jacket on, my man!"

*"Sawatdee!"* The girl was in hear early twenties, with the high cheekbones of the Meo tribespeople, her hair braided into a circle on top of her head. She wore a tight sarong made up of bright orange, copper, and red horizontal rings, and a white blouse decorated with silk roses.

"Have a seat." Fletcher rose to pull a chair out for her, but the girl motioned for him not to bother and took the one beside Cordova instead.

"'Morning." Corky forced a polite nod, then resumed concentrating on the tea leaves swirling about at the bottom of his porcelain cup.

*"Sabaidi-ru?"* She giggled softly, and Cordova's eyeballs rolled toward the ceiling. *"Poot cha-cha noi.* My English poor, so please talk slow, okay?"

"For sure, gorgeous." Fletcher could not take his eyes off her face. If he had to get married, this woman had the kind of perfectly exotic features he wouldn't mind waking up to for the rest of his life. But she was ignoring Snakeman, for the most part.

"Are you Americans?" she asked Cordova.

"CIA," he replied dryly.

"CII?" She did not seem to understand.

"Corky"—Fetcher laughed—"you card." He turned to the girl again. "Yah, we're Americans, honey. Here to find an old Thai friend of ours."

"Oh! How nice. Have you been to see Wat Phra Singh yet? It is Chiang Mai's largest temple. Six hundred years old, too. Old, musty. Very romantic." She batted her long, natural eyelashes at Cordova.

Oh great, he thought. Suddenly she was babbling a hundred words a minute—the chick's a bona fide travel guide. "Is that the one we passed on the *samlor* ride over here?" Fletcher kept talking to her. "The one over on Lamlap Road?"

"Yes, very good. Lamlap Road! You speak very good Thai name." She seemed to notice the Snakeman for the first time, and his evil, Death-to-Traitors grin curled Fletcher's lips.

"Actually," Cordova said, "we were trying to look up an old friend."

"'Look up?'"

"Find. Trying to find an old friend."

Her elbows on the table, and forearms vertical like an amber temple, the girl clasped her hands Thai-dancer style, only to rest her chin on the knuckles. "And her name might be?"

"It's a 'he,'" Fletcher said. "His name is Thaweekarn."

"*Anukul* Thaweekarn?" the girl did not exhibit any overall excitement, but Corky did.

"*Yes!*" he shook the table slightly. "It is very important that we find him. Can you help us?"

"Everyone knows Mr. Thaweekarn." Her eyes dropped to the cup of tea Snakeman had poured her. She puckered her lips and stirred the tea leaves with a toothpick.

"We need his address," Fletcher said. "Can you write it

254

down for us?" He and Cordova exchanged smiles. Neither man thought it would be so simple.

And it wasn't. "Everyone knows Mr. Thaweekarn," the girl repeated. "But no one know where exactly he stay."

"No one knows? Why not?" Agitated, Cordova bumped the porcelain cup in front of him, and tea overflowed onto the mint-green table cloth.

"Mr. Thaweekarn very important man. Own many things Chiang Mai, but stay closer Burma. Most probab'ry in high mountains near Burma border," she said confidently, keeping her eyes lowered. "Chiang Rai, or Chiang Khong. Maybe Muang Prow. I do not think you will find anyone tell you he have home Chiang Mai."

"She wants *baht*," Fletcher told Cordova outright. "And I ain't got the bucks to spare, bud."

The girl's eyes shot up, stinging Snakeman. "I don' want your money," she said. "People not go find Mr. Thaweekarn. He come to them."

"And just how, exactly, does 'he come to them,' dear?" Cordova ran the edge of his finger along her wrist. The girl's flesh was very warm to the touch. Brody the Whoremonger had once told him that was a bad sign . . . that it was an indication she might be carrying something contagious.

"You write down name on piece of paper," she whispered, glancing around mysteriously. "You stay this hotel?" Fletcher and Cordova both nodded. Her dark almond eyes narrowed, taking on a sinister cast for the first time. "I take to someone. If Mr. Thaweekarn want talk you, his man come see you."

"Good." Cordova nodded, rubbing her forearm gently.

"You looking to buy Buddha grass, okay?" Her smile was an all-knowing accusation.

Cordova did not hesitate. "Yes," he said. "Buddha grass, and opium. Bookoo opium, honey. To take back to the GIs in Nam, okay? You tell your friend-of-a-friend that: 'Buddha grass, opium, GIs in The Nam.'"

"We'll deal with a middleman the first meeting," Fletcher

said, "but after that, we only talk to Mr. Thaweekarn—you got that, honey?"

"I got," the girl said. She suddenly had something more important to do in life than try and sell herself to two johns in the hotel restaurant, so she stood up without any farewells and started walking briskly to the lobby.

"What do you think?" Cordova watched her rush through the front doors, climb into a *samlor*, and disappear down the hotel's winding main drive.

"I think we just may be digging our own grave, Corky-san. Yep, I truly do."

"How so?" He refilled their teacups.

"Suppose we do strike paydirt and make contact with this scrotebag. Then what? You were talkin' opium to that cunt, brother. Where we gonna get the *baht* to even come across with a halfway decent bluff?"

"You worry too much about minor details, Snakeman. All I wanna do is get in the same room with the fuckwad so I can cancel his ticket."

"Mr. Big's gonna send a middleman, *Khop*, and the middleman's gonna wanna see some *baht* up front. I fucking guarantee it. And what about Sugar's kid?"

"What about him?"

"What if the Thai cops are workin' their own investigation, trying to rescue the little guy—and I can just about guarantee you they are, him bein' the son of a policewoman killed in the line of duty—and we go and throw a stick into the spokes of their investigation? Huh? What if that happens?"

"Alley-alley," Cordova leaned back in his chair and shook his head from side to side. "You worry too much."

"Bullshit. You don't worry enough!"

"Let's just play it by ear, and see what happens, okay? We'll hang around this dump another seventy-two hours, and if it don't pan out, we'll book back to Bangkok."

"Seventy-two hours?" Fletcher's laugh was a dry, worried

256

one. "That'll just about put us AWOL, amigo. You fucking well *know* that train ain't going to be on time, either."

"Mellow out, okay?" Cordova glanced at the check, was happy with what he saw, and decided to order some more food. "So we miss our hop back to The Nam . . . so what? You know the colonel. He'll cut us some slack. Especially after we explain what went down here. Shit, I'll even take back some documentation, if that'll take a load off your mind."

"Documentation?" Fletcher's laugh was one of sheer hopelessness.

"Hell, by the time this is over, the boys back in Echo Company'll probably be readin' about us in *Stars & Stripes*. We won't *need* no documen—"

"Well," Fletcher interrupted him, "I want a gun. I think we both oughta get one. And I'm not talkin' lousy pea-shooters. If we're gonna dick around with big-time dope dealers, then we need some heavy-duty hardware."

"You get caught with a firearm in Thailand these days, and you're looking at a death sentence, my friend. The communist insurgency has really put a damper on the right to bear arms."

"The last people I'm worried about are the cops." Fletcher stood up and brushed crumbs from his new, made-in-Bangkok safari shirt. "But playin' games with local drug kingpins is downright suicide if you don't plan on having the capability to defend yourself, Corky."

"So what's your hurry? Where you goin'?"

"Downtown to barter for some of that 'hardware.' I just hope this place has a black market."

"Good luck."

"After you're done stuffin' your face, I suggest you go up to our room and wait for me to get back. Don't let anyone in, and that includes *poo-yings*."

"You used to be a lot of fun, Snakeman." He sighed for Fletcher's benefit. "But lately you've been turnin' into a real dud. Lighten up, okay?"

"I coulda picked Hong Kong or even Honolulu." Fletcher

257

turned and left, muttering to himself. "But no, I gotta baby-sit the Cork in Bangkok . . . where I'm catchin' more stress in seven days than seven *months* workin' hatch-60s in The Nam!"

"Ya love it and ya know it, Snakeoil!"

"I'll be back by high noon," he said saluting Cordova with a middle finger.

"I'll have the *poo-yings* lined up in the hallway for your selection, master."

# CHAPTER 23

## Sisters of Mercy Orphanage

"Thank you."

Lt. Maddox's eyes went wide and she smiled. "Oh! So you *can* speak some English after all?" She handed little Tamminh another cookie.

The cute girl nodded her head eagerly. She did not take a bite out of the cookie, but placed it in her blouse pocket beside the first one.

"Aren't you going to eat them?" Maddox dropped into an American-style squat, heels up off the ground. Tamminh immediately imitated her, except that the soles of her feet remained completely flat.

"No, thank you," she said innocently.

"Later, maybe?" Maddox brushed a piece of bark from the child's eyelash.

"Yes, maybe, thank you, when Saint Pat come back?" The acknowledgment became a question in one breath.

Maddox hoped her expression didn't change, and that, if it did, the girl wasn't mature enough to notice. Soldiers from the First Cav's Echo Company were taking heavy casualties at Phung Du. It was getting so bad, a hospital ship had taken up station off the coastline, and critical cases were being transferred direct from there to Saigon and Tokyo. "He will come back as soon as he can, dear. I'm sure he misses you very much, too."

"Saint Pat same-same papa-san for Tamminh. He tell me."

"You would make Numba One Girl." She searched her memory for words from the Vietnamese language classes. "Numba One daughter . . . *con gai!*"

"Ahhh." She suddenly looked and sounded five years older. "*Con gai . . .*" Tamminh stared at the floor, mulling it over in her mind. "Yes."

"Where did you learn such good English?" Maddox knew there was no way Patterson could have taught her so much in such little time.

"Before," Tamminh's little hand swept out to encompass the entire grounds of the orphanage, "Tamminh stay here. When parents kill. Stay here with nun. Learn French and English. They say someday I can be nun, too. Never be hungry 'gain. When grow. But now I stay uncle's family. One year now. Tonight stop. Uncle's family *di-di.*"

"*Di-di?*" Maddox thought the girl would tell her they fled the fighting. *Di-di* was Vietnamese for "go."

"*Fini.* Die." She clasped her fingers together, inverting them, then pretended her hands were a butterfly, trying to fly away.

"Oh, Tamminh, I'm so sorry." Maddox hugged the girl, clutching her close.

"Forget." She smoothed the lieutenant's white locks back as if consoling her instead. "Uncle Numba Ten. Always do bad thing Tamminh." Her face became sullen, and she went silent.

"What have we got here?" A husky Latino with sergeant stripes on his jungle fatigues towered over Maddox. Hands on his hips, he stared down at Tamminh with eyes narrowed menacingly.

The girl jumped back with a start.

"Danny!" Maddox waved her finger at the medic. "You're scaring her. Now tell her you're sorry."

Doc Delgado, as the men called Echo Company's most experienced corpsman, was a dark-complected, thirty-five-year-old Chicano of medium height, whose stocky frame once boasted rippling, rock-hard muscles back in the barrio. But since arriving in The Nam a year ago, the long hours and mental trauma of seeing so many American boys mangled and mutilated by war had left him broken in body and spirit. The weight was still there, but he rarely worked out anymore, and the boxer's physique was going soft.

Things were looking up lately for the buck sergeant, though, and he had Lt. Lisa Maddox to thank for that. For the first several months in-country, they had spent the long shifts between missions in the aid station, caring for the sick and wounded, and she was always there afterwards, too, when he needed someone to talk to, someone to bring him down gently off the adrenaline high, coax him home from the guilt trips. She was even there when he needed someone to keep him warm after lights-out, which was strictly against regulations —fraternization between officers and enlisted men, that is. Even more of a bombshell was when Chopper pilots Lance Lawless Warlokk and Clifford The Gunslinger Gabriel, who had been competing unsuccessfully for the lieutenant's affections for the past six months, caught her and her buck sergeant in the buff together, playing doctor at the advanced skill level. They could have turned Maddox and Delgado in, of course, ruining both their military careers—and embarrassing Lisa's father, who was a hotshot general down at Saigon's Puzzle Palace—but warrant officers the world over are notorious for being "good old boys" who try as often as possible to look the other way when minor infractions of the rules are observed. Especially when the regs involve games of chance or affairs of the heart. That's why doorgunners treat warrant officers with more respect than "real" officers, and call them "Mister" instead of "Sir."

261

"Tell the girl you're sorry," Maddox repeated, before shifting into pig Latin, "or tonight you don't get your ud-pay ulled-pay!"

"I'm sorry, I'm sorry!" Delgado feigned a minor anxiety attack.

"This is Tamminh." Maddox introduced the girl and Delgado bowed like a prince, removing his helmet and tucking it against his stomach.

"Pleased to meet you, *Co* Tamminh."

Tamminh giggled when he called her "Miss," which was usually reserved for the older girls. "Please meet you."

"Yes, yes. Please meet you, too."

"You please meet me?" Tamminh's tiny hand touched her heart, and Maddox's smile faded slightly. "I please meet you, too."

"Uh, we're startin' to sound like a broken record around here." He looked over at Lisa for help.

"She's Corporal Patterson's little friend," Maddox said.

"Ahhh." Delgado's eyes went suddenly lifeless, and Maddox saw him swallow over her words. "Yes." His eyes blinked rapidly for a couple of seconds. "Little Tamminh. I've already heard so much about you."

"Excuse me."

Delgado and Maddox both turned to find two Vietnamese Catholic nuns leading about a dozen orphans through the corridor. "Yes, sister?" The lieutenant rested her hand on Tamminh's shoulder. The gesture seemed almost protective, and a slightly offended look came over the nun.

"It is time to take the children for their shots and examinations."

"Of course." Maddox smiled, pushing Tamminh forward gently, but the little girl's eyes flew wide with horror.

"They shoot me?" Tears filled her eyes, and her tone was asking "already?" as if these orphanage people were really no different from the communists after all. "Tonight?"

262

"Oh, no, no, honey!" Maddox dropped to one knee and clasped her hands. "Not gun shooting, but this kind." She rubbed the vaccination scar a Green Beret medical team had left on Tamminh's arm two years before.

Tamminh winced with apprehension. "Oh." She made a monster face. "That worse!" Everyone standing there envisioned the same thing: some doctor puncturing the children's arms with a long syringe needle.

"Be brave." Delgado patted her on the rump as the nun led Tamminh away with the others.

"Tell Saint Pat 'bout this!" she pleaded, the tears sliding down her cheeks now. She tried to wipe them away. "Tell him come rescue *con gai*! They going to shoot her!"

Delgado laughed at the little girl's antics, but Maddox's face was serious when he looked back at her. "I saw you freeze up a moment ago," she said. "When I mentioned Corporal Patterson." She moved closer and took his hand, ignoring the lower ranking enlisted men who walked past without bothering to hide their stares. "Is there a problem?"

"I just came from Phung Du. Just rode my tenth med-evac slick outta that hell. 'Numba Ten' means *badddd*, and it definitely was the pits, Lisa. It's a clusterfuck, if you'll pardon my French. I don't think the head knows what the tail's doing out there." She heard Delgado's teeth grinding from the stress.

"Our side?"

"Yah, unfortunately."

"What about Saint Pat? Something about Corporal Patterson's name struck a raw nerve when I mentioned him."

"We're missing about three squads of men from Echo Company," Delgado revealed without any dramatics. He stared at the puddles of blood on the floor in the triage area, then at the little girl disappearing down the narrow corridor with her fingers interlocked across the top of her head, pretending she was a prisoner. "Patterson is one of the men they think accidentally got zapped by some of our own napalm."

263

Corporal Patterson lay on his back, watching flares float past overhead. They were so bright, he could no longer see the stars beyond, only jagged trails of silver smoke against the night sky after the flares fell to earth. Tracers arced back and forth over his position—green from the VC side, red from the Americans two hundred yards away, and glowing white from some hotshot freelancer deep within the bamboo.

Saint Pat was lying alone in a dry streambed, cut off from the rest of Echo Company in Phung Du. Dead bodies of men who'd been his buddies lay all around him. Patterson, too, was dead, for all intents and purposes. He was pretending to be, hoping the enemy would ignore him—if they could even see him. He certainly had enough blood on him to pass for a corpse—other men's blood. His rifle was destroyed by some of the 600 steel balls that decimated his squad when they walked into the Cong claymore ambush.

He could hear the dull thump of 61mm VC mortars being fired from the tree line off to his left. They passed well overhead, landing with muffled blasts in the Cavalry positions. The Americans responded with barrages from their 60 and 81 mike-mikes, and both sides screamed the pain of their dead and dying into the night.

The First Cavalry Division had done well in Ia Drang and Plei Me, proving themselves and the air-assault Airmobile concept to any doubters in the other Infantry units, but Patterson was worried about the turn of events here in Phung Du–3. Was Saint Pat going to escape by the skin of his teeth again, one last time? Would he be able to make it back to Sisters of Mercy and take little Tamminh under his wing?

He tried to visualize her, but all he could see was the face of the man who had died in his arms an hour earlier, the soldier whose body he was now using for cover against the smoking waves of shrapnel striking his position from all sides. He tried to think what it would be like taking her to a baseball

264

game, or the movies—wouldn't she just get an everlovin' charge out of Bambi or Dumbo or Sleeping Beauty? But rolling concussions swept over him, one after the other, and all he could think about was making himself flatter than was humanly possible, blending in with the earth. Distinguishing between objects on the battlefield which would afford more cover, which would not.

There was movement in the mangroves a few yards from his head. He didn't want to acknowledge it—the Cong would be putting bullets into the heads of every American they found, or running them through with bayonets—but there was no mistaking the blur of dull khaki in his peripheral vision. The NVA wore khaki. Brown, and sometimes green. Charlie wore black pajamas and ammo belts. He knew he was about to die.

He glanced up and saw the bulging whites of an insane-looking man's eyes glaring in his direction, then staring down right at him. A *black* man, carrying an American-made M-60!

Patterson did not blink. He feigned death again, death that had left a warrior with his eyes open, staring up at the floating flares. He concentrated on staring past the man as he walked through Saint Pat's field of vision. His eyes did not follow the soldier because he was not looking at a fellow American, come to rescue him. This guy was a guerrilla. He was wearing a red Cong headband, and though he carried a Hog-60, belts of ammo for a CKC Chinese assault rifle hung across his chest like a giant green X.

Patterson had heard about him—the black deserter who roamed Binh Dinh Province with the communists, carrying his M-60 and his hatred in his fists. He was known to beat American P.O.W.s, and ran with a Caucasian, who carried a thumper. A Caucasian who played an eerie little flute before firing his M-79 rounds into U.S. positions.

They had only been rumors until tonight, though. And there had been other stories rampant at base camp during the move from Ia Drang to this avowed communist sanctuary.

Allegations that a C.I.A. agent gone rogue was carrying out atrocities in the Binh Dinh area were what first brought an M.I. team to the Phung Du area in the first place. Their investigation revealed nothing to substantiate claims The Agency was behind the midnight raids where pregnant women were disemboweled or gang-raped while their husbands and children were forced, at gunpoint, to watch. But a search of the area did reveal a growing communist influence and sympathy in Phung Du, and the area was included in the sweep that became Operation Masher–White Wing.

C.I.A. Agent John Graves' face always came to mind whenever Patterson heard the stories. Graves was certainly a colorful, soldier-of-fortune-type character, who disappeared into the rain forests on clandestine missions for months at a time. Whenever he returned to the rear echelon, haggard and glassy-eyed, black and blue, bulletholes in his jeep or knife slits in his ruck, he always, without exception, bought the house a round of drinks—often trying to use currency that wasn't South Vietnamese or American—and proceeded to complain about lax U.S. policy in Southeast Asia. "We need to invade the North," he'd always say. "Invade in force, kick the Ho outta Hanoi, and it'd all be over in a matter of days."

"That's precisely *why* we don't invade North Vietnam," the reply was always the same. "This clusterfuck would come to a screeching halt, Johnny-boy. And where else could guys like you and me—where else could all us gunship jockeys have so much fun?"

"Gun*shit* jockeys!" was Graves's usual rebuke. And he would disappear for another month or two, waging the war on his own terms, in his own style.

Patterson often wondered if the man's elevator went to the top floor, or if all his "missions" were actually sanctioned by the War Room at MACV. But he knew Graves was not the kind of maniac who went rabid under a full moon, molesting women and children, raping, pillaging, and plundering. Johnny-boy was definitely *dinky-dau*, but he had too much

266

class to stoop that low just for kicks and a little job satisfaction. Patterson didn't think he was even a double-vet.

And he didn't think the black man toting an M-60 through the bamboo was an American.

There were plenty of black Cubans running around The Nam, acting as advisors to the guerrillas. In North Vietnam, they were often responsible for the most brutal torture inflicted on American prisoners of war. That's who this dude had to be, Saint Pat decided: a Havana whore. Patterson could smell it on him. A sleazeball. *If only I had one lousy frag left . . .*

But he remained frozen, and the Negro slowly continued through the razor-sharp reeds. Patterson listened to the man's tongs sinking in the moist sand only inches from his head. *Tongs!* The creep *had* to be Cong.

He could hear eight-inch artillery pieces discharging their shells two or three miles away, and as the projectiles screamed in, the machine gunner heard them, too. He hustled off through the elephant grass, disappearing in the fog before the first explosions struck the sandy plain.

The barrage lasted about five minutes, during which time Patterson felt as if he was floating in the middle of an atom bomb's mushroom cloud. Though his eyes were tightly closed, and he kept the palms of his hands clamped over his ears, a brilliant light show began bursting inside his head. His temples throbbed from the splitting headache, and he felt himself screaming as chunks of shrapnel the size of fists slammed into the earth all around him, never striking flesh.

Moments after it was over, and he lay there curled up in the fetal position, numb and trembling, bursts from a K-50 Cong submachine gun and several Russian-made K-44 carbines erupted on the other side of the tree line.

American mortars began descending onto the position, and suddenly people were leaping over the bushes, many right on top of him in their haste to escape the imminent barrage.

One young communist landed in the sand beside him and fell forward with his knees and hands gouging Patterson's

267

chest as he clawed his way to safety. Patterson groaned as the air was knocked from him, but the guerrilla didn't even seem to notice. Several more frantic Cong raced past on either side, and then it happened.

He saw her.

The last one in the group. Long, black hair flying behind her as she glided through the bamboo, constantly glancing back as if monitoring the progress of pursuers. A woman to the front and side of her, clad in black pajama bottoms and an olive-drab blouse, fired the K-50 back at shadows moving through the jungle after them.

But Patterson didn't care about any of that. He didn't care about the girl with the submachine gun, or the shadows that might even be his buddies, Americans come to rescue him! The only thing Saint Pat concerned himself with was the last woman. The woman with the defiant smirk on her face, even as death chased her through the rain forest.

It was her! It was Xuyen Thi Vau, the Cong cadre leader who had ambushed his entire platoon in Ia Drang Valley! It was the bitch who captured him, stripped him naked in front of her whole squad, did her best to humiliate him, then took a hammer and nailed a VC flag-patch to his shoulderblade.

She had, in the end, allowed him to live. And that had been her one mistake.

As she rushed up to his sandbar and leaped over him like a track star clearing hurdles, Patterson reached up, grabbed an ankle, and pulled her out of the tracer-lit night, down on top of him.

268

# CHAPTER 24

## Chiang Mai, Thailand

Corky and the Snakeman were on their fourth six-pack of *Singha* when the knock came at their hotel-room door.

"Wait one." Fletcher lapsed into GI radio jargon as he glided to the window, sure-footed, despite the unusually high alcohol content of his blood.

Fletcher looked down from their top-floor, second-level room.

"See anything?" Cordova pulled the grease guns out from under the bed, removed them from their straw boxes, and slipped them under the bedspreads of Fletcher's rack.

"A dark blue Renault," Fletcher responded after a moment.

"Aren't they supposed to be black?" Cordova asked cryptically.

"Well, it's got black, tinted windows. Will that do, Sherlock?"

Without waiting for an answer, Fletcher sauntered over to the door, removed the chain, and slid the bolt back with a loud crack. Cordova kept one hand under the bedspreads, finger on the grease-gun's trigger. "Hope this thing works," he muttered under his breath.

"It better work," Fletcher said, pulling the door open. "I hocked your new Seiko for it."

"I hope you got a good deal on whatever you traded your watch in for," a middle-aged woman, dressed in a conservative, Western-style pants-suit, appeared in the doorway. She had only caught the last half of their conversation.

"I hope so, too." Fletcher motioned her into the room.

"This is far enough, thank you very much." She smiled slightly, but it was a cold, impersonal smile.

Cordova gave her the once over, concentrating particularly on her shapely figure. She was Oriental, but he didn't think she was Thai. The face was too "round" for one with Siamese blood, he decided. Maybe Burmese, or even Chinese.

"Can we offer you some *Singha*?" Cordova held out a half-empty bottle.

The woman frowned distastefully. "Thank you, no." She glanced around the room with a critical eye. "You are just passing through," she deduced by the lack of personal furnishings.

"This is our first week in Chiang Mai," Cordova admitted. "Nice town you've got here."

"And just what exactly did you want of Mr. Thaweekarn?" she asked suddenly.

"We're just in from Vietnam," Fletcher began their hastily invented cover story.

"Oh? Vietnam . . . interesting."

"It has its possibilities," Cordova interjected, "for mercenaries and soldiers of misfortune with a yen for killing and a knack for survival. Us? We'd just as soon stay on this side of the Golden Triangle."

"Our year in The Nam's almost up," Fletcher continued, "and there's not much waitin' for us back in The World."

"From what I've heard," the woman said, "all GIs *can't* wait to get back stateside."

"You've been to the U.S.A.?" Cordova asked her.

"Six years," she revealed. "Columbia University, 'fifty-six to 'sixty-two."

"Interesting."

270

"Anyway, we don't anticipate returnin' to Asia in the near future"—Fletcher sat down on the edge of the other bed—"and see this as our chance at the big time."

"There's *bookoo* boys in Bong Son who could sure go for a little recreational drug abuse right about now." Cordova tossed a *Bangkok Post* onto the serving tray next to the door.

The woman glanced down at a front-page photo showing two American soldiers leading several blindfolded VC prisoners past a burning hut at gunpoint. "Yessss . . ." She drew the word out slowly. "Vietnam has been in the news quite a bit lately. Operation . . . Smasher, is it?"

"Masher." Corky chuckled softly. "Only now they've started calling it Operation White Wing. The liberal lunatics back in the States were raisin' Cain about the first code name. I guess LBJ figured White Wing would placate the doves in D.C."

"So how much do you propose to purchase?" Finished with small talk that bored her, she glanced over at an AWOL bag tucked partially beneath one of the beds.

Fletcher already had the money out. He pulled a large bundle of hundreds from within his shirt. "Ten thousand U.S. to start." His face was without emotion of any kind, but Cordova's eyes lit up at the sight of all the greenbacks.

Fletcher waved him silent and threw the bundle onto the bed farthest away from their visitor. "Ten thousand to start," he repeated, adding, "Until we get an opportunity to sample the product."

"We will require half the money up front," the woman told them.

"And the other half upon delivery." Snakeman nodded. "Exactly how I had hoped you would see it."

She started toward the bed, but Fletcher blocked her way. "Not so fast, cutes," he said. "How do we know you really represent Thaweekarn?"

"And how do we know *you* are not DEA?" She slapped Fletcher suddenly and pushed him off balance.

271

The minor assault must have been a signal, Cordova decided, because just as Fletcher brought his fist back, five burly Chinamen rushed into the room. They were not brandishing weapons, but every one wore a safari suit with a suspicious bulge along the left inner wasitband.

"Ah-so!" Fletcher held out his hands, karate style. He was grinning ear to ear, feeling the challenge—and the booze. "Come on, motherfuckers. I'm ready! How do you want it? One on one, or all of you at the same time."

The man nearest Fletcher grabbed the doorgunner's wrist with little trouble and whirled him around until he was up against the closest wall. Two of the others immediately commenced frisking Snakeman.

The remaining pair as well as the woman seemed to be ignoring Cordova and the wad of money on the bed.

"No guns," the searcher reported, tossing a wallet over his shoulder.

The woman caught it with one hand, flipped through the photo section, then emptied the rest of the contents out onto a writing desk.

"We're not cops," Cordova said calmly, sounding bored as he shifted about on the bed.

She rattled off a declaration in what he thought was Chinese, and one of the thugs nodded. Cordova picked out two words: Vietnam and GI. "Why can I find no Leave papers amongst these?" she asked. "Or 'R and R orders,' I believe you call them."

Cordova allowed another little laugh to reinforce his cool demeanor. "That's a long story." He decided the truth wouldn't hurt. "They were stolen down in Bangkok. Along with my watch." The woman's eyebrows rose slightly. "My *old* watch," he added.

"What is your service number?" she asked Fletcher.

"What's your bust size, bitch?" Snakeman, true to form, shot back. He didn't like being roughed up in front of a wit-

272

ness who could return to Echo Company and tell the guys Fletch allowed five lousy zips to get the best of him.

"Answer her, Snake." Cordova sighed.

"Thirty-six, twenty-four, thirty-six are my measurements," the woman stated calmly. "Now it is your turn."

Fletcher complied, and the woman's eyes compared what she heard with the numbers on his military ID card.

"Any good secret agent would have had that fucking memorized long before taking 'such a dangerous assignment,'" Fletcher said.

The woman in the black pants-suit frowned. "We will take a chance on you," she decided.

"Well, *we* just elected not to do business with *you*!" Cordova pulled the grease gun out from under the bedspread. "Take a fucking hike, Jack!"

"But I thought . . ." The woman seemed genuinely shocked for the first time.

"I don't like the way your bullies manhandled my pal, Snakeman." Cordova stood and motioned the six Chinese back out into the hallway. "We're no longer going to deal with you. Tell Thaweekarn to give us a call if he likes the color of our money," Corky had picked up the wad of bills and now tossed it up and down enticingly, just before slamming the door in the woman's face.

Fletcher placed his ear against the doorframe and listened to their footsteps fade down the hallway. He waited a few more seconds, then exploded right before Cordova's eyes. "What the hell is wrong with you?" He rushed over and grabbed the front of Corky's shirt. "I bust my balls to get this thing set up, complete with equalizer insurance"—he knocked the barrel of the grease gun away—"and greenbacks, and you go and—"

"I couldn't just sit there with a straight face and watch you pull ten thou outta the air like that, Snakeman! Jesus H.! You didn't even warn me about comin' up with that much dough! Did you rob the bank of Chiang Mai or something?"

273

"If you woulda just played along"—Fletcher grabbed the "wad of bills" from him—"we'd be on our way to the big deal by now." He pulled the thick rubber band off the wad, and blank sheets of green-tinted paper were revealed.

"Oh, wonderful." Cordova looked as if he was about to throw up. "Where the heck did you get something as stupid as that?"

"Stupid?" Fletcher produced his most offended expression. "It cost me five bucks down on the black-market."

"Black market?"

"Same joint I bought the grease guns."

"And just what did you propose to do once *they* popped off your silly rubber-band and found the funny money instead of hard currency?"

"Well."

"I'll tell you what would have happened." He tossed the grease gun onto one of the beds. "You and yours truly would have ended up facedown in the Mae Nam river, you shitbucket!" Cordova was pacing back and forth in front of the window now. "Sometimes I just don't know how you make it from day to day."

"Takes talent," Fletcher walked over and put his arm around Cordova's shoulder. "And it's *'cause* I got a best buddy like the Cork who looks out for me, amigo!" He smiled brightly.

Ten minutes after they had begun arguing, another knock came at the door.

Cordova grabbed one of the guns and braced himself against the bathroom doorframe.

When Fletcher pulled the latch back, they found a short, scared-looking schoolgirl standing in the hallway. She held an envelope out to the American and ran off before he could say anything.

"Should I go after her?" He looked to Cordova for guidance.

"Fuck it." Corky snatched the envelope away and ripped it

274

open. "'Mr. Thaweekarn will meet you day after tomorrow, February 2nd, at the elephant-logging contest in Chiang Rai. He will make himself known to you.' Welp, I guess we've reached the point of no return." He handed the note to Fletcher.

"Unsigned." The vacationing doorgunner folded it back up, slipped it into the envelope, and placed both in a shirt pocket.

"Yep." Cordova walked over to the window and began watching the Thai girls weaving rugs and garments at the tourist trap across the street. "Unsigned. We're not dealin' with the Better Business Bureau here, Snake." His voice had turned deadly serious.

"No shit."

"What I'm tryin' to say is, I wouldn't hold it against you if you bugged out . . . decided to call it quits and beat feet back down to Bangkok."

"Then I'd have to return to The Nam, too." Fletcher cocked an eyebrow at him.

"You know"—he stared at the wad of phony bills for a second—"I think it's best things worked out this way."

"You mean bypassing the middle man?"

"Right. I'm sure this Thaweekarn isn't fool enough to show up alone, but at least now we don't have to worry about coming up with the *baht*."

"Lucky us," Fletcher said sarcastically.

"We can just show up at the elephant-logging contest, or whatever it is, eyeball everyone, then act on our instincts."

"Our instincts?"

"Sure. If the dude looks hinky, we take him down then and there, kick the shit out of him, and break his legs until he tells us where Sugar's kid is."

"But if . . ."

Cordova nodded. "But if we get that . . . 'gut feeling' about the little shit, then we'll lay back, follow him home without

275

introducin' ourselves, find out where he shacks, and call in the Cavalry."

"*Our* Cavalry?" Snakeman looked perplexed.

"I wish. A gunship or two would be nice." Cordova stared at himself in the mirror. "Actually, I had the Thai National cops in mind, dude. They're the next best thing."

"Can't have it all."

"But we're gonna rock and roll with what we got!" Corky danced over to the bed, picked up the grease gun, and slapped it back and forth from palm to palm.

" 'Cause we got soul, and that's a lot!" Fletcher exchanged a fist dap with his Latino brother, then both soldiers slid the weapons under the bed and went out hunting for ladies of questionable virtue.

# CHAPTER 25

## Quan Loi, Fifty miles North of Saigon

Brody's hand shot out and grabbed Dep's wrist as she started to knock on the door. The forefinger of his other hand came up to his lips, urging silence. Dep responded with an irritated expression.

"What's wrong?" she whispered. This was the apartment of her sister, Lin. Nothing more. But he waved her silent, a rare angry streak showing through in his own eyes.

Brody tried the doorknob, and, as he sensed in his gut long before they reached the top of the stairs, something was wrong. The door opened without a sound.

They exchanged looks, and he entered in front of her, wishing now more than ever that he'd relieved one of the bandits back on Thunder Road of his revolver.

It was a small, one-room flat, similar to the buffet he had spent his first nights with Dep in. Lin's bed was smaller, and Brody took this as a good sign: it wasn't a hooker's rack. Maybe she was into some other kind of trouble besides pimps and prostitution.

The bed was against the wall adjacent to the door, not beneath a window, like Dep's had been. Lin's apartment was on one side of a hallway, so the only window was the balcony on the other side of the room. He noticed its bamboo partition had been drawn back, but there was nobody outside that he could see. Moonlight filtered down through the mosquito netting.

The apartment building across the alley seemed only five or six feet away, though the drop between dwellings was a good fifty or more. Maybe she was a cat burglar, he thought. Brody moved to the middle of the room, his eyes still on the balcony. From this angle, he had a good view of the ARVN military reservation down at the bottom of the hill, several hundred meters away.

Dep moved past him swiftly, entering the only other room in the apartment, the bath. Before he could say anything, she was pulling on a string, and a bare lightbulb in the ceiling flashed on, blinding them both. There was no one in the bathroom, either, and Brody rushed beside her and turned the light off.

Allowing his eyes a minute to readjust to the dark, Brody walked slowly around the room, taking in the sparse furnishings.

Besides the bed, there was only a small table and a dresser. The bureau had no mirror, and there were no nightstands or chairs of any kind. Like Dep, Lin piled packages of rice and noodles high on the table. There was a hot plate and rice cooker, but no stove. Most Vietnamese didn't need one, Dep had told him many a time when he offered to try and order her one from the PX catalog. Why would they, when so many vendor's stands cluttered the streets below in all Vietnamese towns, selling everything from soup and meat dishes to steaming sugarcane cubes and entire barbecued hogs, hanging by their legs from a pole over the baggies of ice coffee and coconut milk slices. There were no posters or decorations on the walls, as in Dep's Cholon flat. And Brody could not find one of the usual family altars anywhere. Not even a Buddha statue, or urn full of *joss* ash.

He moved over to her bureau and quietly slid the top drawer open. It was still full of clothing.

"What?" Dep resented his invasion of her sister's privacy, and she rushed over to see what he was doing.

Brody held up a beautiful purple *ao dai*. "At least she still lives here," he whispered. "Or at least *some*body lives here."

"It is Lin's." Dep gently took the garment from him and slowly folded it carefully, as if its neat and perfect creases were lined with gold leaf.

A scraping sound reached Brody's ears, and he returned to the balcony. The pitter-patter of light feet in the distance lured his gaze to a rooftop across the alley.

"Dep." His voice grew harsh, and he moved back out of the moonbeams, into shadows. "Get over here. I think you better see this."

When she joined him at the edge of the balcony, he pointed across the alley, and Dep's breath left her in a gasp.

"Is that her?" he asked softly, placing a hand on Dep's shoulder to remind his woman she had someone there to support her, to comfort her in times like these.

"Yes." Dep's voice cracked slightly when she spoke, and Brody rushed over to the kitchen table and grabbed a fish-gutting knife.

Lin was crouching along the edge of the rooftop on the next building over. She was dressed entirely in black, and held an old Garand M-1 to her shoulder.

It appeared to Treat Brody that she was aiming at someone down in the South Vietnamese military compound at the bottom of the hill.

Dep grabbed Brody's wrist, bringing his hand up so that the knife sparkled between their faces. "What are you to do with that?"

"Nothing." He swallowed hard. "If I don't have to." Brody's chin motioned out past the balcony, to the figure crouching along the edge of the roof next door.

"Let's leave, Bro-dee, please," Dep pleaded. "Now I don't want to know!"

"Well, I do!" He jerked his hand free. "Besides, you just can't leave her out there like that. She's headed for a world of hurt, honey-san."

Brody didn't wait for her decision. Silent as a panther and feeling The Nam in his blood, he climbed up onto the balcony railing, slipped the knife between his teeth, dropped into a crouch, and jumped as hard as he could.

*A pirate I ain't!* He groaned as his body slammed against the brick wall of the apartment building on the other side of the alley. His forearms caught the edge of the roof opposite where Lin was crouching, and he could hear Dep gasp as his legs dangled out into space.

His elbows already rubbed raw as he tried to pull himself up, Brody was well aware he had to move fast—Lin had surely heard all the commotion. But he was still weak from the beating on Thunder Road, and a shocking revelation suddenly struck him: He might not have to worry about Lin's reaction at all. He just might drop. But before he realized it, some inner strength propelled his thighs and twisted his waist. His feet were swinging over the edge, and he was rolling onto the dried-tar roof.

He kept rolling once he got there. All the way to a ventilation duct. Without pausing to assess the situation, he relied on gut instinct again, and, keeping to the shadows, darted in the direction he'd last seen Dep's sister.

They slammed into each other before Brody was halfway there. Lin dropped her rifle as they tumbled, and the weapon discharged. A single green tracer sailed off toward the stars and abruptly dropped back toward earth, burning up in the night.

"Stop! I'm your friend!" Brody yelled as they wrestled with the knife, not even sure if she spoke English. "Your sister! Your sister, Dep! I'm here with your sister!" But the

280

words had no effect on her, and they rolled closer and closer to the edge of the roof.

Out the corner of his eye, Brody could see that Dep was balanced precariously on the balcony railing, trying to imitate his daring, but she could not bring herself to jump.

"Dep!" he called to her. "Dep! Tell her who I am!"

Lin was extremely tough for a woman only half his weight. She was no martial artist, but she was determined to overpower Treat Brody and kill him with his own knife.

Dep was shouting at them in Vietnamese, but the she-wolf in Brody's arms was hearing nothing except the animallike sounds coming from her own throat as she growled at him.

"Jesus, woman!" He almost lost control of the knife for a second, and the blade left a deep gash across the palm of his hand.

*"Con de hoang!"* She called him a bastard and spat in his face.

"I hope that wasn't my lifeline!" Brody knew he was being cursed at, but tried to concentrate instead on maintaining control of the weapon. Blood from his hand was quickly spraying them both. Their faces became smeared with crimson as he tried to hold her forehead down and she slapped back wildly.

Brody did not realize how close they'd gotten to the roof's edge until it was too late. Lin tried to knee him in the groin, and to avoid it, he rolled over onto his back. The natural instinct of a fighter was to use the momentum of that movement to propel one's opponent off and away from him, and before he could stop himself, Lin flew over his head and off the edge of the roof.

He both released her wrists and grabbed—fighting the natural instincts again—and her weight dragged him to the edge, too. Brody had managed to keep hold of her, and now she dangled out into space as he had done, her only bond their clasped fingers.

Dep's scream broke the sudden eerie calm as Brody tried to keep hold of Lin's hand, but his grip was weak, and she was slipping loose. Slipping loose, yet still managing to slowly pull him out over the edge with her.

He stared down into her eyes and hate flashed back at him —pure, unadulterated hate. She was not holding on for dear life. Lin was resolved to her fate, but she was determined to take him along in the process.

"No!" Dep screamed as she watched her man sliding closer to the edge and Lin losing her grip. "No, Lin!"

The Quan Loi sniper was now digging her fingernails into Brody's wrist, and as the pain shot up through his arm, he knew it was time to decide. He loved Dep, and he tried to love Lin, but there was no choice.

*"Con de hoang."* She muttered the insult again, renewed strength gripping his wrist like a vise, like a steel claw, and Brody struck. He pounded their arms against the brick wall, over and over again, until the defiant, hate-filled snarl faded from Lin's face, and she dropped to the concrete below.

# CHAPTER 26

## Phung Du

Viet Cong and NVA Regulars appeared to be in control of the An Lao Valley, which proved to be an unexpected turn of events. Green Beret Delta teams were calling for help. They were calling for gunship support-and-extraction from the First Cav. But Moore's people were surrounded and pinned down on the plains outside Bong Son.

Col. Moore could not free his brigade to assist the Special Forces people, but he could certainly radio other units to get on the move.

Directives were sent to the First of the 9th Squadron to locate and rescue the men trapped in the An Lao. Artillery support would be provided the 7th Cav's Alpha Company. Their cannons would be mounted on a hilltop east of the An Lao. The 12th Cavalry at Phu Cat, currently being held in reserve for emergencies just such as this, would race to the 7th Cav's aid as soon as some arty softened up the enemy positions.

If Patterson expected a scream from the woman he was pulling down out of the night sky, he got more—much more.

Kim dropped onto him like a wildcat, slashing with her fingernails, going for his eyes, as her rifle, knocked from her hands, stuck into the sand, buttplate up, like the weapons at a bodybag memorial, waiting for someone to place helmets on them.

"Hey, goddamnit!" He fended off her blows at first, but she was not slowing down—had in fact commenced to kick with her feet, too, as they rolled in the sand and she came out on top from sheer momentum. She slashed at him again, gouging a deep wound in his cheek, and Patterson struck her with his fist.

The force of the impact threw her off of him, but failed to knock her out. She was on her feet again before he could blink, before he could even rise to his elbows. On her feet and charging!

She had the rifle in her hands again, had scooped it up as she rolled away from him. But the chamber was empty. She found that out when she tried to fire at him from the hip.

"Wait!" he yelled as she continued her rush toward him, the rifle's bayonet fixed and gleaming in the dark. Flares popped overhead, but she did not seek cover.

"Tonight you die, *du ma!*" she screamed down at him, the lips curled back from her teeth like a rabid dog's.

"Wait!" he called again, wanting her to recognize him, wanting her to remember that night, the night she had both tortured and set him free. True, he had waited all these weeks, dreaming about finding her in the jungle, but resolved to the probability he would never see her again. Vietnam was too big, and this was not the Ia Drang, where her guerrilla cell had captured him and annihilated his platoon. True, he had prayed for the chance to pound a few nails into her himself, but now that he saw her again face to face, death and madness in her eyes, he wanted to reason with her, to connect. They had both survived that night in the Ia Drang, and by shedding his blood yet deciding not to kill him, Kim had—whether she knew it or not—formed a bond with Saint Pat. He wanted to talk to her. He didn't want to kill her after all.

Patterson's instincts took over as she thrust the blade down at him. Since he was unarmed, all he could do was kick.

"Wait!" he cried again, knocking the bayonet aside several times with the soles of his jungle boot. But then she faked to the left and ran the blade into his thigh.

An uncontrollable scream left his throat, though he didn't feel the pain immediately, and then she was practically on top of him, and jabbing away again.

*Slash, thrust, jab!* In the flash of an instant, he saw himself back in boot camp years earlier, on the confidence course, "killing" dummies.

And then the icy reality of cold steel slammed him from his fantasy: Kim had run the blade into his belly.

The blow caused him to curl up into the fetal position again, and he grabbed the rifle's brown handgrips, disbelief creasing his features, refusing to let go. Blood spurting from his gut sprinkled onto his fingers, and the sight of it drained him of all his power.

Recognition sparked in her almond eyes—recognition, and a sudden trace of compassion, and she didn't rip his stomach open as she withdrew the bayonet.

But then without warning she stabbed him again. In the chest. Twice. And Patterson felt himself falling backward . . . backward and down . . . into the bottomless pit. He must be hallucinating now, because he was sure he saw her rise to her feet and run off into the night. But she was suddenly back by his side, her full, sensuous lips brushing his ear, and she was whispering something. Whispering death.

The words exploded suddenly like bombs echoing in a canyon, yet the noise did not hurt his ears. He locked eyes with her as she seemed to float beside him, down through the shaft of darkness. "You are going to your death because of *me*, Corporal Patterson! Breathe your last breath into my mouth, so I can carry your soul and your strength onto other battlefields!"

Her long, black hair had become golden flames, her sunken cheeks the face of a skull, her eyes the glowing green of a cat's, and he refused her.

Patterson refused to kiss her, and submitted to the voices calling from the pit instead. He closed his eyes and she was gone.


North Vietnamese soldiers were firmly entrenched north of Phung Du's corpse-cluttered cemetery in a dot on the map called Tan Thanh.

The area was a honeycomb of underground tunnels and bunkers, and the NVA were determined to hold their ground when Moore rallied his troops and headed north from the graveyard battleground.

On the second day of Operation Masher, after Buchanan's counterpart motivated his men out of the trench of death where so many civilians had given up, elements of the First Cavalry Division swept the area north of Landing Zone 4, clashing with three platoons of NVA Regulars.

After over two hours of bitter fighting, artillery and gunships were finally called in, and the enemy melted back into the bamboo, leaving forty-four of their comrades behind for Moore's body count.

As the mist turned crimson, and twilight fell over the plains, the Cavalrymen from Bravo, Charlie, and Echo Companies of First Battalion set up a defensive perimeter a little less than a mile from the fierce firefight and dug in for the night. The men from 2nd Battalion and survivors of the 12th Cav took up positions along LZ-4, and within the tombstones of the cemetery itself.

The next day, following a night of harassment from snipers and infrequent mortar barrages, the troopers moved out to search the nearby hamlet. It was January 30, a date they would all remember well, for it was their appointment with the tunnel rats of Tan Thanh.

The communists opened fire on the first arriving squads shortly before zero eight hundred hours, showering the Americans with an unexpected wall of impenetrable lead. More artillery was called in, and after strafing gunships further softened up the area, the Cavalrymen counterattacked.

Duels with machine guns, grenades, and even pistols escalated into hand-to-hand combat as the Infantrymen reached the center of the ville, only to find themselves surrounded by spiderholes glowing with muzzle flashes.

Once again, the gunships came in handy, and when one suicidal squad of sappers bolted into the open, intent on facing off a treetop-swooping Huey, the Americans on the ground cut them down easily. Other communists fled through the trees, only to be chased down by fast-thinking grunts and the gunship pilots themselves, who would compete with the Cavalrymen to reach retreating enemy soldiers first. U.S. Forces suffered only light casualties, but Charlie lost a hundred men at Tan Thanh.

The next day, Alpha and Echo companies again rose before the dawn. They rose before the Cong, too, catching Charlie with his pants down in Luong Tho. But they must have been sleeping ten to a tunnel, Jacob Vance would reflect later, for a blinding firefight erupted, lasting well past high noon.

The battle became so intense, drawing both sides into hand-to-hand combat again, that American commanders could not call in artillery for fear of killing their own people with friendly fire.

Bravo and Charlie Companies from the 7th Cav were eventually able to reinforce the besieged units, and Vance and Zack, among other leaders under fire, were given a chance to drag their wounded back out of the kill zone.

Artillery was then called in once more, and as dusk ap-

287

proached, Alpha Company C.O. Capt. Tony Nadal, with over a dozen of his men seriously wounded, requested a Dustoff. "It's bad," he told Col. Moore over the radio. "Bookoo bad! Need a med-evac *rikky-tik*!" But the Colonel glanced at the western horizon and shook his head. There are strange evenings in The Nam now and then when there is no twilight. It's dusk, and then it's dark. No in-between. This was one of those nights.

"Negative," he told Nadal regretfully. Trying to set a chopper down in a hot LZ after dark was suicide. The wounded would have to try and hang on through the night. Moore would make sure they got help with the first light of day.

"It's a no-go!" Nadal told Zack and the others as they lay against the dunes of sand, watching flares float past on the muggy breeze. Many of the men were keeping pressure bandages applied to the unconscious wounded.

"Shit!" Lt. Vance could only shrug his shoulders as Chappell and Nelson cursed. "They're just gonna fucking let us die out here?"

"Some of these guys aren't gonna make it, Lieutenant!" Zack agreed with the privates. "I know there's nothin' we can do"—bullets slammed into their position on all sides as he spoke—"but it's just a godawful shame, I'm tellin' you, and—"

"Maybe we could try something." Vance volunteered a plan as he low-crawled closer to Leo.

"I'm game if you are." Zack motioned the men in their squad closer.

Captain Nadal was holding up his hand for silence. He had been talking into the PR-25 headset, and now they could faintly hear rotorblades slapping fog in the distance.

"Nadal, you did it!" The other captain, the one with the patch over his eye, was among them now, having burst forth from the darkness.

"Pays to know people in high places." Nadal's eyeballs

288

rolled skyward, toward the flares, and Vance flipped him the thumbs-up.

Zack recognized the winged horse painted across the Huey's snout immediately. "*Pegasus!*" he shouted as the helicopter came into view, hovering directly overhead.

"They already got the bitch repaired!" Nelson shouted as everyone rose to their knees and began firing outward in a complete if not crude circle of barrel flames.

Zack stared hard at the gunship's belly. "That's not Gabriel behind the stick," he muttered.

"It's Bruce Crandall!" Nadal shouted above the roar of their rifles. "He owes me one!"

"*Major* Bruce Crandall?" Zack stopped shooting for a moment.

"The one and only! Gunslinger's riding shotgun."

"Well, aw-*right!*" Zack switched from automatic to semi and began popping off two- and three-round manual bursts at wildly different points in the cloak of darkness enveloping them.

It was pitch-black, except for the occasional flare or shower of tracers, and Crandall was unable to swoop in for a flaring descent because of the terrain. The Americans were pinned down dead center in the middle of the hamlet, with palm trees rising up into the night all around them. He would have to drop straight down from a vulnerable hover.

With bullets whining only inches over his head, Nadal chose the best possible LZ—a very small clearing within the clump of palms—and began directing the Huey in, using the radio and a small GI flashlight.

Crandall wasn't sure why the flickering light he was guiding on kept going out. He couldn't see the ground, or the trees, because of the intense darkness pressing in on the LZ, but every time he was about to abort the landing attempt, the lance of light shot up through the wisps of fog again.

"Let's rock!" Zack ordered, as the blacked-out Huey's outline appeared faintly overhead. The men switched their rifles

289

to full automatic again, and laid down cover fire in a 180-degree pattern, forcing many of the enemy to stop shooting and duck behind their trees or sandbars.

Chappell and Nelson, hearing the monstrous rotors clip a few palm fronds overhead, suddenly realized how close the metal predator was. But before they could worry very much about the hazards of lying beneath a helicopter that could be shot down at any moment, Crandall executed a perfect landing and *Pegasus* was on the ground.

"Let's move it! Let's go!" Zack and several men began lifting the wounded, while the rest continued firing into the surrounding tree line.

"Six max!" came the shout from the cockpit window.

*"What?"* Chappell couldn't believe his ears. "We've got *thirteen* W.I.A.'s here, Gunslinger!"

"Sorry, kid, but we're gonna have to make a vertical take-off—same way we came in." The downblast covered some of his words.

"And for that you've gotta be light!" Crandall added as the chopper's rotors kept beating at the muggy, unyielding heat without slowing.

Lt. Vance glanced around frantically, his heart in his mouth. Someone was going to have to decide which men went into the Dustoff. And which stayed behind.

# CHAPTER 27

## Sisters of Mercy Orphanage

"Do they give you this kind of service in An Khe?"

Doc Delgado stared down at the head of blond hair bobbing up and down slowly over his crotch with renewed appreciation. "No," he sighed, leaning his back against the headboard, "can't say as they do."

Lt. Lisa Maddox suddenly took in as much as she could, dropping her lips nearly to its base, then teased the flaring head again with her tongue. "And how do they talk to you when you stop by their parlor in An Khe for a steam-'n-cream?" she purred. "Those boom-boom girls, do they talk dirty to you, Danny-boy?"

His hands cupped the sides of Lisa's head lightly, directing her mouth back where he felt it belonged. "They . . . talk . . . very . . . dirty . . . to me." Delgado began to groan slightly. He started smoothing her hair down with the palms of his hands as she worked to please him.

"Don't pet me like a dog," she snapped suddenly, gnawing on him until he yelped.

He was about to tease back, when there came a thump against the door of her quarters, and they both froze. "What was that?" he whispered harshly.

"How the hell do I know?" She sighed and he began to shrink while they waited.

"Did you lock the door?"

"It doesn't have a lock."

"Oh, great! Really great!" Delgado couldn't believe he was still whispering.

The doorknob began turning, and they both held their breath.

Maddox and her favorite medic had just completed forty-eight hours straight in triage. The captain in charge of the makeshift aid station gave them both six hours off to recuperate, and they had raced to Lisa's hooch, where tinfoil was taped against the windows to keep out the sunlight. Maddox worked mostly nights, so she was a day sleeper, and because it was difficult to sleep during sunlight hours in Vietnam, the Sisters of Mercy had seen fit to loan her the only air conditioner at the orphanage. They also allowed her use of a small structure at the edge of the compound, which had once been a storage shed but which Maddox, along with the help of Delgado and some of his Echo Company buddies, converted into her hooch.

The door swung open and a burst of sunlight blinded the two lovers just as Lisa slid up onto Delgado, pulling a sheet over her haunches as she did.

"Oh, *Lieutenant!* So sorry, so sorry!" An embarrassed housegirl with fresh bedsheets piled high atop outstretched arms, who had yet to see a man without his pants on, backed out of the hooch and rushed off without closing the door.

Delgado sounded perturbed but not highly upset. "We needed that like we needed a hole in the head," he said.

"She won't say anything." Maddox stared at the open door for a moment, then resumed kissing his chest as she fondled the buck sergeant. With the insides of her thighs riding his hips, Lisa opened herself up to him, grunting as he lanced into her. She allowed her full weight to press down on Delgado as she wrapped her arms around him. She enjoyed letting the man do all the work during a second round of sex, while she hung on for the ride.

But the medic's entire body went rigid suddenly, and he gently rolled Lisa onto her side. "I can't." He withdrew without warning, dragging another gasp from her. "Sheets or no sheets, I don't care if they're all walking zombies out there. I can't do it with the damn door open, Lisa." He slid off the bed, pulling the single sheet from her as he did and wrapping it around his waist.

"Oh-oh!" As he stood in the bright doorway, hand on the knob, a big, brown, short-haired mongrel rushed past through the harsh sunlight outside. The dog was howling and running around in tight circles as it moved from one side of the orphanage to the other. "We got trouble!"

"Is that the mutt Spec4 Brody asked you to keep an eye on for him?"

"Yep!" Delgado rushed back inside and began pulling on his trousers and boots.

"While he was down in Saigon or over in Plei Me or wherever he went?"

"Right. Choi-oi's his name, mayhem's his game. Disappeared the same day Treat left, and I just assumed The Whoremonger had a change of heart and took the little fuck along without tellin' me."

"I hate that name." Lisa sat up on the edge of the bed, not bothering to cover her breasts as they swayed heavily from side to side with the movement.

Delgado did not miss the body language. "What name?"

"The nickname. Whoremonger."

"Boys will be boys." Delgado picked Maddox's uniform up off the back of a chair and threw it to her. "Let's go!" he said, a sudden urgency in his tone. "I'm surprised we've had *this* long!"

"This long? What are you talking abou—"

"You've a short memory, Lisa."

The mortars began descending on the Sisters of Mercy orphanage before he could help her find her bra.

Seven of the children were already dead before Maddox and Delgado got their clothes back on. They were lying out in the open, between the compound's small church and the main gate, their chests torn open by shrapnel, or limbs shredded and mutilated. One small girl had been decapitated, and Maddox thought about Tamminh for a moment, but she had no time now to search for the head, to see if it was really Saint Pat's little girl whose life had been so unfairly snatched away from her.

"You take triage, and I'll make sure all the kids are in the shelter!" she yelled to the medic as they raced, hand in hand, through the swirling columns of bomb smoke.

"Always giving the orders!" He laughed before ducking into the portable Aid station. "Even in the sack!" With a smile, she directed an obscene gesture at him, and Delgado responded with, "You wish!"

"One of these days, maybe," she told herself as she watched him sprint into the series of Quonset huts. "One of these days."

Maddox tried to concentrate on the children as she checked each of their special hiding places, but her father's face kept flashing in front of her eyes.

Deep inside she knew the General would not approve of her life. Military tradition ran high in the Maddox clan. They'd had a man in West Point for each of the last six generations, and even though the General's only child turned out to be a she, papa's little girl became an officer, too.

She felt he knew about her and Delgado. During her bimonthly visits down to Saigon, where she would visit him at his office in the war room, she noticed a change recently. Where before he had always been so warm and physical, hugging her even in public and lapsing into baby talk—"How's

294

papa's little girl?"—he now was cool and distant. Often staring at her with that tight, all-knowing grin and gleam in his eyes, a gleam that said, "you little devil, you." He disapproved. Yes, she knew it now, the more she thought about his behavior of recent months. He knew, and he disapproved, yet he seemed to admire her daring. That was the reason for the gleam in his eyes, the tight grin. She wondered what the men were telling him, and who they were. Not that it really mattered. Ia Drang and now Bong Son had taught her there were more important things in life than what people thought about you, even family. Don't mean nothin', as the old Nam slang goes. But it hurt Lisa deeply.

Her father had attempted on several past occasions to have her reassigned under his command in Saigon, but Lisa protested, refusing all transfers offered her. Many of the women she worked with failed to understand her motivations, and often teased her about passing up an eight-and-skate job at 3rd Field for the harsh realities of triage in the boonies. But Lt. Lisa Maddox did not want to work in the city. True, the shifts at 3rd and 17th were not eight hours at all, but twelve and twenty-four, often longer, depending on casualties, and an assignment there could be very challenging, both mentally and physically, as well as rewarding, rank-wise. But Maddox had volunteered for Vietnam because she wanted to be close to the action.

She had found love in a tough yet tender man who made his living on battlefields of death but could still find a gentleness in his heart for her. Delgado could have left The Nam long ago, but he remained. He extended over and over again, so he could stay with the boys, so he could be there when the newbies and the pogues and the twinks, and all the FNG's needed him. Even though The Nam was killing Doc Delgado. It was killing him from within, and Lisa hoped to be able to change that. Somehow. If they could only survive the NVA backlash to Operation Masher.

"Goddamnit!" Maddox yelled at Choi-oi. The dog had

scampered between her legs when a string of mortars exploded nearby, nearly tripping her up. "Go find yourself a foxhole, *ass*hole!" She pulled the cover off a trashcan, but the little boy who spent most of his time hiding inside it was not there.

"Good!" she muttered, racing to the next hiding place. The kids were finally learning. Aluminum and cardboard would not stop shrapnel.

"Choi-oi!" she kicked at him but missed as the mutt jumped in front of her again, trying to get her attention. "I'm *busy*!"

But the animal persisted, finally growling until she stopped dead in her tracks, shocked at his ugly behavior. Had the mongrel gone mad? Had he finally caught rabies from one of those bitches in heat he was always courting beyond the bamboo or deep inside the concertina? She had even found him fornicating with a black German Shepherd—probably AWOL from a sniffer team—in the middle of a posted mine field one time. The Shepherd didn't make it out, and Choi-oi whined around camp for a week, mooching compassion.

Choi-oi barked and took hold of her wrist. His jaws closed firmly, but not hard enough for the teeth to break flesh. The dog began dragging her in the opposite direction she wanted to go, but Maddox had no choice—if she did resist, Choi-oi was obviously going to get nasty.

"This better be damned important," she snapped, "or you're gonna be the main ingredient in a Yarde pot o' dogmeat soup tonight!"

Choi-oi whimpered and wagged his tail in reply, but kept pulling hard, his big black eyes bulging as he drooled saliva all over the lieutenant's arm.

Brody's pet dragged Maddox nearly all the way back to where she started, near the main gate. He released her as they passed between two helicopters beginning to take off, and ran over to a jeep parked beside the triage conex.

"What *is* it, Choi-oi?" Her pace slowed as she glanced at the headless child near the fenceline. Someone had thrown a

296

poncho liner over the body, but a succession of mortar blasts had blown it off again.

Choi-oi barked in reply, stopping beside the jeep, then jumping into the front seat and out the other side, back down onto the ground.

"Goddamnit!" She stamped her foot at him and the interruption. "Not now, you little jerk! No time for a joyride *now*!"

She started to leave, to resume the search for lost and terrified children, when Choi-oi went wild again, barking nonstop.

Maddox glanced back at the jeep and noticed the splotch of crimson across the inside of the windshield. It was as if someone had thrown a red snowball against the glass from the rear of the vehicle.

His tail still wagging furiously, Choi-oi leaped back into the jeep, hopped over the front seat into the back, and toyed with something under the gun mount for a moment. When he climbed back up onto the frame radio, a misshapen, mutilated face stared back at Maddox. Suspended from the long strands of black hair clenched tightly between Choi-oi's teeth, was something one of the first blasts of shrapnel had torn from an unsuspecting body: the severed head of a little girl.


Lt. Jacob Vance watched the line of Dustoff helicopters come in with the dusk. The battle for Phung Du's sandy plains had ended.

Lisa Maddox and Doc Delgado stood on either side of him. The army nurse wiped grimy sweat from her brow with an olive-drab GI towel. "I'm glad it's over."

"It's never over, Lt. Maddox." Zack was there too, watching the last of the med-evacs swoop in to disgorge their bloody cargo at the aid station. "We're headed into the An Lao tomorrow. Bossman doesn't like the way Charlie's taken over the valley, doesn't like the way the Green Berets nearly got annihilated up there last week. Bein' outnumbered a thousand

297

to one," Leo reflected, "don't see how they *avoided* gettin' annihilated!"

Special Forces had sent some of their crack Delta recon teams into the An Lao during the last week of January, only to find the area so saturated with enemy troops that they could not conduct infiltration missions. And they could not even pull out. Charlie was everywhere. NVA machine-gun nests seemed more plentiful than bird nests.

One team was succcessfully extracted by First Cav rescue choppers, but a second was ambushed three times by communist patrols and half its people killed. Their bodies had to be left behind as the survivors fought for their own lives now. Four men of Team 3 were also killed in an ambush, and the Delta mission leader, Major "Chargin' Charlie" Beckwith, was wounded as his gunship raced to their rescue.

When it was all over, seven of the seventeen original recon troopers were dead. Three had sustained serious wounds, and the bodies of three Green Berets were never recovered.

The communists had dealt the Americans a harsh blow in the An Lao, and now the First Air Cavalry Division was about to attack the valley in force, intent on cleaning out the festering wound.

Zack spotted *Pegasus* among the slicks pranging in across the warped but unyielding tarmac. Major Crandall was no longer in the cockpit—he was back with his regular unit, Alpha Company of the 229th Assault Helicopter Battalion—and Leo recognized Gabriel The Gunslinger manning the cyclic.

Smiling at the memory of such a close call, Zack reflected on the night they spent eating lead splinters in a place called Luong Tho.

Not only had Crandall been able to land in the tight LZ under fire and take out six of their most seriously wounded, but he also returned a second time, and a third, until every trooper that needed medical aid, got it. The heroism he displayed that evening *got him* a DFC, America's second highest award for valor.

After all the gunsmoke cleared, nearly 170 enemy soldiers lay dead in the Vietnamese cemetery at Phung Du. The First Air Cav lost 13 brave and gallant gunship warriors. Another 33 would win the Purple Heart.

"Well, if it ain't Saint Pat!" Chappell and Nasty Nel rushed up to the first stretcher being lowered from *Pegasus*'s cabin.

"You made it!" Zack was right behind them. Delgado and Nurse Maddox rushed up too. "We thought you were a goner, boy!"

"Nobody could find you, Patterson!" Lt. Vance grasped his upper arm warmly.

"We looked, too, Pat!" Chappell said. "We searched for you *every*where, man! What the hell happened?"

Patterson rubbed the blood-soaked bandages covering his chest and stomach. "Had a run-in with a Cong bayonet," he told them, and Vance cringed as he envisioned an enemy soldier plunging the blade into the corporal's belly over and over. "And the bitch wore black."

*"Bitch?"* Nelson's eyes went wide.

"But you're gonna be all right?" Crandall cut in, worried when he read the look of urgency in the stretcher-bearers' eyes. He glanced over at Maddox. "He *is* gonna be all right, right, Lieutenant?"

"Saint Pat'll make it," she said confidently, waving the corpsmen on, but Patterson reached out and grabbed Maddox's hand, forcing them to stop again. Choi-oi, attracted to all the excitement, crawled out from under a water trough and began barking for the wounded infantryman's attention. He stood up on his hind legs, draped his forepaws over the edge of the stretcher, and began licking Patterson's chin.

"Tamminh!" he said. "Where is she, Lieutenant? I really been thinking about her these last twenty-four hours. I've been thinking about nothin' 'cept her! I'm takin' her back, ma'am. I've made the decision. It's final. I'm going to adopt her. I

299

don't care what it takes: Tamminh's goin' back to The World with me!"

"Okay, okay!" She patted his forehead lightly. "Don't get your blood pressure up." Maddox swallowed a hard, dry swallow, and she glanced over at Zack for support.

"She's around here somewhere, kid," he said. "You just get into the O.R. and heal up *rikky-tik*, understand? We'll find her in the meantime."

"Great! Appreciate it, you guys, really I do!" Patterson waved at them all as the medics carried him into the Quonset hut.

"Who's this Tamminh kid Saint Pat was talking about?" Zack confronted the army nurse after they'd taken Patterson out of earshot.

Lisa Maddox stared up at the big black bald-headed sergeant in silence. Her cheek began to twitch under the stress, and then a lone tear edged its way down her face. Without saying anything, she turned around, kicked Choi-oi in the rump, and walked back toward the operating room, agonizing over how she was ever going to tell the corporal that his little daughter-to-be was dead and buried.

# CHAPTER 28

## The Briarpatch P.O.W. camp, Xom Ap Lo

Shawn Larson peeked through swollen eyelids down at the two rats on the floor. They seemed the size of tomcats from his vantage point. Both rodents had risen up on their hind legs, but still couldn't reach his nose.

The Professor was hanging upside down, suspended from the ceiling by wires wrapped around his wrists and ankles. Twine kept his hands and feet knotted together.

The rats were drawn to him from their lair in the sewer pipe by the drops of blood falling from his chin and forming a pool on the shale floor two feet below his face. The rats could almost reach his nose with their gnashing incisors, but not quite. Whenever they did come close, he would try to swing his body from side to side until they dropped back onto all fours from frustration.

Larson was unsure why the filthy animals were toying with him. He knew from twelve months in the underground bunkers of An Khe and Ia Drang that rats in Vietnam could leap a dozen feet if they really wanted to. Maybe these were fat rats. Maybe they had already had their meal for today— someone else's nose, or lip, or ear, in a cell down the row.

The camp was not what he had expected from a P.O.W.

compound. It certainly was not like what they had trained him to expect in Basic, where drill sergeants still thought you were going to Bataan or Saipan. But he hadn't expected that. The Professsor, during the long trek through circles of jungle he was sure they'd already marched him through before, had envisioned small bamboo cages in a concertina-enclosed compound. But the cellblock they had thrown him into was constructed of rusty iron bars and two steel convex containers welded together over a rock floor. They were under cover of a roof of some sort, but because he had been bound since his arrival, he was unable to tell much more about the place. Not even if it had been constructed inside a cave, a tunnel complex, or just an old barracks. He never saw sunlight, or darkness for that matter. A lightbulb was constantly burning only a few feet in front of his face.

He did remember, however, arriving under cover of darkness and passing between several wooden structures, which gave him the impression they housed him not in the main area of the installation but along the edge somewhere, away from most of the day-to-day activity.

Suddenly, the rats scampered back into their hole of a toilet, and Larson felt the fear again—the fear Igor, as he had come to nickname the interrogator, had conditioned him to feel each time Larson heard the stocky Vietnamese's footsteps approaching. Igor, who spoke choppy English with a Soviet accent, seemed to dislike The Professor intensely. Larson couldn't decide if it was simply because he was an American, or for reasons having to do with the private's inability to provide satisfying answers to crucial questions. Logistical questions, and probes of a military intelligence nature.

He had laughed at first, telling Igor the brass didn't even let him know when the surprise urinalysis tests were coming up. But the interrogator had found nothing funny in that, and promptly tightened Larson's bindings until his shoulders popped out again, dislocated for the fourth time.

Igor had a special knack with paper clips and pliers. He

302

would straighten the clips out, making one long five- or six-inch wire, and go around poking people in the eye. Oh, it was not quite that simple, of course. Igor liked to experiment.

His assistants would hold the prisoner still—one guard alone being utilized to keep the Arvin or American's head perfectly still—and Igor would gently place the tip of the wire against the prisoner's eyeball, slowly increasing pressure until the pain became unbearable. Sometimes the prisoner would jerk about from the excruciating agony. Other times, Igor himself would get a bit overzealous. In either event, the prisoner's eyeball always suffered sudden puncture or complete rupture. The Briarpatch's top truth-or-consequences trickster would then go on to the next candidate, often using the same paperclip, over and over.

When he tired of wires, Igor pulled out his pliers. Perfectly good teeth were extracted left and right—though one could not be expected to maintain adequate oral hygiene on pumpkin soup and *manioc* once a day for long. Anesthetics, naturally, were out of the question during this exercise in self-discipline.

"Good morning, Private Larson." Igor entered his daydream by slamming the iron bars shut behind him.

Larson forced himself to look up as far as possible. Igor was alone. "Eat shit and die," he muttered, convinced this was the day. The day he would meet his Maker.

"Oh, *ho-ho!*" Igor laughed, slapping his belly like some Southeast Asian Santa Claus. "Funny man this morning. Very good, very good. Still a challenge."

"*Is* it morning?"

"Maybe. Maybe not."

"You're a slimeball, Igor." Larson tensed, and the man rammed his knee into the small of his back like Shawn knew he would. The Professor swung back and forth under the lightbulb, spitting up blood.

"Slimeball? What is slimeball, Private Larson?"

"Can we just cut the chatter, Igor, and get on with it?"

303

"Get on with it?" The interrogator feigned confusion as he rubbed his chin. "Get on with it?"

"Today. Today's the day. I know it. I can feel it in my gut."

"The day? What day are you speaking of, Private Larson? It is not Tet for us, and it is one month since your own New Year's. A birthday, perhaps? Would you like to exchange Valentines in two weeks?"

"Bite the big one, Igor." Blood was running down into Larson's nose, and he sneezed crimson spray onto the Vietnamese. Igor rammed him with a knee again, for his efforts.

"Don't you know proper manners?" he screamed. "Were you raised in a barn? Was your mother a water buffalo? You should cover your face before you sneeze, Private Larson. It is only a routine courtesy to others in the room." Igor whirled Larson around and pulled on the twine, making sure it was still tight.

"Can we get on with it?" Larson asked. "I don't have any teeth left, you son of a bitch, and there's no feeling left in my arms. I'm a cripple, no doubt about it. I'm all broken up inside and I don't have nothin' to live for anymore, so can we just get it over with?"

Igor dropped into a squat in front of The Professor's face. "Are you telling me you think today is the day you die, Private Larson?"

"Yes." The word was barely audible.

"But Private Larson, we could not let anything that serious happen to you. It is against the Geneva Convention to execute prisoners of war in your category. You are a nobody, a nothing, with no information to enlighten my mornings, no out-of-the-ordinary war crimes to confess to."

"Thank you."

"But I like you, Private Larson. I really do."

"You're . . . loads . . . of laughs, too . . . Igor."

"Thank you." The interrogator slammed the palm of his hand against Larson's nose, crushing more cartilage. The bone had yet to penetrate the American's brain, however. Larson

304

found himself praying for that to happen. It would mean quick death, an easy way out.

The impact of the blow swung him backwards, and Igor kept his hand out. When Larson came swinging back, his face struck the hand again, not as hard this time. He bounced away, only to return, like a pendulum, over and over. Igor did not lower his hand until The Professor was completely still.

"You have only been here a week, Private Larson." The interrogator ground his teeth loud enough for Shawn to hear. "How can I justify ending your misery when there have been prisoners staying here as our guests for several years already, undergoing exactly what you are going through? Now how could I ever justify something like that to my superiors? The others are suffering the same treatment as yourself, my friend."

*Years?* The thought struck Larson like another blow from Igor's fist. How could he ever endure *years* of this? "End it, Igor. Today." Larson's whisper took on an urgent tone. "I have money. Stateside. My family is rich. I'll get them to send you as much as you want."

"You hurt my feelings, Private Larson." Igor laughed. "Honestly, you do!"

"I'm not asking you to release me. I'm not trying to ransom myself out of this mess. I just want you to kill me. Promise you'll end it, and I'll sign anything you want."

Igor laughed louder this time. He slapped Larson gently, then followed through with a vicious kick to the American's tailbone just as Shawn least expected it. "You are a very entertaining foreigner, Private Larson." Igor's face grew somber. "I know you are tired of the treatment you have received here. I am tired of—how you say? Dishing it out. But you remain untruthful, my friend. You personally insult and offend me."

"And now you're going to tell me why," Larson replied, with as much sarcasm as he could muster.

"I know you have no money, Private Larson. Your family does not exist. Your father and mother abandoned you and a sister because of the girl's medical condition. It is regrettable, but please do not lie about wealth you do not have."

"Would it matter if I *was* into big bucks?"

"Oh, most certainly." Igor ran his pliers across the iron bars once. The sudden, unexpectedly sharp sound sent a shudder through the Professor. "But you are poor people—a peasant-soldier, like myself. And you are not even really a patriot, are you, my friend?"

"Why . . . do . . . you . . . say . . . that?"

"The MPs."

"What?"

"We know, Private Larson. We *know*. About the drugs. You were under arrest for smuggling drugs. Being transported to LBJ via Phung Du when your transport helicopter was shot down. You are nothing more than a criminal, Private Larson. A drug peddler. If you were my son, I would be ashamed." Igor's voice was filled with mock contempt.

"What a crock, funnyman."

"A crock?"

"Yah," Larson bluffed with little confidence, knowing full well none of it mattered anyway. He had lost the game of chance long ago. "I've only been here a few days. There's no way you could have found out all that information in such a short amount of—"

"You were not the only prisoner to make the long journey from Phung Du to Xom Ap Lo." Igor lifted a chain from inside his shirt. It was a necklace of molars. He slipped it up over his head and dangled it in front of the Professor's swollen eyelids.

"You're trying to tell me one of my buddies—a *Cavalryman*—ratted on me, is that what you're saying?" He was surprised at the surge of esprit de corps that surged through his veins, if only for a moment or two. Larson knew Igor was lying about there being a traitor. Two other Americans had made the trek to Xom Ap Lo with him. None of them had been allowed to converse, and there was always two or three

NVA positioned between the Americans as they marched through the rain forests trails, but Larson knew the three were complete strangers, all from different companies of the 7th. There was no way either man knew about his sister, not even by reputation, and the drug bust had occurred minutes before the rescue mission where they were shot down. Half his closest friends didn't even know about that yet.

"I know why your eyes are brown, Igor." Larson decided to try a new approach.

"Because I'm so full of bullshit?" The interrogator laughed.

Larson's reflexes were shot. His wit did not seem to be working well lately, either, and he could not formulate an insult or rebuke. He just hung there, suspended from the ceiling, upside down, swinging slowly back and forth, waiting to see what would happen next, yet not really waiting at all. Events no longer mattered to him. He would not hold his breath for Igor anymore.

"Did you think that, with all the blue-eyed, long-nosed devils I have had to put up with over the years, I have not already heard that one, Private Larson?"

The Professor did not reply.

"You have not eaten in two days, my friend. I would like to bring you something special today: steamed rice—not a large helping, to be sure, but rice nonetheless. And cucumbers. Greens. Some snow peas. Would you like that, Private Larson?" Igor slapped him suddenly, but Larson no longer felt the pain.

Larson had withdrawn into himself, preparing for death.


Igor hadn't tortured him in over a week, and this morning he'd received more rice than he could eat. The day before, they'd finally removed the bindings, and though, twenty-four hours later, he still could not move his arms, Igor instructed one of the guards to hold the spoon for him.

It's gotta be good old LBJ, Larson told himself. President Johnson came down hard on these bastards with Arc-Light, and they've seen the error of their ways.

That evening, Igor appeared in front of his cell carrying something. It was Larson's old rucksack, the one he had been wearing when he was captured.

Igor kicked the pack over, stooped, pulled a notebook out, and The Professor's eyes lit. His journal! He hadn't thought about it at all since the first day he'd been taken prisoner.

"You enjoy writing," said Igor. It was not a question, but a statement of fact. The interrogator had read it. Probably all the way through. That's what all this had been leading up to, all this Mister Nice Guy routine. Igor and his little evil gnomes were up to something.

Larson ignored the instinct to remain silent. "Yes," he said.

"You threaten to 'commit suicide,'" Igor frowned, "over and over. Repeatedly. Nearly every entry. Yet here you are today. Still."

"It was kind of a joke in my unit," he admitted.

Igor tossed the notebook in through the bars. "Well, now is your opportunity to catch up on your writing, Private Larson."

"Oh?" he asked softly, without moving to retrieve the journal.

"You seem so obsessed with death." The interrogator turned and started walking away down the corridor. "Well, now you can reacquaint yourself with it. Your own."

"What?" Larson sat up on his steel rack, feeling the pain race through his shoulders with the movement.

"Write, Private Larson." Igor laughed. "You have just had your last meal. Tomorrow at dawn, you die. Write about what it feels like to know you are going to die in thirteen hours."


When they came for him early the next morning, Larson had scribbled nearly a dozen new pages into the bent and filthy notebook. For five or six hours after the interrogator left

him, he'd been unable to pick up the pencil, unable to participate in their sick little game. But then, as the loneliness and
reality of pre-dawn settled into his bones, he began writing.
He wrote swiftly, and with a vengeance, feeling he could write
a whole book if they would just grant him one more day.

He heard footsteps, and then they had arrived. A guard
slammed the iron grill back, and Igor snatched Shawn's journal out of his hands.

"Remember when you first came here?" Igor asked, as they
led him out to the cement wall.

"Yes." Larson glanced about wildly as the sun struck him
for the first time in many days. Trees overhead—their lush
green branches alive, waving. He felt the life all around him
thriving despite this horror of a camp in its midst, and in his
heart he knew he did not want to die after all.

"You pleaded with me to kill you."

"Yes, Igor. I remember."

"I told you that I couldn't kill you. Because you were low
man on totem pole."

"What?"

"Seniority, remember? There were so many other men
who'd been here longer than you, Private Larson, remember?
So much longer. So many years they had put up with us, and
you . . . you were in such a hurry to leave the Briarpatch. You
hurt our feelings, Private Larson. Truly you did."

"I'm sorry."

"But your time has come." Igor beamed as they reached
the cement wall. "Have you done your homework?" He motioned to the notebook. Larson nodded. "Good, good! Then
we will have something to remember you by."

He positioned The Professor with his back against the
center of the ten-foot-high wall as six NVA soldiers carrying
rifles marched out from their barracks. "Goodbye, Private
Larson." He pulled a blindfold from his back pocket and
started to apply it when the American objected.

"I would rather not," he said, remembering Snakeman and

309

Brody The Whoremonger and all the Echo Company troopers he'd survived Void Vicious with, only to fall victim to the girls of Tu Do Street. He remembered something The Stork had once said, too, and he lifted his chin to Igor. "I want them to look me in the eyes when they kill me." Larson tried to remain brave, but he was trembling uncontrollably.

"Very well." Igor did not seem very impressed.

"Because I'm going to come back, you SONS O' BITCHES!" he shouted suddenly. "I'm going to come back and fucking *HAUNT* every last one of you mothers!"

Igor's hand came up, as did the rifles. In Vietnamese, he issued the command to aim. Though Shawn wanted to stare with bulging eyes down the barrels of the American-made M-14s, he found himself whimpering now, and closing his eyes tightly in anticipation of the explosions snatching his life away.

"Fire!" Igor commanded in English, and the Briarpatch's quiet courtyard was suddenly filled with the clatter of a dozen firing pins slamming against empty chambers.

Igor erupted into laughter, and a drained Shawn Larson sunk to his knees.

Two guards ran over, grabbed The Professor, and dragged him back toward his cell. Igor issued a directive in rapid-fire Vietnamese, and they paused until he could catch up with them.

The interrogator forced Larson's notebook against his belly roughly until the prisoner of war doubled over. "Your sissy diary," he muttered. "Last night you wrote about what it feels like to know you are going to die. Now write about what you just experienced."

Igor laughed to himself as he slammed the iron grill shut and walked off down the corridor.

310

# CHAPTER 29

## Saigon

"I think you'll do just fine, Mr. Brody. Report for work at seven o'clock tomorrow morning, and I'll have our security chief show you around the plant."

Brody shook the personnel manager's hand, nodded, and left the downtown Saigon offices of Trans-Pacific Architects & Engineers whistling a cheerful tune. He had three sets of guard uniforms under one arm and a permit authorizing him, as an American civilian, to carry a firearm.

Dep had shown him the classified ad in the Saigon *Post*. Trans-Pacific periodically advertised for Nam vets, especially ex-military police, to fill the supervisory ranks of their large security force, and Dep took him down on Le Loi and showed him where he could have the fake DD214 discharge papers created. Since they were phony, he opted for a 95-Bravo MOS, as well: MP instead of doorgunner. "But I don't have a lot of street beat experience," he told the personnel manager. "Mostly gunjeeps in the boonies, payroll convoy escorts through hostile territory . . . things of that nature."

And that had impressed them. "We really would rather have someone who is familiar with heavy armament than a skate who has only carried an unloaded pistol and never had to pull it," the manager replied. "You'll do just fine, Mr. Brody." Pay was US $1,400 a month, nearly ten times what he was making as a doorgunner. He would work with a couple dozen other Americans, riding around Saigon in blue unmarked jeeps, checking on the Vietnamese security personnel who guarded TPA&E installations across the sprawling city of three million.

Brody had changed his name on the DD214, too. Not his last name, for he'd hate to run across an old buddy in a bar and have the man call out his old name if he was going by something new. Brody changed his first name. That way, if someone happened to call out "Treat" in mixed company, he could always claim it was just a nickname. The DD214 read "Bobby Joe Brody." And he'd changed the service number, too, just in case they ever ran a background check on him or entered his stats into the AWOL computer. He hoped the deception was complete enough.

On the way home, he stopped along Nguyen Hue—"Flower Boulevard" many called it—and purchased a beautiful bouquet for Dep. She had had it pretty rough since Lin's death, and kept to herself, rarely talking. She politely declined offers to see a movie or dine out, and preferred to sit on the balcony, watching flares float along the edge of the city at night.

She was out there again when he arrived home, squatting tirelessly on her haunches, thighs flaring and sensuous as ever, a bowl of *pho* between her bare feet, untouched. It was not even dusk yet, but the glaze was in her eyes, and when he waved his hand slowly back and forth in front of her face, she didn't blink, flinch, or even seem to notice.

"I brought these for you," he said, turning on the tap water to wash out a vase. His voice reached her through the mental fog, penetrating to her world of hurt, her realm of *dau*, and she turned to stare at him for a long time.

After he put the flowers into the vase, he held it up for her inspection. "You like, or you no like?" Brody shrugged his shoulders when she did not immediately answer, and took a can of Pabst from the small PX fridge. She finally left the balcony. "How much did you spend on them?"

"Nothing is too expensive for my precious honey-san." He kissed her forehead. "Next time, I will make it a dozen roses. I promise."

"We can not afford this." She sounded angry.

"No sweat. Forget it. You needed something to cheer you up. You're welcome. End of discussion."

"I am going out tonight," she stated matter-of-factly.

"What?" he said, knowing her answer all too well.

"Out. I'm going out. On street. I'm going out to trick. We need money."

Brody chuckled skeptically. "Oh, really?"

"You think I want to?" She assumed a defensive stance. For days she had been wearing nothing but a sheer beige nightgown. As the flares passed behind her out the balcony, he could see the outlines taking shape where her long, sleek legs came together, and he felt an excitement heating in his loins.

"Do you want anything to eat?" He changed the subject, hoping she didn't walk over toward the doorway and spot the bag containing his new uniforms.

"You think I'm joke?" She grabbed his arm.

"No, I don't think you're joking." He smiled warmly, and her countenance softened.

"I don't want to do, Bro-dee, but need rent doll' tomorrow. It's fifteen doll' that we no have."

Brody wanted to laugh. *Fifteen dollars!* And in two weeks, he'd have seven hundred.

"I will find nice man, not GI. Take hotel Cholon. I know place. Only short-time, Bro-dee. Not stay all night. Dep come back, sleep with you. No worry, okay?"

He fought the disgust he was feeling in the pit of his gut, gently took hold of her arms, and brought her closer until their noses were practically touching. "I don't ever want to hear

313

you talk like that again, okay?" He kissed her lightly, then withdrew to gauge her reaction.

"But what about bills, Bro-dee? What about—"

She hadn't been listening at all, and he silenced her with another, longer kiss, then took the employment papers from his pocket and handed them to her.

"Fourteen hundred smackers a month!" He whooped, dancing around in a little circle as she read in frozen silence. "On that many greenbacks in Saigon, we can live like royalty!"

A full minute passed before his excitement waned and he realized she did not share his enthusiasm. "What's wrong, honey-san?" He rushed over and hugged her, but she leaned her head back, away from his, as if she needed distance to focus on the swirl of emotions within his eyes.

"I did not really think you would get the job," she finally said, breaking away from him and returning to the balcony.

He followed her outside, and they watched the glowing orange afterburners of a distant Phantom, climbing the twilight skyline. "Aren't you happy?"

"It was two week ago I recommend you think 'bout job with TPA&E," she said. "Now I learn more. They check, Bro-dee. They check everything. Police, C.I.A., everything."

"So? I haven't done anything." He knew what she would say next.

"Soon your time . . . your thirty days be up." Dep stared at the stars. "You be AWOL, then deserter. TPA&E, they find out, Bro-dee, you *bic*?"

"I'll worry about that if and when the time comes," he said. "For now, we should enjoy life, Dep. This is Saigon. For us, there might be no tomorrow. Hell, a rocket could decide to drop right down and—" She held her hand up, cutting him off, but then he said, "I know, I know: in Nam, words have power. Say and it will happen. I'm sorry." He grabbed her hand and slapped the narrow, open palm against his mouth.

Dep did not laugh at his antics. He was sure that would have broken the ice, but she showed no emotion whatsoever.

314

"Lin leave diary," she told him after they watched several more starbursts drift by on the humid night breeze. "I read most of it while you were away today."

"I'm sorry about Lin." The words left him as a tortured whisper, and that made Brody feel strange inside. He rubbed at the scabbed-over knife wound on his hand.

"Was not your fault."

"I know that." He looked up, hoping to lock eyes with her, but she was still staring out at the stars. "But do you? Do you really believe that it was not my fault?"

"In her diary, Lin blame me," she said, tears streaming down her face now, yet he did not go to her. "That why . . . now I know why we no find family pictures anywhere her room. She rip up."

"I'm sorry, Dep."

"Lin write about she hate me. She hate all Vietnamese girls sleep with American men."

"You had to survive." He tried to choose his words carefully, but they were coming out wrong. "You got to meet me, didn't you?"

"'Treat Bro-dee, the Whoremonger.'" Her voice dropped very low as she spoke. "What that say about me?" Her lips were trembling, and he knew she would break down and begin sobbing again soon.

"Nothing, Dep. It's just a nickname my goofy buddies gave me long before I ever met you, honey-san."

"Lin was right." Dep turned her back on him. "I am trash. A whore girl. Numba Ten pros'itute." Her words were becoming slurred. She had been hitting the bottle while Brody was gone. A bottle he didn't know they owned. "I should be dead. Not Lin."

"Don't torture yourself like this." He moved to her side and held her tightly, nibbled on her ear. She did not push him away for once, and Brody could tell she needed the warm, human touch after talking to Lin's ghost all day. "It will get better," he promised her. "Please be patient with me, okay? We're going to be so happy, Dep."

"What about tomorrow?" she asked, forgetting the guilt over her sister for now. "The rent. It is due tomorrow. I told mama-san we can not pay. She already bring embassy sec'tary by this afternoon...look at room. We have move by morning. You have plan, Bro-dee?"

"No problem," he lifted his shoe up onto the balcony railing and pulled his pants leg up. "Bro-dee have a plan..." And he opened the secret ankle pouch, but the gold coins were gone.


As he approached the apartment building, Brody glanced up at the balcony out of habit. For the first time in over a week, Dep was not sitting out there in her daily daze, staring off into space when he got home from work.

Maybe she finally snapped out of it, he decided, whistling cheerfully as he approached the back alley that led into their housing project. Things would be better now, he was sure, now that he had this new job, now that they'd have a steady paycheck coming in.

Not that he enjoyed the work that much. True, it was easy money—cruising back and forth across Saigon, never keeping to any set schedule or routine in hopes you could catch one of the guards sleeping on duty. Only a week, and it was already boring, a repetitive game.

He missed his buddies in Echo Company fiercely. And he was feeling guilt now, guilt over deserting. Not that he'd actually deserted yet. He still had a few days before his thirty-day leave was over, but it was the principle of the thing: he wasn't planning to go back. He was going to stay here in Saigon, Pearl of the Orient, Sin City. He was becoming a professional REMF: a rear echelon motherfucker. And Treat "Bobby Joe"

Brody hated himself for it. He hated it even more than he hated The Whoremonger in him.

"You want paper, Joe?" He had almost tripped over a newspaper boy with no legs. A kid who'd been to hell and back before the age of ten, who'd lost his legs to a random rocket attack on the city of sorrows, yet maintained the guts to traverse the town, selling papers for a dong or two. And Brody had the gall to feel sorry for himself.

"No thanks, buddy." He wanted to pat the boy on the head, but that was against Vietnamese custom, so he dropped into a squat beside him instead. "I want you to go buy yourself something." He handed the boy a ten-dollar bill, still refusing the newspaper. Brody didn't want to read about the body count in Bong Son again. "Anything, kid. Just go have yourself a good time."

That was when he looked up and saw it for the first time. Smoke. A little, curling wisp of black smoke, lingering in the doorway of his balcony down the block.

Brody ran. He ran faster than he had ever run before in his life. He took the stairs up to his apartment three and four steps at a time. He was there in a flash, not knowing what it all meant, but so frightened it took him several seconds to get his key in the door.

Unlocked, it swung open as soon as he turned the key.

The smoke was rising from a wok on the kitchen table. It was not a food smell—some type of paperwork was on fire. He glanced around the room, but Dep was nowhere in sight.

On the floor beside the entrance to the balcony, he saw Lin's diary. The back ripped down the middle, its pages were scattered across the floor. He watched a breeze from the balcony take hold of one and carry it out onto the warm afternoon wind.

*The balcony!* He thought of Lin, and in his mind he saw Dep, wracked with guilt all these days, jumping over the railing to her death.

Brody rushed out onto the balcony and stared down over the iron grill bars, but there was nothing on the blacktop below except some more pages from the diary.

He returned to the kitchen and pulled the wok's plug out. It was not papers burning in the wok, but photographs. Black-and-white pictures!

Using chopsticks to fish one out, he glanced at the wall over their bed. The color portrait of the two of them, painted by a Tu Do Street artist in bright oils on black felt, was still in its place. The pictures curling up in the wok were Dep's family photos! He looked over at her ancestral altar: they were all gone, turned to ash.

Water trickling down onto tile reached his ears, and a terrible fear suddenly overcame Brody. He thought his knees might buckle, that he might pass out, so intense was the evil premonition. He dropped the chopsticks on the floor and rushed into the bathroom.

She was waiting for him there.

Lying in the tub, several hours gone. Naked, as when she came into Saigon's twisted little world. Dep's wrists were slashed to the bone. Her weight was shifting, her head beginning to sink now, forcing water over the edge of the tub.

He wanted to go to her, but he couldn't bring himself to move through the bathroom's doorway. He wanted to take hold of her, to lift her in his arms, smooth her hair back out of her face. But the ugly gashes across her wrists held him back, prevented him from helping, from going to her, going to his woman. In her face he thought he saw Koy's likeness flickering for a moment. He thought he was going to be sick.

He stared at her breasts, floating in the crimson-streaked water, and at her face, still not peaceful, not even in death. Her eyes were closed tight, against the terror of what she was doing, it seemed, fearful of what she might find on the other side of the *joss* smoke.

# Tan Son Nhut Airport, Saigon

Brody was glad to be back in uniform. The uniform of the United States Army, a First Air Cav combat patch on his right shoulder, and not a security guard's.

As he waited at Tan Son Nhut Airport for the chopper that would ferry him back to Echo Company, he glanced over the newspaper's headlines again. They were still looking for the salt-and-pepper team, a black deserter and his white turncoat buddy, who were rumored to be running with the Cong. "Gooood *luck!*" Brody shook his head sarcastically. Every man in the Division dreamed about nabbing those two, but they were still out there somewhere, setting booby traps and running hit-and-run ambushes.

He scanned the story beneath it. The NVA were retreating from the Bong Son plains under heavy assault by the First Air Cavalry. They were withdrawing toward the northwest, after two fierce weeks of heavy combat. The official body count was 603 dinks, though the brass was estimating another seven or eight hundred bit the bullet, too. Seventy-seven Cavalrymen lost their lives in the first phase of Operation Masher, and that didn't count the 42 killed in the crash of their C-123.

Brody concentrated on the news stories, but he was thinking about Dep. He couldn't get that picture of her out of his mind: lying in the tub of crimson, her face drained of blood. He would carry the image with him the rest of his life; of that, he was sure.

She had left no suicide note. Only a small slip of paper concerning a transaction. It was in Vietnamese, and Brody had it translated. Dep had not been a communist, but the paper confirmed his suspicions about his missing gold coins had been correct: she had taken them after reading Lin's diary. Taken them and donated his hard-earned gold to the Viet Cong cause.

319

Only the week before her death, they had talked about suicide. Some depressed GI had entered a pact with his Vietnamese girlfriend after CID disapproved their marriage request. A suicide pact. Still naked after making love, they stepped into the shower, slipped a live grenade between the woman's breasts, and hugged each other to death.

That would be too painful, Dep had mentioned in passing as she carved up the mangos. Being blown to pieces was just not Buddhist.

Yes, Brody had agreed. If one had to go, there were definitely less painful ways to "pull the pin." He'd read up on the subject, in fact, and come to the conclusion that an overdose of sleeping pills was probably the easiest way to kill oneself, though some experts theorized the victims suffered pain in the form of internal suffocation while they were unconscious. The only other method was slitting one's wrist with a razor blade, and bleeding to death.

"Using razor blade?" she had responded with a shocked, disbelieving look. "Would be too painful, Bro-dee!"

Not if one climbed into a tub of hot, steaming water first, he told her. The hot water deadened the nerve endings, until you didn't even feel the razor.

Treat Brody's guilt weighed heavy on him as he waited for the flight that would free him of Saigon: Like most homes in tropical Vietnam, their apartment did not have hot running water.

# CHAPTER 30

## Chiang Mai, Thailand

There were other Westerners at the elephant-logging contest, so Fletcher and Cordova did not feel vulnerable or out of place. They arrived early—long before the huge pachyderms —and managed to socialize enough with a group of Nam vets from "down under" that they had developed rather convincing Aussie accents of their own after a few hours. "Just in case any underworld types try to feel out the crowd." Snakeman had nodded confidently.

The sun was directly overhead now, however, and although this was still Thailand, the usual midday heat that plagued them from Bong Son to Bangkok was nonexistent. A cool, mountain breeze drifted down from Mae Chan Pass near the Burmese border, home to the Mae Kam tribespeople. A fine, silver mist clung to the treetops like angel hair, but rarely dropped across the playing field to obscure visibility on the ground.

The "playing field" was a vast plateau of short reeds and grass. Deep pools of mud dotted the plateau here and there. Some elephants—obviously "warming up" for the contests— rolled around in the mud, applying their beauty cream while vigilant, ever-watchful owners kept an eye out for their every need. Dusty cows, their great tusks nearly as long as Snakeman was tall, lumbered back and forth in front of the crowds, balancing bigger and bigger logs on their curved shafts of ivory.

"Ain't this great?" Fletcher took the new Instamatic hanging from a plastic band around his neck and tried to snap off a quick shot of several Yao maidens floating past in their traditional costumes of color: black, richly embroidered dresses adorned with bright beads representing every color in the rainbow, and large pieces of flattened and intricately shaped silver jewelry. But the virgin nearest Snakeman waved her hand in front of the lens, frowning. "Huh?" He slowly lowered the camera, flushing.

"They think it's bad luck, mate," one of the Australian soldiers said, joining Fletcher and Cordova.

"Flashbacks of The Nam," a disappointed Snakeman muttered, replacing the camera's lens cap.

"Ro't. They think it captures thar' soul. Brings 'em ah worlda hurt, *savy*?"

"We *savy*, mate." Cordova extended a hand.

"On leave from Veeyet-Nam, eh?"

Snakeman nodded. "Ia Drang Valley."

"Binh Dinh Province," Cordova amended their unit history slightly.

"Ahhh, yo! Binh Dinh's bad newzzz. Bloody commie sanc' if thar ever were one."

"You pinned *that* tail on the water buffalo," Fletcher muttered, watching the group of Yao girls closely as they sauntered off through the crowd. He wondering what it would be like to fuck one.

" 'M from down Delta-way m'self." The Aussie pulled a snapshot from his waterproof wallet to reveal a pose showing three deeply tanned, bare-chested men with hair bleached blond by years under the tropical sun sitting atop an American Marine tank.

"Leatherneck Armor." Cordova examined the photo closely but was unable to make out the unit markings on the tank. "Tread-heads."

322

"Meatmasher waiting to happen," Fletcher added, losing interest in the women and the elephants, "iron boxes, filled with courage."

"What the heck you ramblin' on 'bout, Snakeman?"

"Nothin'."

The Aussies eventually went their way, inviting the two Cavalrymen to join them for a *baht* bus ride to Chiang Saen. "Goi'n to riverraft down the Mekong into the roo'ins of King Mengrai, mates! You oughtn't ta miss it: used to be the capital of Siam long 'bout seven hundred years ago! Maxim-majestic, I dare say!"

Cordova declined with a warm smile. "We've got an appointment with a first-class prick!" he said, as the group clamored aboard the same type of vehicle two American GIs had been riding when they were robbed-'n'-rolled then murdered, down in Pattaya the day before.

"Eh?"

"Nothin', mates! Have a good time!"

"Rie-et! Well, if ya happen to change yor minds, look us up at the Rama Hotel. We sleep in the sticks, but we always *eat* at the Rama!" He raised a fist in salute, and the two Americans both responded with thumbs-up gestures.

"Good group o' dudes," Fletcher decided, eyes scanning the crowd for women of questionable virtue again.

"Yah." Cordova was looking for persons a bit more sinister in appearance. "Too bad they weren't going to hang around a bit longer. We might be able to use 'em."

"I'm sure they'd love to help us kick ass and take names," Snakeman read his thoughts, "they came across as a bunch o' fun-loving clowns. But don't sweat it, Corky. We can handle whatever comes up. You just gotta have a little more faith in your buddy the Snake, okay?"

Affection for Fletcher warmed Cordova inside as he realized how strong their bond had become during the last week. There were times back in Ia Drang, at the Tea Plantation, when the tension between them could have been cut with a

323

knife, but he sensed all that was changing. He just hoped they didn't have to prove anything to each other under fire.

They'd spent nearly an hour before breakfast trying to conceal the grease guns beneath Windbreakers, but no matter what method they used, conspicuous bulges were visible, and they didn't need to attract that kind of attention from the police. So they opted to risk an unarmed, public contact with Thaweekarn and just hope for the best.

Depending on the number and appearance of the drug kingpin's entourage, they would make a decision on whether to initiate a confrontation in Chiang Rai, or follow the gangster back to his headquarters—*if* they were able to. The two Americans' own demeanor left little to be desired: Cordova thought they blended in well with the other tourists, and the Air Force sunglasses might help them pass for any in the population of GIs visiting the festival. Hopefully—Corky kept his fingers crossed—all Westerners looked alike to the Thai pushers. They would make a conscious effort to maintain a low profile, too, keeping to the fringe of all congregations while remaining alert. It was a long shot, he decided, but they just might survive their excursion to the valley of elephants and opium poppies.

Anukul Thaweekarn was good. His men had the two off-duty doorgunners cordoned off from the rest of the crowd before either Fletcher or Cordova knew what was going down. "This will be the last time we ever meet face-to-face," the tall, gaunt-looking Thai said, twisting a pencil-thin mustache with narcotics-stained fingers.

His men had the Americans backed up against a huge elephant. The animal's left front leg was chained to a thick stake, anchored securely to the ground behind a line of vendors' tents, and it shifted nervously from side to side on hearing the well-dressed warlords's threatening tone.

324

Fletcher kept glancing down at the enormous hooves rocking back and forth behind him. "How much of the product do you require?" Thaweekarn asked from behind dark sunglasses.

Cordova removed his own. "Enough to set us up for life." He grinned confidently. "We're headed back to Vietnam, where a lot of our buddies are waitin' for—" He began the routine story, and one of Thaweekarn's bodyguards lunged forward, doubling the Latino over with a mean slug to the belly.

"Hey!" Snakeman pounced, nearly ripping the man's ear off with a blinding series of swinging *tae-kwon-do* chops. The Thai was down and out before he knew what hit him, but three other hoods were all over Fletcher before he could whirl on them.

They rolled to the ground just as Cordova got his wind back and started to throw a fist at the kingpin himself. Thaweekarn drew a 9mm automatic. "Be my guest," he said softly. "Kiss the widow-maker."

Cordova watched Fletcher slide out from under the pile of kicking, punching Thais, and Snakeman was quickly standing beside the Cork again, breathing hard, fists raised, a gash across his cheek. His lower lip was rapidly swelling. "You fuckers don't play around." His nostrils flared.

A group of tourists passed nearby, and Thaweekarn lowered the pistol. He motioned for his men to back off. "You're a first class fuckwad, did you know that?" Cordova was clutching his belly. "Okay, so we've *proved* ourselves. Do you want our business, or not?"

Thaweekarn did not speak immediately. He stared at them from behind the black sunglasses for several seconds, then chuckled softly. "I am not going to sell you even a spoiled shot of leg," he hissed, and Cordova could see the knuckles of his gun hand go white.

"Fucking fine." Fletcher turned to leave. "We'll just buy from someone else—Madame V, down in Chon Buri . . ."

325

"Yah." Cordova nodded. "We heard she's got more first-grade Buddha grass than she knows what to do with."

"You amateurs are not here today to purchase drugs." The automatic came up again.

"Not from you, anyway." Fletcher spat at the the ground. "That's for fucking sure."

"You were at the Soi Nokyung incident," he announced, and Cordova felt a chill run through him. They knew. Thaweekarn knew who was in the commandeered taxi that had chased his trucks through the streets of Bangkok the week before. "You have continued to meddle in matters that are none of your concern. And now you are going to begin your journey to a higher plain of enlightenment."

The two Americans locked eyes, and Fletcher's fist flew down and back as hard as he could throw it, striking the elephant near its genitals. The monster mammal trumpeted an ear-splitting scream, and rose up on its hind legs, ripping the stake out of the ground. The chain attached to its left hoof swung around wildly, striking several of the bodyguards in the head, but missing Thaweekarn.

Snakeman grabbed Cordova's wrist, pulling him beneath the elephant before the beast's front legs dropped to earth again. "Move it or lose it!" he yelled.

"Where to?" Corky was still clutching his belly.

"Those trees! I saw some taxis lined up back there somewhere. We can play a repeat of Friday night at the fights and borrow one until—"

The two unarmed doorgunners skidded to an abrupt stop as they rushed through the tamarinds. The cab drivers were all gone, and the only vehicle in sight was a dark blue Renault.

The attractive woman who had visited their hotel two days earlier stood in front of the sedan's black-tinted windows. She held a pistol in her hand and a blatant glare of contempt in her eyes.

326

* * *

"I would like you to meet Mr. Chatri." The opium warlord of Chiang Rai, dressed in a three-piece suit instead of armor, dropped a collection of news clippings on the table in front of Fletcher and Cordova. The tall, stocky Asian standing in the doorway twenty feet away made no effort to shake hands or further acquaint himself with the two Americans seated at the table.

Snakeman glanced at the machine-gun-toting guards positioned between himself and the newcomer. Their faces held no expression, their eyes no silent message. "Fuck it," he said.

Corky was looking at the newsclip on top of the recently assembled pile. Mr. Chatri was pictured in nearly every article. The stories identified him as a professional Thai kickboxer.

Chatri was not the kingdom's champion, but he held an odd record of sorts: he was a contender, and five out of his last ten opponents had died from injuries they sustained in the ring with him.

"I take it you're trying to intimidate us slightly?" Cordova knocked the papers off the table, onto the floor. "Big fucking deal. And we're both members of Hog Heaven. That and five *baht*'ll get you a cup of Viet ice coffee."

"Mr. Chatri is very famous in Thailand," Anukul Thaweekarn said. "He has many friends. He would not be able to purchase his own meal anywhere in Bangkok."

Snakeman Fletcher leaned forward, locked eyes with Chatri, and directed an obscene gesture at him, smiled, then leaned back in his chair again. "Fuck it," he repeated. "Don' mean nothin'."

Through the open doorway, Cordova noticed a group of children being led toward a large, circular-shaped building in the distance. His eyes narrowed, but he could not make out

327

faces—they were too far away. Besides, he consoled himself, they were all wearing uniforms, as if from a private school.

"Please follow me." Thaweekarn spoke politely to his two prisoners, but the guards standing behind Fletcher and Cordova jabbed them in the lower back with rifle butts when they took their time responding.

They had been waiting in the small, box-shaped lobby of a mansion that rose up along the hillside for several stories. Thaweekarn appeared to be leading them toward an outdoor arena of sorts—his own private martial arts stadium.

"Because I was amused by your crude attempts at damaging my operation," he said, "I am willing to give you a . . . 'fighting' chance, gentlemen . . ."

"Let me guess," Fletcher interrupted sarcastically. "You've decided not to kill us outright. That's why you've been saving us for two days without your guards delivering so much as a single black eye. You're going to let us get into the ring with Chartruse the fairy here, right?"

"*Chatri* has a very leathal foot." Thaweekarn smiled.

"No sweat." Fletcher walked up to Chatri and held out his hand. When the Thai reached for it, Snakeman slapped him viciously across the chops with his other hand.

Knocked off balance and backwards by the force of the open-handed blow, the martial artist let out a yell and prepared to charge, but Thaweekarn held up a fist and the entire compound went silent. "Save for later," he said, glancing at the Americans. "First, we have ceremonial. Drink, eat . . . sample your last *poo-ying*, if you so desire." He motioned toward a carnival-like tent set up at the entrance to the stadium. It was crowded with Thaweekarn's people.

"What happens if we win?" Fletcher asked. "Do we get to go free? Like in the movies? Or do you hold a grudge?"

"I have not even considered it," Thaweekarn replied.

"Oh?" Fletcher folded his arms across his chest and tilted his head to one side.

"Mr. Chatri is undefeated," he said. "The only reason peo-

328

ple come to watch him kick-box anymore is to see whether the man foolish enough to challenge him lives or dies."

"I just have one question," Cordova said.

"And what would that be, my friend?"

"Do me and the Snakeman get to fight him together, or will it be one on one?"

"Oh, one on one, my friend," Thaweekarn sounded surprised by the question. "Definitely one on one. With your gun hand tied behind your back."


The Snakeman pivoted, curled at the waist, and kicked his foot out suddenly, catching Chatri, the kick-boxer with the lethal feet, square in the jaw. The Thai champion went down hard and, though he was exhausted from nearly thirty minutes of fending the madman off with just his heels, Fletcher dropped his entire weight on his opponent, using his knees as weapons now.

Chatri responded like a human accordion, flinging Fletcher off as he sprang back to his feet, but the doorgunner had some tricks waiting in the wings, too. He whirled again, knowing full well the kick would throw him off balance if he failed to connect.

Fletcher felt the satisfying crunch of nasal cartilage under his heel. The Thai was having trouble compensating for the difference in height. Chatri was used to fighting much shorter boxers.

Using the scissors maneuver, Fletcher leaped up and caught the dazed champion's throat in his legs and dropped hard, twisting violently as both men struck the ground. Fletcher was on top.

Thaweekarn's bodyguards could all hear the notorious martial artist's neck snap, but before they could react, the Americans, as if on cue, dropped onto their haunches, slid their manacled wrists underneath their feet until the handcuffs were in front, and sprinted toward one of the stadium's side exits.

More guards immediately blocked them, of course. Thaweekarn had all avenues of escape covered—except the main entrance.

Fletcher sprinted toward it, Cordova hot on his heels, as two bulky gunmen rushed to try to head them off. Discharges in the sky overhead suddenly sent most of Thaweekarn's people seeking cover, and Snakeman looked up to see a huge green-and-brown National Police helicopter hovering over the arena. Additional officers were pouring through one of the rear gates, and Thaweekarn abandoned his plans to do away with the Americans.

He ran for the main exit, too, and disappeared into the crowd that had formed to see why the gunship was hovering there.

"There he goes!" Cordova spotted the drug kingpin weaving in and out of the tourists, heading for the building they had watched all the children filing into earlier.

"Fuck him." Fletcher, breathing hard, dropped to his knees.

"I'm gonna get him!" Corky ran over to one of the cowering gunmen, disarmed him with a blinding First Cav offensive hand-to-hand combat technique, then chased after Thaweekarn, waving a revolver with a six-inch barrel.

The opium king found himself trapped when Cordova entered the private schoolhouse before he could make good his escape. Thaweekarn knew what the police wanted, and why they had finally zeroed in on Chiang Rai: the cops' kids his people had snatched in Bangkok.

The time for Thaweekarn to escape into the Burmese hills with a little personal safety insurance was also ripe. Only the man in the doorway—the Mexican from Vietnam—stood in his way.

"Leave now, and I'll forget this ever happened!" the kingpin warned as Cordova started down the stairwell, his gun arm

330

locked at the elbow, the "borrowed" Smith & Wesson pointing at Thaweekarn's face.

Thaweekarn was holding one of the children in his arms for protection. His other hand also brandished a pistol, but he didn't appear ready to use it, and Cordova sensed this. Several children were huddled at his feet. One little girl was quietly crying as she tried to hide her sobs in her hands.

"Drop the kid!" Cordova yelled. The boy was one of the children from the shoot-out at the police family apartments. Sugar Prasertkwan's boy.

"Please let me go," the child pleaded in English, using the language they were using.

"The child dies unless you back right up those steps the same way you came down."

Cordova kept walking toward Thaweekarn, and the drug lord placed the barrel of the pistol against the boy's temple. "Don't do it," Cordova muttered, holding his own revolver aimed at his face. "I mean it!"

Upstairs, doors were being slammed open. Boots were stomping across the floor overhead. He could hear Snakeman, calling his name.

His attention diverted momentarily, Thaweekarn glanced up at the stairwell as several police officers began entering the basement. Cordova chose that moment to fire.

The tremendous discharge became an explosion of screaming children as the bullet slammed into Thaweekarn's nostrils. The force of the impact flung him backwards, off his feet. Cordova scooped up the child as the opium kingpin's automatic clattered across the floor.

The boy was whimpering, but there was strength in his arms as he clung to Corky. The American held the little face to his chest, shielding it from what was making a rookie police officer rush to a corner and vomit.

"My mother," the child kept to English. "Why won't my mother—"

But then the boy's eyes lit up, and he tried to jump from

331

Cordova's arms. He screamed for joy and lapsed back into Thai as he recognized the two uniformed policewomen rushing down the stairwell, pistols drawn.

Sgt. Sugar Prasertkwan had returned from the dead. Her partner, Officer Sawang Chatsungnoen, had apparently come along for the ride.

## Bangkok

"We appreciate the letters of reference or commendation or whatever you want to call them." Corky Cordova leaned across the short chain-link fence at Don Muang Airport's Customs counter and kissed Sugar on the lips.

She pulled away, a reprimanding gleam in her eyes—not in public, it told him. Sawang reached out and shook Corky's hand. "It should be enough to get you back into your unit without any trouble," she said. "Have your CO teletype Bangkok Metro if there's a problem."

"We're really going to miss you ladies." Snakeman bowed as the announcement of their flight came over the PA. "I guess we better get going."

"You can always come back for another visit." Sugar winked at Cordova, and Fletcher grabbed the man by the elbow and started leading him over toward their gate. Corky blew her a kiss and, smiling warmly, she wiped away a tear and waved.

"Imagine that." Cordova shook his head. "Their deaths ... the newspaper reports ... the whole thing, a scam. They couldn't get away with that crap stateside, could they, Snakeman?"

"Well, like Sugar told us: She and Sawang were due to testify against that Thaweekarn creep in a major drug case, and when all the death threats against them escalated into an actual shoot-out at the Temple of Dawn, their superiors decided it would be safer to lead everyone to believe the primary witnesses against Opium Warlord Numba One were dead, and unable to testify."

"Some 'warlord.'" Cordova grinned. The word made him think of Vietnam, and that made him eager for the flight back to his buddies in Echo Company. He was ready to get back to the action.

# GLOSSARY

*AA*   Antiaircraft weapon
*AC*   Aircraft Commander
*Acting Jack*   Acting NCO
*AIT*   Advanced Individual Training
*AJ*   Acting Jack
*AK-47*   Automatic rifle used by VC/NVA
*Animal*   See Monster
*AO*   Area of Operations
*Ao Dai*   Traditional Vietnamese gown
*APH-5*   Helmet worn by gunship pilots
*APO*   Army Post Office
*Arc-Light*   B-52 bombing mission
*ArCOM*   Army Commendation Medal
*Article-15*   Disciplinary action
*Ash-'n'-Trash*   Relay flight

*Bad Paper*   Dishonorable discharge
*Ba Muoi Ba*   Vietnamese beer
*Banana Clip*   Ammo magazine holding 30 bullets
*Bao Chi*   Press or news media
*Basic*   Boot camp
*BCT*   Basic Combat Training (Boot)
*Bic*   Vietnamese for "Understand?"
*Big-20*   Army career of 20 years
*Bird*   Helicopter
*BLA*   Black Liberation Army
*Bloods*   Black soldiers

***Blues***   An airmobile company

***Body Count***   Number of enemy KIA

***Bookoo***   Vietnamese for "many" (actually bastardization of French *beaucoup*)

***Bought the Farm***   Died and life insurance policy paid for mortgage

***Brass Monkey***   Interagency radio call for help

***Brew***   Usually coffee, but sometimes beer

***Bring Smoke***   To shoot someone

***Broken-Down***   Disassembled

***Buddha Zone***   Death

***Bush ('Bush)***   Ambush

***Butter Bar***   2nd Lieutenant


***CA***   Combat Assault

***Cam Ong***   Viet for "Thank you"

***Cartridge***   Shell casing for bullet

***C&C***   Command & Control chopper

***Chao***   Vietnamese greeting

***Charlie***   Viet Cong (from military phonetic: Victor Charlie)

***Charlie Tango***   Control Tower

***Cherry***   New man in unit

***Cherry Boy***   Virgin

***Chicken Plate***   Pilot's chest/groin armor

***Chi-Com***   Chinese Communist

***Chieu Hoi***   Program where communists can surrender and become scouts

***Choi-oi***   Viet exclamation

***CIB***   Combat Infantry Badge

***CID***   Criminal Investigation Division

***Clip***   Ammo magazine

***CMOH***   Congressional Medal of Honor

***CO***   Commanding Officer

***Cobra***   Helicopter gunship used for combat assaults/escorts only

***Cockbang***   Bangkok, Thailand

***Conex***   Shipping container (metal)

***Coz***   Short for Cozmoline

***CP***   Command Post

**CSM**   Command Sergeant Major
**Cunt Cap**   Green narrow cap worn with khakis

**Dash-13**   Helicopter maintenance report
**Dau**   Viet for pain
**Deadlined**   Down for repairs
**Dep**   Viet for beautiful
**DEROS**   Date of Estimated Return from Overseas
**Deuce-and-a-Half**   2½-ton truck
**DFC**   Distinguished Flying Cross
**DI**   Drill Instructor (Sgt.)
**Di Di**   Viet for "Leave or go!"
**Dink**   Dergogatory term for Vietnamese national
**Dinky Dau**   Viet for "crazy"
**Disneyland East**   MACV complex including annex
**DMZ**   Demilitarized Zone
**Dogtags**   Small aluminum tag worn by soldiers with name,
  serial number, religion, and blood type imprinted on it
**DOOM Pussy**   Danang Officers Open Mess
**Door gunner**   Soldier who mans M-60 machine gun mounted
  in side hatch of Huey gunship
**Dung Lai**   Viet for "Halt!"
**Dustoff**   Medevac chopper

**Early Out**   Unscheduled ETS
**EM**   Enlisted Man
**ER**   Emergency Room (hospital)
**ETS**   End Tour of (military) Service

**Field Phone**   Hand-generated portable phones used in
  bunkers
**Fini**   Viet for "Stop" or "the End"
**First Louie**   1st Lieutenant
**First Team**   Motto of 1st Air Cav
**Flak Jacket**   Body armor
**FNG**   Fucking new guy
**FOB**   Fly over border mission
**Foxtrot**   Vietnamese female
**Foxtrot Tosser**   Flame thrower

***Frag***   Fragmentation grenade
***FTA***   Fuck the Army

***Gaggle***   Loose flight of slicks
***Get Some***   Kill someone
***GI***   Government Issue, or, a soldier
***Greenbacks***   U.S. currency
***Green Machine***   U.S. Army
***Gunship***   Attack helicopter armed with machine guns and
    rockets
***Gurney***   Stretcher with wheels

***Ham & Motherfuckers***   C-rations serving of ham and lima
    beans
***Herpetologist***   One who studies reptiles and amphibians
***HOG-60***   M-60 machine gun
***Hot LZ***   Landing zone under hostile fire
***Housegirl***   Indigenous personnel hired to clean buildings,
    wash laundry, etc.
***Huey***   Primary troop-carrying helicopter

***IC***   Instillation Commander
***IG***   Inspector General
***In-Country***   Within Vietnam
***Intel***   Intelligence (military)
***IP***   That point in a mission where descent toward target
    begins

***JAG***   Judge Advocate General
***Jane***   Jane's Military Reference books
***Jesus Nut***   The bolt that holds rotor blade to helicopter
***Jody***   Any American girlfriends
***Jolly Green***   Chinook helicopter

***KIA***   Killed in Action
***Kimchi***   Korean fish sauce salad
***Klick***   Kilometer
***KP***   Mess hall duty

* * *

*Lai Day*   Viet for "come here"

*LAW*   Light Anti-Tank Weapon

*Lay Dog*   Lie low in jungle during recon patrol

*LBFM*   Little Brown Fucking Machine

*LBJ*   Long Binh Jail (main stockade)

*Leg*   Infantryman not airborne qualified

*Lifeline*   Straps holding gunny aboard chopper while he fires M-60 out the hatch

*Lifer*   Career soldier

*Links*   Metal strip holding ammo belt together

*Loach*   Small spotter/scout chopper

*LP*   Listening Post

*LRRP*   Long-Range Recon Patrol

*LSA*   Gun oil

*Lurp*   One who participates in LRRPs

*LZ*   Landing Zone


*M-14*   American carbine

*M-16*   Primary U.S. Automatic Rifle

*M-26*   Fragmentation grenade

*M-60*   Primary U.S. Machine gun

*M-79*   Grenade launcher (rifle)

*MACV*   Military Assistance Command, Vietnam

*Magazine*   Metal container that feeds bullets into weapon. Holds 20 or 30 rounds per unit

*Mag Pouch*   Magazine holder worn on web belt

*MAST*   Mobile Army Surgical Team

*Med-Evac*   Medical Evacuation Chopper

*Mess Hall*   GI cafeteria

*MG*   Machine gun

*MI*   Military Intelligence

*MIA*   Missing in Action

*Mike-Mike*   Millimeters

*Mike Papas*   Military Policemen

*Mister Zippo*   Flame-thrower operator

*Mjao*   Central Highlands witch doctor

*Monkeyhouse*   Stockade or jail

*Monkeystrap*   See **Lifeline**

*Monster*   12-21 claymore antipersonnel mines jury-rigged to detonate simultaneously

*Montagnarde*  Hill tribe people of Central Highlands, RVN
*MPC*  Money Payment Certificates (scrip) issued to GIs in RVN in lieu of greenbacks
*Muster*  A quick assemblage of soldiers with little or no warning
*My*  Viet for "American"

*Net*  Radio net
*NETT*  New Equipment Training Team
*Newby*  New GI in-country
*Numba One*  Something very good
*Numba Ten*  Something very bad
*Nuoc Nam*  Viet fish sauce
*NVA*  North Vietnamese Army

*OD*  Olive Drab
*OR*  Operating Room (Hospital)

*P*  Piasters
*PA*  Public Address system
*PCS*  Permanent Change of (Duty) Station (transfer out of RVN)
*Peter Pilot*  Copilot in training
*PF*  Popular Forces (Vietnamese)
*PFC*  Private First Class
*Phantom*  Jet fighter plane
*Phu*  Vietnamese noodle soup
*Piaster*  Vietnamese Currency
*PJ*  Photojournalist
*Point*  The most dangerous position on patrol. The point man walks ahead and to the side of the others, acting as a lookout
*PRG*  Provisional Revolutionary Govt. (the Communists)
*Prang*  Land a helicopter roughly
*Prick-25*  Pr-25 field radio
*Profile*  Medical exemption
*Psy-Ops*  Psychological operation
*PT*  Physical Training
*Puff*  Heavily armed aircraft

340

**Purple Heart**   Medal given for wounds received in combat
**Purple Vision**   Night vision
**Puzzle Palace**   The MACV HQ building


**Quad-50**   Truck equipped with four 50-caliber MGs
**QC**   Vietnamese MP


**Rat Fuck**   Mission doomed from the start
**Regular**   An enlistee or full-time soldier as opposed to PFs
   and Reserves, NG, etc.
**REMF**   Rear Echelon Motherfucker
**R&R**   Rest and Relaxation
**Re-Up**   Re-enlist
**Rikky-Tik**   Quickly or fast
**Rock 'n'Roll**   Automatic fire
**Roger**   Affirmative
**ROK**   Republic of Korea
**Rotor**   Overhead helicopter blade
**Round**   Bullet
**RPG**   Rocket-propelled grenade
**Ruck(Sack)**   GI's backpack
**RVN**   Republic of (South) Vietnam


**Saigon**   Capital of RVN
**SAM**   Surface-to-Air Missile
**Sapper**   Guerrilla terrorist equipped with satchel charge
   (explosives)
**SAR**   Downed-chopper rescue mission
**Scramble**   Alert reaction to call for help, CA or rescue
   operation.
**Scrip**   See **MPC**
**7.62**   M-60 ammunition
**Sierra Echo**   Southeast (Northwest is November Whiskey,
   etc.)
**Single-Digit Fidget**   A nervous signle-digit midget
**Single-Digit Midget**   One with fewer than ten days remaining
   in Vietnam
**SKS**   Russian-made carbine
**Slick**   Helicopter

**Slicksleeve**   Private E-1
**Slug**   Bullet
**SNAFU**   Situation normal: all fucked up
**Soggy Frog**   Green Beret laying dog
**SOP**   Standard Operating Procedure (also known as Shit Output)
**Spiderhole**   Tunnel entrance
**Strac**   Sharp appearance
**Steel Pot**   Helmet
**Striker**   Montagnarde hamlet defender
**Sub-Gunny**   Substitute door gunner

**TDY**   Temporary Duty Assignment
**Terr**   Terrorist
**"33"**   Local Vietnamese beer
**Thumper**   See M-79
**Ti Ti**   Viet for little
**Tour 365**   The year-long tour of duty a GI spends in RVN
**Tower Rat**   Tower guard
**Tracer**   Chemically treated bullet that gives off a glow en-route to its target
**Triage**   That method in which medics determine which victims are most seriously hurt and therefore treated first
**Trooper**   Soldier
**201 File**   Personnel file
**Two-Point-Five**   Gunship rockets

**UCMJ**   Uniformed Code of Military Justice
**Unass**   Leave seat quickly

**VC**   Viet Cong
**Victor Charlie**   VC
**Viet Cong**   South Vietnamese Communists
**VNP**   Vietnamese National Police
**Void Vicious**   Final approach to a Hot LZ; or the jungle when hostile

**Warrant Officer**   Pilots
**Wasted**   Killed

**Web Belt**  Utility belt GIs use to carry equipment, sidearms, etc.

**Whiskey**  Military phonetic for "West"

**WIA**  Wounded In Action

**Wilco**  Will comply

**Willie Peter**  White phosphorous

**Wire**  Perimeter (trip wire sets off booby trap)

**The World**  Any place outside Vietnam

**Xin Loi**  Viet for "sorry about that" or "good-bye"

**XM-21**  Gunship mini-gun

**XO**  Executive Officer

**'Yarde**  Montagnarde

**ZIP**  Derogatory term for Vietnamese National

**Zulu**  Military Phoenetic for the letter Z (LZ or Landing Zone might be referred to as a Lima Zulu)

Fly with the men of First Air Cav as they swoop down on the Cong-infested swamps of the Mekong Delta to blast Charlie off the muddy waters of the rivers in Cam Son in their next bloody battle . . .

CHOPPER #4: RED RIVER

## ABOUT THE AUTHOR

THE AUTHOR served with the United States Army in Southeast Asia for three years, where he received the Bronze Star Medal. His unit was awarded the Vietnamese Cross of Gallantry. He has written eighteen other adventure novels on the Vietnam War under several pseudonyms, and alternates between homes in the Orient and Little Saigon, USA.